ECHOES OF DARKNESS

ALSO BY CHERYL CAMPBELL

SCIENCE FICTION

Echoes of War (#1), *Echoes Trilogy*

FANTASY

Burnt Mountain: The Monster Within (#1)
Burnt Mountain: One in the Chamber (#2)
Burnt Mountain: Do and Die (#3)
Burnt Mountain: Rhyllia (#4)
Burnt Mountain: When Heroes Fall (#5)

ECHOES OF DARKNESS

**BOOK TWO
IN THE ECHOES TRILOGY**

CHERYL CAMPBELL

SONAR PRESS

Published by Sonar Press,
Augusta, Maine, USA, 04330

Published 2020
Printed in the United States of America

ISBN: 978-0-9897608-6-7 (pbk)
ISBN: 978-0-9897608-7-4 (e-bk)
Library of Congress Control Number: 2020907482

Formatting by Katherine Lloyd, The Desk

Mom
1940-2020

CHAPTER

1

Sixty years ago—before the Wardens started the war to take Earth and eliminate humans—the drive from Belfast, Maine, to Bangor had taken forty-five minutes, longer during tourist season. Today, two hours into the drive, the small convoy of Commonwealth trucks picked their path over battered roads left unmaintained for six decades.

After Mary declined her offer to take over driving, Dani forced herself to remain alert for a Warden counterattack. They could strike anywhere, anytime. Dresden sprawled in the back among the gear crammed on the seat with him. He was supposed to be standing in the hatch, manning the gun mounted to the top of the truck, but he'd bailed on that job an hour ago.

Dani's truck was the last in the three-vehicle convoy, and she hated the unchanging scenery of the rear of the truck in front of them. She leaned forward and cast her gaze up the slope along the driver's side as they traveled over a road carved into the hillside. On her side was a steep, tree-covered slope down to a river. She rocked as Mary guided the truck around a deep crack in the asphalt.

Mary cast a glance at her. "Jesus, Dani, relax."

"You can come back here with me," Dresden said. "I'll help you relax."

Dani's eyes remained trained on the landscape. "You can get your ass back up to the gun."

Dresden yawned. "God, you're in a mood."

Dani reached for the radio. "They're too close. Wright needs to back off the lead vehicle."

Mary caught her hand. "They're fine."

"I like the reckless Dani who tries to commandeer Warden helos by herself," Dresden said. "This stressed out version is far less fun."

She scowled back at him. "Fuck you."

He laughed.

Mary said, "You've been like this since we left this morning. How are you not exhausted? I'm beat."

Dani perked up. "Need me to drive?"

Mary waved her off. "No! You don't have to be on duty all the time. Just be a passenger." She softened her tone. "I appreciate your attention to detail, but we've made supply runs a dozen times the last couple of months with no problems."

"I know," Dani grumbled.

Dresden released a loud, obnoxious yawn. "As soon as we ditch this cargo, I'm going to Aunt Hattie's for ale and women. Mary, you in?"

Mary snorted. "You can't handle Aunt Hattie's women *or* men."

The truck rocked when it struck another pothole. Dani's shoulder, already sore from prior collisions with the door, smarted.

Outside her window, sunlight glittered on the river's surface. She smiled, although sunny spring days in Maine were deceptive. The temperatures crept up during the day before plummeting again overnight. The moisture in the ground from melted winter snow and ice created a mud season to remind Mainers that summer was not arriving anytime soon.

Mary shifted in her seat, and Dani realized why she was so attracted to her. Mary's posture was perfect, and the sunlight played off her light-colored hair, elegant jawline, and cheek bones. *Regal*, Dani thought, finally putting a word to how she viewed Mary. When her friend's head began to turn her way, Dani shifted her gaze to avoid being caught staring.

Dresden and Mary continued their chatter, but Dani didn't listen; she felt a bit embarrassed. She scanned the slope between the road and river. The roads being in such disrepair might cause them to go over the edge into a catastrophic roll into the river. The two trucks ahead carried munitions and gear. Dani, Mary, and Dresden were hauling food and medical supplies from Portland to an outpost in Belfast, with the remaining contents destined for Bangor's barracks.

"Isn't that right, Dani?" Dresden asked.

Dani buckled her seat belt. "You should put your seat belts on."

He scoffed at her remark. "Did you hear anything we just said?"

Dani scanned the area again. "If we go off this road, there isn't much to keep us from rolling to the bottom."

Mary laughed. "My driving isn't that terrible. Why would we go off the road?"

Dani finally looked at her friend. "Maybe because the roads are shit and could fall away beneath us? Or a boulder off that hill could knock us off? Or the Wardens could attack?"

"Relax," Mary said. "You're making me insane, darling. You normally make me insane in a good way, except, disappointingly, it never goes anywhere."

A flush crept up Dani's neck anytime Mary started flirting. She shifted her shoulders to try to hide it while she moved her gaze from the hillside, across the road, and down the slope toward the river.

The truck rocked side to side, and Dani unclipped her seat belt. She twisted to face Dresden. "Dres, get on the gun or put the goddamn seat belt on." She leaned across Mary and pulled the shoulder strap out. Dani paused, her face inches from Mary's.

"Put your arm through."

"That's not where I want to put it."

Dani sighed. "Please, Mary. I don't want you to die."

Mary released the steering wheel and passed her hand through the opening between the shoulder and lap straps. "I like this. *A lot.*"

There was no way for Dani to hide the redness she knew was flowing into her face, so she hastily fastened the belt into place.

"Mmm, so do I," Dresden said. "Will you fasten mine?"

"Shut up," Dani snapped back at him, and she clipped her belt back on.

Mary leaned toward Dani. "Feel free to reach across me like that again. I'll have you right here."

A nervous laugh escaped Dani. She leaned forward to peer out the windshield, far too embarrassed to look at Mary.

Dresden bumped the back of Dani's seat. "You're so tense."

"We never caught all the Wardens that escaped Portland," Dani said.

"So? Only stragglers were left. They'll never come this far north."

"And they never thought we'd go that far south. Their complacency is exactly why we were able to attack and win. I'll be ready when they show up."

"*When* they show up? If they were going to retaliate, they would've done it months ago. They don't give a shit about Maine."

"You still won't catch me sleeping on duty."

"You're an alien. You get another shot at life when you die. Me and Mary don't. You should be the one relaxing."

Dresden understood the basics of normal regeneration by alien Echoes, but only a few people—Mary included—knew what happened to Dani with a regen. Hers wasn't the standard process of an Echo returning to a healthy, young adult body with memories intact. Dani's regens were more like a train wreck where she returned to a child's age with zero recollection of her prior lives.

Mary intervened. "Dres, shut the fuck up."

He stretched and leaned back in his seat. He sighed. "Next time she dresses up like a Warden, she might end up shot instead of punched."

Dani closed her eyes for a moment. Friendly fire—so she'd been told—had ended her first three lives.

Mary spoke up. "Give it a rest. Talk about something other than dying, please."

"We'll all end up dead at some point, right? No point looking for it out the window."

In her peripheral vision, she noticed Mary watching her. Dani kept her gaze on the hillside.

"Die in your sleep; that's the way to go," Dresden said.

Mary shot him a glare. "One more word and you're walking to Bangor."

They sat in silence for a moment before Dani spoke again. "I'd rather see it coming."

Mary grinned. "You know who I'd like to see coming?"

Dani resisted the urge to meet Mary's eyes, though a smile played at the corners of her mouth. Flirting had resumed, and Dani didn't mind the topic change away from death. An odd shadow crept along the hill. "Shit."

Mary shook her head and smiled. "No, not—"

Dani reached for the radio mike to alert the others, then shouted at Dresden. "Ten o'clock! Get on the fucking gun."

Mary gasped. "Incoming!"

Dresden scrambled topside, but the shadows on the hill moved into the light and became Wardens. They attacked. The initial blast destroyed the first truck in a ball of fire, which sent the second truck airborne. Mary jerked the wheel hard to the right.

The second truck flipped and struck the road upside down, and the edge of the roadway crumbled. Dani's truck slid down the slope toward the river. Dresden's lower half disappeared through the hatch. Tree limbs lashed the vehicle, and glass shattered when it began to roll. Mary screamed, but Dani couldn't do anything to help herself or her friend. The truck slammed into something that stopped the roll but sent it into a slide. The truck rolled again, then skidded to a stop on its side. Dizziness and darkness swallowed Dani's mind.

CHAPTER
2

A drop of something splashed on Dani's cheek. She groaned and opened her eyes, surprised that she was not where she expected to be. Instead of her bed or a bunk in the barracks, she lay in a mix of rocks, mud, bits of tree limbs, and broken glass. She was on her right side, and the dripping on her cheek continued. Dani shifted and grimaced when flashes of pain shot through her.

Her arms and hands were scraped and bleeding. She was still in the truck, with parts of the landscape inside it and around her. Dani made small movements throughout her limbs and decided nothing major was broken. She wiped at her cheek and blood smeared her palm. She turned to find her friends.

Mary hung from her seat belt.

"Shit! Mary!"

Dani fought with her seat belt to free herself. Mary was motionless. Blood ran in small streams from the left side of her face. Dani's hand trembled when she placed her fingertips against Mary's neck. She couldn't feel a pulse.

"Mary?"

Her friend groaned. Dani placed her palms on the sides of Mary's face and kissed her bloodied forehead. "You're alive.

Thank you for being alive." She glanced to the rear of the transport, but didn't see Dresden. She remembered him being thrown from the vehicle when the road broke apart.

Dani looked around the vehicle, organizing her next move. "Think!"

She looked at the radio, and the mike was gone. She'd had it in her hand until the truck went off the road.

The Wardens would search the transport. If they found Mary, they'd kill her. When they found Dani and learned she was an Echo ... the memory of the Wardens' reconditioning process made her shudder. They would turn her into one of them, adding her to their army to rid Earth of all humans.

Dani had her pistol, but she didn't know how many Wardens were on the hillside. She'd seen two, and she might be able to fight a pair of them if she had the attack advantage. But she was at a major disadvantage being outnumbered and with less fire power. Attacking was not an option.

"Mary, wake up."

Mary's eyes fluttered, and Dani wiped them clear of blood.

"We're leaving the truck. Put your arms around me."

Mary winced and groaned with her movement. Dani looped one arm around her friend and planted her feet against anything that would hold their weight. She pulled her knife and cut the seat belt. Mary sagged against her, and Dani struggled to hold her. She sheathed her blade and put her other arm around Mary.

"You have to help me, or I'll drop you."

Mary nodded and opened her eyes again. "I'm sorry we crashed."

"You're a shit driver."

Mary tried to smile, but her face was pinched with pain.

The two of them worked together to maneuver Mary over the scattered food totes and out through the broken hatch in the rear. Once on the ground, Dani guided her away from the wreckage. She wanted to grab a med kit, but she didn't know where the Wardens were or where the kits might be buried beneath the other supplies. She decided to find a place to stash Mary first.

She wasn't sure how far they'd gone, but Dani stopped when she found a level area and a tree with a broad trunk. She eased Mary to the ground and helped her lean back against the tree. Mary was covered in blood, and her skin was ashen. Bits of glass were embedded in her face. She didn't move her left arm much, so Dani guessed it might be broken with some fractured ribs in the mix too. She tried not to think of internal injuries.

"Where's Dres?" Mary asked.

"I don't know." Dani pressed her plasma pistol into Mary's hand. The energy weapon was no match against Warden quake grenades, but it was better than nothing. "Stay here and take this."

"No."

"Take it, Mary. I'm going back to get a med kit and look for Dres."

"I'll go with you."

"No. I'll be right back."

"Promise?"

"Yes. Because if I don't come back, you and Oliver will steal my damn dog." She smiled when Mary did.

Dani left and refused to look back. She had never seen so much blood covering someone who was alive. She needed to grab at least one med kit, preferably two, out of the truck. Weapons, food, and gear to help them through the cold, damp night would be useful too, but she promised herself she wouldn't get greedy. The med kit was the top priority.

She slipped back through trees and around rocks as she scrambled up the slope. The mud quieted her movements but slowed her pace. Dani looked for Dresden during her ascent but didn't see him. As she neared the truck, she stopped and listened. Hearing nothing, she resumed moving.

She crawled in through the rear of the vehicle and began moving totes and the packages that had spilled from them. She found her field bag and threw it out the back of the truck. Dani grabbed the handle of a black case that contained the spare radio, but as she extracted it from the mess of gear, she had only the top part of the case's lid. The bottom part and the radio were buried.

"Goddammit."

A blast from somewhere on the road above made her start tossing the totes and food rations aside with more haste and less caution.

After finally finding a med kit, Dani struggled to free it from the debris. Her heart seemed to beat out of control, and sweat burned the cuts on her face. Once the kit was in her hands, she shifted to throw it out of the truck. She froze when she heard a voice.

"Third one is down here."

"Nuke it," a second man's voice said.

The third voice was a woman. "Let's check it first."

"I'm not going down there," the first man said.

"Scared of getting dirty?" the woman asked.

Shit! Dani moved toward the rear with the med kit and spotted Mary's jacket. She grabbed it and found Mary's rifle underneath. The truck slid a few feet before stopping. Dani lost her balance and her back struck the gear totes beneath her. She resisted an urge to cry out when the corners of the totes jabbed her.

Loosened gravel and mud trickled down past the front of the truck.

"You get stuck down there, I'm not coming to help you," the second man said.

The woman's voice was much closer now. "There are food rations scattered all over."

Dani took a deep breath to calm her mind. She'd been almost stepped on by a Warden during the attack on Portland, but she had been hidden in a snow drift and wearing a CNA skin at the time. She couldn't hide among the totes. Dani crept to the rear of the truck and paused. She glanced out and didn't see the other two Wardens. The truck had rolled far enough down the slope that she assumed they were on the road and out of sight. The female Warden was coming for the transport. Dani didn't see or hear her, so she slipped out the back.

She silently picked her way over rocks and broken tree limbs. If the Warden took the time to search, she'd see Dani's boot prints in the mud going away from the truck. She couldn't worry about that now, and tucked behind a boulder. She eased herself to one knee and lowered the med kit and jacket, keeping the weapon. Upon spotting the female Warden moving around the truck, Dani aimed the plasma rifle at her.

Her finger touched the trigger, but she hesitated. Assuming the sights weren't off after the beating the weapon had taken in the tumble, Dani wasn't a great shot at distance anyway— definitely not good enough to make a decapitating head shot. A Warden could regen after taking a fatal hit to the chest or abdomen, and she would have to attack again during that vulnerable regen time to permanently end the enemy. Even *if* she managed to remove the woman's head, the other two Wardens remained a problem, and Dani didn't know where they were. Plus, she was outgunned. A plasma rifle was nothing when the Wardens were taking out transport trucks with quake grenade launchers.

She cursed under her breath and eased her finger from the trigger. She'd shoot only if the Wardens followed the tracks she and Mary had left. The female Warden took several packages of food rations before going back up the slope. Dani lost sight of her but could hear their voices.

"No bodies in there but a shitload of blood," she said. "They're wounded and will die from exposure tonight anyway."

"Can I nuke it now?" the second man asked.

"Light it up," the woman said.

Dani ducked. A second later a deafening explosion ripped the truck apart and shook the ground. She remained in place until the ringing in her ears lessened. She slipped the rifle's strap over her shoulder and crept up the slope. She spotted the three Wardens walking down the road one hundred yards away. They rounded a bend in the road and were gone. She reached the road and crept toward the burning second truck. Three bodies in pools of blood were in the roadway, and Dani didn't need to approach them to know they were dead. The first truck, deformed from the direct hit by the quake grenade, was engulfed in flames. She quickly searched for Dresden but didn't find him.

She left the road, picked up the med kit and jacket she'd left at the boulder, and continued down until she found her pack. Dani lumbered under the load, fighting increasing stiffness as she scrambled toward the area where she'd left Mary.

She was gone.

Dani dropped the gear and followed boot prints for several yards. Mary emerged from behind a thick tree, and Dani rushed to her. She caught her before she fell, and Mary released the pistol to embrace her as she sobbed against Dani's shoulder.

"Christ, Mary, what's wrong?"

"I thought you were dead."

"I'm fine."

"You were stupid to go back. You can't regen if you're in pieces."

"I was out before they blew the truck."

Mary continued to hold on to her. "What the hell took you so long?"

"I had to look for Dres, but I couldn't find him."

Mary sniffled and took a deep breath. "The others?"

"Gone." She extracted herself from Mary's embrace to slip her arm around her waist. "I got a med kit. C'mon."

Once she had Mary seated, Dani left to retrieve the pistol. She returned and draped Mary's jacket around her shoulders. Mary looked like shit, and Dani wanted to make a fire, but that was too risky. She removed a light from her pack and dug through the med kit while the sun crept below the horizon, taking the daytime warmth with it.

CHAPTER 3

Dani rummaged through the medical gear. She'd wrapped Mary's left shoulder to keep her arm close to her body as a splint, but Mary wasn't deterred by being reduced to one arm. She lifted her rifle with her right hand, tucked the stock into her shoulder, and balanced the end of the weapon on the top of her boot. She peered through the scope and adjusted the sights.

"Would I have missed the Warden if I'd shot at her?" Dani asked.

Mary nodded and continued her adjustments until she looked up. "She'll shoot straight for you now."

Dani removed a vial of plasma expander from the med kit. "Me?"

"I can't shoot it with one arm."

"I can't shoot it with two arms," Dani said.

Mary laughed, then winced. She placed the rifle on the ground and touched her sore ribs.

Dani removed a second vial from the kit. She affixed the first vial to the healing patch adhered to the back of Mary's hand. The vial clicked into place, and the liquid inside flowed through the patch and into Mary's hand. The skin on her hand luminesced for a moment, then returned to normal. Dani swapped out vials and repeated the procedure.

Mary took a deep breath and closed her eyes. "That is *good* shit. Takes all the pain away."

Dani picked up the MedPanel and pointed one side of the glass-like device toward Mary. The black screen filled with a myriad of images and grayish text. Some of it she understood— most of it she didn't, including the blinking red text. She shook her head and frowned. "I gave you another dose of plasma. The panel says your volume is good with the expanders, but your blood counts are a little low. The blood transfusion vials in our truck went up in flames with everything else. There is shit blinking at me on this display, and I don't know what it means." She tossed the panel aside. "Fuck it. Just don't die on me."

Mary slurred, "I shall do my best to not die."

Dani slid closer to Mary and adjusted her headlamp before picking up the healing pen and hemostats. "Ready?"

"There can't be much more glass left in my face."

"This is the last round and won't take as long."

Mary twitched when Dani's hemostat touched one of the tiny shards of glass embedded in her skin. Dani pulled the glass free, then touched the end of the pen against the wound. The skin cells replicated to stop the bleeding and close the cut, leaving a small pink scar. She moved to the next piece of glass that needed to come out.

"The smoke from the trucks was easily visible before nightfall," Mary said. "I was hoping some area Brigands might show up by now."

Dani adjusted Mary's head to face forward again. "No sane Brigand would come here with quake grenades going off. We're overdue for returning to the base with no comms regarding the delay. Houston will send someone." She plucked another piece of glass out, then applied the pen.

"You have a lot of faith in her."

"She's always kept her word, which is a nice change from the usual CNA bullshit."

Dani continued her work until the last shard was out.

"How bad is the scarring?"

"Minimal. I'm pretty good with a pen."

"Guess it's a good thing I only help Aunt Hattie manage the brothel's books now. A scarred-up whore is bad for business."

Dani turned Mary's face to look into her eyes. "*Never* use that word around me—especially about yourself."

Mary lowered her gaze. "I'm sorry. I guess I'm just feeling particularly pathetic tonight."

Dani had enough moonlight to continue working, so she turned her headlamp off. She poured water from her canteen over a cloth and used it to wipe blood from Mary's face.

"Pathetic? You're never that."

Mary caught Dani's hand. "What are you thinking about when you stare at me when you think I can't see you?"

There was nothing to stop the redness that filled Dani's face, and she was grateful the night helped conceal it. She was relieved when Mary released her hand. She swallowed a few times. "I'm not trying to be creepy, but it's like admiring … art."

"*Art?* That's quite the compliment."

Dani nodded.

"Do you ever wonder why I worked as a wh— on my back for a while?"

Dani fiddled with the cloth. "Sometimes. It seemed like a job beneath you. I mean, you're smart and know how to fix things. You could find work doing other stuff."

"You thrive as a Brigand, Dani. I lived that life of scavenging and being forced to find food to live another day. I hated it. Aunt Hattie had better-paying work. She offered me a few different jobs, and I took the one with sex. It was my choice.

Everyone who works for her gets the best food and money. She looks out for her people. We're not slaves or servants. We can stop anytime we want."

Dani rinsed and re-wet the cloth and resumed cleaning. "Why *did* you stop?"

"So I could be involved in Portland. It wasn't about me making as much money as I could anymore. There were bigger things happening, and I wanted to be a part of them."

Dani half snorted a laugh. "Today probably has you rethinking that decision to be a volunteer for the Commonwealth."

Mary touched Dani's arm with a light caress that made Dani's face burn hotter than before.

"Not at all," Mary said.

Dani swallowed hard and rinsed her cloth again. "Almost done."

"It's just blood. Stop wasting your water on it."

She stopped and stared at Mary for a moment. "Red isn't your color," she said before leaning in and kissing her.

Mary smiled. "You prefer me wearing yellow."

Dani's face felt like it was on fire.

"Do you know how long I have waited for you to do that? Of course, you do it when I'm high and won't remember."

Dani passed her fingertips over Mary's new scars before pulling Mary closer. "You'll remember." Dani kissed her deeply. She dropped the cloth and wrapped her arms around Mary, who flinched when Dani's hand touched her injured side.

"Sorry," she said, loosening her embrace.

Mary kept her close. Dani responded by again covering Mary's mouth with her own until they heard a scuffling noise. Their lips parted, and she helped Mary stand. Once on her feet, Mary placed her hand on Dani's shoulder to turn her around. She used her finger to tap on Dani's back and drew a line with her fingertip.

Dani nodded, and Mary removed the pistol from Dani's hip.

Mary wanted her to swing to the right to go around the location where the noise came from, and Mary would go left. Dani didn't want to leave, but if the Wardens were back, they needed to split up. She picked up the rifle, moved without a sound, and periodically paused to listen for someone or something else moving. Several minutes passed, and she figured the noise was caused by some animal until she heard movement before seeing the outlines of two people. She crept forward and then froze when she heard a third person breathing.

She was only a few yards from the man, and she inched the rifle to her shoulder. She found his silhouette and aimed. He moved in the darkness, and Dani's finger touched the trigger. Something about him seemed familiar. She ceased all movement, even breathing. She would have stopped her heartbeat if she'd been able to.

She drew in a slow breath and crept closer.

He holstered his pistol. "Clear."

Three other men echoed, "Clear."

Dani shook her head. "Gavin?"

The man spun, snatched the rifle from her hands, and swung the weapon back at her, striking her with the stock in her right shoulder. She cried out and crashed to the ground.

A light turned on, and Gavin loomed over her.

"You're still hesitating," he said.

She had always hated those words. During the years he had taught her how to fight, he had mocked her with them each time he kicked her ass. Anger began to turn to rage at being on her back, in the mud, and hearing those words again.

His head rocked to the side when struck. He stumbled, then fell with a second blow to his skull. Mary was on top of him in an instant and thrust the end of her pistol into his mouth. Gavin released the rifle and raised his hands in surrender. He waved off the other three men as they approached with weapons aimed at Mary.

"If you ever touch her again, I'll take your fucking head off," Mary said. "No regen, asshole."

Gavin nodded, and Mary withdrew the weapon. Dani remained on the ground, clutching her throbbing shoulder, and stared open-mouthed at Mary.

"Gonna keep lying in the mud?" Mary asked.

Dani rolled to her knees and stood. She rubbed her sore arm.

Mary raised her arm. "I need you to help me. Meds are wearing off."

Dani scrambled to her feet, looped her arm around Mary, and helped her back to their place near the tree. She didn't bother to look at Gavin but listened to the men speak.

"Well done, Cap. You just got your ass handed to you by a one-armed woman."

"You know them?"

Gavin grunted in response.

"Did you know the one with the rifle had you in her sights the whole time?"

"Kelsey, they look like they can use a medic," Gavin said.

"You've been a medic longer than me," Kelsey said.

"Mary just sat on my chest and put a goddamn gun in my mouth. You really think she wants me anywhere near her? Go! Corey, Jamie, set up a perimeter," Gavin said.

Dani grinned to hear their exchange. Mary had humiliated Gavin in front of his team, and it was perfection. She eased Mary to the ground and winced to see how pale her friend's face had become. She took the pistol from Mary and slipped it back into her holster. "Swinging for the fences at Gavin's head took a lot out of you."

Mary smiled and nodded. "Worth it."

"Have to admit I'm jealous as hell."

"I love that rifle. Make sure you get it back from him."

"I will."

Kelsey arrived and put his weapon on the ground before moving closer. He shrugged out of his pack and knelt. Dani passed him the MedPanel and waited while he assessed Mary. He asked Mary a few questions and checked her wounds before turning to Dani.

"Please don't tell me I fucked something up," Dani said. "If I did, just fix her."

He chuckled and shook his head. "You did a great job. You could flip into combat medic training if you ever wanted to." He removed a few items from the med kit. "Ready to assist?"

Dani's gut knotted. "With what?"

He turned his attention to Mary. "Your shoulder is dislocated, and you have a few smaller fractures in your upper arm. Putting things back where they belong will go a long way in helping the pain."

"Knock my ass out and get on with it," Mary said.

Kelsey snapped a series of vials to the patch on Mary's hand. When the medications entered her veins, Mary's breathing slowed and her chin dipped to her chest. Dani helped the medic place her on her back.

Mary looked up at her. "Dani, feel free to take advantage of me when I'm out. You, too, Kels."

Dani adjusted Mary's head to a more comfortable-looking position. "What did you give her?"

"A cocktail that won't let her shoot either of us when we fix her shoulder. Wait. Are you the Dani who crippled the Bangor barracks?"

Gavin touched the bleeding wound on the side of his head. "She's the one."

"I'm both impressed and pleased to meet you, Dani. You

and Mary are the only Brigands to ever get the jump on us. I'd heard the Bangor Brigands were the best stealth artists in the Northeast. I understand now why you make great sabs," Kelsey said.

"Best saboteurs the volunteers have," Gavin said. "Enough mooning over them. Get to work."

Dani shot him a glare. "Kinda hoped that with some time away you might be less of a dick, but that didn't happen. Dresden was in our truck and thrown when we went off the road. Do something useful and find him." She turned her full attention to the medic. "What do I do?"

After helping set Mary's shoulder, Dani shivered, but she couldn't tell if she was cold or sick from putting Mary's shoulder back in place. She didn't have time to rest yet. Kelsey finished treating Mary while Dani started a fire. As it burned brighter, she shifted from her knees to her rear.

Kelsey knelt beside her and checked the cuts on her face and arms. He scanned her with the MedPanel, then placed a patch on the back of her hand that made the skin beneath the patch tingle.

"What's that for?" Dani asked.

"Drugs. You've been running on adrenaline too long. Time to rest."

"How did you find us?"

"We've been in New Hampshire for months and were hiking for Bangor. Houston's orders. We took out a trio of Wardens, then spotted the smoke from the transports."

They both turned when Gavin, Corey, and Jamie started down the slope with Dresden on a field-made stretcher.

"Kels, we have our work cut out for us," Gavin said.

Dani sat up straighter.

Kelsey snapped a vial into the patch on her hand. "You're off duty."

The warm fluid entered her veins, and Dani shuddered. "Oh, shit."

"Good stuff, right?"

She moaned and blinked when her vision blurred. He helped her lie back and covered her with his jacket. She stared up at the tree limbs above and could not have risen if she had been set on fire. All soreness left her, and for the first time all day, her shoulder stopped aching. The tree limbs changed from black shadows to multicolored lines. Sparks from the fire grew golden wings and flew upward. Somewhere in her mind she knew the medication was causing the crazy visual effects, but she didn't care. They were beautiful. Her head lolled to the side, and her leaden eyelids closed.

CHAPTER

4

Miles had wanted to leave the Bangor base to meet Dani in Belfast, but Colonel Houston had denied his request. His assignment as a glorified security guard for Houston's meeting annoyed him, but he obeyed his superior officer's orders. A dozen or so people had arrived in Bangor from other states and Canada over the last few days to meet with her. Strict security was maintained as each visitor was checked for weapons. The final visitor passed through the scanners, and Miles frisked him—same as he'd done for all others entering the room.

The man lowered his outstretched arms. "All good?" His neatly trimmed beard matched his short, black and gray hair. He wore military-issue fatigues with a name patch of Cameron. He had no other insignias on his uniform to indicate rank or origin. He wasn't CNA.

Miles waved the man on. *Not from the States or Canada*, he thought. *Not with that accent.*

He followed the man through the door and closed it behind him. He stood beneath the giant plaque with the Commonwealth of North America's logo on the rear wall. Miles had the same emblem on one of the patches on his uniform. He'd been in this small auditorium many times, but his most memorable was when Dani used the room—while it was full of midlevel officers—to disable the barracks as a way to gain the CNA brass's attention. And gain it she had. Her brazenness had intrigued Houston and started the formation of a Commonwealth-Brigand partnership to take the fight to the Wardens for a change.

Miles pushed the memories aside to focus on the others in the room. Colonel Houston leaned against the long desk at the front of the room and folded her arms. Once the last person was seated, she stood up staight and eyed each of the visitors.

General Ramos had traveled up from Boston to be present, but he let Houston do all the talking. Miles wasn't sure why the general felt the need to be in Bangor for this gathering.

"You've bugged the hell out of me and my superiors for information on our success at Portland," Houston said. "This is the meeting you've requested. We haven't been trying to withhold any information, but we couldn't afford to lose precious time for a dozen different meetings about the same thing." She waved her hand and said, "Welcome to Bangor and the room where the CNA-Brigand partnership began. Some believe Portland was a stroke of dumb luck. It wasn't. It's no secret we're eyeing Boston, so don't bother asking me questions about that city. Ask whatever you want about Portland. I want to do whatever I can to help you retake your target regions from the Wardens.

"Fighting them isn't easy. The enemy is composed of Echoes who strive to see *all* humans dead, and they recondition and add captured Echoes to their army. Use your Echo allies to help plan your battles. Attacking Wardens on their turf will end in loss of life, but we proved that they can be beaten by uniting Commonwealth troops with civilian Brigand forces. This war is far from over, and we need to help each other. However, don't bother asking to borrow any of my officers or Brigands who served with us to take Portland. If I don't shoot you first for making such a stupid request, the answer will still be no."

She grinned. "I'd say that I was kidding, but I'm not. I think that's about it for ground rules. We're only discussing Portland, and if you try to take any of my people, do so at your own peril. Are we clear?"

Heads nodded, and Miles refused to share Houston's grin. He kept his face stone-like, but he was amused by the wide-eyed looks on some of the faces. It was a common reaction when people met Catherine Houston for the first time.

"Good. Captain Miles Jackman was part of the Portland attack, so he will also be answering your questions." She gestured toward Miles. "Fire away."

For four hours, Houston entertained any questions they had and offered suggestions on how the visitors might retake key cities and territories. She asked Miles to provide his input at times, which he did, but Miles was more concerned about the last man he'd allowed into the room. Cameron never spoke during the entire session.

Houston finally dismissed the group. "We're done for the day, but please use the remainder of your evening in Bangor to enjoy yourself. We no longer have Brigand and CNA territories, so you are welcome to wander off base as desired. We'll reconvene at the same time tomorrow."

Cameron remained, so Miles approached him.

"Happy to help you with directions on how to get around town," Miles said.

"Very kind of you, Captain. Colonel, I wished to speak with you about Boston. I'm Major Cameron with the Commonwealth of Europe."

Miles repressed his grin as Houston bored into the visitor with her gaze. He'd been on the receiving end of that glare before. Even watching her torment another with it made his insides twitch.

"You were not listening earlier. I will not discuss tactical plans with you, Major," Houston said.

"You don't understand," Cameron said. "I want to *help* you with Boston. London is the center of Warden activity in the UK."

"You help us with Boston, we help you with London. Is that it?" Houston asked. "Did you bring the British army with you to attack Boston with us? No? Fuck off. How is that for understanding?"

Cameron laughed. "I'd heard you were a tough customer, but that doesn't cover it at all. Colonel, I'm here to help you with Boston regardless of what happens with my country later. We need new ideas on how to handle London, and I want to learn from you and your team. I understand three Brigands crippled this base to gain the CNA's attention. I want to meet them."

Houston stared at Cameron while several seconds ticked by. No one could see through lies like she did, and Miles wished he had her skill at doing so. When she nodded, the Colonel signaled that Cameron had spoken the truth.

"We have only two of the three alive, and neither are in town at the moment," Houston said. "Dani will be back tonight, and Captain Marcus will be here in another day or two."

Miles's eyes snapped to Houston. She'd failed to tell him Gavin Marcus was back from whatever he had been assigned to do in New Hampshire. Gavin had treated Dani like shit before they broke up, and Miles would be more than happy to put his fist through the man's face.

"Good. This Danny. When can I meet him?" Cameron asked.

Miles approached the Brit. "Dani's been on assignments for the last two weeks. *She* will not be bothered on her first night back."

Cameron nodded, his smile small. "Understood. Tomorrow, then. Good night to you, Colonel and Captain," he said, and left.

"Prick," Miles muttered.

"Miles, I want your full attention," Houston said.

He turned and faced his commanding officer.

"Gavin is due back any day. I know you despise the man, and for a valid reason—probably more than one. Don't go starting any shit with him on my base. If you want to brawl, do it off-site."

"Yes, ma'am."

An alert sounded on her panel on the desk, and she checked the message. A frown crossed her face. "Fuck."

Houston never looked stressed. Even after no sleep for an inhumane amount of time following the Portland battle, she had never lost control of her emotions. Whatever the message was on her panel, Miles knew it was bad news.

"Miles, grab a med and tac team and take two helos. Our transport from Belfast to Bangor is overdue. No contact with them since they left Belfast a few hours ago."

"Shit. Dani and Mary were with them."

Houston nodded. "Find them."

He saluted and bolted for the door. He used his comm to order his teams together as he rushed to his quarters to grab his gear. His son met him at the door and jumped aside when Miles barreled through. Brody wagged his tail and followed Miles through the apartment.

"Dad, what's wrong?" Oliver asked.

Miles pulled gear from his trunk. "I need to go out tonight. We have an overdue transport, and I don't know how long it will take to reach them."

"It's Dani."

Miles turned to his son. "How did you know?"

"You wouldn't look so panicked if it was anyone else, except maybe me. Let me go with you, Dad. *Please?*"

"Not a chance, Ollie. Stay with Brody. If it starts getting late and I'm not back, you can stay with the neighbor."

"I want to go!"

"We're not arguing about this." Miles slung the pack over his shoulder. "I'll send you a message as soon as I know she and Mary are safe."

Oliver's eyes widened. "Mary's missing too?"

"Not missing. Overdue. There's a difference." He gave his son a quick hug. "I love you." The tears forming in his son's eyes made his chest hurt, but Miles had to leave. He needed to find Dani for himself *and* for his son. "I'll send you a message."

CHAPTER 5

"Contact," the pilot said.

Miles nodded. "I see it." A signal had been fired from the ground, and he followed the soaring red flare's trail downward. Ground flares were lit to indicate a place to land and glowed like tiny red lights. "Take us down and radio back to base that we have initial contact."

The pilot began the descent toward the road. Miles wished for a quicker landing, but he knew that was his own impatience to know Dani was safe. He hoped he'd see her on the road, but instead, Miles spotted two men he didn't recognize. His hand went to the plasma pistol holstered at his hip as he led the tactical team off the helo. He'd worn alien gear and pretended to be a Warden before, so these could be Wardens pretending to be Commonwealth. Carelessness got people killed, so he kept his hand on his weapon for now.

"Report," Miles said as he approached and the second helicopter landed.

"I'm Corporal Corey, sir. This is PFC Jamie. We're part of the CNA out of New Hampshire and came upon your transport after it was attacked by Wardens. The Wardens are dead, but of your people, six dead, three wounded, one seriously."

Miles removed his hand from his pistol and forced the lump out of his throat so he could speak. "Where are the survivors?"

"Down the slope, closer to the river," Corey said.

Miles began barking orders. He left part of his tactical team with the helos as guards and sent the med team and remaining tac soldiers with Corey. "Jamie, is it?"

"Yes, sir."

"Talk to my pilot. Relay information back to the base, then load the dead on the helos," Miles said. He didn't wait for the man's reply before giving orders to the tactical team. Once he had everyone in motion, he left to join the others headed for the survivors. He jogged past two smoldering trucks and didn't see the third. He followed the group led by Corey as they turned off the road to start down the hill. He saw the third truck on its side and smoking.

Two of his medics knelt next to two other men as they worked on someone lying on his, or her, back and not moving. *Shit. Please don't be her. Please don't be her. Boots are too big; it's a man.* His fears eased a fraction.

He recognized Mary's blond hair before he saw her face. A medic helped her stand, and a second medic blocked his view of another person seated next to her. Another medic moved, and Miles gasped to see Dani sitting on the ground. The medic helped her up, and her eyelids drooped. She had dried blood on her face, with more blood on her arms and clothes. She looked terrible, but she was alive.

"Miles!" Mary put her arm around him and kissed his cheek. "I'm so happy to see you."

He smiled and kept his embrace light since she had one arm wrapped in a sling-like device. He started to reply but stopped when Gavin stood after kneeling next to the injured man on the ground. His hands were covered in blood, and he wiped at his forehead with the back of his forearm.

Mary's eyes followed Miles's gaze and she snorted. "Yeah. Look who turned up."

"Miles," Gavin said.

Miles didn't bother with a response.

Dani approached and threw her arms around Miles's neck. "I knew you'd come," she said.

Miles glanced at Mary when Dani continued to cling to him. He and Dani had been lovers in her former life, but those memories had vanished with her last regen. She hadn't shown him this kind of affection since before her death, so her actions now bewildered him.

Mary patted his shoulder. "I'm really glad to see you. Kels, the medic, gave Dani the good stuff. She's a little shitfaced. Dres is in bad shape. He was thrown from the truck when we went off the road."

Gavin spoke as he approached. "Both femurs have compound fractures, and he has internal bleeding. Kelsey and I got him somewhat repaired, but he'll need extensive surgery."

Miles tried to pull Dani off his neck, but she didn't let go. "Take him up to one of the helos with the med team for evac."

Gavin nodded. "We're almost done prepping him for load and go."

Miles nodded. "Good."

Dani kissed Miles. "I love you."

He nodded and smiled. She said the words through a haze of medically induced inebriation, but he appreciated her show of affection. He couldn't help but also be pleased that Gavin, Dani's asshole of an ex, was there to witness it. When Miles spoke, his words were true. "I love you, too."

"How's Oliver? Brody?" Dani asked.

"Both are fine." Miles called to one of his tactical soldiers as he unwound Dani's arms from him. "Elmore, grab a medic and escort Mary and Dani to the road and put them on the medical helo."

"Yes, sir," Elmore said.

Dani started the hike up the hill with the medic while Mary lingered with Elmore. Kelsey and the others lifted Dresden on the stretcher to carry him out.

"Thanks for your help, Gavin," Miles said.

Mary shook her head. "Don't be too appreciative yet, Miles. If anyone gets to kill him, it's me."

Miles frowned. "You want him dead *already*?"

"Dani got the drop on him but didn't shoot. He struck her for hesitating."

Miles's confusion turned to anger. He directed his glare at Gavin. "You hit Dani?"

Gavin tightened his jaw and didn't answer.

"Abusing her before wasn't enough?" Miles slammed his fist into Gavin's jaw, and the man stumbled until he dropped to one knee. Miles stepped toward him, then stopped. He took a deep breath and returned his attention to his duty instead of his personal grudge. "Elmore. I gave you orders."

"Yes, sir," he said, and he urged Mary to the path up the hill while she continued to grin at Miles.

"Thought you said you had friends in Bangor, Cap," Kelsey said as he and the other medics carried Dresden past while Gavin remained on his knee. "Must be different friends from these folks."

Mary's laugh echoed through the trees.

Miles stepped in to help the medics carry Dresden. His knuckles ached from the blow, but he didn't care. Gavin rubbed his jaw as he righted, and Miles didn't bother looking back at him again.

The mud and steep slope hindered their ability to quickly move Dresden, but once they reached the road, they walked at a brisker pace to meet the helo. Dani was strapped into her seat, and her head rested against Mary's shoulder. She slept despite the noise from the helicopter, and Mary gave Miles a tired smile.

Once Dresden was strapped in, Miles hopped back out and gestured to the helo pilot to leave. He and Gavin were the last ones to climb into the remaining helicopter. As it left the ground, Miles pulled his comm from his pocket and sent Oliver a quick note.

"We don't have to be friends, but we do have to work together," Gavin said.

"I can do my job. Can you do yours without inflicting some kind of pain on Dani for the enjoyment of hurting her?"

"I trained her to be a fighter. She asked me to train her harder than before, and I did."

"You beat her, Gavin. Call it whatever the hell you want, but you beat her, and not just physically."

"How the fuck do you think she's alive?"

Miles laughed at his absurd remark. "Are you really trying to take the credit for her surviving a quake rifle shot to the chest?"

"I had given her my CNA armor, so she had an extra layer on that no one else had. *That's* how she survived, you fucking moron. So, yeah, I'm taking some of that credit."

"The transport attack? She survived that because of you?"

"I'm not talking about only today. She's tougher because of how I trained her. Dani fought Rowan and lived. I saw the feed of her in the med bay with that psychopath. Mary would have died in the same situation. Colonel Houston could not have done what she did that day. Dani will survive because of *me*. Not you. Not Mary."

"Leaving her in a field hospital as soon as she woke up from surgery—how exactly did that save her life?"

Gavin remained silent.

"You know you fucked that one up. She knows it too. There will come a day when you will pay."

Gavin laughed. "Ah. The human is now giving the Echo a warning about karma. That's perfect. I've already lived enough lifetimes to make your single, insignificant existence on this planet a nonevent. You're a fool for loving an Echo. Dani will outlive you. She'll watch every human she loves die while she continues on." He paused. "Unless she regens and forgets all about you. Again."

Miles clenched his hands into fists, but he refused to lose control of his anger. "Stay away from her."

"Or what? You'll kill me?" Gavin leaned his head back against the seat and closed his eyes. "Get in line."

Miles took a deep breath and relaxed his fingers. His gaze fell on the dead beneath the blankets in the rear of the helo. He thanked any Echo or human gods who might be listening that Dani wasn't one of the people under a blanket. His chest ached to remember her telling him that she loved him. He hoped it was true.

CHAPTER 6

Dani stirred when Brody pressed his wet nose against her cheek. She cracked one eye open, and the dog licked her face until she rolled over to leave the bed. She ached all over, and she sat on the side of the bed for a moment while Brody jumped to the floor. His tail wagged, and his eyes never left her. She winced when he barked.

"Okay. Okay," Dani groaned. She stood and pulled a pair of tattered jeans from the back of her chair and put them on. She stopped for a moment and realized she couldn't remember returning to her room at Hattie's. She glared at Brody when he barked a second time. He wiggled in response. "You can be a real pain, B." She decided her tank top and jeans were enough clothing to escort the dog out. They left the room, and Dani paused. The cool air made the skin on her arms prickle, but she didn't bother going back to her room for another layer. She trudged barefoot to the rear of Hattie's multiroom house that operated as living quarters, a brothel, and a pub.

Brody diverted from his path to the back door and entered the kitchen. Dani followed him, unsure why he delayed going outside to relieve himself. A man with a neatly trimmed beard whom she'd never seen before gave the dog a piece of his toast.

"Careful, he's vicious," Dani said.

The man smiled. "We've already met."

"We have?"

"I meant Brody. I met him early this morning when the boy dropped him off. I think his name was Oliver."

Shit. Dani didn't remember seeing Oliver this morning. She opened the back door. "Brody. Out."

The dog left the man and headed outside. She closed the door and passed her hand over her face, wishing her mental fog would lift.

"Hungry? I can make more toast," the man said.

The man had an accent that was pleasant to her ears, but she wasn't in the mood to chat. She shook her head and tried to remember something from last night. She started with the transport going off the road. She and Mary were together, Gavin showed up, the medic—what's his name—drugged her, and that's when things got *really* fuzzy. *Miles? Was he there or a dream? A helicopter, maybe two.* She recalled nothing of the flight back to Bangor. Dani had been in the infirmary with Mary, they were treated, Dani was released, but Mary needed to stay a little longer. *How did I get home?* Hattie was in the mix of memories somewhere.

Hattie came into the kitchen. "It's alive!" She cackled at her quip.

Dani turned and leaned back against the door for added support "Hattie, I'm losing my mind. I can't remember much from last night."

The older woman grinned. "I'd think you'd be used to forgetting shit, honey."

Dani winced.

Hattie waved her hand. "Fine. Bad joke." She turned her attention to the man in her kitchen. "What the hell are you doing in here? This isn't a bed-and-breakfast. Get out! Dani, have a seat at the table before you fall over."

The man started to leave and stopped. He pulled the chair out for Dani to sit. She eyed him for a moment before sitting.

"I'm Cameron—Cam," he said.

"Dani."

"I've heard about you." He stumbled when Hattie shoved him.

The older woman stalked him, a menacing finger pointed at his face. "The next time I tell you to leave, it will be with my foot up your ass."

He backed away, and Hattie stared at him until he disappeared through a door to the interior of the house. She sat across the table from Dani.

"Where's Mary?" Dani asked.

"Sleeping. The doctors released her an hour or so after you. I brought you home, and you passed out. Oliver dropped the mutt off before he went to school this morning. I let the dog into your room, and you didn't wake when he got on the bed with you."

"Dres?"

"Alive, somehow. He'll be in the infirmary for a while."

Brody barked at the door, and Hattie stood before Dani could get out of her chair. She let him in, then went to the pantry.

"Ask the rest of your questions now while I fix you something to eat. You have a busy day, and so do I. The new brothel in Portland is opening. I'm heading there tomorrow and will be gone for several days." Hattie dug through her cabinets. "Coffee? Yes, you'll need coffee."

"Why?" Dani asked.

Hattie turned and winked at her. "Trust me."

After eating, bathing, and dressing, she felt more awake. She left with Brody and walked the few miles to the barracks, figuring she should find Colonel Houston. Dani's volunteer status didn't require her to follow Commonwealth military protocols like Miles had to, but she assumed Houston would want to see her after yesterday's transport cluster fuck.

She neared Houston's office and stopped when six people she didn't know approached her at once. Brody released a low growl.

"Is that her?"

"I think it is. Dani Ireland."

"No. She's not in uniform. She could be anybody."

The voices ran together, and Dani wasn't sure what the people were talking about. She turned to face one who spoke, but then another one said something. She had turned again, ready to flee, when a hand snagged her upper arm. She relaxed upon recognizing Miles.

He pulled her from the middle of the group.

Once they were clear of the others, Dani found her voice. "What the hell was that?"

"I'll let Colonel Houston fill you in."

Dani walked with him, and he led her through another, larger group that was gathered near Houston's office. Once inside, Dani took a deep breath and felt more confused than ever.

"Ah, Dani," Houston said. "Welcome back. How are you feeling?"

Gavin stood next to Houston's desk but didn't speak.

Dani shrugged. "Wondering if I should panic."

Houston laughed. "Best get it over with now if you're going to unravel. Meeting starts in twenty minutes. Your timing is perfect. We have a dozen or so folks here to talk to us about Portland. They're from areas across North America plus one from Britain. Miles and I entertained them yesterday, but they're more interested in speaking to you and Gavin."

"About what?"

"Portland. Were you listening?"

Dani shook her head. "I don't understand. I can't do this today."

Houston shifted to a counter near her desk and poured a cup of dark liquid. She passed the cup to Dani. "Best to drink it in one gulp. Tastes like shit, but it'll wake you up."

"I've already had some coffee."

"This isn't coffee. Drink it and let's go," Houston said, and she left with Gavin.

Dani remained in the office with the mug in her hand and stared at Miles. "Is she serious?"

Miles nodded.

Dani closed her eyes for a moment and sighed. "Fuck." She gulped the liquid and shuddered. The drink tasting like shit was an understatement, and she resisted the urge to gag. She left the cup on Houston's desk and followed Miles and Brody out.

She did feel far more awake by the time they reached the room where the visitors had gathered. Dani passed through them and waited near the front of the room with Gavin and Houston while Miles screened each guest before allowing them to enter. She recognized the man from Hattie's kitchen that morning.

Gavin leaned in and whispered. "I want to talk to you later."

"Fuck off."

Once everyone was in the room, the session began. Dani and Gavin were pummeled with questions for the next five hours. It would have continued longer, but Houston ended the meeting. People began filing out, and Dani tensed when the lone general in the room approached her.

He extended his hand, and Dani pulled her eyes from the mass of ribbons, pins, and other stuff on his uniform to meet his gaze and take his hand. He hadn't spoken once during the questioning.

"I'm Santi Ramos. It's an honor to finally meet you," he said.

She noticed he'd dropped his title when introducing himself. "Thanks?"

He smiled, released her hand, then turned to Houston. "You underestimate her, Colonel."

Houston pressed her lips closed. Dani knew that look. The colonel was physically preventing her desired response from coming out.

"I'll work on improving that, General," Houston said.

Dani wasn't sure what was going on between them but didn't care. Ramos left and she was finally feeling like she could relax when Cameron approached.

"Remarkable work your group did with Portland," he said.

"Session is over, Major Cameron," Houston said.

He nodded and grinned. "Interesting dynamic here with the way others hover around you to keep you protected," he said to Dani. "Quite interesting."

Once he left, Dani headed for the door too.

"Can I talk to you?" Gavin asked.

Dani continued her retreat. "No." Brody trotted to catch up to her. She was almost free when Houston spoke.

"Dani, we need to debrief about yesterday."

"Not today."

"Be in my office first thing tomorrow morning."

Dani didn't bother responding. Miles held the door open for her to leave. She paused on her way out. "Thank you."

"Anytime," he said.

She used Brigand trails to return to Harlow Street and avoided the more commonly used roads between the barracks and Hattie's brothel. She gave Brody his food in her room and left to find Mary.

Dani knocked on her door. She waited a few seconds before the door opened, and Dani's heart skipped a beat. Mary wore only a T-shirt that almost reached the middle of her thighs.

"Were you sleeping?" Dani asked.

"No."

Kelsey walked by in the interior of the room, completely naked. Dani frowned.

Mary stepped into the hall and closed the door behind her. "Why are you here?"

"To see how you were doing. We almost died yesterday. Remember?"

"I remember everything. Do you?"

"No, not everything. I do recall kissing you." Dani waved her hand toward the door. "I'm confused why you have the medic in there."

"Him and not you, is that what you mean?"

Dani passed her fingers through her hair. "Maybe. I don't know. You flirt incessantly with me. When I decide I'd like us to be more than friends, you brush me aside. It's a ton of mixed messages, Mary."

"You don't remember what you told Miles last night, do you?"

"When?"

Mary chuckled and shook her head. "You're a walking disaster. You told him you loved him."

Dani's mouth opened, and she could only stare at her friend.

"Granted, you were a bit hammered after the drugs Kels gave you, but I've never seen you so happy. Miles arrived on-site, and you went for him in a way you've never approached me, Gavin, or anyone else."

The word *no* was on endless repeat inside her mind; she couldn't speak, so she just shook her head.

"It was very sweet, Dani. You obviously love him, but you can't get your heart and mind on the same page. The drugs took down whatever barrier has kept you from telling him before."

Dani's gut knotted. She had been starving after the long meeting, but now she was nauseated.

"I had every intention of moving things forward with you until Miles showed up. Your reaction to his arrival changed things. I won't get between you and him."

"Christ, Mary, there is no me and him."

"There is. You just haven't figured it out yet. I won't flirt with you anymore. I am truly sorry for the confusion I created in doing so."

"But—"

"I'm happy to see you up and about, but you look like shit. Get some rest. I'll see you tomorrow." Mary stepped back through the door and closed it.

Dani's eyes burned with tears, and she wasn't sure why she wanted to cry. The mix of emotions between Mary sending her away, the horror of learning she'd told Miles she loved him, and physical exhaustion drained her. She wasn't sure what to do, so she escaped back to her room and sulked.

CHAPTER

7

The next morning, Dani met the Brit in the kitchen again when she let Brody out.

"Morning," Cameron said in a cheery manner that made her want to punch him.

"Hattie's gonna kill you for eating her food again."

"This time I paid for breakfast. She's happy now. Everyone calls her Aunt Hattie but you. Do you work for her when you're not fighting Wardens?"

Dani opened the door and looked out, but Brody was off in the taller grass tending to his morning routine. "We're in-laws."

"Mother-in-law?" he asked, then took a bite of his bread.

"Sister-in-law." Brody's head came up, and he bounded through the grass in the opposite direction from the house. She closed the door and growled.

"Really? Quite the age gap to be a sister-in-law. Your brother, or sister, I guess, who married her must have been young or you're actually an Echo with a recent regen. Which is it?"

"Brother."

"Where is he?"

"We're *not* talking about this." Since Brody wasn't in a rush to come back, Dani went to the kitchen and sliced off a couple of chunks of bread.

"Not much into mornings, are you?"

"Not when I've had a shit night. Move," she said, gesturing with the knife for him to vacate his current location.

He stepped aside from where he leaned against the counter, and Dani found a jar of jam in the cabinet he'd blocked. She used the knife to spread the jam over one of the pieces of bread. Once finished she stabbed the blade into the bread so the handle stuck upright.

He stared at the knife handle. "I'd love to talk to you about London when you're a bit less, um, hostile."

"London! Have you lost your mind, whatever your name is?"

"Cameron. Cam is fine too."

"I have enough to sort out with Boston. You're on your own with London."

Brody barked at the door.

"Finally." She left the kitchen area with her bread. After she opened the door, she gave Brody the plain piece, which he gulped down.

"How come the dog gets to attend meetings with CNA brass?"

"Like me, he's part of the Brigand army."

"I'm happy to help you with Boston, Dani."

"If Houston agrees, maybe I'll let you."

She ate her bread on her way back to her room. She dressed and then headed to Houston's office, not caring that she'd missed the "first thing" time frame.

Dani told Houston everything she recalled from the transport attack until she got to the parts where she didn't remember the details. Kelsey's drugs had done a number on her. She told Houston to ask Mary about the missing parts of her story, then bolted for the planning room. She didn't want to be present when Mary gave her side of the story, certain she'd die of embarrassment if Mary told Houston about Dani declaring her love for Miles while wasted.

She stared at a giant map of Boston projected on the wall, but her mind was elsewhere. Brody leapt from his place on the floor and rushed to the door. Dani smiled when Oliver entered with a daypack slung over his shoulder. He greeted Brody on his way to her, and they hugged.

"I'm so glad you're back," Oliver said. "I wanted to see you last night, but Dad said you were tired after the meeting."

"I was. Sorry."

"Well, I guess I can forgive you if you promise to have dinner with us tonight."

"Oh, uh." She didn't want to see Miles just yet.

Oliver's shoulders slumped with disappointment.

"Tonight's fine," Dani said, and Oliver smiled. The kid could talk her into anything, and she hated that.

"Mind if I hang out here and have lunch while you work?"

"No, not at all."

He sat on the floor with Brody and opened his pack. Brody's ninety pounds of bulk leaned against the thirteen-year-old, waiting for a treat.

Dani returned to the map. She picked up a panel from one of the tables and made a few notes, but ultimately, she did a lot of staring at the map while her mind wandered.

She closed her eyes for a moment when a memory of Rowan, a Warden who had tried more than once to kill her, returned. She replayed the events in her mind—the pain of being shot in the back by a plasma pistol and of him sticking her arm with a needle. She shuddered to recall the fire that had burned up her arm from the medication he gave her to turn her into a Warden. Memories of fighting him and being stabbed pushed to the front. She startled when a hand gripped hers, and her eyes flew open.

"What's wrong?" Oliver asked, looking up at her. A few more inches of teenage growth spurts and he'd be looking down at her.

She shivered and pulled her hand from his grasp.

"You've been standing here for almost an hour and haven't spoken or moved."

She couldn't believe she'd lost an hour.

"What's wrong?"

Dani took a deep breath and decided to tell him everything.

"I keep remembering my encounter with Rowan. He's relentless, Oliver. I live with this constant fear that he's not done with Maine or me. I am always on edge, waiting and watching for him to show up. Mary dismisses it as paranoia, but three Wardens took out our transport in seconds."

"You think Rowan ordered it?"

"I don't know. I think that's what bothers me the most—well, that and I don't have a clue what to do about Boston."

"You worked with Gavin and planned Portland to perfection."

"Perfection?" Dani said, and she laughed. "Hardly."

"The plan was perfect; everyone says so, except the Wardens screwed parts of it up. Gavin's back. You can work with him again."

"We're not on speaking terms."

"You gotta be now. This war can't drag on forever because you're mad at him. I know he wasn't nice to you, but you make a good team when you're plotting against the Wardens."

Dani opened her mouth to argue her point, but her comm chirped. She checked the message and sighed. "I gotta go. Houston beckons."

"I'll walk with you on my way back to class."

"Her office is nowhere near your class."

He shrugged and offered her a crooked smile. "That's okay. I can be a little late."

"Am I a bad influence on you?"

He nodded and widened his smile.

"I can live with that."

"Can Brody come back to class with me?"

"Sure. He's bored with me today."

They parted ways at the building where Houston's office was. Dani entered and found Gavin and Houston waiting for her.

"This can't be good news," Dani said.

"We've lost contact with Boston," Houston said.

Dani's eyes widened. "Our intel contacts?"

Houston nodded.

"Dead?"

"We don't know yet. If we're lucky, it's just a technical problem with comms, and they'll reestablish contact in a day or two. What do you have for me for an attack?"

Dani's shoulders slumped. "Not a goddamn thing."

"I figured. You've been struggling with this too long, which is why I called Gavin back from New Hampshire. I need the two of you to sort your shit out and come up with something for me *now*. Get your asses in the planning room and don't come out until you have something."

Dani shook her head, and Houston held up her hand.

"I don't want to hear it, Dani. There's something in the way you two work together, and I need that spark back. As individuals trying to plan an attack, you suck. Planning room. Go." Houston pointed at the door.

Dani left the office without speaking to Gavin until they were back in the room with the wall-sized map of Boston.

"Did you know this is why she called you back?" she asked.

"No. Listen, I'm sorry, Dani. I was an asshole for hitting you with the rifle. You are the only person to ever sneak up on me, and it pissed me off. I was mad at myself, not you, but I took it out on you. I'm sorry."

"You have a habit of doing that, and you're not done apologizing for all the other shit."

"I know. But we'll be here forever if I do that instead of figuring out what the hell to do about Boston."

He reached for her hand, and she slapped it away. "We are on working terms only."

Gavin shoved his hands into his pockets. "Understood."

They worked long hours over the next few days. Houston was happy with their progress, but she had them pause their efforts. Contact with Boston did not return, and an attack on Boston couldn't happen without intel. If the colonel needed to send people into the city for recon, she wanted to be closer to the target. She ordered many of Bangor's CNA and volunteer Brigand troops to Portland. Dani was among them.

CHAPTER

Dani stood in the middle of the floor inside a giant warehouse near Portland's wharf district. Miles, Javi, and Gavin stood next to her, and she tinkered with the settings on her helmet while they waited. Houston's R&D techies took the Warden helmet tech they had stolen during the Portland battle and had made tweaks to it to create the version she wore today. She tapped a tiny knob on the side to adjust the visor's visibility. She could see Miles's face inside his helmet as if no visors existed between them.

She didn't like the rest of the outfit. The suit clung to her frame, and the boots had strange soles that made her feel like she was standing in mud even though the warehouse floor was concrete.

Houston's voice came over her ear comm. "We discovered some novel Warden tech the week after we took Portland. It took us some time to figure it out, and today you'll have the chance to give it a test run in this building. We have almost every square inch of this place lined with projectors and sensors."

Dani looked around for the woman but didn't find her.

"The techs have taken every 2-D and 3-D map and scan of Boston to create a digital version," Houston said.

The warehouse interior changed to a cityscape of war-torn Boston in an instant. Dani stood on a street surrounded by the rubble of bombed-out buildings throwing shadows across the street, with the sun setting in the west. She turned in a full circle with her mouth agape.

Houston continued. "We can control contours, structures, and even weather patterns to mimic any conditions in Boston."

Clouds formed overhead, and the sun disappeared. Rain fell and created streaks down the front of Dani's helmet. She turned her palm up, but no water touched her skin. "Holy crap," she muttered.

"Everything is simulated. It will look as real as we can make it, but, as you can see, you don't actually get wet. Your helmets are equipped to add to the experience. So, if there is a fire ..."

Flames suddenly swarmed the remains of a building, and smoke filled the street. A blast of heat surrounded them. Dani thought she was hallucinating, but she actually *smelled* the smoke.

"... you will feel the temperature change, and we can introduce scents to make everything more realistic. The Wardens are sharp bastards. We'll thank them for this tech when we rip Boston from their grasp."

The flames disappeared, and Dani laughed. "This is great!"

Houston continued. "Behind you is the heap of what's left of city hall. Keep going beyond it and you'll reach the harbor. Keep city hall to your back and you'll go into the interior of the city. Roam around, check things out, and find a way to breach the city. The sim is postwar projections and what we know of Boston present day. Go to work."

"Wait," Dani said. "We're inside a warehouse, which is a finite space. If we walk around, we can only go so far. How are we supposed to explore the full city?"

"The squishy shit on your boots allows you to move around,

but they double as a treadmill of sorts. You are walking across a digital city, but the measured distance will keep you within the confines of the warehouse unless you go crazy and try to walk to New Hampshire—then you'll go into a wall. Got it?"

"We'll be moving while the scenery around us changes based on the sensors in our suits?" Dani asked.

"Yes."

"We can walk or run, but we won't be covering the exact same physical distance we would if we were outside. Right?"

"Yes."

Dani remained curious. "What if we split up? How does the sim work then?"

"Split up and find out for yourself."

The comm chirped off; Houston was done answering questions.

Gavin frowned at Dani. "You pissed off the boss. Nicely done."

"Which way are you headed?" Dani asked.

"To the harbor. I want to see what kind of water access we may have."

"I'll go the other way. Miles, care to wander?"

He smiled, and they left Gavin and Javi at city hall.

They walked a quarter of a mile, and Dani stopped at the top of a crater in the middle of the city. Brush lined a few areas of the slope leading down to the bottom of the crater, but the rest of it was scorched land, uninhabitable by any plant.

"Shit," Miles said. "The Wardens didn't hold back when they torched this area."

"This was Boston Common. On the other side is the Boston Public Garden."

Houston's voice sounded inside her helmet. "Dani, your heart rate just spiked. You good?"

"Yeah."

"Being here is bringing back some memories," Miles said.

Dani shrugged. "Guess so."

She hurried past the former park and gardens to go down what she knew was Boylston Street. She continued until she reached the rubble of one of many buildings. "This was Trinity Church."

"Nothing left now."

The church had beautiful architecture, and Dani had a flash of an image of the inside of it. She turned to Miles and smiled. "I remember this church. The library is up here. C'mon." Her attempted sprint was clumsy as she adjusted to the boots. She figured out the motion of the spongy soles and jogged down Boylston for a block to arrive at the library that was also rubble. "I loved this place. So many books." She frowned and continued down the street.

Miles stayed at her side. "The sim is bringing back memories you lost a long time ago."

"Jace said we lived here before the war when I was a child. My first regen wiped all that out."

"You've had other memories return, but this is different."

"They've never come back with such clarity. Usually things are fuzzy, and I can't tell what's a real memory and what's a dream. I'm just glad they're good memories."

They reached another area that used to be a park. This one wasn't a charred hole in the ground, but the shrubs and other plants were overgrown. "This was a garden."

"I bet it was nice before the war," Miles said.

Dani nodded and resumed exploring. She turned left on Fenway and walked with the garden on her right. She reached what used to be Evans Way Park and cut through the weeds growing there. She made a few more turns to end up on Longwood Avenue. The streets were buckled with heavy damage from decades of no maintenance and littered with debris, but there were a few buildings left that hadn't been leveled by the war.

Dani led Miles past a long row of destroyed buildings. "This was the Harvard Medical School campus." She froze when she recognized Boston Children's Hospital. It was a rubble heap like the other structures, but in her mind, it was intact. She blinked and shook her head. The hospital loomed before her. "This isn't possible."

"What's wrong?"

Her breathing quickened, and her feet wouldn't move.

"Dani," Houston said. "Your heart rate is significantly elevated."

All she heard was her thundering heart beating inside her chest and ears. Miles touched her shoulder, and she glanced at him before fixing her eyes back on the hospital. She trembled, and the deafening noise of explosions erupted. A jet passed low over the buildings and fired a missile that struck the hospital, and the hospital exploded into flames, smoke, and dust. Dani stumbled in her rush to turn around, then bolted.

The remaining buildings were present and intact again. They seemed somehow larger than before, and her brother sprinted beside her. Jace urged her forward, shouting at her to keep going. Her lungs ached with the sustained sprint, but they eventually stopped and hid inside a school. Alarms and explosions continued across the city, and Dani closed her eyes and huddled in the corner of a classroom with her brother and other people hoping to escape the destruction.

When she opened her eyes, she was at a window in the classroom. The Wardens were in the streets, executing everyone. When the Wardens left, she and Jace knelt in the pools of blood left by dozens of dead—the bodies of their parents among them.

"Dani!"

She blinked several times and recognized Miles. He held her arm with a firm grip.

"End the fucking sim," he said.

"It is off," Houston said. "We terminated the feed to her helmet when her heart rate went through the roof. I have a medic coming to you."

The voices inside the helmet panicked her. She fought to remove the gear and clawed at the straps. Miles helped her unfasten the clasp, and Dani threw the helmet aside. Sweat poured down her face, and she couldn't take a deep-enough breath. She collapsed to her hands and knees, Miles next to her.

"Christ, Dani, calm down. You're safe."

She tried to free herself from his grasp, but he wouldn't release her.

"Whatever you saw wasn't real."

She stopped fighting and leaned against him. Her uncontrolled shaking slowed the longer he held her. Javi and Gavin arrived, and as they knelt to check her, she recoiled to avoid their touch. A stranger appeared next to them, and the panic in her mind began to rise again.

Miles held his hand up. "Everyone, just back off."

"I'm the medic," the woman said.

"I don't care."

Gavin didn't leave. "She needs a sedative, Miles."

"She doesn't. Go away."

Javi urged Gavin and the medic to leave. "Let's give her some space."

Dani lost track of time. Miles was with her, and that was the only thing that made her feel a shred of sanity. She might have passed out or fallen asleep; she wasn't sure. She no longer trembled, the terrible tightness in her chest was gone, and her legs below her knees were numb. She remained wrapped in Miles's arms on the floor in the warehouse.

"I'm sorry," she said.

"It's okay. How do you feel?"

She sat up slowly and shifted her legs. "Better, I think. I can't feel my feet. How long have we been here?"

Miles shrugged. "Doesn't matter."

Dani pulled her sim boots off, wiggled her toes when sensation returned to them, then stood. Miles stood with her and rubbed the side of his hip.

"We sat there long enough for your ass to go numb?"

"It's fine."

She shook her head and passed her hand through her hair. It was dry and not sweat-soaked as she expected. She checked her watch. They had entered the sim this morning for training. It was now late afternoon, and she winced. "I'm so sorry."

"Don't worry about the time. Please tell me what happened in the sim. What did you see?"

She began pacing. "Jace's journal says I was eleven when the war started. We were in Boston the day the Wardens attacked. When I saw the hospital, I remembered everything from that day and the days following the attack. Jace and I hid, but the Wardens slaughtered my parents in the street with hundreds of other Echoes and humans. They weren't taking Echoes at that time—just murdering anyone who wasn't a Warden." Dani wiped at her fresh tears and took a few deep breaths to slow her escalating anxiety.

"Your memories returned, but they also sparked a hallucination. I'm so sorry. If any of us had known the sim would set you off like that, we would not have put you in it."

She sighed and headed toward the gear room to change out of the suit.

"If you don't want to be alone, you can stay in my quarters tonight. I can bunk with Oliver."

She shook her head. "Brody's already with Oliver, so he can stay with you another night if that's okay."

"Sure. Whatever you need."

"I'm going to Hattie's. I'll sleep there."

"I'll walk with you."

They removed their gear but didn't speak much on the walk back to Portland. She appreciated his company. Gavin, Javi, and Houston sat at a table in the brothel's pub with mugs before them. They stood when Dani and Miles entered.

"Sorry for losing my shit today," she said to them before turning to Miles. "You can tell them what happened if you want. I'm too tired to care either way. I'm going to bed. Thank you for staying with me through it." She hugged him and then left.

Dani made it to her room, locked the door, and leaned her back against it. She slid to the floor and hung her head. More tears fell. She desperately missed her brother.

CHAPTER

9

His infant daughter's eyes remained fixed on Rowan as he held her close. Like her brother, she was of pure Echo lineage, and Rowan adored her. Katy's birth had been the best thing to happen to the family since their confinement to Boston. Losing Portland stung his pride every day he was forced to remain in a city when he desired to be elsewhere. Maine was never far from his thoughts, but he'd promised Curtis he would follow Vice Regent Aubrey's orders—for now.

Rowan carried his daughter into the kitchen, and Devon made a whooshing sound as he ran past them, holding a toy plane. Rowan didn't mind the noise, and neither did the boy's little sister.

He smiled at his daughter. "Your mother thinks I can't handle being left alone with two children, but I'm not the one who hired a nanny to help me."

She yawned, and Devon continued out the other side of the kitchen with his plane.

"This isn't that hard, is it?"

His son collided with something in another room. There was a crash followed by the start of a long wail, and the doorbell chimed. The sound startled Katy, and she began to cry.

"Fuck," Rowan muttered.

Rowan ignored the door and went to his son. Devon lay on the floor clutching his knee, and the plane was in three pieces next to a toppled decorative table.

"Gotta watch where you're going when you fly that thing," Rowan said.

"I hurt my knee," Devon said between sobs.

Rowan shifted Katy, still crying, to hold her with one arm and took a moment to console his son until the sobbing diminished to a sniffle.

"Let's see who is here. I bet it's Uncle Curtis."

Devon wiped the streaks of tears from his face and limped to the door. He pushed the button on the pad next to the door, and the door slid open. Devon's scowl changed into a smile.

Curtis knelt and hugged the boy. "Rough day?"

"I broke my plane."

"That's terrible. Your dad can fix it, I'm sure," Curtis said. Katy's crying continued to escalate. "Rough day for you too, sir?"

Rowan rolled his eyes. "Come on in while I put her down."

Once his daughter was settled in her crib, she quieted and closed her eyes. He fixed Devon a snack while his son played with toys so Rowan could meet with Curtis in his office.

"Ana is out for a walk and then making a food run to pick up our rations. I think she got lost," Rowan said.

Curtis chuckled. "Giving her a break from the kids is nice of you."

"What do you have for me?"

Curtis glanced into the room where Devon played. "I have news on Portland. Try to remain calm and maybe wait until we're not in your home if you want to kill me."

Rowan's eyebrows went up.

"I have a spy deep inside Portland—one of my former aides when we were there. I'm not giving you a name or any details about my contact to keep you protected should the VR find out and this goes to shit. I'll be the one to take the fall." Curtis removed a slender panel from his pocket and passed it to Rowan.

After Rowan touched the screen, an image of a woman wearing Brigand clothes appeared. "Dani," he growled. He flipped through the images and sneered at the woman's face. "These are recent?"

"Yes, sir."

He slammed the panel down on his desk. "I *told* you she was still alive. Goddammit, Curtis."

Curtis lowered his gaze to floor. "The quake rifle shot would have killed any human or Echo. I was clearly wrong about her being human." He brought his gaze up again. "But she didn't regen. We were right there over her, and she never regenned."

"She's an Echo."

Curtis nodded. "My contact has confirmed that the CNA and Brigands know she is nonhuman."

Rowan's brow creased as a new thought entered his mind. "What if she did regen, but we just didn't see it happen?"

"You mean like a mutation or something? Her body doesn't glow when she dies?"

"Yeah."

"We'd have to get her into the labs to find out for sure. The fucking humans—" Curtis glanced at Devon, who seemed undisturbed by the conversation. "The regen glow always gives us away after we die. If we had a way to eliminate that part of our genetics and continue to regen, the humans would have a much harder time ID'ing us."

"Right. We need to go to Maine."

"We can't. *You* can't. The VR is just waiting for you to screw up."

Rowan sighed and stared at his desk. He folded his arms and

paced. Curtis remained silent. He had worked with Curtis for decades, and both had been through several regens. Dani was the direct cause of Rowan's two most recent ones. It didn't matter that they were more than a decade apart. She needed to die. He stopped pacing and lowered his arms. "How do you contact your spy?"

"I send a ping through our linked comms. A return ping means we are clear to talk."

"Send it now." Rowan shifted to close the door to the office.

"No need to close it, sir. The voice is distorted, so you can't tell who it is, or their gender. Only I know the contact's identity." He removed a small device from his pocket and pressed a few buttons. "Code name is Crow."

Rowan closed the door anyway. "That kid hears everything. When he repeats your reference to the 'fucking humans' to his mother, I'll tell Ana it was you and not me who taught him that one."

"She hates the humans as much as we do."

"Right. She won't care about that part. She'll be livid that Devon now has context for his new vocabulary word."

"Understood. Any chance I could talk Devon into forgetting what I said?"

Rowan laughed and shook his head. Curtis's comm chirped, and Rowan moved closer to Curtis, who held the comm between them.

"Crow, nice work on the recon photos," Curtis said.

"Thank you, sir." The spy's voice came through the device distorted, and Rowan couldn't tell if the person was male or female.

"Continue gathering intel on the CNA and Brigand volunteers, paying particular interest to Houston and her contact with others."

"Yes, sir."

"Do you have eyes on Dani?"

"Yes, sir. She's well protected by the others here when they're around. Her schedule is erratic at times. When she is alone, it's never part of a routine when she takes off or where she goes. She's impossible to track when she's alone and outside of populated areas."

Rowan leaned toward the device. "Crow, this is Rowan. I understand you were one of Curtis's aides, so you know who I am."

"Of course, sir."

"I need you to extract Dani and bring her to us."

There was a pause.

"Do you copy?" Rowan asked.

"Yes, sir. I ... I just don't know how that will be possible."

"I can't leave Boston or I'd drag her out of Portland by myself. She must come to me. We think she may have a genetic enhancement that will benefit all Wardens and end this damn war and the humans forever."

"Understood, sir."

"Any news on their plans for attacking Boston?" Curtis asked.

"Nothing yet. General Ramos was on the base for a few days, but I don't know the reason for the visit. May have just been routine. Captain Marcus is back in town, but no word on attack specifics other than rumors and speculation. Rogue Wardens hit one of their transports, so security has been tighter than usual."

Rowan was undeterred by this news. "Do what you can to gather intel, but Dani is the priority. If you can't capture her, make her come to me."

"Yes, sir."

Curtis ended the transmission and returned the device to

his pocket. "Why did you mention Dani's genetics? We don't know if that is even true."

Rowan shrugged. "It doesn't matter if she has an enhancement or not. Is Crow loyal to the Wardens?"

"No less than you or I are to establishing Earth as the new Ekkoh home planet."

"Anything to end the humans sooner rather than later is an excellent motivator."

"I understand. This is why you need to be regent, or at least vice regent," Curtis said, smiling.

"Speaking of which …"

"We have numerous allies, sir. The politics around a leadership change are sensitive, but I have players in motion to unseat the VR and move you into the role. Remain patient. It will happen."

Rowan opened the office door. Devon's head popped up, and the boy smiled. The front door opened, and Ana entered. Rowan took the packages from her hands and kissed her. Devon stood on his toes to hug her waist, and she returned the embrace.

"I was beginning to think you'd gotten lost," Rowan said.

"Maybe a little," Ana said. "Curtis, you're staying for dinner."

"I have to—"

"Stay for dinner," Ana said, finishing his sentence.

Devon looked up at his mother with a beaming smile. "Goddammit, Mommy, I broke my fucking plane!"

Ana's smile disappeared. "Oh, okay. Where's your sister?"

"Sleeping," Devon said, then returned to his place on the floor among his toys.

Ana shifted her gaze to Rowan and Curtis, and the men escaped for the kitchen. She joined them, her glare piercing. "Neither of you are getting out of this that easily."

"Ana, I am terribly sorry," Curtis said. "Devon overheard me, so his swearing is my fault."

She shook her finger at him. "You'd take the blame for anything to keep Rowan out of trouble. Not this time."

Rowan kept his mouth shut. The only thing he and Curtis could do now was endure her wrath.

CHAPTER 10

Oliver had just finished pulling his shoes on when his father called to him from the other room.

"Breakfast is on the table."

"Almost ready, Dad."

He had one shoe laced when the chime to their door rang. Oliver stopped and listened, waiting for someone to tell his father he had to leave again. He never expected to hear Dani's voice.

"Hey, sorry to drop by so early," she said.

"Dani, hey. Come in."

Oliver thought her voice didn't sound right. He didn't bother tying the laces on his other shoe before darting out of his room with Brody racing him for the door. He saw the shadows under her eyes and knew she hadn't slept well. She managed a tired smile when he and the dog arrived. She patted Brody's side when he leaned against her legs to gain more contact and attention from her.

"Would you like to eat with us?" Miles asked.

"No, but thank you. I'm actually here to see if I can borrow Oliver for the morning," Dani said.

"Me?" Oliver asked.

"Yeah," she said before turning her attention back to Miles. "I know he has school today, but I need his help. I'm going back into the sim."

Miles shook his head. "It's too soon."

"I want to do this, and I want Oliver to go with me."

"Dad, *please*, can I go?"

"Dani, you can't put him through what happened to you yesterday."

"I won't. I'll be in the sim, not him. He'll be in the control booth or wherever the hell Houston was yesterday, yapping through our helmets."

Oliver wasn't sure what either of them were talking about, but he didn't care. Dani came to *him* for help, and he'd skip class to go with her even if his father didn't grant him permission. His father and Dani debated a bit longer before his dad relented.

"We're going now?" Oliver asked her.

"No. Tie your shoe and eat first."

Oliver knelt, laced his shoe, then rushed to the table. He gobbled the food his father had made for him.

Miles sighed. "How do you do that? I have to stay on him to do things, but you say one word and he jumps."

Dani shrugged.

Oliver forced the final half-chewed bit of bland, CNA rations down his throat, gulped a mouthful of water, and was back at Dani's side. "Now?"

"Thanks, Miles. I'll bring him back to class when we're done."

Oliver followed her and Brody out. He turned and gave his father a quick wave goodbye before closing the door. She didn't speak again until they were beyond the barracks.

"The short version is Houston has a computerized simulation of Boston. She loaded images of what it looks like now, and

I unraveled yesterday. It brought back my memories of the initial Warden attack on the city when I was a child. I panicked, Oliver. I absolutely fucking panicked."

"Oh." Oliver frowned. He'd never seen Dani lose control before, and his insides knotted with concern.

She continued. "I've already got the tech guy setting up for me to reenter the sim. You'll be with him, monitoring me. My heart rate starts climbing before I realize I'm stressed. When you see that, your job is to talk to me like you do when we're throwing rocks. Know what I'm talking about?"

"Yeah."

She gave him more details about what she had experienced in the sim, and Oliver felt sorry for her. The specifics about how her father and mother died weren't in the journal Jace had left for her when he died.

They arrived at the old warehouse and proceeded past the guards, and Oliver's eyes widened when they entered the building. A man greeted them with a grumbled hello.

Dani handled the introductions. "Anton, this is Oliver. You'll tap him into the audio feed so he can speak to me and see what I see through the helmet's simulation. Oliver, this is Anton. You and Brody will go with him to wherever he goes to run this place."

"I can't have a dog around my gear," Anton said. "This is *my* control room. In here, I am a god! What I say is the law." He took a step back when Dani glared at him. "Or, maybe I use tweezers all afternoon to pick out the dog hair from the electronics. Yeah, that's a good plan. Let's go."

Oliver grinned and left with Anton. The big man spoke lovingly about the sim's capabilities as they went up the stairs toward the control center.

"The brains of this operation," Anton said with a wave of his hand toward the endless display panels and blinking lights.

"Well, that's not true. I am *the* brain behind this operation, and I tell *these* brains what to do. Dani freaked out in the sim yesterday, so what's your role?"

"To keep her from freaking out." Oliver walked to the wall of glass and peered down to the empty warehouse floor.

"She's changing into her sim suit, and we'll stay up here." Anton then directed Oliver to a chair and reviewed what the sim could and couldn't do. "Questions?"

"Many. How—"

"Save them for later." Anton placed a tiny comm into Oliver's palm. "Stick that in your ear. You can hear her and speak to her through it, but you'll see what she sees during the sim on these screens—unless she sees other things in her mind that aren't on the screen. If that happens, well, we're screwed."

"I won't let that happen."

Brody sat next to the chair, grew bored, and sprawled on the floor for a nap. Anton frowned at the dog. "How?"

"Do you have any images of Bangor in your database?" Oliver asked.

"Why?"

"Show me."

Anton shrugged and went to his console. He displayed images on the panels in front of Oliver.

Oliver pointed at his screen. "This one of the river, flip it so we're looking at the river from the Bangor side, not Brewer."

The image changed on his screen.

"Good. Shift it to the right. More. Keep going. There. Load that. Actually, can you give me control to flip between it and the Boston sim?"

Anton pressed a few buttons on his console, then looked up. "Press the blinking button on your right to change them."

"Hey, street urchin," Dani said through the comm.

Oliver brightened. "Yeah?"

"Can you see me?"

Anton gestured to the wall of windows overlooking the sim floor. Oliver hopped up and ran to the glass. Dani stood in the middle of the warehouse floor and looked impossibly tiny.

"I see you." He waved at her through the glass. "Can you see me?"

"Nope. I'm having second thoughts about this."

Oliver darted back to his chair. "Your heart and breathing rates are already going up. Take some deep breaths. I'm going to control what you see through your helmet, okay? We won't even start with Boston."

"Okay."

Oliver checked the monitor with her vital signs. Her heart rate had already started slowing. *Good. This is good.*

He caught Anton's eye and nodded. The perspective on his screen changed as the image converted to what Dani now saw through her helmet.

"You recognize this, right?" Oliver asked. "This is the river where we skip rocks."

"Yeah."

"We'll start the sim of Boston where you started it yesterday and go through the same course until you started to run into trouble. I'll flip you back to this river scene at times, and you'll talk only to me. I'll switch the images to help you adjust out of the stress response and kinda reprogram how you think of and remember Boston. The trick is to catch it early enough, so you have to be honest with me and tell me when you're anxious."

"I figured you'd just talk me through it. Good idea about changing the overall response, but how the hell do you know how to do that?"

"We were having a lot of thunderstorms when I was told Mom had died. I hated thunderstorms after that, but a counselor helped me retrain how I reacted to them."

"Huh. I'm impressed, Oliver."

"This stuff takes time, too. We can't fix you in one day."

"I'll take what I can get. It has to be better than turning into a scared rabbit and bolting."

"Or this could be a massive failure, and we break your mind permanently and turn you into a slug."

Dani's laughter erupted through his earpiece, and Oliver smiled.

"Ready?" he asked.

"I think so."

With the image of the riverbank in Bangor showing through Dani's helmet, Oliver talked to her in a conversational manner and told her about one of his classes the previous day. Her heart rate remained normal. He pressed the button, and the image changed to Boston. Her heart rate increased slightly before slowing again. Oliver instructed her to begin retracing her steps, and once she started moving, he told her about one of his walks with Brody after class the day before. He continued talking to her as she moved through the sim.

Anton appeared at his side and kept his voice low. "In a few minutes, she'll reach Longwood Avenue. This is where she started losing it."

Oliver nodded and kept his eyes on her vitals monitor. Her heartbeat increased by a few beats per minute. Oliver pressed his button again. The image on his screen and what was projected to Dani's helmet changed back to the Penobscot River. He talked to Dani until her vitals returned to her relaxed state and warned her before shifting the image back to Boston.

They repeated the image changes and then stopped the sim once Dani could see an image of the Children's Hospital's rubble without her heart rate spiking. Oliver's neck and back ached from staring at the screens and being in the chair for so long. When he checked the time, he winced. He'd missed most of his classes.

He and Brody rejoined Dani after she changed out of the suit. "How do you feel?" he asked.

"Tired. I could not have done that without you."

"In my sessions with the counselor, we never went that long."

Dani shrugged. "I don't have the luxury of taking my time to sort through this. We could be hitting Boston in the next few months, and I need to be able to go into the city at any point and know I won't lose my shit."

"You need to repeat what we did today, over and over, until you're retrained on how you respond to the images that make the bad memories return. It's okay that they return, but you'll learn how to deal with them in new ways that are less panicky."

"Miles may kill me if I pull you out of school every day, but I'll ask Houston to intervene. If she wants my ass in Boston, she won't have a choice but to make special arrangements with your teachers."

"It won't take as long next time to get you to where we ended today. It's like learning to ice-skate. First time you suck, but with practice you get faster at figuring out how to move on the ice and fall less."

"You're scary smart for a street urchin. Thanks for helping me with this."

He gave her a broad smile, proud to be able to do something for her for a change. She'd saved his life last year, and he'd do *anything* for her.

"I'm starved. Wanna ditch the rest of the school day and go to Hattie's for food?"

He answered with a vigorous nod.

"Great!" She clapped her hand on his shoulder, and they left the warehouse with Brody trotting ahead of them.

CHAPTER

11

Oliver swallowed the last bite of his food and leaned back in his chair. "Why did you want to go back into the sim so soon?"

Dani took a long drink of water from her mug before answering. "Once I got past feeling like complete shit last night, I was angry. I have to be part of the Boston invasion. I need to do this."

"Why?"

"The Wardens slaughtered my parents."

"Boston is revenge?"

Dani took a moment to consider her response. She had declared Boston as the next target long before the memory of her parents' deaths had resurfaced. "Part of me wants revenge, yes. I'd be lying if I said I didn't. This war has been going on long enough. It has to stop. Too many have already died."

Hattie appeared beside their table. The older woman folded her arms and glared down at the dog lying on her floor, then at the pair seated at her table. "You and the kid devoured enough food to feed three men."

Dani looked up at Hattie and grinned. "Oliver is a growing boy."

Oliver was horrified to be blamed for the food consumed; Dani laughed.

Hattie responded with a grunt. "Bullshit. When was the last time you ate?"

Dani scrunched her brow. "Um …"

"That's what I thought. I guess you'll learn to eat more regularly if you pass out enough times."

"I will try to do better, Hattie. I promise."

"I'll believe it when I see it. Be ready to work your ass off tonight to repay me."

"You said family got to eat for free."

"You? Yes. The mutt and Oliver, no."

Oliver sat up in his chair. "I can work too, Aunt Hattie."

Dani gave him a dismissive wave and addressed Hattie. "I'll fix whatever equipment you have in the basement that needs repairs."

"Yes, you will. Weren't you supposed to be somewhere this afternoon with Mary? Training or something?"

"Shit."

"Love your reliability. Glad I'll never be in combat next to you." Hattie scooped up the empty plates on the table.

The remark stung, and Dani frowned. "That's not fair."

The older woman glanced out the window of the dining area of the brothel's pub. "Explain it to them," she said with a nod toward the window, then disappeared.

Dani sat up straighter to look out. She groaned and sank back into the chair. Miles and Mary were among the group of six headed toward the pub, and Houston was with them. Colonel Houston loved eating at Hattie's, as did most everyone else in Portland, but Dani knew that once Houston spotted her in the pub, she was in for an ass chewing.

"What did you miss today?" Oliver asked.

"They were forming new fireteams to begin practice

maneuvers for clearing structures similar to ones we'll have to breech in Boston."

"That was training for Brody too, right?"

Dani nodded and sighed.

"Oh. You're in trouble."

Dani glanced around, deciding which exit to take to evade the colonel. She couldn't leave Oliver, so he'd have to go with her. The door opened, and Brody bolted to greet Mary as she entered. *Too late.*

Kelsey came in behind her, followed by Houston. The colonel crossed the room with long strides to Dani's table. Miles arrived right behind her.

Houston stood with her hands on her hips. "Not surprised to find you here."

"It's my fault," Oliver said. "I kept her in the sim too long, and I talked her into coming here after so we could eat."

Dani gasped at his attempted lie.

Houston glanced at Dani and then Miles before turning her gaze on the teen. "Oliver, you're a terrible liar, just like your father. I do like that it was your idea instead of Dani's. She looks ready to crap herself. The trick about conspiring to create a cover-up is that everyone involved needs to be in on the lie. Work on that. It'll help you be a more problematic teenager for your father." Houston broke into laughter at her own quip.

Mary, Kelsey, two men, and a woman Dani didn't know were at the bar buying mugs of ale.

Dani stood and addressed both Miles and Houston. "Oliver helped me today, and the hours in the sim were gone before I realized the time. I need him to help me reprogram my fear response, and we need to be in that sim every day."

Miles shook his head. "He can't miss that much school."

Houston shrugged. "I'll have his teachers rework his assignments so he gets the content he needs." She turned to Oliver.

"You'd walk through fire to help Dani. I know you're going to agree to this, but I'll ask it anyway. You will have extra homework every day you're with her and not in class. Can you handle that?"

Oliver nodded.

"Dani, you'll have extra training time to make up for today and any other times you miss. You'll also reschedule your time with Gavin on planning sessions for Boston. I don't care if you don't sleep again for the next month. This work will happen. Understood?"

"Yeah," Dani said, figuring she'd regret this arrangement later.

"Problem solved." Houston turned toward the bar. "What the hell is taking so long? Where's the ale?"

"Coming!" the woman said. She had her eyes focused on not spilling anything from the two mugs in each hand. She placed them on the table before Houston and passed one to the colonel. She turned her eyes to Dani, and her mouth dropped open.

Dani wasn't sure why the woman stared at her. She glanced at Miles, but he didn't offer any answers.

The woman's look of shock changed to one of happiness. She shrieked and threw her arms around Dani, kissing her.

Dani tried to back away, but the woman remained attached. She pried the woman off her and took a step back. The name on her uniform said Bishop, and Dani didn't remember ever knowing a Bishop. She held her hand up to keep the woman from approaching again. "Who are you?"

The woman laughed, but after a moment her smile faded. "Are you serious?"

Dani lowered her hand and refused to meet Miles's eyes. She'd forgotten him with her most recent death, so whatever pain she was causing the woman now, Miles could relate.

"Uh, my memories, they can, um ..." Dani decided to skirt

around the problem that she couldn't remember her prior lives like normal Echoes. "Sometimes I have gaps."

"Gaps? What kind of gaps?"

She didn't want to try to explain. "Who are you?"

"Alex. I'm *your* Alex. Really, Dani? Nothing?"

Dani shook her head.

"Alexandra Bishop. No memories of me? *Us?* How could you forget *us?*"

The commotion gained attention from others in the pub, and Mary, Kelsey, and the other two men gathered at the table. The last thing Dani wanted was more attention. Miles kept his gaze fixed on her, and she felt heat welling from her insides that would make her start sweating any second now.

Dani, however, remained curious about Alex. "When and where did I know you?"

"This is a brothel," Alex said, approaching Dani again. "Let me take you to one of these rooms. You'll remember."

Mary stepped between them and prevented Alex from getting any closer.

"Oh. You're with her?" Alex asked Dani.

"Not. At. All," Dani said with a flat tone that earned her a sharp glare from Mary.

"Dani, we were together, here, in Portland, before the Wardens attacked. You look the same, so you're obviously not the human you said you were. Anyway, I bought it during the attack, but friends got me out before the Wardens got their hands on me. Fucking reconditioning. Want nothing to do with that."

Dani wanted nothing to do with anyone right now. She leaned down to speak to Oliver and lowered her voice. "Anything in Jace's journal about an Alex? I don't remember her being mentioned."

Oliver shook his head. "She's not in the journal, but maybe

Jace didn't know about her. She's right about you thinking you were a human during that life."

"Okay," Dani said, except nothing felt okay at the moment. "I'll come by in the morning to grab you."

"I'll be ready."

Dani straightened and addressed Houston, Miles, Mary, and the others. "Hattie has work for me. B, let's go." Brody's tail wagged as he walked beside her to leave. Her quick escape was derailed when Miles caught up to her.

"Wait," he said.

"Don't bother asking me about Alex. I don't know who she is or if I was with her at the same time I was with you. I don't remember!"

"Christ, Dani, calm down. I wasn't going to say anything about that."

She took a deep breath and muttered an apology for snapping at him.

"Do you need any help with whatever Hattie has you working on?" he asked.

"No, but thank you for offering. I'll see you in the morning when I come for Oliver."

He nodded, and she left, darting through the brothel and avoiding everyone. She jogged down the steps to the basement. Hattie had left enough things for her to fix to keep her working late into the night, a daunting task that was far better than facing the awkwardness upstairs.

CHAPTER
12

D ani stood outside Colonel Houston's office and tried to clear her mind of the extraneous shit clouding her thoughts. She and Mary were barely speaking, and Alex's presence didn't help. Cameron would appear at random times to chat, and Miles and Gavin were tense with each other and now with Cameron, too. She did her best to avoid them all, but training and tactical planning forced them together.

She stretched her neck and took a deep breath. Dani activated the chime, and the door opened. She stepped through and strode across the room to stand before Houston's desk. The colonel's eyes remained down while she scrolled through the feeds filling the panels on her desk.

"What is it, Dani? Took you long enough to ring to come in."

"Please tell me you have something up your sleeve for Boston."

Houston lifted her head. "Why?"

"Because there is no fucking way we can breech Boston without something else for resources, tech, weapons, anything. We'd have to throw millions of troops at Boston—losing most of them in the process—to take the city. And we don't have millions of troops. Gavin and I have been through every scenario.

He thinks there is something we're missing and can take it with what we have. He's wrong."

"Continue working with him and come back when you have a solution."

"There isn't a solution to this, Catherine!"

"When you first proposed Boston, you told me you had ideas."

"I did, and they won't work. We don't have the resources to make a land *and* sea attack. You didn't reveal the sim tech until a couple of weeks ago. What else do you have that you're hiding? We need something else to make this attack even remotely feasible. Anything from the Boston contacts?"

"Comms remain spotty, so there is a technical problem. I'll need to send a repair team down if they don't get it fixed soon."

"Give me *something*."

Houston leaned back in her chair, but Dani was familiar with this tactic and didn't move except to fold her arms and continue to stand before the colonel. Minutes ticked by in silence before Houston spoke.

"Ever hear of the Ancients?"

"The original Ekkohrians who came to Earth centuries ago? *Those* Ancients?"

Houston nodded.

"They're myths."

"What if I told you they aren't?"

"Prove it."

Houston leaned toward her desk and tapped a few items on one of her panels before leaning back again. "Take a seat. It'll be a few minutes."

Dani frowned, shoved her hands into her pockets, and paced instead of sitting. Houston resumed working. Minutes passed, and Dani considered sitting down. Then the door opened and Hattie entered.

"There's your proof," Houston said. "Hattie is an Ancient."

Dani couldn't speak.

Hattie scowled at the colonel. "Nicely done, Catherine. Just drop the fucking bomb on her."

"Oh, like you never dance around topics."

The two continued their bickering, but Dani could only stare at Hattie. The woman didn't deny the claim that she was an Ancient, and Dani wondered how many other things she didn't know. She eased into a chair. She'd always thought Hattie was a history buff or at least an Echo claiming to be human, but Dani had never imagined that Hattie might be an original Echo who had settled on Earth.

"Is this true?" Dani asked when she found her voice.

The women stopped arguing, and Hattie turned to face her. "Yeah. Have to keep this a tight secret since there are only a few dozen of us left. We remember the ships and the tech that brought us here. If the Wardens knew I was an Ancient, they'd burn Maine to the ground to capture me. They are desperate for that kind of information."

Houston stood. "Thankfully, Hattie is on our side. She's already reached out to a few other Ancients who are coming out of hiding and on their way to Portland. We have early specs put together for planes and other weapons to use against the Wardens. Once we have the final designs, we can start building. We won't have much of a new arsenal ready for Boston, but we'll have enough to give us an advantage. The size of that advantage will depend on how quickly you and Gavin can put a plan and timeline together for us."

The colonel projected a 3-D image from one of the panels on her desk, and the form of a jet unlike anything Dani had ever seen rotated before her. Houston grinned and waved her hand at the projection. "The Wardens won't have the ability to detect this plane until it is already dropping its payload on them."

Dani stared at the projection. "Gavin doesn't know about the new tech?"

"No."

Dani's anger exploded. "Why the hell have you been riding our asses about a plan when you were holding back on the tech the whole time? Christ, Catherine, we can't accurately plan an invasion when we don't know about key resources."

"Bullshit. You planned Portland using only what we had plus some ingenuity. I expected the same for Boston, and you delivered."

Dani shook her head. "What? We don't have a plan yet."

"For all of your intelligence, sometimes you're a fucking idiot," Houston said, and Hattie burst into laughter.

"She *is* right, you know?" Hattie said.

Houston terminated the image of the plane and brought up a map of Boston. Dani recognized the markings and notes she and Gavin had made on the map days earlier.

Houston pointed at the map. "This is the plan that will give us Boston. Delta-5."

Dani shook her head. "We deep-sixed that one already."

"Un-deep-six it and fine-tune. Look at the date on the map. This is the one you worked on the longest, then tossed the day after you panicked in the sim. You've lost your confidence. Since that day, your performance in fireteam trainings has plummeted. You get your ass shot up with paint rounds. Those little bastards hurt when you get popped, but you're not adjusting. You're going to blow yourself up if you don't pull yourself together."

Houston was annoyingly right. Dani was peppered with tiny bruises where she'd been shot with rounds of orange and yellow paint. In one of the training sessions, Dani had dropped one of the fake explosives that would've blasted her entire team to bits in a real scenario. She hung her head and closed her eyes for a moment.

"Catherine, give us a minute," Hattie said.

"Getting kicked out of my own goddamn office. This is a new one," Houston grumbled as she left.

Once Houston was gone, Hattie spoke. "You already know you're not getting a touchy-feely pep talk from me, right?"

Dani nodded, bracing herself for the imminent tongue-lashing.

"Your head's a mess, kid. You're letting all this shit with Mary, Miles, Gavin, and now Alex get to you. Let them sort out their own problems with each other. Stay in the sim with Oliver so you can handle being in Boston when it's time to go. If you panic in the city during the battle, you die."

"I know."

"And stop all the goddamn sulking. It's pathetic. Get your ass back in the planning room with Gavin. D-5 will work."

"We did the sneak attack thing with Portland, Hattie. They'll see it coming."

"No, they won't. This is far more advanced than what you did with Portland. Take another look at D-5 from *inside* the sim; you'll see. You're entirely too stressed out. Get yourself laid. I know a place that can help with that," Hattie said, cackling.

Dani couldn't help but laugh with her.

Hattie waggled a finger at her. "I'm serious about getting laid."

"Yes, I know. What about the planes and other tech that is coming?"

"Since we don't know exactly what will be ready in time, plan like you don't have it. We'll adjust the tech to the plan, not the other way around."

"Why come forward now? Why did you wait?"

"We needed to see how things played out in Portland. The Ancients who are left, we couldn't come out of hiding until we knew those oppressed by the Wardens had finally had enough and were ready to fight back. You didn't just take Maine back from the Wardens, you fucking humiliated them. Plus, you didn't score one win and stop—which is exactly what Houston wanted to do. Remember?"

"Yeah."

"You turned her around, persuaded her to go after Boston. You're ready to attack the Wardens' core. Take Boston, and the rest of New England will fall from the Wardens' grip. The Ancients couldn't ignore that initiative and sit by and watch any longer. We're ready to help."

Dani nodded, though her mind struggled to catch up.

"You can't tell anyone about me, the other Ancients, or the tech," Hattie said. "Catherine and you are the only ones who know what I am."

"What did she do when you told her?"

"She practically shit herself and wanted to put a security detail on me, for Christ's sake. Like that wouldn't draw attention."

"Did Jace know?"

Hattie shook her head. "I told him I was a human. I tell everyone I'm human. I planned to tell Jace the truth if he regenned, but when he didn't … well, it didn't matter. No one expects to see an old Echo. It's easier to sell the human story once you look like an old fart." Hattie gave her a toothy grin and headed for the door.

Dani followed the woman out. "I'm still not processing all this and your history."

"I tend to stay in denial about the whole thing, especially since I'm related to the assholes who started this war. I'm tired, Dani," she said, and sighed. "But I want to stick around a bit longer in Maine. When I'm ready to get rid of this shell, I'll disappear like I always do and regen someplace new where no one knows me."

"Wait. What? You don't get to leave like that! You're my sister-in-law."

"Let's argue about this and pretend you have a say in the matter after the war is over. Yeah?" Hattie left her before Dani could respond.

Dani headed for the planning room. She was early for her meeting with Gavin, but she wanted to spend some time reviewing the Delta-5 plan by herself. She also needed time with her thoughts. She had to keep Hattie's history concealed from her friends, and she didn't like this new burden at all.

CHAPTER 13

Dani ached with a couple dozen new bruises. She stood with her fireteam, her shoulders slumped. Miles, Flynn, and Alex stood with her. They appeared just as tired and disappointed as she was. Even Brody sat with his head lower than usual. Dani's team had worked closely with Mary's, and the other team gathered to stand together next to them. The side of Mary's face was painted with yellow where she had taken a sim round in the head while trying to get Dani out of the line of fire. Dani's gut remained knotted. A real round would've taken her friend's head off. Cameron, Elmore, and Ibsen joined Mary. Everyone had smears of paint on them somewhere, including Brody.

Javi walked the length of their line, shaking his head. "I'm re-forming your teams. This bullshit has gone on long enough. If you were able to work together as a cohesive unit, you'd be doing it by now. You're done for the day and will have your new teams tomorrow. Get out of here."

Dani passed her hand over her face and sighed. A hand landed on her shoulder.

"C'mon, I'll buy you a pint," Mary said.

Dani walked with her as they left the training grounds for

the city. She noticed a lump on the side of Mary's head and winced. "I should be the one buying you a round. I am so sorry you took that one in the head for me."

Mary touched the lump. "Looks worse than it is."

"Liar. That shit hurts."

Mary smiled.

"I apologize for acting like an asshole lately, and I'm sorry for the remark I made about you in front of Alex," Dani said.

"I hurt your feelings, but, you know …" Mary jutted her chin toward Miles, who walked ahead of them with Elmore. "Why are you not doing anything about him?"

"I don't know, Mary. I can't pull myself together lately. The last thing I need is a relationship."

"How is it working with Gavin this time?"

Dani shrugged. "The man is a tactical genius. He's not trying to win me back, so that's a relief."

"Cameron is gorgeous, is he not?"

"I guess."

"And Alex?"

"Why all the questions?"

Mary shot Dani a glance and smiled. "We haven't talked in a while. Dres is back in the ranks. Did you know that?"

"No. That's great news!"

"Javi is genuinely pissed at us, but I think Dres being back is also part of the reason for the shuffling of our teams. That and his throat is sore from screaming at us all the time."

"I'll take Javi yelling at us over Gavin."

"If Gavin even looks at you crooked, Miles will slug him again."

Dani touched Mary's arm, and they stopped. "Again?"

Mary resumed walking and told Dani about the altercation the night Miles arrived after the transport was attacked. She couldn't believe the news or that Mary had waited so long to fill her in on that part of the night. They were the last ones to arrive at Hattie's, and Miles held the door open for them. Brody raced ahead, followed by Mary, then Dani.

"Thanks," Dani said.

"I'm happy you two are speaking again," he said. "Neither of you have been pleasant to be around."

Mary continued forward. "Shut up, Miles."

He chuckled. "Correction. Mary remains unpleasant to be around."

Dani laughed, and some of the tension left her. It had been too long since she'd been able to sit and laugh with her friends. She grabbed a seat at a table, and Cameron and Alex sat next to her, one on each side. Both placed a mug of ale in front of her.

"Oh, uh, Mary was getting mine," Dani said.

"These will get you started," Alex said, sliding a mug closer. "Still a cheap date, right?"

Not only was Dani a cheap date, but she turned into a babbling idiot when drinking alcohol. Only Miles and Mary had seen her in that embarrassing state. The last thing she wanted was Alex or Cameron to see her that way—or maybe Alex already had at some point in one of Dani's prior lives. She didn't know.

Mary arrived holding two mugs, spotted the ale in front of Dani, and passed her extra mug to Miles.

Elmore raised his mug. "To the two worst fireteams in the CNA-Brigand army."

The group laughed as they touched mugs and drank. Dani enjoyed the mix of conversations that followed and was content to just listen. Gavin and his team arrived, and Mary's attention shifted to Kelsey as if no one else existed. Dani realized Mary truly cared for him. She envied Kelsey a little. But Mary was happy, and that made Dani smile.

Alex dropped her hand below the table and placed it on Dani's thigh. Dani's smile vanished. Alex's hand traveled to the inside of her leg. She relocated Alex's hand back to her own lap, took a final drink from her mug, and stood. She caught Cameron watching her; he'd seen the interaction with Alex.

Dani retreated to her room in the back of the brothel with Brody, changed clothes, and wiped the paint smears from her face and arms. She paused in front of the small mirror and touched the scar on her neck. It was a constant reminder of Jace giving his life to save hers. Part of her loved the scar and the memories of her brother. Another part of her hated it. She put her jacket on and pulled the collar up to hide the old wound. She reached the kitchen to slip out the back with Brody and found Miles leaning against the counter, waiting for her.

"You okay?" he asked.

"The group thing isn't doing it for me. I'm going for a walk."

"What's on your mind?"

"Comms are intermittent with our teams in Boston. Houston thinks it's the tech."

"If she sends a team down, you want to go."

"Yeah."

"As long as Oliver gets to keep Brody while you're gone, he'd tell you to leave today."

Dani smiled at his joke.

He shrugged. "If the comms are broken, you're the best one to fix them. You do it all the time for Aunt Hattie."

She tilted her head, confused. His answer wasn't what she'd expected. "I figured you'd try to talk me out of it."

"Nah. I'll go with you into Boston. Enjoy your walk."

She and Brody left to wander through Portland. Before the Brigands and CNA in Maine joined forces to retake the city, Portland had been a hazard for war-displaced civilians. The CNA operated under orders to capture Brigands to add them to their waning ranks to replace those killed by Wardens. At least those were the stories Jace had told her.

Dani's roaming took her out to the wharfs, then back across the peninsula. She stopped and, somewhere in her mind, recognized the place as B Block. It was somewhat cleaner than she remembered.

Dani continued through the block, picking her way around collapsed portions of buildings and debris. She didn't know where she was going, but she knew where she was and how to make a quick exit if needed. She spotted other Brigands in the area but didn't stop to talk to them. A man and woman stared at her as she walked by, but neither said or did anything. Dani figured Brody's presence had something to do with that. He stayed by her side and remained alert.

She arrived at a place she remembered so vividly, she froze. She turned in a full circle, taking in the alley. She walked a few more yards to where the alley opened up, and gasped. "Holy shit."

Dani closed her eyes and tried to recall the details of when she'd been here before. This was where she'd first met Miles in her previous Echo. He was an officer with the Military Police and had caught her stealing CNA food rations. He could have arrested or just shot her, but instead he'd lowered his weapon. They talked through the night while sharing the food. The next night he was on duty again, and she returned with some of her stolen rations. They made out more than they talked or ate that time. The following evening, he was off duty, and she took him to where she lived and introduced him to her body.

A pleasurable shiver coursed through her with the memories. She regarded Miles as a friend, but in her prior life, they had been lovers. *Fuck. I cannot deal with this now.* She took a deep breath. *Figure out what to do with Miles later.* She opened her eyes and retraced her steps from the alley to the place where she and Jace had lived.

Dani found the door to her old room slightly ajar and

pushed it open, the hinges shrieking in protest. The room was unlit, dusty, and empty except for two broken totes on the floor. More memories surfaced, and she reconstructed the room in her mind. She had kept totes of gear to one side of the room, and often worked by candlelight at a small table at the far end of the room. A tattered blanket on the floor next to the table was where her prior dog named Brody had slept. The thin, lumpy mattress on the floor against the wall opposite the totes was where she had slept—where she and Miles had slept.

Multiple images of them together and naked filled her mind, and she leaned her shoulder against the door frame for balance. The fifteen-year gap since her last regen had taken her memories of him, but then a few had started to resurface last year when she was with Gavin. *Because that wasn't a mind fuck or anything. And where was Alex during this time? When was I with her?*

Dani's wanderings in B Block hadn't brought back any memories of Alex. The woman had claimed they were together during the same time she was with Miles. She didn't know why Alex was a void yet memories of Miles returned at random times. Miles had been a void too, until she met him again through Oliver.

She groaned and lowered her head into her palm. "And I told Miles I loved him."

Brody's growl snapped her head up.

"What are you doing here?" a middle-aged Brigand woman asked her.

"Sorry. I got a little lost. I'm leaving."

"If you're lost, how are you going to leave?"

She was shit at lying. "I'll figure it out." Dani left the area, but she stopped again at a half-broken table lying on its side. She squatted and passed her palm over the wood. This was where she'd sorted her tools and she and Jace would plan their day of scavenging. She wished she could better recall what his face looked like then. Footsteps approached, and she slipped away with Brody before anyone else spotted her.

It was after dark by the time she returned to Hattie's. Her walk was supposed to help ease her mind, but instead it had added more jumbled memories to the mix. She used the back door to enter the kitchen, and Hattie looked up from where she was making a cup of tea.

"You look worse than when you left," Hattie said.

Dani grumbled a response, grabbed something to eat for her and Brody, and left for her room, desperate for a better day tomorrow.

CHAPTER
14

Dani rubbed her eyes. She and Gavin had been staring at the map too long. The Delta-5 plan did show promise, as Hattie and Houston said it would, but Dani was skeptical.

"We've put this thing in the sim, and it works up until here," Gavin said, waving his hand through the projected image of Boston and the section that glowed in yellow.

She rested her hands on her hips and looked at the map. She moved around the table to view it from a different angle. She'd made this walk several times already without any new ideas.

Gavin continued grumbling. "We don't have the data to know what we'll encounter when our mainland troops move in toward South Boston and South End. We're working blind. This is why we scrapped D-5 the first time."

A few seconds ticked by in silence.

"Say something!" Gavin barked.

"What is there to say? You won't shut up for two goddamn seconds. *I'm thinking!*"

She returned to the yellow portion of Boston. They needed more intel. Period.

She turned to suggest they go to Boston to get the data, but the door slammed shut as Gavin left.

"Asshole!" she said to the closed door.

Dani stomped out of the room, not to follow him, but to go to Colonel Houston. She arrived outside her office and didn't bother with the chime before barging in.

Houston glanced up from her desk before resuming her work.

Dani strode forward. "I need to go to Boston to fix the comms so we get our intel on time and not when shit happens to be working one day and not the next."

"I need you here."

"You need me *there*, Colonel. Delta-5 may not work if I don't have all the data. I can't know that for certain until I have the information I need."

"I'll send Gavin's team down to find our contacts and put a fix in place."

"I'm going too. None of the plans he and I have worked on include a retreat. Once the attack starts, it continues regardless of what happens. There is no white flag for us. When we engage, there is no retreat or surrender. The Wardens will slaughter us if we try either."

"I'm quite aware of how the Wardens deal with their human and Echo prisoners, Dani."

"Then you need to be aware that before I propose a final option for attacking Boston, knowing many will die for it, I have to know it will work."

Houston finally looked up and leaned back in her chair. "I appreciate your concern for others, but I need you in Portland."

"I don't care what you need. Send me with your blessing, or I'll fucking go without it."

"What if you get down there and lose your shit?"

"I won't. I'll be fine."

Houston drew in a long breath and released a sigh. "I'll put you on the team."

"I need Miles to go too."

"Absolutely not. Take Mary instead."

"Mary stays; Miles goes."

Houston stood and leaned her palms against the top of her desk. "Exactly when the hell did you decide you could start giving *me* orders?"

"When you put me in charge of planning Boston."

"You're asking for trouble by putting Gavin and Miles together on a mission like this. They've already had one altercation."

"You know about that?"

Houston laughed. "I know everything that happens around here."

"I need Gavin's tactical experience, and I need Miles. I'm willing to risk a conflict between them to get the comms up and the data we need to finish planning D-5." Miles was her anchor, and the one person who had gotten her past the point of complete panic in the sim. She wanted him in Boston with her in case she wasn't "fine" in the city. Dani didn't want to admit this to the colonel, but guessed the woman had already figured that part out.

"Fix the comms and get your ass back here to finish the plan on your own."

Dani cocked her head to the side. "On my own?"

"If I'm sending Gavin down, I'll keep him and his team there for a few other tasks."

"Like what?"

"You don't need that information."

Arguing with Houston was frustrating, so Dani relented. "Miles and I will come back, and Gavin and his crew stay."

"When do you plan to leave?"

"Tomorrow at dawn."

Houston laughed as she returned to her chair. "You haven't

asked Miles yet or you would leave tonight. He'll agree, of course, but you really know how to spring shit on people. Taking lessons from Hattie?"

"He knows I was thinking about going to Boston and already said he'd go."

"Get out. I have work to do."

Miles agreed to the trip and short departure time, but his mood shifted when he learned Gavin was going too.

"Why him?" Miles asked.

"Houston picked him to go—him and his team. It's not like it will just be the three of us. Plus, he's staying down there for some other crap she wants him to do. You and I will return without him."

"I admit I'm okay leaving him there."

"He's not that bad."

"He *hit* you, Dani."

"We trained together for years. I knew what I was doing when I asked him to train me."

"So when he hit you with the rifle after the transport crash, that was training?"

"He was being a dick then, which is what you're starting to be now, so back off." Dani took a moment to calm her growing anger. "I need to go. I need to talk to Mary about training with Brody while we're gone."

"Mary isn't going?"

Dani shook her head.

"Good luck with that conversation. Come by later to see Oliver and Brody."

"I will."

Mary was in the middle of drills with her fireteam when Dani found her at the training complex. She waited for her friend, saying "Hello" or nodding as members of Dani's former team passed by as they left the complex. She tensed when Alex's steps slowed as she neared.

Cameron gave Dani a small smile as he put his arm around Alex's shoulders. "C'mon, you owe me a pint for saving your ass from the sniper today."

Dani felt like she owed *him* a pint for saving her from an awkward conversation with Alex.

Mary came out last in her bulky, paint-spattered gear. *Christ, she looks amazing in anything.* Dani cleared her throat and shifted her thoughts in other directions. Mary was with Kelsey—not her. It really was that simple.

"Hey," Mary said. "You're waiting for me, so this probably isn't good news."

"It's good, but you won't like it. I'm leaving in the morning for Boston to fix their comms."

"I can be packed by then."

"You're not going. I need you to be Brody's handler for a while. This will be no surprise, but Oliver has him now."

"Let someone else be his handler. Javi can do it."

"Brody is better with you than Javi. There's more. Gavin's team is assigned to go with us—or we're going with them—I'm not sure how that works. Doesn't matter. Kels is shipping out tomorrow."

"Shit."

"I know. I'm sorry. Houston will keep them there after we're done. I don't know for what or for how long."

"You keep saying 'we.' Who's going with you?"

"Miles."

Mary grinned. "Good decision. Last time you made a trek with one other person, you fucked him." She shrugged before continuing. "Sure, it was Gavin the Asshole, but hey, you're not perfect."

"Oh, shut up."

They walked together away from the training grounds, and Dani spoke again. "Can you do something else for me while I'm gone?"

"God, you're needy."

"Keep an eye on Hattie, please."

"Aunt Hattie doesn't need anyone looking after her. Hell, she's running the civilian side of things for both Bangor and Portland right now. The woman's a machine."

Dani picked her next words carefully. "She's still human and can use someone looking out for her for a change."

"Yeah, I'll make sure she's okay."

"Thanks, Mary."

"Let's pick up the pace. This is my last night with Kels before he ships out; I need to make sure it's one he remembers," Mary said, and she winked at her.

CHAPTER

15

Dani had already said her goodbyes to Brody and Oliver, and she feared crying if she spent more time with them. She pretended to inspect her plasma pistol while waiting for the rest of the team to gather. Miles spent an extra few minutes with his son, and Mary and Kelsey kissed as if they'd never see each other again. What Dani didn't expect was Cameron's arrival. She holstered her weapon as he approached.

"Glad you're putting that away instead of aiming it at me," he said.

She gave him a small smile. "Thanks for diverting Alex yesterday."

He shrugged. "I saw how uncomfortable she made you the other day. If she's trying to make you remember her, she's doing it the wrong way. Stay safe on this trip and come back soon. I won't be able to keep up with Aunt Hattie's work pile on my own."

Gavin arrived with Corey and Jamie in tow. "Let's go!" Gavin said.

Miles hugged Oliver once more. The boy had seen his father leave many times before, and Dani silently promised Oliver she'd make sure Miles returned home.

They climbed into the transport truck and rode in it until they reached the New Hampshire line. From there they met their guides and hiked south for five days until meeting their contacts north of Boston. It took them another three days to find their spies in the city.

The tension in Dani's neck and shoulders worsened each day as they neared the city. Miles would discreetly ask how she was, and she always responded with a quick nod. Her nervousness about panicking in the city diminished once she changed tasks to hands-on repairs. After two days of creeping through the city, using sewers for cover, checking comm equipment and making minor fixes on minimal sleep, Dani's head sagged lower while she tinkered with an emitter in her lap. Someone took the device from her hands, and she looked up and blinked. Her headlamp beam fell on Miles's face.

"Go to sleep, Dani."

She reached for the emitter, and he didn't give it back.

"Miles, I need that to fix the broken relays."

"Work on it tomorrow. We don't even know where the relays are."

"Yeah, we do. I figured it out earlier, based off the signals. The relays at Briggs Field by MIT and Thatcher Street by Knyvet Square are down. That's why we can't get any info out of South End."

Miles dug into his pack and pulled out a map.

Gavin joined them. "What's going on?"

"Dani says two relays are down. MIT's Briggs Field and Knyvet Square."

"Okay." Gavin scratched at the bristles on his jaw while he reviewed the map. "You two can take Briggs, and I'll do Knyvet Square."

"Good idea," Miles said.

Dani sat up straighter. "Good idea, my ass. You're both

trying to keep me away from the hospital. I know Knyvet is by Children's. I'm going." She dismissively waved her hand at Gavin. "You do whatever errands Houston has for you. I'm on repair detail, and you can't sideline me."

"I'm not sidelining you, just dividing up the work," Gavin said.

"Bullshit."

Gavin didn't give up. "I know how to fix relays."

"You're a damn moose when you do it. We don't have the spare parts lying around to replace the shit you break in the process." Dani rubbed her eyes as a wave of fatigue washed over her. "Fuck, I'm tired." She turned her attention to Miles. "I'll sleep for a little while, but I'm doing both relays."

Miles relented. "They're both yours."

The men bickered in hushed tones, but Dani didn't care. She shifted her pack closer and leaned across part of it. She rested her head on her arms and dropped into a deep slumber within minutes.

She woke hours later with a terrible cramp in her neck, and Miles appeared with CNA rations for her. Dani massaged the side of her neck. "Why did you let me sleep so long?"

"I tried to wake you earlier. You told me to fuck off, so I let you sleep longer."

"Oh. Sorry. I don't remember doing that."

"Hungry?"

"I need to pee first."

After she'd eaten and drunk a cup of some sludge that Gavin claimed was coffee, she felt somewhat awake.

Gavin started giving orders. "Spend the day organizing and

cleaning your gear. We'll stay tucked into this hole until nightfall, then move to MIT."

Kelsey, Jamie, and Corey nodded, but Dani shook her head.

"We're losing valuable time," she said.

"Someone slept so long that we lost our window to leave."

"Someone? Don't give me that passive-aggressive shit. We need to reach MIT today so we can meet at the rendezvous point tonight to cross into the city."

"Sun's up. We already know they watch the sewers here. You want to walk through Boston in broad daylight?"

"Why not?" She pulled a device from her pocket. "I can find their surveillance equipment with this so we can avoid being seen."

"Seen by cameras, maybe. What about being seen by Warden patrols?"

"Christ, Gavin, you act like we were never Brigands. Moving undetected is what we *do*."

"You're the only Brigand, Dani. The rest of us are CNA."

"Stay here then. I'm going to fix the comms." Dani turned away from him to grab her gear. Gavin's large hand clamped on to her upper arm, and he spun her around. Before she could react, Miles had his pistol up and pointed at Gavin's head.

"Let her go," he said.

The men stared at each other for a moment and neither moved. The other three men on Gavin's team reached for their weapons, but Miles's pistol remained steady and aimed at Gavin. The corner of Gavin's mouth twitched a second before he released her. She refused to rub her arm where he'd held her, and Miles kept his weapon up.

"You're under orders, Miles, just like me," Gavin said. "Houston would never give us permission to enter the city during the day."

Miles shrugged. "If we had operational comms, we could ask

her. Dani, get your pack. Gavin, meet us at the rendezvous and we'll cross the river with your contacts to enter the city's interior tonight."

"If she dies, it's on you. *Again.*"

Dani was sick of Gavin's constant attacks on Miles. "Being a bit dramatic, don't ya think? I'm not dying today."

"Did you say that the last time? You know, when he shot and killed you? Or you don't remember?"

"Fuck you." Dani slipped her pack on, and Miles holstered his gun. He picked up his pack and rifle, and they left together.

They moved through the city toward Briggs Field undetected. Only one Warden patrol came near them, but they easily avoided the enemy.

Dani checked her scanner. "Relay is that way. Camera is this way," she said, and she turned to head to the camera.

"Wait. I thought we were avoiding the cameras."

"I want to know how they work. I should be able to tap into the feed."

"Without getting caught?"

"Anton would be the best one to do this, but I think I can manage it."

Dani stopped at the base of a building and looked upward. The old, rusted fire escape was something of a death trap.

"No. No, this is a *bad* idea, Dani."

She shrugged out of her pack and pulled several items from it, stuffing the pockets of her fatigues. "Give me a boost."

Miles shifted his rifle out of the way and grumbled while he helped lift her to reach the lower rung.

The fire escape groaned with her added weight. "I don't think it will hold us both. I'll be right back."

She climbed up the mix of landings and ladders to reach the roof. She did another quick scan and found the camera. While working from behind the lens, she used her knife to pry open the rear casing. She attached wires from the camera to a small panel she pulled from one of her pockets. The panel showed what the camera detected. She entered a few commands, and half of her screen displayed lines of code being extracted from the camera. She waited until sixty seconds passed on her watch before deleting the commands and disconnecting the wires. After reattaching the casing, she gathered her things and headed for the fire escape.

She started down the ladder and reached the highest landing without any trouble. Dani looked down and spotted Miles pacing in the alley below, his rifle ready. She had a great view of the city, but her admiration of the skyline was cut short when she noticed a Warden patrol headed toward their location. "Shit."

She scampered down the fire escape as quickly as she could without making too much noise. When Miles looked up, she signaled to him that a patrol was coming, then increased the pace of her descent. The fire escape's bars and bolts shuddered with her movement and began pulling away from the building. She leapt from the lowest landing.

A jolt of fiery pain shot up her leg when her boots struck the ground and her right ankle rolled with the impact. Dani refused to cry out. The lower half of the fire escape separated from the upper half and the building. Miles had her pack in one hand and threw his other hand around her waist.

He leapt to the side and turned so his pack broke through the smudged window first. He pulled her with him, and she vanished inside the building as the mass of broken and twisted metal crashed into the alley. They scrambled away from the window and hid among the dust, filth, and destroyed furniture.

The Wardens arrived and checked the area around the building.

"It's just the fire escape coming apart," one Warden said.

"Thing is old as hell. Prewar. I'm surprised it hasn't fallen before today."

"Let's go," a second Warden said.

Dani and Miles waited for several minutes after they left. Her ankle swelled inside her boot, and blood trickled down Miles's face from a cut on his scalp. She stood and drew in a sharp breath with her first step.

"Broken?" Miles asked.

"Just pissed off." She took a few more steps and nodded. "I'll be fine." She picked up her pack and bit her lip when her ankle protested under the added weight. Dani refused to complain. She shouldered the pack and limped toward the broken window.

"Did you at least get what you wanted off the camera?"

"Yeah," Dani said. She turned and smiled at him.

He wasn't smiling. "Was it worth it? That was a really close call with the Wardens."

Her recklessness had almost gotten her captured and Miles killed. She sobered a bit. "The patrol wasn't in sight when I reached the roof, or I wouldn't have stayed. I'm sorry that didn't go as planned. But we need every advantage—even small ones—we can get. I think I pulled enough data off the feed to give Anton a nerd erection."

"I didn't need that visual. I *really* didn't."

The trip to reach the relay at Briggs Field took more time than expected because of Dani's injury. Once there, she found the device hidden in an old storm drain. She had to lie on her belly to access it, and Miles passed her the tools she needed and kept one hand on his rifle. The repair took her longer than she wanted, but Dani finally got the unit working again. She and Miles packed up the gear and slipped away from the former college campus.

They arrived at the meeting location well after nightfall, but

Gavin didn't bother yelling at either of them for their lateness. Dani spotted a woman talking with Gavin and assumed she was their contact. He didn't ask why Dani was limping or why Miles had blood on his face.

"This is Corporal Allyss," Gavin said. "She's our guide tonight. We're meeting another contact on the other side of the river, and they'll both take us into the city."

Dani introduced herself and Miles to the corporal and shook the woman's hand.

"Glad you made it," Allyss said. "You got the relay fixed?"

"Yep. One more to go."

"Two were busted? No wonder we couldn't figure out what the hell was wrong with the comms." Allyss gestured for them to follow her.

"Wait," Gavin said. "Kels, fix Dani's limp first. Then we'll leave."

Dani started to argue, then realized that being inside the city on a bad ankle was a terrible idea. She wouldn't be able to run if they hit any snags. Dani began unlacing her boot for Kelsey.

"What? No argument?" Gavin asked.

"Don't get used to it," Dani said, and removed her boot.

CHAPTER
16

A slow smile crossed Rowan's features while he watched the thin man strapped to the stretcher struggle against his restraints. The half-starved Brigand man's neck and forehead veins bulged with exertion, and his dark complexion turned crimson. The R&D team had made great strides with reconditioning techniques, and new Echoes were added to Warden ranks every day. They were no longer limited to reconditioning only those who regenned to a childhood age. They could now convert men and women in their twenties and sometimes thirties. The higher ages were more difficult, but since the twenties were a common age range for Echo regens, Warden troop numbers continued to grow.

The medical staff in the R&D room placed electrodes on the man's chest and head before sticking a large-bore needle into the bend of his arm. They removed the needle and left a flexible catheter in place, which they attached to clear tubing linked to a bag of medication hanging from a pole. They had more advanced and less traumatic ways of administering the medication, but the archaic method of using needles, bags, and tubing always provided the most effective results.

Curtis oversaw the operation and never stopped taking

notes on the small panel in his hands. He moved almost vulture-like as he circled the man on the stretcher. No one heeded the Brigand's endless begging for mercy. When the sobbing began, Rowan's smile vanished, and he stepped forward.

"Let me do it." Rowan despised the weakness of tears most of all. An Echo should never beg for their life. Ever. They would regen anyway—well, provided they weren't caught in an explosion or suffered decapitation, but … begging? *Sobbing?* Rowan sneered at the man as he removed the clamp on the tubing to allow the medication to flow into the man's arm.

The Brigand released a deafening scream as the medication burned through him. The scream was replaced with a few gasps, then nothing. It was a relatively quick death, compared with other ways of dying. Rowan left the stretcher and moved away to allow the medical team back in. They tended to the bags, swapped out medications, and checked the restraints.

Rowan's thoughts drifted back to Dani. He'd had her on a stretcher in Portland and had just started giving her the preconditioning meds. He remembered her scream of pain, which lasted only a second or two before she slashed her knife at him and the tubing. That encounter was the third time he'd crossed paths with her, and she'd still gotten away. She was a good fighter and would be a great asset as a Warden once he captured her.

The Brigand man's body began to glow and writhe beneath the restraints. He self-healed from the trauma of Brigand life, starvation, and always existing on the edge of death. He transformed from a gaunt, malnourished middle-aged man to a healthier, younger man around twenty-five years of age. His chest rose as he drew in his first ragged, post-regen breath. He ceased writhing except for an occasional twitch. Curtis ordered the second infusion to begin, and a different type of fluid traveled from the bag, through the tubing, and into the man's veins.

"How soon will you know?" Rowan asked.

"Within an hour. This new cocktail is showing faster recoveries and is about 60 percent effective on the first go."

"You're working on higher efficacy, yes?"

"Of course, sir."

"Very nice work, Curtis. I'd like to speak to you in my office for a moment, and then you can return here."

Curtis glanced at his subject, then nodded to Rowan.

He knew his friend was reluctant to leave his research, but Rowan noted Curtis's loyalty to him. They left the bay for the sterile-looking white walls of the R&D corridors. Rowan glanced into the two tech development bays as they passed and made a mental note to check on those departments that day. They arrived at his office, and he closed the door behind them.

Curtis wanted to return to the lab, so Rowan didn't bother offering him the option to sit. "You've been neck-deep in the lab the last several days. Your progress with the reconditioning process is remarkable, but I do need information on other matters." Rowan moved to stand behind his desk.

"Your orders are unchanged, sir. You're not allowed to leave Boston. I've looked into a transfer to Portsmouth, but the VR isn't budging. Others support retaliation and attacking Maine, but Aubrey won't listen."

"She's an idiot." Rowan began pacing.

"I'm trying, sir. Give me time. I'll make it happen."

Rowan scowled, dismissed Curtis, and continued pacing. His movement stopped when his comm chirped with a message from Crow. He returned to his desk in two long strides and pulled up the transmission. He paused before opening the comm. If caught, he would be found guilty of disobeying orders and possibly guilty of treason for having a spy in a location from which he was forbidden to operate. Rowan opened the comm anyway.

"Go ahead," he said.

Crow's voice, as usual, came through distorted. "I have files to send you when you're ready to receive."

"Send them now."

"Yes, sir."

A light on the top of Rowan's desk lit, and he tapped it. Images of people appeared, and he scanned the faces. He recognized Colonel Houston and Captain Gavin Marcus, but the others were new to him. He paused at a low-light image of Houston and Marcus in an embrace. He flipped past it and paused longer. A *child?*

"I know Houston and Marcus. Who are the others?"

"The older woman is a human they call Aunt Hattie," Crow said. "She runs the local brothel and offers board for Dani if she's in Bangor or Portland. Dani doesn't usually stay on base in the barracks."

"A motherly figure. Good." Rowan could get to Dani through others in her life.

"The younger woman is Mary Smith—another human and close friend of Dani's. There is sometimes a tense dynamic between them like they may have been lovers at some point. I'm not sure."

"Okay." Rowan paused on the image of Mary. She had what many men or women would consider attractive features, but because she was human, she repulsed him.

"The man is Captain Miles Jackman, human."

"What is it with her and the goddamn humans?"

"Jackman is another friend, but it's his son, Oliver. She's close with the boy. It's like he's a little brother of sorts."

Rowan had no problem with sacrificing a human child to get to Dani.

"Houston keeps Dani busy with anything and everything. I don't understand that dynamic yet. Dani and Marcus were lovers, but something happened around the Portland battle that ended it. There is a lot of tension between them, but she cares for him to an extent."

"How do you mean?"

"He tends to be an asshole around her, and she hasn't shot him yet, sir."

"What about the relationship between Houston and Marcus?"

"They're having an affair and have been able to keep it hidden. I noticed a look that passed between them once and kept watch on Houston. Marcus showed up at her quarters two hours later and didn't leave until just before dawn."

"Brilliant work, Crow."

"Thank you, sir."

"You're making more progress for me on the outside than my people on the inside in Boston. Keep at it and find a way to get Dani here."

"I'll do my best, sir. She's currently in the field, but I don't know where. She went somewhere with Captain Marcus's tactical team and Captain Jackman, but that's all I know. I don't know the location or the intent of the mission."

"Find out and let me know as soon as you can."

"Yes, sir."

Rowan ended the transmission and flipped through the images again. He had an idea for getting around the vice regent's orders and avoiding a charge of treason. He would use pieces of this new intel from Crow and merge it with other official documentation to prove that the CNA in Maine required additional investigation.

Fuck Curtis's political tactics. Rowan went right for Vice Regent Aubrey's throat. He didn't care what kind of activity was traced during his research. He was the head of Research and Development in Boston; it was his job to dig for information.

He pulled up all data on known Brigand and CNA contacts in all of New England. He had six states to research, and Maine just happened to be one of them. Rowan would propose a better way to identify and locate the enemies resisting Warden rule. This included plans for him to lead the wide-reaching attack to slaughter the humans and capture the Echoes.

If Aubrey acknowledged the data, she'd have to send troops in. Rowan added pieces of Crow's intel into his report but was careful to mix it in with other official info from the Warden database. Any viable solution to end the war would get him a face-to-face meeting with not just the VR but the entire governing council in Boston. He wouldn't be turned away.

If she ignored the report, it would backfire. The Wardens knew Houston was coming for Boston. The city had been publicly declared the next target by the CNA after they took Portland, but Aubrey refused to take the claim seriously. The CNA colonel wasn't a brilliant tactician, but she had people around her who were—Gavin Marcus being one of them.

He looked over his report one last time, then sent it. He had more research to do, but Rowan took a break to return to the tech bays. He inspected new equipment and weapons, and lifted the newest version of the quake rifle, admiring its light weight.

"Have these been in the field yet?" he asked the technician.

"No, sir, but they have passed all lab tests."

"Round up our R&D field troops. I'll take this one and join in the maneuvers. We start in one hour. Knyvet Square is a good place to work. Make it happen," he said without waiting for the technician's reply. Rowan *really* liked the feel of the new quake rifle.

CHAPTER

17

The last thing Dani wanted was to deal with more sewers after spending so much time in them beneath Portland, but those sewers were the reason their attack on the city had been successful. Like Portland, Boston's actual sewage went through a reclamation-recycling process instead of being dumped into the bowels beneath the city. The stink and filth of stagnant water and whatever else mixed in with the muck made her stomach turn more than once. She refused to whine about any of it. Allyss and her partner, Richter, navigated the system with ease, which meant they had spent way more time down here than Dani wanted to imagine.

Richter stopped at a junction in the pipes and pointed upward. "Relay is up there by the street level."

Allyss shook her head. "We've both worked on it and can't get the damn thing to cooperate more than occasionally. I'm curious to see what kind of magic you can work. Especially with it in a shit location. Tight as hell up there."

Dani tilted her head and cast the beam of her headlamp into the narrow tube posing as an access drain with an even narrower ladder. She hadn't had great luck on ladders lately. The others also cast their beams upward and groaned.

Kelsey chuckled when he addressed Gavin. "Good thing Dani opted to fix both relays, Cap. You wouldn't fit in that tube even if we greased you up."

Dani snorted and ignored Gavin's scowl.

Miles slid out of his pack. "Dani, tie a rope around your waist. I'll tie on the tools you need at this end and you can pull them up."

She handed her pack to Kelsey so she could dig through it. Dani filled her pockets with a few items while Miles removed a rope from his pack. She took one end and tied it around her waist, then pulled her uniform top off so it wouldn't restrict her movement while working inside the tube.

"Ready?" Miles asked.

"Not yet." Dani removed her belt and holster to pass off to Jamie. She was left in her tank top and trousers, and she was about to get worse than filthy. "Okay."

Gavin positioned himself beneath the tube and laced his fingers, palms up, for Dani to use as a step. She placed her boot into his hands, and he lifted her up. She grabbed a ladder rung, pulled herself up, and began the climb.

The task of taking the relay apart and figuring out why it wouldn't cooperate kept her mind off the stench. Having to haul up additional tools one by one slowed the process, and she was exhausted by the time she got all the circuits on the relay operational.

She'd been on the ladder so long that her knees and hips were stiff. Her descent was far from graceful as she half slid, half climbed down. Corey and Miles caught her as she came off the bottom of the ladder and stumbled in the knee-deep slush.

"It's fixed?" Richter asked.

"Yeah," Dani said. "There was a lot of shit on the circuits— some were fried, so I rebuilt most of the relay piece by piece." She looked for a clean area of skin on her arms to wipe grime from her face, but she was covered.

"Richter will take you back the way we came," Allyss said. "You can clean up in the river and rest for a while before leaving." She removed a panel from her gear bag and moved to stand below the relay. "I'll be here a while sending data, but I'll see you before you go."

Dani pulled her panel from her own pack and passed it to Allyss. "Send this too."

"Love note to Mary?" Gavin asked.

"It's certainly not to you," Dani said.

The others in the sewer chuckled. She returned her attention to her pack to find something to wipe her face. She found a somewhat clean shirt and used it to wipe away the worst of the filth. She'd need a dozen baths and a scrub brush to get fully clean again, but she'd take what she could get for now. She followed the others and didn't argue when Miles carried her pack for her.

They stopped in a less flooded area of the sewer, and Dani found a dry-ish place to sit. Everyone was beyond tired, but they stayed busy. Gavin and Richter checked the exit and stood near it with their rifles ready. Miles and Jamie prepped food, and Dani drank deeply from her water bottle while Kelsey readied another bottle for her once she was finished with the first one.

"Cap has a soft spot for you, ya know?" Kelsey said.

"Huh?"

"He's a tough bastard, but he turns soft around you."

"Him slugging me with the butt of a rifle wasn't soft."

"Yeah, that was rather mean of him. Other than that incident, he becomes a different person around you."

"Bullshit. Did he ask you to talk nicely about him to me?"

He shook his head. "It's just an observation."

She traded bottles with him and frowned when Gavin approached.

"Nice work getting the comms up."

She hadn't expected a compliment from him. "Thanks. Hey, what do you think of sneaking into South End for a look? We have recon data gaps we can fill if we do some poking around ourselves."

"Not a chance. As soon as I can get you out of here, you and Miles head north. It's not up for debate. My team has work to do here that doesn't involve you, so I need you gone."

"What work?"

Gavin shook his head.

"Fine. Keep your secrets with Houston, but don't get yourself or your team shot up while you're here."

"Careful. I might think you care," Gavin said.

Dani didn't bother with a retort. She didn't have the energy.

When she and Miles stopped north of Boston, Brigands gave them more supplies. Once packed, she and Miles were off again.

"What's on your mind?" Miles asked. "You haven't said much since we left the city."

"I don't like Gavin and the others staying behind. He's doing something for Houston that I fear will get him killed."

"I like the others on his team. Gavin," Miles said, shrugging. "I'm okay never seeing him again."

"Asshole."

"Yes, he is."

"I meant *you*," Dani said, and scowled. "He's on our side and a good fighter. I know you hate him, but don't wish him dead because of your stupid grudge." She increased her pace, and the argument set the tone for the rest of their trip back to Portland.

CHAPTER
18

Allyss had sent volumes of data in the days Dani and Miles hiked back to New Hampshire and returned to Portland by boat. A weather system in the Atlantic made the lobster boat ride slow and rough. Given how many times Dani *thought* she would puke over the side of the boat, she decided that chumming the water only three times during the trip wasn't so bad. Back home, sleep, several baths, time with Brody, and a little more sleep had her back in the mood to work.

Gavin wouldn't be in the planning room with her, and Dani wasn't thrilled with the idea of sorting the new data and finalizing the plan by herself. Houston hadn't told her yet if she'd be partnered with anyone else, and no one showed up. Oliver and Brody had spent so much time together while she was gone that Dani allowed the routine of Brody going to class with him to continue. She missed having her dog with her.

After hours of analyzing the files sent from Allyss and Richter, she loaded much of the data to a palm-sized panel and headed for the door. The door opened before she arrived, and Alex stood before her.

The other woman's eyes widened with surprise for a split second before softening as she smiled. "Hi."

"What are you doing here?"

"Looking for you."

"Why?"

"I, uh, wanted to apologize. I didn't mean to make you so uncomfortable that you'd leave the table, much less Portland. Where have you been?"

"Busy." Dani shifted to move around Alex, but the woman didn't move.

"Wait, Dani. Please just give me a chance."

"I don't know you. If you want my trust, earn it." Dani went around Alex and left.

She arrived at the warehouse, and the MPs guarding the entrance recognized her and let her pass. She paused for a moment and wondered what was different about their uniforms. Something had changed. They had the large patches on their shoulders declaring them military police, and they carried plasma pistols at their hips. She'd seen Miles in this same rig many times. She returned to the guards and scanned their uniforms.

"Ma'am?" one of the men said.

"Tranqs." Dani lifted her gaze from their duty belts. "Where are your tranq pistols?"

"Colonel Houston had us stop carrying them."

Dani frowned. "You used them on Brigands to capture them and bring them into CNA ranks."

"We haven't done that since the vols joined us against the Wardens."

"Where do you keep the weapons now that they aren't in use?"

The MP shrugged. "Colonel Houston could tell you."

"Thanks." Dani reentered the warehouse and found Anton in his control center. He looked like a gargoyle hunched over his workstation. His head came up, he blinked several times, and he grinned as he left his chair.

"You wouldn't believe the shit I can pull off the Warden cameras now, based off what you sent me. I can get right into their main feeds without them knowing. You're a genius for getting me that data," Anton said without taking a breath.

Dani winced and took a step back from him. "That's great. You can use a shower—a few of them actually."

"Oh, yeah, probably." He scratched at his patchy semblance of a beard.

"Here," she said, handing him the panel.

He took the device and hurried back to his station. He synced it into his system and whistled. "This will take a while to render."

"Render?"

"Uh, compile. Put all the guts into the right sequence. Render."

"How long?"

"Thirty minutes at least."

"Set it to do whatever, go take a shower, shave, and change clothes. I can't work closely with you when you smell like something Brody would roll in."

He laughed, then realized she was serious. He nodded, tapped multiple things on his station, then left. Dani found a comfortable chair and sank into it. She closed her eyes for a moment, and when she felt a hand patting her knee, she bolted upright. Anton jerked his hand back. His beard was gone, his hair was clean and pulled back from his face with an elastic band, and he wore different clothes.

"Thanks for not shooting me," he said.

She rubbed her hands over her face and sighed. "I'm not armed."

"Oh. Right. The sim is ready."

Dani pushed herself up from the chair and followed him to the panel array. The modern-day map of Boston with complete sections of South End and South Boston was displayed before her.

"Load it with Wardens based off the data we have on their patrols," Dani said. The screens blinked as they reloaded, and the forms of Warden patrols appeared in the streets in and around the city. "Can you add in a factor of uncertainty to make them periodically change their patrol routes?"

"Like random activities?"

Dani nodded.

Anton tapped more things on his station, and Dani's screens blinked again.

She headed for the door.

"What are you doing?" Anton asked.

"Suiting up."

"Oh, no. Wait. Wait! You need Oliver here."

"I don't," Dani said without slowing her pace. She took the stairs down to the lowest level to the gear room. She changed out of her clothes and into the suit, noting her elevated heart rate, and took a few deep breaths. The tension in her shoulders eased, and she took another deep breath before pulling the helmet on.

She arrived at the door between her and the active sim and pushed it open. In an instant she was back in the city, and her heart rate quickened.

Houston's voice boomed inside Dani's helmet. "What the fuck do you think you're doing?"

"I—"

"Shut it down, Anton," Houston said.

The city disappeared, and Dani was standing on the warehouse floor with nothing around her but blinking sim transmitters. Houston approached from the other end of the warehouse with quick, determined steps. Dani jerked her helmet off and refused to wait for the colonel. Instead, she strode toward the woman to close the distance faster.

"I can handle being in the sim. Everyone needs to stop hovering over me like I'm going to break."

"You *did* break. I'm trying to keep you from breaking yourself again."

"I can do this. You want a solution for Boston? This is how I get it for you."

"Not today."

"Goddammit." Dani threw the helmet. It bounced across the floor, the visor shattering in the process. "Let me do my fucking job! I know how we can get past the Wardens *and* breach Boston, but I need to be in the sim to run through it a few times."

Houston stared at Dani. "How?"

"We used the sewers in Portland. This time we go right at them. Topside. Anton can jack up their camera feeds so we go in undetected, and we take out any Warden patrols we encounter. We'll move in waves, similar to Portland, and use tranqs on the patrols."

"Tranq pistols? You want us to wage war on Boston with *tranquilizers?* Why don't we just take slingshots, Dani?"

"We can take them out quietly instead of blasting our way in and being detected. Plus, if we shoot them with plasma rifles or pistols, they'll just regen some minutes later and be back in the fight. We'll never last against an army that won't die if we don't get a head shot every time. And we'll lose time waiting to kill them mid-regen."

"So we put them to sleep instead of trying to kill them?"

"Oh, we kill them. Subsequent waves move through later and permanently dispatch the Wardens while they're sedated. Have your lab folks ramp up the tranq juice to keep the bastards out for hours. Also have them adapt cartridges to rifles and pistols with better range than the standard MP tranq pistols."

"The Wardens will see our armies moving in long before we get there."

"We're not sending the entire army until much later. We'll use select fireteams to go in first and start taking patrols out at the beginning of their shift and plant explosives. We'll have ten hours to do our work while Anton transmits cleared sector messages from the patrols back to the base."

"Ten hours isn't enough to take Boston."

"No, but it's plenty enough time to get in and wreak some havoc. At shift change, the oncoming Wardens will know something is wrong. That's when we start blowing things up. The chaos will disorganize them, and that is exactly what we need to happen."

"Okay, so in ten hours that gets us from the perimeter into the city. What's your plan to take the city in its entirety and penetrate their HQ?"

"Delta-5."

Houston frowned.

"I need time in the sim to work out the exact details," Dani said.

The colonel paced for a few minutes while Dani waited. When she stopped and looked up, Dani realized that the expression on Houston's face was the same as when she had interrupted her in the sim. Houston looked like she was in pain.

"What's wrong?" Dani asked.

"Meet with Javi to select your fireteams and put everyone in the sim. You're not going into it alone, and I'll skin Anton alive if he allows it."

Dani shook her head. She expected Houston to agree to her plan, but the woman was hiding something. "Catherine, *what* is wrong?"

"Gavin's been captured."

It took Dani a moment to find her voice. "When?"

"Yesterday."

"And you're only telling me this now?"

"I tracked you here to tell you, but things got sidelined with you trying to go into the sim alone."

"The rest of his team too?"

"Our contacts confirmed Jamie and Corey were captured too. Kelsey is missing at this time."

"So you know where they are and have sent a tac team, right?"

"There will be no rescue, Dani."

"We have time—"

"No rescue."

"We have to try!"

Houston shook her head.

"Christ, Catherine, why not?"

The colonel cast her gaze downward and shifted her stance as though she were debating whether to leave or stay.

Dani tried a softer tone. "Why not?"

"I can't use CNA troops to go in after a civilian."

"They're *all* CNA. Gavin is one of *your* troops."

"The New Hampshire CNA has already written off Jamie and Corey. They are humans and are likely already dead. They won't risk sending in an extraction team for Kelsey without knowing where he is or if he's alive. I can't authorize a CNA team from Maine to go after Gavin when he's not part of the Commonwealth."

Houston turned to leave, and Dani caught her arm. "What are you talking about?"

"Everything about Gavin's rank and incorporation into the CNA was a lie. With his skill sets, I knew if I added him to Commonwealth ranks, those above me would take him out of Maine. He was never CNA, and he didn't know."

"He's an Echo. He'll be reconditioned if we don't get him out."

Houston's anger exploded. "I know how the Wardens operate!"

Dani had never seen the colonel lose control, and it startled her. Houston grimaced just before tears filled her eyes.

The colonel brushed the tears away. "This is killing me more than you know. I love him. Fuck. I don't even know how or when it happened. I'd send him on missions, and he always came back. *Always.* I justified taking him into my bed because I knew he was technically a Brigand."

Dani didn't know what to say. She was reeling from the knowledge that he'd been captured and his service in the CNA was a lie. Now *this*? She passed her hand through her hair. "There has to be a way to find him and get him out. Did he have a comm you can ping for his last location?"

Houston shook her head. "He's gone. As much as I hate to admit it, he's gone."

Tears stung Dani's eyes. She and Gavin argued more often than not, but that didn't mean she wanted him dead—or worse, reconditioned. "Who else knows he's been captured?"

"It's quiet for now, but it won't stay that way long. The Wardens always openly mock us when they capture our people. Everyone will know soon enough."

"Let me be the one to inform Mary about Kels."

Houston nodded and wiped the remaining tears away. She squared her shoulders, and Dani watched as the woman's face turned to one of pure business.

"Remember the other orders I gave you," Houston said. "I'll put things in motion today for the tranq weapons' mods. The work on Boston doesn't stop because of this setback. Deep-six Delta-5; it won't work." She turned to leave.

"What? Why? You said it would. Now it won't?"

Houston didn't slow her pace. "You'll figure it out."

Dani stood in the middle of the warehouse floor, alone. She

didn't want to admit that Gavin, Corey, Jamie, and possibly Kelsey were lost to the war. Many had died in the fight to retake Portland, some from her own fireteam, but those losses didn't weigh on her as heavily these.

She had experienced a glimpse of the reconditioning process at the hands of Rowan, and she shuddered at what the full conversion meant for Gavin. He'd become a Warden, and Gavin's Marine Corps background, combat experience, life as a Brigand, and natural ability to be one tough bastard meant he would be a key Warden asset. He knew Houston and others in the CNA well. He knew their tactics, tech, and practically everything else about Maine's branch of the Commonwealth. If the Wardens wanted to breach Portland, Gavin could walk them right up to Houston's front door.

Another thought struck her. He knew the details of Delta-5. *God. Dammit.*

She needed a completely new plan to attack Boston. Gavin knew every plan they'd worked on over the last several weeks. If the CNA tried any of them and Gavin was working for the Wardens, he'd have measures in place long before the CNA arrived. This changed *everything.*

But he couldn't tell the Wardens what he didn't know. He didn't know she'd taken the data from the camera, so they had that advantage. Dani mentally listed the few things Houston had for intel that Gavin wouldn't know about: Hattie's history, the new jets, pending tech from the other Ancients, cameras, tranqs, the initial topside sweeps, and whatever rabbit Dani pulled out of her ass for an alternative attack.

"This is more than a fucking setback, Catherine," Dani muttered to the empty warehouse.

CHAPTER 19

The news of Kelsey's possible capture devastated Mary as much as Dani thought it would. As the evening wore on, she stayed in Mary's room while her friend drank herself into a stupor and passed out. Dani gathered the mugs and empty pitchers of ale and brought them to the kitchen. She'd hoped to leave them, grab something to eat, and go for a walk, but Cameron and Alex sat at the small table in the area. Given the sullen expressions on their faces, she knew that word of Gavin and his team's capture had spread.

Alex rushed toward her. "When were they captured?"

"How did this happen?" Cam asked.

"Anything new from the Wardens?"

They fired questions at her so quickly that she scowled and brushed past them. She started washing the mugs and tried to ignore them.

"What can we do to help?" Alex asked.

"Grab a towel and start drying," Dani said.

"No, I meant—"

Dani spun around, surprised by her own anger and a growl in her voice. "There's nothing we can do to help them. We're fucking helpless to do anything. We don't know where they are, so we don't know where to go to even try to rescue them. We have *nothing*."

Alex winced with Dani's outburst and left.

Dani turned back to the sink. She had the dishes scrubbed in minutes and had nothing else to wash. She looked for something else to do, but the counters were clear.

"Dani," Cameron said.

"Fuck off."

"I'm sorry I rushed you with so many questions. It was inconsiderate. If there was any possible way for us to help Gavin and his team, I'm sure you've already considered it."

Dani picked up the towel on the counter and began drying the dishes she'd washed. Once they were dry, Cameron placed the items into the cabinets where they belonged. She headed for the door, and he caught her hand.

"I'm truly sorry for your loss, Dani."

She pulled her hand from his and spotted Oliver standing in the doorway between the kitchen and the hall leading out to the rest of the brothel. Brody bounded in and came to her. She patted the dog's shoulder, appreciating his presence.

Cameron muttered a goodbye and left.

Dani dropped into one of the chairs at the table. "Don't ask me what the rescue plan is, because there isn't one."

"I wasn't going to," Oliver said as he sat next to her. Brody squeezed between them and sat so they could pet him at the same time.

"Christ, Oliver, I'm sorry. I didn't mean to snap at you too."

He nodded and tilted his head. "You and Dad have borrowed mannerisms off each other. He runs his hand through his hair when he's thinking or stressed. You do the same. I think he picked that up from you when you were together in your prior Echo."

"Oh. Maybe." Dani shrugged. "I don't recall much from that life."

"Have you ever noticed that you swear like Dad?" Oliver changed his tone to mimic his father's voice. "'Christ, Oliver, how can you have so many socks on the floor and none of them match? Christ, Oliver, why is it that Dani can ask you to do something once and you trip over yourself to make it happen, but when I ask, I have to do so repeatedly.'" He grinned. "A few years ago, I looked up my birth record just to make sure my first name was actually Oliver."

Dani's slowly forming smile broadened. "Which it was."

"Nope. It was Christ."

She laughed, and it felt good. It also tore down what was left of her emotional wall, and tears fell. She closed her eyes, but didn't try to stop the tears from coming. Oliver's hand covered hers, and he remained silent.

She sniffled a few times and opened her eyes again. "I just feel so helpless."

"I know the feeling. It sucks," Oliver said.

Dani looked at her young friend. "Is this what you go through every time Miles has to leave?"

He nodded. "I feel the same when you leave too. I can't do anything but wait until you come back."

"That's horrible. I'm so sorry you go through that each time, Oliver. It must be unbearable when we're both gone."

"It's a little easier when you're gone together. I know you'll look out for each other. You'll make sure the other one stays safe."

Dani recalled Miles pulling her through the window with him to dodge the Warden patrol. She would've done the same for him had the roles been reversed.

"Brody has to work as a combat dog, but when he's not doing that, he's your dog, Oliver."

The teen's eyes widened. "You're *giving* him to me?"

"He's been your dog for a while now; he was just mine by title. I get visitation rights."

Oliver smiled and nodded. "Since you've had a rough day, do you want him to stay with you tonight?" he asked.

"No, but thanks. It's late and you have class tomorrow. I need to check on Mary."

They hugged, and as Oliver and Brody left, Dani headed to the basement to find something to fix. She found a solar panel that looked like it had been struck by lightning. She threw several tools and parts into a duffel and took them back to Mary's room.

Mary remained passed out on her bed, and Dani adjusted the blanket to pull it up to Mary's shoulders. She kept the lights low, lit a few candles, and sat on the floor with the gear. The fried panel would keep her hands and her mind busy for several hours.

CHAPTER
20

Rowan stood out of the way while the medical team buzzed around the man strapped to the stretcher. Capturing Gavin Marcus had been a huge success, partly because of new intel from Crow. Marcus's involvement with Houston on both CNA and personal levels would give the Wardens a major advantage over the CNA and Brigands in Maine. As expected, early interrogations and torture of him had been useless. When Rowan threatened the lives of the two humans they'd also caught, Marcus stayed firm. Even the humans refused to talk when nearly beaten to death. They were loyal to their cause the same way Rowan was committed to his.

Curtis wanted to kill the humans, but Rowan—though tempted—had other plans for them.

One of the medical techs finished inserting the needle into one of the bulging veins in Marcus's arm and turned to Curtis. "We're ready, sir."

Rowan stepped forward with Curtis.

"Are the cameras running?" Rowan asked.

"Yes, sir," Curtis said.

"Perfect." Rowan moved closer to Marcus. "You took Portland from me, and you'll help me take it back. I'd tell you not to bother trying to fight the restraints or resist the medication so things go easier for you, but please, do resist. It'll be more entertaining for your people in Maine when I send them the feed. Once we're done with the reconditioning process, you will be a Warden and you'll tell me everything."

Marcus pulled against restraints that didn't move. Sweat dripped from him as he struggled, and Rowan grinned.

"Did you know that you are nowhere to be found in the CNA records?" Rowan asked. "I thought it was a mistake or that your records were locked down with the tightest security, but then I realized it was no mistake. You're not in the database because you're a Brigand. There is no Captain Gavin Marcus. It's a false title you've been dragging around with you since the Portland battle." Rowan enjoyed watching Marcus's determined resistance diminish a little with this revelation.

"My guess is Houston—I imagine you call her Catherine when you're in her bed—kept you out of the CNA database for a reason. Easier for her to fuck a civilian than it is an inferior officer with the CNA's cumbersome rules," Rowan said. He smiled.

He laughed when Marcus fought the restraints hard enough for the devices to cut into his skin and make him bleed.

"I'll never understand your thing for human women. We'll fix that problem soon enough." Rowan turned to the medical tech. "Start the infusion."

He took a few steps back and stood with his hands clasped behind his back and a grin on his face. The fluid raced down the tubing into Marcus's arm, and the man's face turned a dark shade of red. He thrashed against his restraints before releasing a deafening roar of pain. Rowan admired the man's strength and determination to fight the inevitable. As the medications reached the peak of infusion, Marcus began to tremble with his ongoing fight, but he lived on for a few more minutes until his strength began to fail. He drew in another deep breath, and his final scream faded as his life ended.

Rowan watched the monitors attached to the man. All signs of life vanished. He glanced at Curtis and caught the man smiling and furiously taking notes.

"Have we ever had one last that long?" Rowan asked.

"No, sir. Never."

Rowan strolled through the bay while waiting for the regen process to begin. A few minutes later he glanced back when the medical staff began murmuring. Marcus's body glowed as it healed and regenerated, and Rowan returned to Curtis.

"I'll notify you when the final phase of induction is complete," Curtis said.

Rowan nodded and left.

He tried to work from his office, but he wondered about Marcus's progress over the next few hours. He didn't have any new messages from Crow, and he was too distracted to research Maine residents. He spoke briefly with his wife and son, promising to be home that night. He passed the rest of his time pacing in his office until he gave up to return to the med bay. Both Curtis and Marcus were gone, so he walked through the facility to the main lab, hoping nothing had gone wrong to force Curtis to rework his IV cocktails.

He passed through the lab to where the technicians told him Curtis was. Rowan stopped after he passed through the entry to the lab bay. Marcus stood in the center of the bay, dressed in Warden patrol gear, and his eyes didn't move as Rowan approached. Curtis circled around Marcus and never stopped making notes on his panel. He glanced up once at Rowan, smiled, then returned his attention to his notes. He had seen Curtis like this before and knew not to bother with any questions. If he did, Curtis would respond with a hasty gesture for him to wait a moment.

While Curtis worked, Rowan examined Marcus. The man's tall, broad frame made him a formidable figure. The Warden gear amplified his appearance. His eyes paused at the newest plasma pistol model in Marcus's holster. Curtis lowered his panel.

"His reconditioning took a bit longer than usual, but it is complete. He's a tough bastard. His memories are intact, excluding those of the reconditioning process, which we removed, but he is now a Warden."

Rowan wanted to be certain and stepped forward. "Marcus, remove your weapon and aim it at my head."

Without pause, Marcus pulled his pistol and pointed it at Rowan's forehead. Rowan moved forward until the end of the pistol almost touched his face. One quick trigger pull and his head would disappear. Curtis fidgeted as seconds ticked by, but neither Rowan nor Marcus moved.

"Lower your weapon," Rowan said, and Marcus complied. "Don't reholster it. You're not finished."

Rowan's newest Warden kept his pistol in his hand by his side.

"Bring his companions from the holding cell to us," Rowan said to Curtis.

Curtis sent for the prisoners, and Rowan continued to examine Marcus while they waited. Once the two humans were dragged in, his attention diverted to the men. Their faces were swollen and bleeding from both old and new injuries.

"Cap?" one of the men said, despair in his voice.

Marcus didn't look at the man, twitch, move, or give any other indication that one of his prior comrades was even present.

Rowan grinned. "Marcus, what do we do with humans?"

"If they have no useful intel, kill them," Gavin said.

"Kill this one," Rowan said, gesturing to the man who had spoken.

Marcus lifted his pistol and fired a single shot. The man fell, and blood poured from the hole in his chest. The second man knelt, but his friend was already dead.

"Goddammit, Gavin," the man said.

"He's a Warden now," Rowan said, proud of Marcus's performance. "Corey, isn't it? You can live a little longer if you tell me how Houston plans to attack Boston."

"Fuck you."

Rowan turned to his new puppet. "Kill that one too."

Marcus fired one shot, and Corey's body fell.

"You may holster your weapon now," Rowan said. As Marcus followed his latest order, Rowan approached one of the cameras in the lab. He looked directly into it. "Gavin Marcus is *mine*, Colonel Houston. If you're brave enough to come for him, I'd love to see you try. We do have a reversal process for reconditioning that I will hand over to you if you successfully take Boston. I'll give it to you myself." Rowan left the camera and returned to Curtis, who had stood motionless throughout Rowan's testing of Marcus's reconditioning.

"Cut the feed there and send it to me. I'll put the best parts together and send it to Houston," Rowan said.

"Sir, we can't reverse reconditioning."

"They don't know that," Rowan said. "Marcus, with me."

He left the lab with Marcus at his side. Once they reached his office, Rowan closed the door and pulled up a map of Boston on his desk.

"First, you're going to tell me every detail of the plan Houston has for attacking Boston. Then you're going to tell me everything you know about Dani."

"Yes, sir."

CHAPTER
21

S weat stung Dani's eyes, but she couldn't wipe it away. A droplet fell from her brow and landed on the back of her already sweat-glistening hand. She worked alone to disarm the training explosives running the length of an entryway she and her fireteam needed to enter. They'd spent the entire day working their way through the toughest part of the simulation using the electronically reconstructed buildings mixed in with wooden structures and fake explosives. Even with fake explosives, if she failed at her task, she'd be blasted with paint, and her fireteam would need to repeat that portion of the drill.

Her sim suit and helmet were impossibly hot. She'd removed her helmet to work on the bomb, but the relief from the stuffy helmet was short-lived once the sweat started dripping down her face.

She'd spent the day battling her mix of emotions over the capture of Gavin, Corey, and Jamie. Kelsey was MIA, and Mary's saboteur training today had been disastrous. Her friend had failed to defuse two bombs and was already covered in yellow paint. Javi was so irritated, he pulled Mary out of training for the rest of the day. Dani was certain Mary was at Hattie's now and well into her pints, and Dani was ready to join her.

"Dani?" Miles said through the comm, so his voice was directly in her earpiece.

She startled with the sound, almost yanking the wrong wire free of the device and setting it off. She took a moment to steady herself.

"What?" she asked with a sharper tone than intended.

"Just checking in. This one seems to be taking a while."

"It'll take longer the more you keep yapping in my ear." The comm went silent, and she took another second to clear her thoughts of Gavin and Mary. The device was more complex than she was used to dealing with, and she needed every bit of her attention on her work. She moved her fingers over the wires, tracing them to figure out what went where and which ones would cover her in paint and which ones wouldn't. *This is such a fucking mess. Wires are bloody everywhere.*

Miles and the rest of her team, including Brody, waited just beyond the blast range for her to finish, the same as they would if the bomb was real. They'd have to wait a bit longer. More sweat dripped into her eyes, but she finally figured out the wiring pattern. She'd need to do four cuts to make two splices, then she could disarm the thing like a normal Warden trip cord. The wires were tightly wound, so the cuts wouldn't be easy. She wove her smallest set of snips through the wires and made the first two cuts. She shifted to begin the third, and Javi's voice interrupted her.

"Dani, I need you to exit training."

"No."

"Houston wants you to report to her now."

"She can wait."

"I'm watching you on the feed. Leave the device and report to Houston. Don't, Dani. *Don't* take it out. Leave the—"

She pulled the earpiece out and placed it on the floor next to her. She finished her final two cuts and created the splices she needed. Once that part was complete, she finished disarming the bomb. She gathered her gear in one hand and her helmet in the other. She stood and wiped her sim suit's sleeve across her face.

"I'm done." When she received no answer, she realized her earpiece was on the floor. She wedged her helmet between her already full hand and her ribs and knelt to pick up the ear comm. She wiggled it into place. "Entryway is clear."

"*Goddammit, Dani!*" Javi's voice boomed into her ear.

She flinched with the noise and dislodged her helmet. She tried to catch it as it fell but missed. Javi kept yelling, but she wasn't listening. She failed to stop the helmet's fall, and it smacked into the fake bomb's paint cartridge near the floor. She turned her head and closed her eyes just before the explosion of paint coated her right side. Paint dripped down her right arm and fingers, so she shoved the tools in her left hand into any available pocket on her sim suit without looking, then wiped her clean hand over her face and eyes to remove the excess paint.

When she opened her eyes again, her fireteam had just entered and Miles, Cameron, Alex, and Dresden didn't bother concealing their laughter. Javi was yelling in her ear, and Dani couldn't remove the tiny comm since it was now the only thing preventing paint from entering her ear canal.

"Christ, Javi, shut up," Dani said. "I'm going. My team doesn't get dinged for this one going off. I had it disarmed until you started screaming."

"Noted. You're the only team to successfully get this far in the sim anyway. Get your ass over to Houston. Don't bother changing out of the suit. Just go."

She removed her tools from her pockets and passed them to Dresden for him to put into her gear pack. She left the warehouse to lumber across the base in the suit and boots to

Houston's office. During the walk she removed the suit's top in an effort to cool off. Her short-sleeved T-shirt was soaked with sweat, but it was paint-free. The paint in her hair and on her face, neck, and right hand was bright yellow. The suit's right leg and boot was also almost solid yellow. The other half of the suit was speckled with paint that had spattered from the initial contact. Dani was certain she'd get yelled at more for getting paint on the floor in Houston's office, but when she entered, both Catherine and Hattie were waiting for her. Neither of them said a word about the paint, and Dani's gut knotted.

"What's wrong?" Dani asked.

Without a word Houston turned a panel toward Dani.

The image of Gavin strapped to stretcher in a Warden medical bay made her shudder.

"This arrived," Houston said before playing the video feed.

Dani was horrified to watch the conversion process take place on Gavin. His screams of pain made her shiver with fear and dread. When Gavin later stood in Warden armor with his pistol against Rowan's head, she silently begged him to pull the trigger. But he didn't. Gavin was a Warden now and obedient to his superiors. She gasped when Jamie and Corey were brought in to join Rowan and Gavin. They'd been beaten and looked horrible. Gavin fired his pistol and murdered Jamie, and she groaned.

"Turn it off. *Turn it off!*"

Houston let the video play, and Dani closed her eyes. She heard Gavin's second shot and the sound of Corey's body hitting the floor. Tears flowed from her eyes, and she placed her palm over her eyes and wept more. She refused to open her eyes, even when she heard Rowan's voice.

"Gavin Marcus is *mine*, Colonel Houston," Rowan said. "If you're brave enough to come for him, I'd love to see you try. We do have a reversal process for reconditioning that I will hand over to you if you successfully take Boston. I'll give it to you myself."

Houston placed the panel back on her desk. "That's the last of the transmission."

Dani allowed herself a few more minutes' time to grieve before wiping her tears away. She wasn't finished mourning for her friends, but since Houston hadn't dismissed her yet, she assumed the woman had more to say.

"You should've sent in a team to rescue them," Dani said.

"It was too late to do anything for them."

"Fuck you, Catherine. I'm beginning to wonder which side you're on." Dani turned to leave.

"Dani, wait," Hattie said.

"Why bother? Careful who you pick for friends, Hattie. Catherine will leave you with the Wardens if they get their hands on you." Dani continued to head for the door.

"What about you?" Hattie asked.

Dani stopped and turned. "What do you mean?"

"What would you do if the Wardens got their hands on me?"

Dani shifted her gaze from Hattie to Houston as she spoke. "Kill anyone who tried to stop me from bringing you home."

Houston's face remained neutral with the direct threat, but Dani didn't regret her words. It wasn't a lie. She knew in her soul she could kill another person if it meant saving Hattie's life.

"What do you think of Rowan's reversal process?" Hattie asked.

Dani returned her attention to Hattie. "It's bullshit. Once the Wardens create a convert, they'd never need or want to reverse reconditioning and lose a Warden. It's a taunt to bait us into attacking prematurely out of hope."

Hattie nodded. "That's what we thought, too."

There was no hope for Gavin. He was Warden material now, and Corey and Jamie were dead. Fresh tears began to burn

Dani's eyes, so she left. She retreated to Hattie's brothel and slipped into the kitchen. She poured herself a mug of ale and drank half of it in a few gulps. Her head began to swim, so she leaned against the counter.

"Dani?"

She turned at the sound of Alex's voice, then returned her attention to her mug.

Alex continued. "I've been thinking. We can do a rescue on our own to find Corey, Jamie, and Gavin. I want to help you. Colonel Houston likes to follow the rules too much. You're a Brigand and can do whatever you want. I'll help you go to Boston."

Dani barked a laugh to think of Houston following the rules while fucking Gavin, who wasn't even in the CNA as Houston had made everyone believe. The colonel was *not* who she appeared to be.

"I'm not joking, so don't laugh. I really want to help."

Dani shook her head and retreated to her room with her ale. She sank into the soft chair in the corner and finished her drink just before someone knocked lightly on her door.

"Go away."

Dani wasn't in the mood for company, but Oliver had never let that stop him before. He and Brody entered, and without a word, Oliver took his pack off and sat on the floor. He pulled out his books and started on his homework while Brody hopped up onto her bed to nap. Dani watched the boy for a moment, and then the tears returned. Oliver shifted his things closer to her and leaned his head against the side of her leg while he worked. They'd been friends long enough for him to know she actually liked having company when she was sad, but he also knew she didn't like being hugged or talked to when upset.

She appreciated his presence. If anyone else had come through her door, she would have rudely sent them in the other direction. The boy was special to her—like a younger brother—and she adored him. She couldn't fathom her life without him in it, but this war was taking everyone from her—one by one. Gavin was alive, but he was just as gone as Jamie and Corey. Dani lowered her head and wept for her friends.

CHAPTER

22

"I 'm glad I came home for lunch," Rowan said as he pulled his uniform trousers back on.

Ana rolled her eyes as she left the bed.

He smiled as her naked form approached.

"Sometimes I hate your fucking job, Rowan," Ana said. "A quick romp in the sack and you're off to play with Curtis the rest of the day. As the mother of your children, I assure you, your priorities are backward."

She sounded angry, but he didn't buy the act. He slipped his hands around her before she could leave, and pulled her close. "Quick? That was a lot of moaning earlier for you to now deem it unfulfilling." He slid his hand to the inside of her thigh and she grinned.

"Ella is a good nanny," she said. "I can send her out with the kids every day for lunch."

"I like that plan."

"Me too." She moved past him to the bathroom. "When you leave, take your gorilla with you. I don't want him here anymore." She turned the shower on.

"We have threats present in the city, Ana," Rowan said, and

resumed dressing. "Marcus was one of those threats until we caught him."

"Three or four CNA soldiers in Boston does not constitute any kind of real threat. I've seen combat, Rowan. I can take care of myself and my family."

"He's here to protect you and the children."

"Devon thinks he's a giant toy and keeps trying to play with him."

"I'll talk to Devon."

"Don't bother. The gorilla goes with you." She ended the discussion by stepping into the shower.

He loved Ana's strength; it was one of the many reasons he'd married her. But sometimes that same strength irritated him. He left the bedroom and found Marcus standing at the front door where he'd last seen him.

"With me," Rowan said.

Marcus followed him without question, and Rowan could understand why she equated Marcus with an ape. Echoes didn't share any human ancestry, but Rowan's newest Warden was indeed a big man. He had done some hand-to-hand training with Marcus and was impressed with his speed and skill. Their rounds of training ended in draws, and Rowan recognized some of the same tactics Dani had used against him. She'd learned well from her former mentor.

Rowan glanced at Marcus as they walked. "When you trained Dani to fight, what were her weaknesses?"

"She hesitates before making a fatal strike. She has never killed anyone other than casualties created with her work as a saboteur. She's never made an intentional, direct kill with her hands or other weapon."

"Unintentional kills?"

"Only one. A Brigand, and she acted in self-defense."

"She's killed Wardens."

"Only as a sab. Never directly."

"Why not?"

"I've never understood her hesitation, but I've seen it many times. She won't take another's life."

Rowan laughed. "She is weak."

"Yes, sir, she is. Use it to your advantage."

"Oh, I will. You're handy to have around. I'm so glad we found you, Marcus."

"Thank you, sir."

When they arrived in the department, Curtis met them and nodded toward the office. Rowan dismissed Marcus and went to his office with Curtis.

"I thought he was watching your family," Curtis said.

"Ana was sick of him hanging around, so he's here now. What do you have for me?"

"Two of the three chancellors here side with us against the vice regent. We also have the ones in Portsmouth and Providence."

"So why haven't they done a vote of no confidence yet?"

"We need the third chancellor here. To move you from department head straight to VR, skipping chancellor, we need a unanimous vote."

"Who is the holdout?"

Curtis stalled a moment. "I don't like you knowing the specifics, sir. This is treason. I will take the blame if things go wrong. The more details you know, the more liable you'll be."

"I understand the risks!"

"Please, sir."

Rowan growled with frustration and paced. The comm inside his desk drawer chirped. It was Crow.

"What's that?" Curtis asked.

"Personal comm. I need to take this."

Curtis paused, then nodded before leaving the office.

Rowan waited until the door closed before retrieving the comm.

"Report," Rowan said.

"Sir, no one is coming from Portland for Captain Marcus."

"No one?"

"No, sir. Colonel Houston isn't sending a team, and none of his associates here are willing to risk capture to rescue him."

Rowan slammed his fist on the top of the desk. "Fuck." He took a deep breath. "So, they're leaving the missing one—the medic—for dead."

"Yes, sir. His status is MIA, but Houston isn't trying to find him."

"What about their spies here?"

"Radio silence, sir. Nothing in or out as far as I can tell."

"I need Dani here. She's vital to our research. Bring her to me."

"I have an extraction plan, but it's flawed. She's too surrounded, sir. I have help here, but we just can't get to her without getting killed in the process. Plus, she is a hell of a fighter. I'd have to tranq her, and that would make her dead weight to transport out, thus slowing us down."

"I want a solution, not excuses."

"I can take the boy," Crow said.

Rowan flipped through the images on his panel Crow had given him before. "Oliver Jackman."

"Yes, sir. He's small and easily accessed. I can alter my plan to take him instead. She'll come for him."

"She didn't come for Marcus."

"Her relationship with Gavin was different. There are others here that Dani is close to. She'd disobey Houston to go to Boston for them, and Oliver is the easiest target."

Rowan considered his options. The last thing he wanted was a human in Boston. He'd have to come up with a lie to cover the boy's presence. A nephew or something. The mere thought of declaring a human a relative, even if untrue, nauseated him.

"How much time do you need?" Rowan asked.

"I can hand him to you in three days, sir."

"What do you need from me?"

"Transport. I'll send you the coordinates and time for pickup from shore by boat and coordinates for an airlift from sea. Once I deliver him, I'll need a low-flying trip back in for an airdrop."

A water transport was easy to arrange. An airlift was trickier to pull off. Rowan would find out what tech Curtis had that they could use to create a field trial for the boat and helo logs to depart Boston. He could make it work. "Will you deliver him yourself?"

"If able to do so, I will, sir. I can't be gone from Portland long without losing my cover. If I don't put the boy into your hands, my associate will."

"Good. Proceed with the plan to take the boy. Come if you can. I look forward to meeting you."

"Thank you, sir."

Rowan ended the transmission. He'd tried baiting Dani to come to Boston but had failed. If Crow was right, she'd come for Oliver.

He left his office for the research area. Curtis looked up from his work as he approached.

"You're smiling," Curtis said.

"I just received some good intel on enemy targets in the region."

Curtis kept his voice low. "We need to stay on our primary objective, sir."

"I've netted more human and Echo captures out of the state this month than the VR's idiots have in the last eight months. My methods are working. Don't question my tactics or my objectives."

Curtis nodded with the rebuke.

"Show me what you have for weapons or scanners that we can operate from air or sea. I want to see the newer tech, what's working today and what's in development." Rowan's anger flashed when Curtis gave him a questioning look. "Now!"

"Yes, sir. Of course."

Rowan could use Dani's presence to dethrone the VR. He'd spin the circumstances as needed and show that her arrival meant an imminent CNA attack on Boston. Her involvement in the Portland battle and subsequent capture in Boston would prove that the current VR's rule of the region was so inept that the enemies of the Wardens could come and go at will. He already knew the measures he'd take to secure his appointment as Vice Regent Rowan and retake Maine without mercy.

CHAPTER
23

Miles turned the damaged helmet over in his hands and sighed. Every time Dani got frustrated in the sim, she tended to toss her helmet—usually before or after a swear-filled rant. Anton had tired of repairing the helmets himself, so as the team had left the warehouse that morning, he had given Miles her most recently damaged gear and said he'd send the rest over. Anton hadn't been joking.

Two totes arrived addressed to Miles. He squatted and checked the gear inside. One helmet had a shattered visor. It remained attached to the helmet, but it had thousands of little fissures across it. The faceplates were designed to take a beating, but maybe not the kind of torture Dani delivered. He checked the rest of the tote and saw that several helmets had various forms of visor damage. A few had cracks across the back or side, and Miles was glad he was not one of Dani's helmets. He shifted his attention to a third tote containing spare parts and wondered if he'd need another delivery.

With several hours' worth of work before him, Miles went to his workstation and started on the helmet Anton had given him. The electronics inside the helmets didn't react well to being bounced off floors, walls, or support beams. He glanced to his left, where Cameron worked on a set of circuits from a solar array that had been damaged by a tree limb falling on it during an afternoon thunderstorm.

Farther to his left, Dani worked on her assignment—a small circuit resting in her palm. Her head moved up and down as she took her eyes from the circuit to the panel display with the schematic and back to the circuit. "This makes no fucking sense," she said.

Cameron's head came up, and Miles sent him a mental warning. *Leave her alone, pal.*

Word had circulated about the deaths of Corey and Jamie. Kelsey had not been found, and Gavin was now a Warden. Miles had no love for Gavin, but he'd never wish reconditioning on the man. The news of Gavin's conversion was a major blow to the CNA in Maine and a massive win for the Wardens. Morale on the base sank, but no one had time to stop working. There was no hope of getting the bodies of Jamie and Corey back from the Wardens, either. Colonel Houston had led a service for them yesterday, and Miles had attended along with many others.

Reconditioning didn't make Gavin a traitor, but it meant he was now part of the enemy's army. Some on the base wanted a service for him too, but since he wasn't physically dead, Houston refused. Miles didn't care either way. If there was a service for Gavin, he'd skip it. The man had treated Dani roughly, and Miles would never respect him in life or death.

"What the hell? You can't route a circuit like this!" Dani said to the schematic on the panel.

"Need a hand?" Cameron asked her.

"*No!*"

Dani's bark made the man scowl, and Miles suppressed his grin. He dug through the tools at his work area to find something to pry the visor off the helmet. He noticed Cameron watching him, and Miles responded with a shrug before going back to work.

Dani's muttering and curses continued, and Miles worked in silence, stopping occasionally to inspect the next helmet in the line to be repaired. He paused at times to marvel at Dani's explosive temper and decided he was *really* glad he was not one of her helmets.

Dani began ranting again at the circuit in her hand. "Who comes up with this kind of rig? These new comms are shit. Schematic may as well be in goddamn hieroglyphics."

Miles didn't respond to her outburst; he knew better. His head lifted when Dani yelped, but he didn't leave his station.

She threw the blood-covered circuit and the screwdriver aside before clenching her injured left hand into a fist. Cameron, ever helpful and unaware of the storm he was walking into, stopped his work to go to her.

Nice knowing you, Cam. She will eviscerate you.

"Let me have a look at that," Cameron said, reaching for hand.

Miles shook his head. *Here comes the first bite out of your ass.*

Dani recoiled from his attempt to touch her. "I don't need you."

Cameron's temper flared along with hers. "I'm just trying to help."

And the second.

"I don't want or need your help," Dani said, scowling.

"You don't need to be rude about it."

Make it a triple.

"Fuck off!"

Cameron frowned and left the gear room.

Rookie.

Miles picked up a clean towel from his station and threw it to Dani. She caught it and turned her glare on him. He returned his attention to the helmet he was working on.

He watched her in his peripheral vision, and she wrapped the towel around her sliced palm where the screwdriver had slipped and cut her. She muttered things he couldn't hear and drew in a sharp breath when she wrapped the towel tighter over the cut. She dropped her hands to her sides and stared at him. Miles feigned keeping his attention on the helmet. He pried the visor off and placed it aside so he could see her reflection in it.

"Miles?"

"Yeah?" He kept his head down while he turned the helmet in his hands.

"Miles!"

With deliberate calm he placed his tool down next to the helmet and turned his full attention to her.

"Why are you here?" she asked.

He waved at the totes. "I'm on helmet repair detail." He knew not to mention they were all ones she'd broken.

"That's not what I mean," she said, snapping at him though he'd done nothing to warrant her anger.

Miles kept his voice even. "I don't understand what you're asking, Dani."

"*Why* are you here? *Why* do you put up with me? I tell Cam to go away, and he does. But you and Oliver, you stick around even when I don't want anyone near me. It's infuriating, and I want it to stop."

"I don't think you could ever be angry with Oliver."

"I have been before."

"When?"

She frowned. "Okay, so it's been a while." She softened her tone. "That's not the point."

Miles gave her a small smile, glad he'd gotten her to calm a bit. "What is the point?"

"I don't know anymore." She shook her head and headed for the door.

He touched her arm as she walked by, and she stopped. He lowered his hand, and she stayed. "We stick around because we love you. Aunt Hattie, Mary, Oliver, and me, too. We all love you, and you're part of our family."

"I'm a train wreck, Miles, and I'm a terrible influence on your son."

"Mmm, yes, that you are, on both counts."

"How are you able to make me calm down so easily?"

"It's not easy. Trust me. You used to chew me up and spit me out into a hundred pieces like you did Cam before I figured you out. People like Alex and Cam adore you, but they don't understand that you don't need rescuing. You are best left to sort out your thoughts on your own. You're not someone who needs another person doting on you. You're a Brigand who has been surviving on your own with each of your lives. Sure, you had Jace helping you when you were a child, but you would have found a way to survive if he hadn't been around—just like you've been doing since he died."

"Except I can't seem to get past my midtwenties before dying again."

"Technicality." Miles shrugged, but the idea of losing her again terrified him. "Like with that circuit and anything else— for the most part—you'll ask for help when you're ready. Every once in a while, you need a nudge, but pushing too early or too hard only makes you retreat more or lash out. If Cam's smart, he learned that today, but he doesn't strike me as terribly sharp."

Dani smiled, then lowered her gaze. "I am so sorry, Miles."

"You're hurting with the deaths of Corey and Jamie. They were good men. I liked them a lot, and you did too. It's okay to be angry. It's okay to grieve."

"Oliver didn't mind me crying the other night."

"He didn't try to hug you, did he?" Miles asked, wincing. "You hate that."

"No," Dani said. She smiled. "I think he figured me out a long time ago."

"Yeah, he's great with people."

"Oliver isn't cut out for war. I mean, none of us should have to deal with this shit, but especially him. He's already a victim with his mother's death. He can't be part of this war as a soldier."

A familiar and uncomfortable ache filled Miles's chest. "No," he said, his voice cracking. "The essence of everything that makes him who he is would be destroyed."

Dani nodded, and Miles allowed his gaze to drift to the helmets. "We have work to do to end the war before it's time for him to enlist."

"Yeah." Dani sighed and headed back to her work area.

"Not that I'm any good with the schematics, but holler if you need a hand with the new comms."

"I'll figure those little bastards out."

"I know you will." Miles pulled the helmet he'd started repairing closer and removed the inner lining to access a relay inside that he was certain had cracked when Dani had bounced the helmet off one of the warehouse's steel beams.

CHAPTER
24

Birdsong was a sound Dani considered pleasant, but with Maine's four-in-the-morning summer sunrises and trying to function on minimal sleep, she wanted to throttle every bird in the county. Since sleeping longer wasn't an option, she rolled over and sat on the edge of the bed. She rubbed her eyes, swollen from another night of grief plus a bit of a hangover.

Dani hadn't gotten much done with the comm circuit when she finally gave up for the night. With memories of Gavin clouding her judgment, she'd pushed her emotions aside to be with Mary. Drinking with Mary was never a good idea. She'd seen Mary drink men under the table, so she knew better than to try to keep up with her friend or risk passing out on the floor.

She stood to dress and took an extra moment to make sure her balance was intact. She left her CNA-issue fatigues on the floor and pulled her battered jeans on instead. She slipped a tank top on and pulled a threadbare tee on over it. When she spotted her reflection in the mirror, she sighed. Dani ran her hand through her unruly hair, which did nothing to improve the mess on the top of her head.

She was dressed like the Brigand she was before the Brigands and CNA joined forces. That seemed like many years ago, but it had only been about a year since she, Jace, and Gavin had taken over Colonel Houston's meeting to prove the Maine CNA was vulnerable and should combine forces with the Bangor Brigands. She and Gavin had been on friendly terms then, and Jace had truly enjoyed breaking into the CNA base that day.

Both Gavin and Jace were gone now.

Dani finished dressing, brushed her teeth, and splashed water on her face. She passed her wet fingers through her hair a few times and frowned at the results. Some causes were just lost. She grabbed her daypack and turned to call for Brody. That was when she remembered he was with Oliver. It would take her some time to get used to not having Brody around, but the dog was better off with Oliver.

She left her room and crept down the hall, careful to avoid the boards that creaked when she passed Mary's room. She arrived in the kitchen and stopped. Both Mary and Hattie sat at the table with mugs in their hands. Her attempt to sneak away unnoticed had crashed and burned.

"Zombies *do* exist," Hattie said, and she cackled. She stood and waved at Dani to join them at the table while she went to the counter.

Dani had learned it was useless to argue with Hattie, so she slid a chair back and dropped her pack on the floor by her feet. Mary's eyes were dark and a little puffy; she'd had a rough night too.

"Why are you up so early?" Mary asked.

"Birds woke me," Dani said.

"Try again."

Lying to her friend was another lost cause. "I couldn't sleep and was sick of lying in the bed feeling like shit. Figured I could at least be up doing something and feeling like shit."

Mary nodded and took a sip of her coffee.

"Why are you up?" Dani asked.

Mary grinned. "Birds woke me."

Dani chuckled and shook her head.

Hattie returned and placed a mug in front of Dani and handed her a sack.

Dani felt the contents of the sack through the cloth and realized Hattie had given her food.

Hattie sat and took a sip of her tea. "You're not dressed to work on the base today, so you're bailing, yes?"

"Am I that predictable?"

"Honey, for the most part, no. You're an absolute wild card except when you're hurting. When that happens, you bail every time. Could set a damn clock by your actions."

"Then what do I do?"

"You sort your shit out and get back to work," Hattie said. She paused. "Which should be by tonight."

"Tonight? No."

Hattie and Mary shared a look before they both nodded at Dani.

"Tonight," Mary said.

"Where are you headed today?" Hattie asked.

Frustrated with their assessment, Dani took a gulp of her coffee and fiddled with the mug without meeting their eyes.

"That mug won't change anything, so stop looking at it for answers while you stall," Hattie said.

Dani shrugged.

Mary leaned forward with her elbows on the table. "Wander over to Portland Head Light."

"It's a bit of a hike from downtown," Dani said.

"You have all day. Go anyway."

"Why there?"

"Miles mentioned it as a place you liked when you lived here before."

"Oh." *Another memory lost with my last regen. The list keeps getting longer.*

They drank in silence for a few more minutes while the birds outside continued to sing their guts out. The birdsong didn't irritate her as much now that she was awake.

Hattie finished her coffee and left the table. "Unlike you slackers, I have businesses to run." She left the mug on the counter and strolled out of the kitchen.

Dani grinned. "Want to bail with me?"

"Nah. I'm on tech repair detail today, covering for a friend who covered for me when I needed time to pull myself together."

Dani stood and picked up her things. She squeezed Mary's shoulder as a thank-you and left. She wanted to tell Mary that Kelsey was alive and would be found, but no one needed false hope. The thought reminded her of Rowan's lie about the ability to reverse Gavin, and her anger flared. She cursed the Wardens and wanted them to pay for all the death and pain they caused.

She was tired and hungry by the time she reached the lighthouse. The five-mile walk on little sleep had her wishing she hadn't listened to Mary, until she looked out across the bay. The lighthouse on Ram Island just across from Portland Head Light had fallen apart, so only the base was left. She couldn't remember if it had always looked that way or had been whole when she lived in Portland before. It didn't matter.

She crawled down the rocks toward the water so Portland Head Light towered above her. She found a place to sit, dug through the sack, and ate, then took a drink of water and put everything back into her pack before making herself comfortable. She leaned back against the rocks, and between the waves crashing on the rocks and the cool breeze coming off the water, was asleep within minutes.

When Dani woke, a shadow was looming over her, and she scrambled to her feet. No one was around, and the shadow was from the rocks behind her. The sun had moved across the landscape. She'd slept for hours. *Shit.* She hadn't intended to sleep the entire day away. Her skin felt hot, and she touched her face. She sighed—she had a sunburn. *Great.*

On her walk back to town, she recalled her fight with the new circuit and schematics. It was part of the Ekkoh tech from the Ancients. The schematics weren't in hieroglyphics, they were in the Ekkohrian language. It made much more sense now, and she knew how it was supposed to work. Dani quickened her pace from a walk to a run and headed straight for the base. She was out of breath when she arrived.

"Dani!"

She stopped as Oliver approached. She gave him a small wave while she caught her breath.

"Why were you running? Where have you been? Why is your face so red?"

"I was at the coast, thinking—sort of." She decided not to admit she had actually been sleeping the whole time. "I got sunburned while there, and now I need to get into the gear room to work on something. Okay? We good? Can I go?"

Oliver shook his head.

"Why not?"

"You made a promise to me."

"I *know*, Oliver. I'm trying. I swear. The thing in the gear room might help us with Boston." She waved toward the building. "I haven't forgotten you. I'm doing everything I can to keep you out of the CNA and this fucking war."

"You promised you wouldn't hurt yourself."

"I'm not. I didn't." She paused, remembering her promise to him the previous year when she was in a dark place after Jace's death. She didn't know why he was bringing it up now. "Oliver, I'm not suicidal."

"When you don't take care of yourself, it's the same as causing yourself harm—even if you don't mean to."

"Oh."

"You look terrible."

She started to defend herself, then snapped her mouth closed, considering his words. She felt like shit and figured she looked like it too. "You're right. I'll do better."

"Have you eaten?"

"Earlier, yes."

"Will you have dinner with us tonight?"

"If that's good with your father, sure. How is Brody?" she asked. She really wanted to ask *where* he was.

"He's great, but he will keep me up tonight. He was with Mary today for training, and he always snores a lot after that. Are you sure you want me to keep him?"

"I miss him, but I know he's happier with you."

"Visit him—and me—whenever you like."

Dani smiled and walked home with him. She was desperate to work on the circuit, but it wasn't going anywhere tonight.

Oliver opened the door, and Brody hopped up from his bed to greet him. "Dad, Dani's having dinner with us."

"If that's okay with you," Dani quickly added.

Miles stood in the kitchen and wiped his hands on a towel. "Always. Where were you today?"

"At the lighthouse." Portland had several lighthouses in and around the area, but she'd been vague on purpose.

"Portland Head. Great place. You always liked going there and would fall asleep. Given the sunburn, I'm guessing you did."

Dani nodded and knelt to pet the dog when he came to her.

It annoyed her a little that Miles knew her better than she knew herself.

"Colonel Houston's pissed you weren't around today."

She kissed Brody on the top of the head and stood. He ambled back to his bed and flopped across it. "When is she not pissed at me for one thing or another?"

Miles shrugged. "This is true. You can help me in the kitchen. Oliver, homework."

Oliver groaned and made a great show of trudging to his room as if sentenced to death. Dani smiled at his antics, glad she'd crossed paths with him today. He meant the world to her.

CHAPTER
25

Dani had the new comms working by midday and proudly demonstrated their operation in Houston's office.

"I didn't show Anton the comms, but I had him run every scan with the Warden tech we have while I was transmitting," Dani said. "He didn't pick up anything."

"Good," Houston said. "You'll train our research techs on the build so we can produce these around the clock. Grab your gear." She picked up a panel from her desk and headed for the door.

Dani loaded the items back into her pack and jogged to catch up to the colonel. She followed Houston across the base toward the warehouses, but they didn't enter the sim as Dani expected. Houston took her past two rows of buildings and through an MP station to reach the final row of structures. The colonel deactivated the security system on the side door with something hidden inside the cuff of her uniform sleeve.

"We mooched the proximity security clearance tech off the Wardens," Houston said. "Handy as hell to unlock doors just by walking up to them. We tweaked the system so it incorporates bio clearance too. No one can pull a jacket off a corpse and get in like you did when we took Portland."

"So how does it work?"

Houston grinned and gestured for Dani to enter the warehouse.

"Oh, please," Dani said. "You're going to act like the proximity crap is top secret? That's the stupidest thing—" Her eyes landed on the four sleek jets inside the warehouse. Crews moved around and on top of them. Cables hung from the ceiling down to the aircraft, and Dani could only stare.

"These are our new birds. Beautiful, aren't they? Straight off Ekkoh designs from the Ancients. One word about this and I'll kill you myself."

"Wow."

"This needs to be kept as quiet as Hattie's identity."

"Yeah." Dani blinked a few times and headed toward the new fixed-wings.

"Put your comms in those birds, and we'll be ready for Boston very soon. Figure out how to incorporate these into your plan. Can you do that?"

"Yeah."

"Got anything more than one-word answers for me?"

"Nope."

Houston handed Dani the panel she'd taken from her office. "You'll need this. Designs for the birds and how to integrate the comms. This device stays here or in my office. Understand?"

"Got it."

"Oh, good. We're up to two words now. Have fun." Houston turned to leave.

"Yep."

Houston shot her a glare, and Dani grinned. The colonel sighed and left, and Dani headed straight for the first jet. She checked the panel, reviewed the specs, and marveled at the design. She went up a ladder to the open cockpit and looked in. Her sense of wonder was replaced with dread. "Well, this is gonna suck."

The pilot's seat was missing, and the instrument panel was half installed. Numerous wires hung loose from behind the instruments, and some weren't connected to anything. She wished Houston hadn't left so quickly. Dani wasn't sure if she was supposed to just do her piece or fix the rest of the wiring disaster too. She climbed into the cockpit and removed her pack. She didn't have much room, so she re-reviewed the schematics on the panel before setting it aside and lying on her back to slide her upper body beneath the instrument panel.

She lost track of time as she installed the comm system and then repaired most of the wiring. Per the specs, two other pieces of instrumentation needed to go in, so she left those wires loose.

"Dani?"

Startled, she whacked her head on something behind the instrument panel. "Ouch. Shit." She slithered out from behind the panel and rubbed her forehead.

"Sorry," Cameron said. "Didn't mean to startle you."

"Head is harder than it looks. What are you doing up here?"

"I'm installing the shielding and weapons components to create the readouts here." He pointed to a long, slender portion of the instruments. "I was just going to get started on this plane when I found you."

"If the rest of them look like this one did when I got here, we'll want to team up to knock this out."

"Sure."

They were tired and hungry when they left after dark and went to Hattie's in search of food. The evening crowd had the place packed, so Dani and Cameron squeezed in at the bar to order.

A group of four locals played Irish music in a corner of the pub. The ale arrived first, and Dani drained half of her mug on the first drink. She was thirsty but forced herself to put the mug down. Their bowls of Brigand stew arrived, and Dani started eating.

Houston arrived at Dani's shoulder. "Sorry to interrupt."

"No, you're not," Dani said.

"I need you to prep several new comm units. They're going to Boston tomorrow."

Dani swallowed her food and washed it down with the rest of the ale. "Yes!"

"You're not going."

"What? Why not?"

"You're compromised and are staying here."

"I'm not compromised."

"You'd bring the comms down and stay to look for Kelsey and probably Gavin too. You're not going," Houston said, and she disappeared into the crowd.

Dani growled with frustration. Someone bumped into her back and she rocked forward. Annoyed with the crowd and angered with Houston for making her stay in Portland, Dani wanted to be away from everyone. She'd deal with the comms in the morning. She waved at the man behind the bar for a refill, and he nodded.

"Thanks for your help today, Cam. Oh, and sorry for biting your head off yesterday, or the day before, whatever day it was. They all run together. Guess we'll finish up the pl— project tomorrow." She had almost screwed up in a crowded area where she could be overhead. She'd make a terrible spy.

"Sure," Cam said. "Wait. You're leaving already?"

"Yes."

Her ale arrived, and she took it and her bowl, weaving through people to the rear of the building and the kitchen. She stood at the counter and finished the stew and the ale. Her head felt both heavy and light after drinking the ale too quickly, but she was still thirsty. Instead of drinking water, she headed back into the pub area, where Alex met her at the bar. Alex gestured for two more of whatever she was drinking.

"Rough day?" Alex asked.

"Started off okay, went to shit, got better, more shit and such, and now I just don't care."

Alex grinned and slid one of the two new mugs toward Dani. They touched mugs, and Dani drank. The taste wasn't unpleasant, but Alex had given her something other than ale.

Alex leaned against her and spoke into her ear. "Do you like it?"

"I'm not sure." She took another long drink from the mug.

"It's noisy in here. Want to go somewhere else?"

The music seemed to be *inside* her head now, and Dani wasn't sure how that had happened. Her vision blurred, and Alex was kissing her. Dani tried to back away, but she was pinned between the woman and the bar. She turned her head to avoid Alex's touch, and the movement made her head swim more. Her balance abandoned her, and she crashed into two other people on her trip to the floor. Feet scuffled around her, and raised voices escalated into shouts. Miles rolled her to her side in time for Dani to see Mary land a trio of solid punches to Alex's face before someone separated them.

Everything went dark, and she started floating. The noise inside her head faded, and she stopped floating. That's when she realized that her world wasn't dark; she had her eyes closed. She forced her heavy eyelids open and released a garbled laugh at her mistake. She recognized her room and comfy chair. Miles and Mary moved around the room and appeared busy, but Dani didn't understand why.

Dani rested her palms on the chair's padded arms and grinned. "I was floating."

"No, you weren't." Mary knelt next to the chair with a vial in her hand. "Alex *will* be floating in the river the next time she tries to get you drunk."

Miles held up a basin. "Will this do?"

"Should catch most of it," Mary said.

Dani didn't know what they were talking about. "Catch what?" She was tired and didn't want to be in the chair. "I want to go to bed. You and Miles can come to bed with me too."

Mary removed Dani's hand from her cheek. "Here." Mary raised the vial to Dani's mouth. "Drink this."

Dani laughed and leaned toward Mary. "You and Miles don't have to get me drunk to sleep with me." A tiny part of her mind registered these as words she should *not* be saying, but her mouth wasn't listening.

"Drink it." Mary helped her drink the vial's contents.

Miles moved in closer with the basin. "How quickly will it work?"

Dani frowned and tilted her head. "I don't feel so—" She pitched forward, and vomiting ensued.

"Oh, wow," he said. "*Wow!*"

CHAPTER

26

"Keep an eye on her, Captain," Houston said. "Dani needs to finish building the comms before noon. Half of them will go with the team to Boston—a team that she is *not* on."

"Yes, ma'am," Miles said.

"Take the other half into the sim and train your fireteams on them. The time is quickly coming for us to begin the assault. By 1600, finish up in the sim and send Dani to my office for her next assignment."

"Yes, ma'am." Miles was Dani's babysitter today to keep her from leaving with the team going to Boston.

"She's in the gear room now, working on the units. Help her finish them on time. She looks like shit. What happened last night?"

"Alex gave her something to drink without knowing Dani had already been drinking ale."

"She looks worse than a mere hangover."

"Mary thinks Alex put something in Dani's drink, but everything was spilled when Dani went down, and Mary attacked Alex. We took Dani back to her room, and Mary gave her an emetic."

"That must have been fun."

Miles's stomach knotted, and he swallowed hard when he recalled his job holding the basin.

"Any proof Alex gave Dani something more than alcohol?"

"No, ma'am."

"Alex is CNA. I can't have this formally investigated without something more than a Brigand's hunch." Houston held up her hand before Miles could protest. "Look, I know Mary and Dani are more than mere civilians, but I have regulations to follow. Did you see anything? Did anyone else see anything?"

"No, ma'am."

Miles hadn't seen Alex and Dani at the bar until Mary said something to him. They saw Alex kissing Dani and Dani's failed attempt to back away. Mary was already in motion, pushing her way through the people separating her from Alex before Dani struck the floor. Within seconds Mary was swinging for the fences on Alex's face.

"If anyone comes forward with any information that Alex tried to drug her, let me know. We'll investigate and charge her if the results warrant it."

"Yes, ma'am."

"Busy day today. Get to it, Captain."

"Yes, Colonel."

When he arrived at the gear room, it was his first time to see Dani since leaving her late the night before in Mary's care. Her face was pale. She glanced up when he entered, then went back to work. For each of his promotions in the CNA, his fellow officers engaged in a drinking game that always left him with a vicious hangover. Bright lights like the ones in the gear room made it worse. Miles dimmed the lights, and Dani sighed.

"Thanks," she said.

"Colonel Houston sent me here to help you finish the build."

"Give me a minute and I'll set up a station for you next to me."

Miles picked up her almost empty mug of water. He left to top it off, returned, and placed it back where she'd had it before. He was glad to see her trying to rehydrate. After the volume of ale and stew he had witnessed leaving her last night, he was surprised she wasn't in the infirmary.

"Thanks," she said. "I'm sorry for what happened last night. I somehow remember most of it, and I cannot begin to explain how horrified I am at the things I said to you and Mary. I don't know why I said them. My brain told me to shut up, but my mouth ... I'm a fucking disaster." She looked away from him and sighed. "I apologized to Mary earlier. She said it wasn't a big deal, but it is to me."

Miles didn't need an apology from her. Like Mary, he felt it was more of a misunderstanding. Plus, Dani had been completely shitfaced, like the night she told him she loved him.

"Apology accepted," he said to end Dani's groveling. "Now, give me a crash-course on how to build these things."

They worked together over the next few hours, and Miles kept her mug of water full to encourage her hydration. On one trip to refill it, he grabbed several bland CNA food wafers and brought them back for her to eat. Her color improved, as did her productivity. They had two totes of comm units put together by the time they were due for delivery to the transport truck. They left the gear room, and Miles carried both totes out.

"I feel like dog food, but I can carry one," she said.

"When you no longer *look* like dog food, I'll let you."

She chuckled, and he smiled.

He dropped off one tote at the truck and kept the remaining

one. "Colonel Houston says we're to take these into the sim to have our fireteams start training."

Dani's eyes lingered on the four-person team making the final preps for the transport south. "Catherine made you my babysitter so I wouldn't leave?"

Miles nodded.

She frowned and led the way to the warehouse. As the others on their team arrived, Miles noted Alex's absence. Mary was present, but he wasn't surprised that Alex was a no-show. Javi and two other teams joined them.

Dani distributed the equipment and instructed them on their use. "Clarity and reception are better with these. No more static when you're underground and someone you need is up top. The range is quadrupled."

Miles noted that Dani's mind was sharper now despite her lingering hangover. She didn't tell the group anything about them being developed off Ekkoh tech or that they were undetectable by the Wardens. Those were things she'd failed to conceal from him earlier that morning when her mind was fogged. She'd sworn him to secrecy, and they'd agreed she'd be a shit spy.

The teams fiddled with the devices while standing in the middle of the empty warehouse until Javi declared playtime over. They changed into their sim suits, and Anton loaded the program.

Dani performed in the sim without any problems from either her illness or her past trauma from living in Boston during the start of the war. They made it through two hours of the simulated attack on Boston using the newest version of the plan Houston had approved. Hundreds of CNA and Brigand troops trained in the sim at different times since they all had different tasks to perform. Anton kept the program running around the clock, eating and sleeping in the control room while the troops did their thing on the sim deck.

Boston and the center of Warden operations was on a peninsula-like area of land. Much of it was bordered by the harbor, but it wasn't as isolated as Portland. Miles led his team through South End down Washington Street toward the city. Other teams moved in to secure the landlocked portion of the region in a pincer attack from two different directions. Per Dani's plan, CNA forces would move in for a seaside assault at the same time to encircle the Warden ops center.

The attack on Boston would likely last days, if not weeks. Subsequent waves of troops would flow into the area once the initial assault started in order to keep fresh troops coming and ultimately overwhelm the Warden forces. It was a good way to keep fierce, constant pressure on the city, choke it off from supplies, beat the shit out of it, and hope no Wardens from other cities came to help them defend it.

The idea that the CNA and Brigands would even go after Boston was ludicrous. Such doubt meant—Dani hoped—that no one would take the threat of an attack seriously. Well, no one but Rowan. He was always the one person she couldn't predict.

Miles held his lead position for a moment to make sure the way ahead was clear. He gestured, and they moved between a pair of buildings, pausing when one of the sim's random Warden patrols neared. His team took cover except for Dani. She stood in the middle of the street and turned in a full circle.

"Dani, take cover," Miles said into the comm. He feared she'd relapsed and was headed into panic mode. "Dani!"

"This is wrong," she said.

"Anton, freeze the sim," Miles said. The approaching Wardens froze, and Miles and his team left their cover. He joined her where she continued to turn in a circle.

"Captain, what's wrong?" Javi asked through the comm.

"Checking something out. One sec," Miles said. Dani continued to examine the surroundings. Dresden arrived and started to speak, but Miles raised his hand and gestured for the team to remain silent.

Dani stopped and removed her helmet. She frowned, but he didn't think she would be destroying another helmet this time.

Miles touched her arm. "What is it?"

"Landscape is wrong. We should be between two overgrown parks right now, and instead we're on a hill and between destroyed buildings. The sim is wrong. If we stroll through this area thinking we have cover and we're out in the open, we'll be slaughtered. Anton, load the most recent topos for this area."

"They *are* loaded," Anton said.

"No, they're not."

"Dani, they are. I don't have anything more recent."

"This isn't right. I'm telling you it's not right!" She winced at the sound of her own shouting and rubbed the side of her head. "Miles, the topography is wrong."

"We don't want to be slaughtered, so what do we do?"

"I need to look at the maps back in the planning room."

"Javi, we need to take a break to revisit the maps."

"All right," Javi growled into the comm. "Get your asses back here as soon as you're done."

"Will do."

"Anton, get this thing going again as soon as they're off the sim floor," Javi said.

Miles and Dani changed out of the suits and left the warehouse. As soon as Dani arrived in the planning room, she began sorting through the stacks of paper maps. She unrolled a long one partway, glanced at it, then tossed it aside. She shuffled through several more.

"Can I help you look for something in particular?" Miles asked.

"I'll know it when I see it. Sit tight. I need you to be my extra pair of eyes."

Miles nodded while Dani focused on the maps.

"There's a problem with the sim layout. I'm not crazy."

"I know you're not crazy."

She paused and looked up at him. "Thanks." Her head was back down as she pored over the maps. "I don't know why you put up with me."

Miles remained silent. He'd already given her that answer and didn't think she needed to hear it again.

CHAPTER
27

Miles held the paper version of the map in his hands and compared it with the digitized one on a large wall panel. "This area of South End where we were is flipped. How did you see that within the sim?"

"I don't know. Just something in my head knew it was wrong." She shrugged. "Something I remembered as a kid when I lived there, maybe?"

Miles pulled up a more general map of the state on the panel. His fingers flew over the keys as he entered commands.

Dani shifted to look over his shoulder. "What are you doing?"

"Need to see if anything is off at a larger scale. At a higher-level review, the general topo is good for most of the state except here." Miles pointed at the map. "Here, only in Maynard, is the other place where I see the topography is off 180 degrees."

Dani groaned. "We'll need to pick apart the rest of the city's maps to make sure everything is accurate before we go in."

"That'll take forever. Maybe Anton can write a program to speed up the analysis."

As Miles looked over the maps on the table, Dani watched him. The scenario felt familiar somehow—like she'd watched him work before—but she had no memory of doing that. From what she could remember of her prior Echo with him, she enjoyed having him as a friend and lover. His was the name that had never been far from her lips when she had been with Gavin. Maybe Mary was right and she just hadn't gotten her mind and heart into alignment yet. When Dani blinked to clear the wandering thoughts, she realized Miles was watching her.

"You okay?" he asked.

"Uh, yeah. Yeah." She nodded, but then winced when a wave of memories of their life together before her last regen arrived unexpectedly, accompanied by dizziness. He had been organizing his MPs to fight the Wardens when she warned him of an incoming ambush.

She remembered a few other pieces from that day—mostly of wanting to run and hide when the Wardens showed up, but seeking Miles instead. She'd risked capture to warn him. Dani figured she must have loved him to do something that defied everything she'd been taught as a Brigand.

Her balance was off, but she didn't fall when she stumbled from the continued dizziness. She realized that if he was in danger today, she'd risk everything to warn him. Mary *was* right. Dani had feelings for Miles that she'd lost with her regen. The dizziness passed, and when she opened her eyes, he was holding her in his arms. He was the reason she hadn't fallen.

"What's wrong?" he asked.

She was already in motion to kiss him. "Nothing." His arms wrapped tighter around her, pulling her so close she couldn't take a deep breath. Dani wanted him in a way she'd never wanted anyone else. His hands and mouth made her entire body flush with an impossibly warm sensation. A tingle coursed through her core when his hands moved beneath her shirt. His mouth left hers and found the side of her neck near her ear. She shivered with pleasure and moaned as she passed her fingers through his hair while his lips wandered.

She backed up until she bumped the table, then released him to scoot her rump onto it. Her knees parted as he approached, and Miles pulled her hips toward him as he pressed his body against hers. They kissed again, and Dani moved her hands to his belt to unfasten it.

Excruciating pain struck her in the side. She cried out, but the blast obscured all other sounds. She and Miles were thrown aside by the force of the explosion. Debris sailed past them, striking them after they crashed to the floor.

She wasn't sure how long she'd been unconscious, but as her mind began to function again despite the throbbing in her head, she knew she was in danger. Sleep beckoned her, but she forced her eyes open and winced. A bright orange light surrounded her, and it took her a moment to realize that the glow was fire. Flames seared her forearm. She groaned with a new and somehow more violent pain in her head. Miles was on top of her, not moving. Blood flowed down his face and neck.

Dani swatted the piece of burning wood aside and didn't bother checking the burn on her arm. Her hands traveled to Miles's head. His pulse was strong but beating too quickly. Her fingers found a gash on the back of his scalp, and his warm blood covered her hand. "Miles, wake up. Miles!"

She reached around him and flung pieces of the table off them. Dani squirmed until she slithered out from under him. She cleared more wood and broken pieces of concrete, then wrapped her arms around him. She dragged him a few feet away from the growing flames and rolled him to his back. A puddle of blood began forming behind his head. She pulled her shirt off, rolled it, and placed it between his wound and the floor. She put her hands on the sides of his face. "Please don't die. I need you."

Her mind raced as she tried to figure out what to do next.

Shouts from outside grabbed her attention as people fought to open the door. Dani didn't want to leave him, but she needed help to get Miles to the infirmary. She scrambled around large chunks of concrete to the door and shoved aside anything blocking her way. The door opened a couple of inches.

"Dani?" Mary said.

Her reply was choked with a sob, so it took her another attempt before she could speak. "Mary!" Dani shoved her hand through the opening, and Mary's fingers closed around her hand. "Miles is hurt."

"You?"

"No." *Am I?* She hadn't had time to check. "The door is blocked. I'll try to move more stuff out of the way, but keep shoving from your side." Dani released Mary's hand and went to work.

Having the planning room in a lower level of one of the buildings had seemed like a good security tactic until now. With no windows present, she didn't have any other way out except through the blocked door or the hole she couldn't reach in the top part of the wall. Smoke continued to fill the room while smaller fires grew. She wrestled a heavier piece of metal aside while Mary left to find more help. Once the door was open a few more inches, Mary squeezed through.

Dani wanted to hug her, but they were running out of time. They fought to open the door more, and Cameron and two other men were able to enter. She wasn't sure how much time had passed, and she had lost track of a few events between helping carry Miles out of the room to his receiving care in the infirmary with several other wounded people. Cameron and the other two men were off again as soon as they deposited Miles on a stretcher. Dani pressed her back up against a wall to stay out of the way and was grateful to have Mary next to her.

She kept her eyes on Miles while the staff worked around him. "What the hell happened?"

Mary turned to Dani. "Rogue Wardens. There were five blasts across the base. The one that hit you was a secondary explosion when the primary one took out a munitions truck. It flipped, and everything inside it ignited when it landed next to the building you were in."

"Have they been caught?"

"No. Reports of how many there were—like the reports of the numbers of dead or wounded—have been unreliable. It's too early."

"What can I do?"

"Stay here. You *are* injured."

Dani didn't question her friend. She ached everywhere, with sharper pains in spots when she moved. She slid into a chair and sighed. As she leaned forward, elbows on her knees, her side screamed at her, so she adjusted her position. She wasn't going anywhere, and her throbbing head curbed her desire to go Warden hunting. She intended to stay with Miles, but then she saw a crying girl with a blood-covered left arm. An unconscious boy was carried through by a woman Dani recognized as one of the teachers on the base.

Mary and Dani shared a glance. Miles was receiving the medical attention he needed, and Dani was desperate to know Oliver was safe. She stood, and a rush of pain in her head arrived. When she opened her eyes, she was seated on the floor with her back against the wall.

Mary smiled and passed her palm over Dani's cheek. "You just scared the shit out of me."

"Sorry."

"How is she?" one of the medics tending to Miles asked.

Mary glanced up at the medic. "Okay for now, but she needs to be checked." She returned her attention to Dani. "You're not allowed to die."

Dani resisted the urge to nod with her throbbing head. "If I promise not to move from this spot, will you find Oliver and bring him back?"

Mary nodded and kissed her on the forehead before leaving.

The staff continued buzzing around Miles, and Dani eyed the chair nearby. She considered going to it, but exhaustion had taken hold of her. She was safer sitting on the floor. She couldn't ignore the protests from stiff joints and a reaggravated ankle injury when she moved, but she managed to shift her position to watch the doorway for Mary's return with Oliver.

CHAPTER
28

Someone kicked Oliver in the side, and he uncoiled enough to poke his head up. One of the older teenage girls lay sprawled next to him on the floor. She'd tripped over him. She scrambled back to her feet and bolted for the door. More students came his way, where he lay between them and the exit. He crawled to the side of the smoke-filled room until he reached a wall. Oliver pressed his back against it and sat there, unmoving.

His thoughts were jumbled, and something wet dripped from his cheek and chin. Two other blasts erupted from somewhere on the base. He trembled uncontrollably as he realized what had happened. The base was under attack, and his school had been hit.

The cries and screams faded once the students able to walk or run scrambled for the door or crawled out windows. One disoriented boy stood in the center of the room, unblinking, his face was covered in blood. Oliver's eyes left the boy to scan the rest of the room.

"Brody!"

His voice was weak, so he called again. He didn't see Brody anywhere in the room. One of the girls who had been playing with him lay on the floor, unmoving. Oliver pushed himself to his feet and continued calling for his dog.

"You have to leave," Oliver told the boy standing in the middle of the room, but the boy didn't move. Oliver never stopped looking for Brody when he took the boy's hand to guide him toward the door. People began arriving to help get children out of the damaged school building. He let one of the teachers take the boy, and Oliver turned to go back for Brody. A man's hand landed on his shoulder.

"Stay here. We'll get the rest of your friends out," the man said.

"I can't find Brody," Oliver said.

"We'll find him for you."

"But—"

The man pushed him aside.

Oliver leaned in to look back into the room, but people were coming and going. They went in with empty arms and came out carrying his classmates. He watched the flow of people for a second, then stepped into the stream to reenter the room. He headed for the area of the classroom where he'd last seen Brody. Arms suddenly wrapped around Oliver's upper body and picked him up.

A man, different from the one who had shoved him, held him. "It's okay, son, I've got you."

"No, I'm not hurt. I need to find Brody."

Oliver squirmed, but he couldn't free himself from the man's grip. The man carried him toward the door, and Oliver's struggle became more desperate. "Let me go!"

The man held him tighter. Oliver freed one arm and pushed against the man. He was carried out of the class, and the man turned down a hall away from where the other injured children were being taken.

"Brody! *Brody! Dad!*"

Oliver's panicked screams earned him a fist to the side of his head. He was both dazed and angered. When his vision cleared enough, he swung back at his captor. His fist landed against the man's jaw, but the man was unaffected. Oliver's hand, however, throbbed. The man threw Oliver to the floor and pinned him, pressing one hand on his head to hold him down. Something sharp pricked the side of his neck. His thrashing against the man's grip slowed as his limbs grew heavy and refused to do what he wanted. He relaxed against his will, and Oliver feared he was dying.

"Dad," he said, and then his eyes closed.

CHAPTER
29

lex paced in the woods near the coast. She watched the lobster boat stacked with traps waiting for her in the bay and the dinghy waiting on the beach, but she was missing her partner and the boy. She heard the sound of approaching footsteps and raised her pistol. Kane arrived, carrying Oliver over his shoulder. She lowered her weapon and scowled.

"You're late." She holstered her weapon.

He dropped the boy at her feet, and his unconscious form rolled to his back. Oliver's cheek was bruised, and he had cuts to his face and chin, with smudges of soot from head to toe.

"Is he even alive?" Alex asked.

"Yeah. The little fucker wouldn't come quietly, so I tranqed him."

She dug through her pack for a moment, then tossed a black sack to Kane. "Put that over his head in case he wakes up."

"He's already seen me, Alex."

"He hasn't seen my face yet. Put it on him and stop arguing. The boat is waiting."

Kane manipulated the hood to open it up more. "You're in a mood."

"You fucked up the sedative in Dani's drink and gave her too much."

"I gave her the right amount."

"It was too much. I told you that others talked about how much of a lightweight she was with alcohol, and you blew it. That was the *one* shot we had at capturing her instead of this little shit," Alex said, waving her hand in Oliver's direction. "Rowan wants Dani, not him."

Kane pulled the boy up and slipped the hood over his head. Oliver groaned and recoiled from the hood.

"Brody!"

The man punched him through the hood. Oliver crumpled with the blow and began crying.

"Shut him up. Tranq him again," Alex said.

Kane stood to pull his tranq pistol. He turned at the sound of a snarl that erupted behind him. The attacking dog sank his teeth into the man's thigh. He howled with pain and fell. The dog tore at his leg, then lunged at his face. Kane put his arm up to protect himself, and the dog's teeth disappeared into his forearm.

Alex scrambled away from Brody. He'd always seemed like such a goofy, harmless dog, but his vicious attack on Kane had startled her. She drew her pistol. Kane kept screaming, and Oliver tried to remove his hood and escape. Alex stomped her foot on the boy's back and pinned him. She had her weapon up and fired at the dog. Her first shot missed, but the second one clipped him. The dog yelped and abandoned his attack on Kane. Brody limped a few feet away and growled at her. Alex aimed at the dog to kill him, but Kane's motion to get away from Brody had blocked her shot.

Alex couldn't shift her position to fire on the dog with her boot still on Oliver's back. "Move!" By the time Kane was out of the way, the dog had disappeared into the brush. She kept her weapon out in case he returned. "Kane, stop whimpering and tranq the kid."

Alex kept Oliver pinned until Kane had medicated him again. When the boy stopped struggling, she removed her foot. She put an I-cuff on him so he couldn't move anything if he woke again, and she secured the hood over his head so it wouldn't come off. Alex turned to her partner. Blood poured from the wounds to his thigh and arm.

"Keep your pistol out in case the dog comes back," she said.

"What? I can make the trip with you."

"Stay here. I'll take the kid, deliver him to Rowan, and return in a few hours."

"I can't stay here. What if they find me?"

"Start thinking up a story to explain your injuries. I'll come back."

She ignored Kane's pleading. He tried to stand, but fell with each try. Alex holstered her pistol and hoisted the boy over her shoulder. He was heavier than he looked. After a few yards of carrying him, her breathing became ragged. She moved out of the tree cover and down toward the beach. The man at the dinghy left the small boat and helped her transfer the boy into the craft. She dropped into the dinghy and fought to catch her breath. He rowed them out to the lobster boat, where the boat's captain waited. He and the other man pulled Oliver on board and then helped Alex on.

"Where's the other one?" the boat captain asked while the crewman anchored the dinghy to leave it behind.

"Not coming. Go," Alex said.

The boat wasn't fast enough for her liking, but they only needed to get into New Hampshire waters to meet the helo. She recovered from carrying Oliver and was back on her feet. They met the helo at the designated coordinates, and the boat crew loaded Oliver into a basket lowered from the helicopter. Alex climbed into the basket with him.

"Stay here and wait for me," Alex said. "I need to be back in Maine tonight."

The captain shook his head. "We can't stay out in the open like this."

"You're on a lobster boat. Put those traps in the water and look like you're doing something productive until I return."

The men shared a glance, and Alex realized that neither of them knew how to fish. She rolled her eyes and gestured for the helo to pull the basket up. She didn't start to relax until the helicopter turned to head for Boston.

"Radio ahead to have Rowan meet us at the helipad. I need to drop the kid and head right back."

"Yes, ma'am," the pilot said.

She leaned her head back and sighed. She touched her fingertips to the aching bruise on her cheek where Mary had punched her the night before. *Fuck, that woman has a mean jab.* She closed her eyes. She didn't intend to sleep; she needed to think of a plan for Kane. Explaining their absence during the attack was easy. Explaining the animal bites to Kane's body was a problem.

She opened her eyes as the helo began its descent, and cursed herself for dozing. Once they landed, the helicopter door slid open, and she recognized both Gavin and Rowan. Gavin reached in and grabbed Oliver, effortlessly hauling the sedated boy out of the helo. Rowan extended his hand to her, and she took it. Alex didn't need any help exiting the helo, but she was too starstruck to decline his offer.

He led her several paces away from the noise of the helo and lowered his head to talk into her ear. Her heart definitely skipped a beat or two from being in the presence of a Warden officer she admired.

"Alexandra Bishop. Curtis's aide. I remember you," Rowan said.

Alex swallowed hard.

"You're Crow?"

She nodded.

"I underestimated your abilities when you were Curtis's aide. You have my apologies. It'll never happen again."

"Thank you, sir."

"You've earned the right to call me by my name, Alex."

She suddenly couldn't speak.

He touched the bruise on her cheek. "Ran into some problems taking the boy?"

"A few," she said, finding her voice again. "I need to return to tie up some loose ends and make sure Dani comes for Oliver."

"I look forward to your return, Alex."

"Thank you, sir."

"Rowan."

"Yes, sir."

He chuckled. "You'll get used to it. A vice regent needs people he can trust at his side, which is where you will be."

"I'm honored, sir—Rowan."

He was one of the most decorated Wardens in the region, and she'd idolized him for years. She felt silly for mooning over him, so she headed back to the helo. She turned and trotted back to hand him her comm. "Portland's security will lock the place down. I can't be caught with this, so I won't be able to transmit any updates."

"Understood," he said.

The boat was in the bay with fewer lobster traps on board. She laughed to think of how many fingers the nonfishermen on the boat had lost trying to figure out how to throw traps and use the pot hauler while pretending to be lobstermen. Alex climbed into the basket, and the helo crew lowered her to the boat. She ordered the captain to leave for Maine as soon as the basket cleared the deck.

When they arrived, she hopped into the dinghy, and the man rowed her ashore and dropped her off. Kane was right where she'd left him.

"Did the dog come back?" she asked.

"No."

"Good. Hopefully it's dead somewhere. You have your story?"

He shook his head.

"You're about fucking useless. Get up." Alex helped him stand. "We're going back with a story that we caught up to the Wardens and fought them, but they got away. We need to beat the shit out of each other so the wounds back up the story of the fight. Got it?"

"Yeah, that's good."

"We'll tell them the Wardens had a dog that attacked you."

"Yeah."

"Hit me."

Her head snapped back with the first blow, and she stumbled. She leaned forward with a groan, and blood poured from her nose.

Kane winced. "Too hard?"

Alex straightened and stalked toward him. "Nope."

They exchanged several blows, and when both were battered and bleeding, Alex deemed it enough evidence of an altercation. She drew her plasma pistol, fired one shot, and relieved Kane of his head. His corpse fell, and Alex wiped at the blood dripping from her nose. She started the walk back toward the base alone.

Several yards into the hike, she spotted Brody lying under

some brush. He growled when she approached, but was unable to get up or attack. He had a hole in his left shoulder, and blood soaked his fur around the wound. He also had burns on his rear legs, which explained why it had taken him a while to catch up to Kane after he took Oliver. She pulled her pistol and pointed it at the dog's head. He continued to growl as she began to squeeze the trigger.

Another thought struck her, and Alex released the trigger. She walked back to Kane's body and took his tranq pistol. She returned to Brody and removed her jacket.

"You're my ticket into Dani's inner circle," Alex said to the dog.

She fired the tranq pistol into his side, and he yelped. Alex dropped the pistol and spread her jacket on the ground. Once the dog was asleep, she moved him to her jacket and removed the tranq dart. He was too heavy for her to carry, so she planned to drag him back to the base. She tossed her plasma pistol near some brush, grabbed the sleeves of her jacket, and started pulling. Her ribs and shoulders ached from her brawl with Kane, but even if the dog died on the trip back, she'd be returning Dani's beloved pet to her and telling a marvelous story of how she and Brody had tracked two Wardens who had kidnapped Oliver but one had gotten away with the boy.

Despite the pain from trading blows with Kane and the strain of dragging the big dog, Alex grinned. *Goddamn, I'm good.*

CHAPTER

30

Dani sat in a chair near Miles's healing pod—one in a row of several pods in the medical bay. The doctor had said his condition was stable but guarded—whatever that meant—and they had moved him from the trauma room to the bay full of pods for accelerated healing therapy. She'd been treated for lacerations, a concussion, dehydration from her prior evening's puking marathon, and blah-blah-whatever the other things he'd said were wrong with her. She had the infusion patch on the back of her hand where one of the medics had attached a series of vials to rehydrate her. Dani refused anything for her headache. She wanted a clear mind, and the pain in her head had lessened some anyway as her hydration improved.

A medic had repaired the deep lacerations to her side where she'd been cut by debris during the explosion. He also started treating the burn to her arm with something wider than a regular healing pen. While he worked, he blabbed on about how burns needed different, slower healing treatments than a standard laceration. She didn't care about any of it. He probably figured the mindless chatter would help keep her calm, but Dani wasn't panicked. She was furious. Mary hadn't returned yet, and she had no information other than the drivel that came out of the medic's mouth. She wanted details on the attack and was glad when he finished and left. That's when she got up to pace.

The flow of wounded coming in to the infirmary had slowed, but Dani couldn't get anyone to give her any information. She'd spotted Houston at one point, but she wasn't able to catch her attention. She couldn't leave Miles. The first time Dani had awakened in a pod, she had thought it was a coffin and panicked. She didn't want him to wake and be alone.

Dani spun when she heard a familiar voice, and gasped upon spotting Hattie. Dani called to her, and the older woman used the towel in her hands to wipe blood from them as she approached.

"You look like shit as usual, but I'm glad you're alive," Hattie said.

"You're bleeding."

"I'm fine. I helped a couple of folks to the infirmary." She glanced at Miles. "He gonna make it?"

"Yeah, but he's not awake yet."

"Stay with him, Dani."

"I will."

"No. I mean *stay* with him."

Confused, she shook her head. "I said I would."

"We have four dead, twenty-eight wounded, and six missing. Oliver is among the missing."

Dani shook her head; he couldn't be missing or …

"Mary, Cam, and others are looking for him. He wasn't in the school—"

"Not in school? Where the hell was he?"

"He was in his class when the blasts hit. His classmates confirm seeing him—"

"Brody will be with him. Did you find Brody?"

"Stop interrupting. We haven't found the mutt. One of the

kids said they saw a man take Oliver. Mary and the others are chasing down leads to figure out where he might have been taken."

"Kidnapped? Wardens attacked the base and took Oliver? Why?"

"Looks like there were two, maybe three Wardens involved. Catherine thinks the attack was a probe. It if had been a full assault from Boston, we wouldn't be standing here talking. We'd be ash."

Dani's pacing resumed. "Houston's an idiot. This wasn't a probe. Poking around and blowing shit up is one thing. Taking a kid is a different thing altogether."

"No buildings or tech were destroyed—well, not the important tech and buildings."

"This attack was a decoy. Remember Rowan's taunt about Gavin?"

"Yeah."

She stopped pacing and fell silent. When the realization of what had really happened registered, she walked to the side of Miles's pod and slipped her hand inside his.

"Rowan wasn't taunting Houston. He was directing it at me. I didn't go to Boston for Gavin, but somehow Rowan knows we'll go for Oliver."

"No, Dani. He's a kid—a *human* kid. He is of no use to the Wardens. Catherine didn't try to retrieve her captured CNA soldiers; she won't rescue Oliver."

"I wasn't including Houston when I said 'we.' The attack is a few hours old now. With the right arrangements, Oliver could already be in Rowan's hands. If that psychotic son of a bitch—"

"Focus, honey."

"Right. Yes. Oliver has been taken."

"I'll start putting some gear together for you and Mary. If you're well enough, you can leave tonight."

"Prep gear for Miles too. As soon as he is able to travel, we leave. He has to go too."

"What about Catherine? She won't allow any of you to leave."

"Fuck her."

Hattie's cackling laughter echoed in the bay. "That's my girl," she said, and left.

Dani lost track of time while she remained with Miles. When she heard Mary's voice, she turned. Brody was covered in blood and not moving in Cameron's arms. Alex looked like she'd been run over by a truck, and Mary helped her to a stretcher in the trauma area while Cameron placed Brody on another one. Medical teams rushed to their newest arrivals, and Dani stepped away from Miles's side to meet Mary. She stayed close enough to see his pod.

"What happened?" Dani asked.

"Cam, Javi, and I found Alex in the woods. She said she found Brody trapped in some debris at the school and got him out. Oliver was gone, but she followed Brody to track him down. They found the two Wardens who had him and killed one, but Brody was shot. Alex went after the one who had Oliver and took a beating. The man who took Oliver got away by boat. Alex was dragging Brody on her jacket to return to the base when we found her."

"Christ."

"Javi checked out the area where Alex said this all went down. Her story matches his findings. There's a man without a head out by one of the coves south of the city."

"Was Oliver hurt?"

"Not badly, according to Alex. The Wardens had sedated him."

She growled with frustration and moved closer to Brody. "How is he?" she asked one of the medics working on him.

"The vet is on the way, and we're prepping him for surgery. He's lost a lot of blood and will likely lose the leg. He's survived this long, so he's tough. If he makes it through surgery, we can grow him a new leg."

Dani nodded and stepped back to allow the staff to care for Brody. She was helpless to do anything for him. She went to Alex's stretcher when the medical crew around her thinned, and Mary joined her.

Alex struggled to sit up and held one hand against her side. "I couldn't stop them from taking Oliver, and I don't know if Brody will survive. He was in a lot of pain, so I tranqed him. I didn't want him to suffer."

"Thank you for going after Oliver and helping Brody," Dani said.

"The other Warden was too strong." Tears formed in Alex's eyes. "I tried, Dani, I swear. I almost had him, but he disarmed me. I'm sorry."

Alex's face was smeared with blood from cuts and bruises from fighting a Warden, and she had a dark bruise on her cheek from Mary's strikes the previous night. Dani felt a pang of guilt in her middle that Mary had pummeled Alex on her behalf. She wasn't sure what to say and started to leave. Alex caught her arm but released it when Mary glared and inched closer.

"I'm not ready to give up, Dani," Alex said. "Oliver is a good kid. Colonel Houston won't try to rescue him, but you will. I want to go."

Dani glanced at Mary. She returned her gaze to Alex and shook her head. "No."

"You're not the only one with a score to settle," Alex said. "I am so sorry about last night. I didn't know you'd already been drinking ale, or I never would have offered you more. I know how sensitive you are to alcohol."

Mary snorted, and Dani ignored her. She considered her

options. Mary had threatened to kill Alex less than twenty-four hours ago. Now Alex had risked her life to save Oliver and help Brody. Fire and gasoline were a less volatile mix than these two women.

"When do we leave?" Alex asked.

"Soon," Dani said, and she left to return to Miles.

As soon as Dani stopped at Miles's pod, Mary was next to her and in her ear.

"Are you sure it's a good idea to have her along?"

"You don't like her, Mary. I know."

"We don't know how much of her story is true. She missed training today. Where was she during that time? She has yet to answer for that."

"You beat the shit out of her last night, Mary. I'd miss training too."

"She can't go with you."

"She went after two Wardens and took one out. She knows how to fight," Dani said.

"Not well enough, or Oliver wouldn't be gone."

Dani turned on Mary. She struggled to keep her voice low. "For fuck's sake, Mary. Can we *not* discuss this until later? When Miles wakes, I have to tell him what happened. I don't give a shit about your personal feelings about Alex. I have to figure out how to tell him that his son is in Boston." *And it's my fault.*

Mary left without speaking.

Dani was tempted to sit in the chair and try to sleep, but she couldn't. She borrowed a comm off one of the medical staff and sent a message to Anton regarding the maps and the problem she and Miles had discovered with them. She wasn't sticking around on the base to finish planning the attack on Boston with the CNA, but she didn't want them walking into a slaughter either. Anton could research and fix the maps without her. She had a different invasion to plan.

CHAPTER 31

Miles woke early the next morning. Dani was glad she was there with him but had dreaded the moment. Now that he was awake, the medical staff moved him and his pod to a room. Once he was settled in his new, more private location, Dani talked to him. He took the news as she expected.

He was both worried and furious, tried to leave the infirmary, and fought Dani and her efforts to keep him in the pod. The lights and alarms he set off inside the pod had medical staff running into the room.

"I've got this," she said, and nodded for them to leave.

He was too weak, so she pressed her hands into his upper arms until he stopped struggling.

"We will get him back, Miles. I won't leave without you, okay? Let them treat you today. I need time to finish putting things together anyway."

"Don't expect me to lie here for days."

"Never. Give me one day. Please. We can leave tomorrow, maybe tonight. I can't stay with you and prep to leave at the same time. Can I trust you to stay here until I'm back?"

"Yeah, but make it quick."

"As soon as we're ready, we're gone."

He took a deep breath and nodded. He relaxed, and she released his arms. He wouldn't be fit to leave the infirmary in a day, maybe not for three or four days, but they couldn't wait that long to go after Oliver. She had to find a way to get Miles out of the infirmary and to Boston without killing him in the process.

She took his hand and laced her fingers through his. She leaned down and kissed him. "I love you. And I'm not saying that while shitfaced."

Miles gave her a tired smile.

"I can't live without both you and Oliver in my life. I'll tear Boston apart brick by fucking brick."

"So will I."

"The Wardens have no idea the hell we'll bring to them for this."

Miles nodded. He was weak, but the determined fire in his eyes hadn't dimmed.

"Rest for now, please. I'll put things in motion so we can leave."

He eventually went back to sleep, and Dani stared out the window of his room. She passed her hand over the back of her sore neck. She had volumes of work to do, and she was already exhausted.

"When was the last time you slept?" Cameron asked.

Dani turned and dropped her hand. He approached, holding a mug and a small sack. She shrugged as an answer.

"Can you leave?"

"Yeah," she said.

"Eat on the way." He reached into the bag, pulled out an oval-shaped object wrapped in a cloth, and gave it to her. "This is from Aunt Hattie."

Dani unwrapped the cloth to find two thick slices of bread

slathered with jam. She lifted one slice and bit into it. She savored the feel of the warm bread in her mouth for a moment, then started chewing as she followed him out.

He glanced back at her. "You kinda have a thing for bread, don't you?"

Dani nodded while she chewed. "It's a Brigand delicacy. I can't scavenge flour from the woods or make it myself. Hattie's my supplier. Where are we going?"

"Houston wants to see you."

"Why?" She took another large bite.

"She didn't say."

She devoured the first slice, and he passed her the mug. Dani took a drink of strong coffee to wash down her food. She took another long drink and handed him the mug before starting on the second slice.

"Brody is doing well this morning," Cameron said. "One of the med techs said they updated you last night after his surgery."

"Yeah."

"Once he's doing better, they can grow a new leg for him. Since he's done CNA ops, he gets CNA healthcare like their regular K-9 troops." He gave her the mug again when she finished eating.

Dani drank the rest of the coffee. "I know. I just don't like having to leave him."

"A couple of kids from the school were visiting him this morning," Cameron said. "He's not alone." He paused. "Oh, you mean *leave* him. How soon will you head out? What can I do to help?"

Dani stopped and looked up at him. "Are you sure you want in on this? You're Commonwealth. Houston could shoot you for treason, desertion, or whatever excuse she wanted. She can ship your ass back to England."

"Only if she catches me."

"I'm not joking, Cam."

"You're going to Boston, which means Miles and Mary will be with you. Miles looks like half a corpse right now. I'm rusty, but I have some medical background. I can help keep him alive and be your field medic when things get interesting."

She would definitely need help keeping Miles alive. "Okay." Dani resumed walking. "You can also help me keep Alex and Mary from killing each other."

"Shit! You're bringing Alex too? You don't like to do anything the easy way, do you?"

She had to laugh; he was right.

Houston dismissed Cameron when they arrived, so Dani was left in the office with the colonel.

"I know how you think, Dani. You're plotting to leave to go after Oliver."

"*You* should've left hours ago—as soon as we knew he was missing. Yet here you are in your comfy office. Did you even consider pursuing the Wardens?"

"I have bombs that went off on *my* base. I'm actively turning this place upside down for intel and leads. Besides, I can't use CNA resources for one civilian. This also means you can't use CNA resources."

Dani's frown deepened.

"Got a transmission from Rowan late last night, except it wasn't actually for me." Houston passed the palm-sized panel to Dani.

She took the panel and pressed the screen.

Rowan stood next to Oliver as he held him by the back of his shirt. Oliver's face was tear-streaked, bruised, and bloodied.

"Look what I found," Rowan said, grinning. "Come and get him, Catherine."

The transmission ended, followed by a set of coordinates. Dani gripped the small panel tighter.

"He has a real hard-on for you, Dani. He captured you once and is not letting it go."

Dani tossed the panel back to Houston's desk, where it landed with a clatter. "Are those coordinates accurate?"

"You know this is a trap."

"Are they accurate?"

Houston pulled up a map on another panel and turned it to face Dani. She pointed to one grid among many on the map. "This whole area is where the higher-ranked Wardens live. It's top-shelf security. You're not getting in there."

"I'll find a way. Transfer the map to the small panel for me."

"Dani, this is suicide."

Dani's patience evaporated. "*Transfer the fucking map!*"

Houston shook her head and started pressing things on the larger panel. The palm-sized one blinked a few times, and Houston talked while she worked. "We're attacking Boston in a month. The planes are almost ready, and we're building the new tech around the clock. Oliver is human, so Rowan can't recondition him. He'll be safe until we get there."

"Safe? Do you even listen to the bullshit coming out of your mouth?"

"I need you here."

"I'm not one of your soldiers, never have been."

"Miles is CNA. He is part of those resources you're not allowed to use."

Dani laughed. "Like you can stop him from going after his son."

"I can put you in the brig for everything you've stolen from the CNA in the past, and that's just for the shit I know about. I'll hold you here if I have to."

"Good luck with that."

Houston handed Dani the small panel. "Research what you

need, but you can't leave Portland. You can't take anything. I'll arrest you and anyone helping you."

Dani left with the device in her pocket and headed for Hattie's brothel. She went straight to the cellar and found Cameron, Mary, Alex, and Hattie there. Stacks of gear, body armor, explosives, and weapons were everywhere. Her eyes widened at the volume of the stash.

"Don't look so surprised," Hattie said. "You always think you're the only one who steals from the CNA." Hattie lifted an older version of a quake rifle from one of the tables containing multiple weapons. "This is all the newest tech plus some of the classics."

"We have five people going, not five hundred, Hattie."

The older woman shrugged and placed the rifle back on the table. "Think of it as a shopping spree. Take what you need and a few extras of what you want."

Mary began placing explosives into an extra pack. "Have a plan yet?"

"Working on it," Dani said.

Hattie took Dani's arm and led her back toward the stairs. "They have things under control down here. Alex and Mary haven't murdered each other yet, so that's a bonus. You're going upstairs to clean up and rest."

Dani was desperate for sleep and didn't protest. She went to her room and stripped out of the clothes she'd been in since the previous day. She bathed with the cold water in the basin, then crawled into bed.

When she woke, the sun had already set.

CHAPTER
32

D ani stood next to an overloaded pack sitting at her feet. She had two more duffel bags of gear next to her pack where she waited within the trees. She was on the base and had wanted to meet somewhere off base, but she figured Miles would have enough trouble making it to this spot, much less one outside the city. As soon as she spotted Miles's form approaching, she left her gear to help him with his. Even in the darkness of the wee hours, she could see his struggle. His breaths came in labored, raspy gasps. His shuffling gait and waning strength didn't give her much confidence he'd last long on this trip. She took his gear and carried it back to her spot. He caught up a minute later, and they waited.

"I know I look like shit," he said once he had enough air to speak. "I feel like it, too, but I'm going."

"I know."

Cameron and Mary arrived next, with Alex joining them within a few minutes. Alex and Mary shared a glare, and Dani sighed. This would be the trip from hell.

"Change of plans," Dani said. She took Mary's arm and led her out of the trees and pointed. "Load everything into that transport truck."

"We can't steal a ride. Everything's locked down. Codes have changed since the attack."

"I'll get the access for the truck while you load. Steal some additional medical gear—whatever Cam needs to keep Miles from keeling over on us. He'll never be able to make the trip on foot. We're taking the truck."

"This will be another rabbit-out-of-your-ass trick to get the codes, but okay."

"Load it with extra fuel too."

"On it," Mary said.

Dani left her and headed toward the officer's barracks. When she arrived outside Houston's door, she activated the chime—repeatedly. She didn't stop until the door opened and Houston's scowling face greeted her. The colonel's hair was barely mussed, and she stood at the door in her bare feet and wearing a set of silky red pajamas. It was like she slept standing up instead of in a bed. When Dani rolled out of bed after waking, she was a staggering mess with blurred vision. Houston's eyes were angry but alert.

"What the fuck do you want?" Houston asked.

"I need access codes for the transport truck I'm stealing."

"Confessing now so I can go ahead and arrest you?"

"Fuck off. I want the codes."

"No."

Houston started to seal the door, and Dani pushed her way through. She drew her pistol and pointed it at the colonel's head.

"Oh, please. Like you'd ever use that thing." Houston turned away from Dani. "I don't know why you even have a pistol. It's just added weight."

Dani growled and reholstered her pistol. She followed Houston into the kitchen. The colonel's quarters were much nicer than the ones Miles and Oliver lived in. Higher rank equaled better everything.

"Tea?" Houston asked as she opened one of the cabinets.

Dani closed the distance between them in two strides and slammed the cabinet door closed. "I'm taking the truck. Give me the access."

Houston folded her arms and leaned against the counter. "Your threats don't mean shit to me."

Dani's hands tightened into fists. "I also want a map of the CNA- and Brigand-controlled routes from Maine to Mass and Kelsey's last-known coordinates."

Houston's mocking laughter ended abruptly when Dani's fist collided with her mouth. She struck the colonel a second time while pinning her against the counter. Dani grabbed fistfuls of the front of Houston's fancy pajama shirt and threw her to the floor. She followed Houston down and immobilized her with a forearm across her throat.

"Give me what I want or I'll beat it out of you, you piece of shit."

Houston managed a small cough, and blood sputtered from her mouth and landed on Dani's hand and forearm. She couldn't speak because of the pressure across her neck, so she nodded.

Dani released the colonel and stepped back.

Houston rolled to her side and slowly stood. She picked up a small towel from the counter and wiped blood from her mouth. "Hell of a jab, Dani."

"Stop stalling."

"You hit me twice and bounced my head off the floor. Forgive me if it's taking more than a few seconds to gather my thoughts." Houston touched the cut on her lip with her tongue and winced. She held the towel to her mouth as she moved toward her office, and Dani followed. "I honestly didn't think you had that kind of physical violence in you. I'm impressed."

Houston set the towel aside to dig through her desk for a

moment. She reached for something inside a drawer, and Dani's hand went to her pistol. She had half expected the woman to pull out a gun and arrest her, but instead she pulled out a panel. Houston activated the device and began typing things into it.

"Multiple counts of treason if you take this and leave," Houston said. "Are you prepared to deal with those consequences?"

"If I wasn't, I wouldn't be here. You won't arrest me or you would've done it already. Your threats don't mean shit to me."

Houston nodded. "So we're done trying to bluff each other. Good. You know I won't arrest you, and I know you won't shoot me. You will, however, beat me to a pulp, so that's good to know going forward." The colonel offered Dani a small grin. "Having an understanding is important. I'm loading the coordinates of the last time Gavin and his team checked in, which was the same spot where you met Richter and Allyss. We didn't find out they were compromised until two days after it happened. There's no way to know exactly where they were when things went wrong."

"I can narrow it down from the coordinates if I know what they were doing. What was the mission?"

"Classified."

"Fuck you."

Houston didn't answer, and Dani stalked closer with her hands closing into fists again. "I thought we had an understanding."

Houston raised her hand, palm out. "I'm not inclined to take a beating if you want to get yourself killed. They were there to assassinate the VR and her advisers, Rowan included."

Dani's eyes widened. "The CNA authorized an assassination?"

"No. I did. Gavin wasn't CNA, remember? They were to take out Warden leadership ahead of our attack. At least that was the plan." Houston handed Dani the panel. She also passed her a device that was an electronic key. "Coordinates, map with travel routes, and the codes to the transport trucks. Dani, don't leave the base with these things. I'll be forced to declare you and anyone helping you criminals."

Dani laughed. "I'm a Brigand. I *am* a criminal." She turned and left the colonel's quarters. When she returned to the transport truck, Mary and Cameron met her.

"Everything ready?" Dani asked.

"Yeah," Mary said. "We're loaded with everything we could possibly need except a pod for Miles. Alex is in the back getting him settled. You got the access?"

Dani handed her the key.

Mary took it from her and caught Dani's hand. "You're bleeding."

"It's not mine."

"Whose?" Cameron asked.

"Catherine's. Cam, get in the truck and keep Miles in one piece."

He muttered a string of curses as he left, but Mary stayed.

Mary waved the key in front of Dani. "You beat this out of Catherine? Have you lost your goddamn mind?"

"Pretty much," Dani said, and shrugged. "Listen. I also got the coordinates of Kelsey's last-known location. They're old and not of much use, but I know roughly where they were headed when Gavin and the others were captured. We can narrow our search for him while we're looking for Oliver."

Mary shook her head and lowered her gaze. "I don't have much hope left that he is alive."

"I know." Dani squeezed Mary's shoulder. "It doesn't look good, but we'll search for him and bring him home either way."

Mary nodded.

"If we haven't found Kels by the time we pull Oliver out, you and I will stay until we do."

"Thank you."

"Thank me later if I don't get us all arrested or killed," Dani said, and she gave her a small smile. "Let's go. You're driving, and I'm navigating."

"Last time I drove, I put us over a ledge. You trust me?"

"With my life." Dani put her arm around Mary's shoulders. "C'mon. I have a map that will put us on CNA and Brigand routes all the way to Mass."

"A map? You got the transport key, coordinates, *and* a map from Catherine? Dani, is she alive?"

"Fucking livid, but alive."

"Oh, that's great," Mary said as they headed for the truck. "Leaving one hornet nest to stir up another one. I may ask you later to remind me why I have you as a friend."

"Can't promise I'll have a good answer for you." Dani climbed into the passenger side, and Mary started the engine.

She held her breath as they approached the outer gate. The guards opened it as they neared, and allowed them to pass without question. Houston was apparently giving Dani and her fellow criminals a head start before issuing statements for their arrest.

"Drive as fast as you can without rattling us to pieces or setting off the explosives in the back," Dani said.

Mary nodded, and the truck surged forward.

CHAPTER 33

Dani reviewed the plan in her mind. She needed sleep, but she needed to stay awake more. They had already completed almost half of the 250-mile trip from Portland to Boston by way of side roads and detours with an agonizing, bumpy, and slow pace. They had to stay well away from Warden-controlled Portsmouth, so they traveled west instead of due south out of Portland. They stopped several hours later in Peterborough, New Hampshire, to rest and check road conditions with local Brigands.

The second part of the trip had them leaving Peterborough for Leominster, Massachusetts, to continue through Maynard to Waltham, where they'd have to leave the truck at a covert CNA outpost. They would proceed on foot from there for the twelve-mile hike to Boston. The good news was Miles looked a bit less like shit than he had when they'd left Portland.

When they stopped, Dani and Cameron split Miles's watches so he could rest longer. Mary covered her own watches and remained awake for Alex's too. Mary would never trust Alex, and Dani didn't bother getting between them on the matter. Alex had stayed quiet most of the trip, and Dani was thankful.

Fatigue clouded her mind, and Dani leaned her head back against the seat's headrest and closed her eyes. A hand patting her arm woke her.

"There's movement in the trees," Mary said.

Dani reached for her pistol and glanced to the rear seat. Miles, Cameron, and Alex were armed.

"Where?" Dani asked.

Mary pointed.

Dani looked out her window and saw nothing at first but trees and brush. She spotted two people behind trees, then located more.

"Stop the truck," Dani said.

"No way."

"Mary, if they were Wardens, they would've already blown us off the road."

Mary slowed the truck to a stop but kept the engine on.

Dani holstered her weapon and reached to open her door. Mary caught her arm.

"Not all Brigands are nice."

"We're surrounded and not fighting our way out of this if they want our shit."

"Surrounded? We're not—" Mary's voice faltered when a dozen armed people stepped from the shadows and trees on both sides and entered the roadway to encircle the truck.

"Oh, fuck," Alex said from the back seat.

"We have quake rifles. We can take them," Cameron said.

Miles shook his head. "I saw only half of the explosives Dani packed, so I'm sure she has at least twice as much squirreled away in here. If we try to fight, one wrong shot turns us into a crater in the ground."

"You know me well," Dani said to him. "Everyone, stay calm." She eased the door open and slid out of her seat with her hands raised.

A man approached her and gestured with his gun for her to turn around. She complied, and he pulled her plasma pistol from her holster, then backed away.

"We're transporting supplies from Portland." Dani grunted when he shoved her against the side of the truck. He pressed the end of his pistol to the back of her head. She closed her eyes and tried to think of a way to not die by having her head blasted from her shoulders.

"No, you're not," the man said. He ordered everyone out of the truck, and his crew disarmed her friends as they exited the vehicle. They were pressed against the side of the truck while it was searched. The man kept his weapon against Dani's head.

The only person who knew their route through the state was Houston. Dani figured the colonel had followed through on her threat to arrest them after all and radioed ahead.

A Brigand woman climbed from the rear of the truck. "They have a shit ton of weapons, explosives, and medical gear."

The man lowered his weapon and grabbed the back of Dani's shirt. He pulled her away from the truck and pushed her aside. "Everyone will walk in front of the truck. Try anything and we'll gun the whole lot of you down."

Dani started down the road. She kept her pace slow until the others were with her. She and Mary flanked Miles while Cameron walked in front of them and Alex put herself between Dani and the armed men and women. The robbers climbed in and on the truck and followed. Dani didn't bother trying to explain their situation or talk her way out of the mess. The man in charge wouldn't care either way. She had no choice but to do whatever he said.

Miles's pace slowed the longer they walked. Dani decided it was time to ask the man to let Miles rest or at least ride in the truck, but the man ordered them off the road. Several people from his crew hopped off the truck and joined him in following their prisoners down a path into the woods while the truck continued on. If he was going to kill them, Dani didn't understand why he needed to take them into the forest to do it when he could've shot them in the road hours earlier.

They reached a camp and passed through guards. The man ordered them to an area in the center of the camp, and they sat on the ground. Dani was tired, thirsty, and hungry, but she didn't say anything. Miles's color improved the longer he rested, but he was exhausted.

A woman approached, and Dani sighed with relief upon recognizing her. "Allyss."

Allyss dismissively waved at Dani's captor. "Jesus, Borerro, they're *not* the enemy."

"Can't be too careful." Borerro kept his gun pointed at Dani.

Allyss stepped between them. "Lower your fucking gun and return their weapons to them. Bring them food and water." She turned and extended her hand to help Dani up. "Great to see you. Miles … oh. Damn, Miles, you look terrible."

"Hi, Allyss," Miles said. Cameron helped him stand.

"What the hell took you so long to get here?" Allyss asked Dani. "For a rescue party, you took your sweet time."

"We left as soon as Miles was well enough to travel. We were on our way to the city for Oliver when your crew stopped us."

"Who's Oliver? You're not here for Kelsey?"

Mary entered the conversation. "You have Kels? *Here?*"

"Yeah. He's sick as hell. We've done everything we can for him, but our medical supplies are depleted."

Dani shifted her attention. "You. Borerro, right?" she said to the man who had put his gun to her head. "Take Cam, Alex, and Mary to the truck. Grab *everything* we have for medical gear and take them to Kelsey."

Borerro looked to Allyss, who waved at him to go.

Someone arrived with a bowl of some kind of soup and

tin cups of water. Miles downed his water in a few gulps, and Dani gave him the rest of hers after she took a sip. The soup reminded her too much of the Brigand stew she'd puked up a few nights ago, so she gave him her bowl despite the gnawing hunger in her gut.

Others from the camp carried their bags of gear from the truck, and Dani spotted Mary hounding Borerro to move faster while they hauled the med kits with Cameron and Alex to another part of the camp.

"Allyss, Houston told you we were coming?" Dani asked.

"No. I just assumed you were here for Kelsey. I sent word days ago to Portland that we had him."

Dani wondered if Houston had gotten the message and kept it secret or if the message never arrived because of comm problems. "What happened to Kels and his team? I know about their mission." Dani dug through her pack to find a bottle of water and CNA-issue food wafers. She ate while Allyss spoke.

"Richter led them in. They made it to Back Bay, and a group of Wardens showed up for weapons testing. They didn't have time to hide and had to engage. They got their asses kicked. Jamie, Corey, and Gavin were captured. Richter and Kelsey managed to slip away, but they were shot up. Richter got a message out to us before destroying the comm so it couldn't be tracked. Then they hid. Richter was dead by the time we reached them."

"I'm sorry, Allyss. I really am."

"We carried him out to bury him. Kelsey is in bad shape, Dani. Is one of your people a surgeon?"

"Field medic," Dani said. She wasn't sure if that was the right title for Cameron. He was vague about his medical training, and she had never asked him about it.

"Hope he's a good one. Who's Oliver?"

"Miles's son. He's thirteen. Rowan reconditioned Gavin and

had him kill Jamie and Corey. The sick fuck sent us the feed
of the killings. He used Gavin to try to bait us to attack. When
we didn't show, he had someone on the inside at Portland do a
small-scale attack as a diversion and kidnap Oliver."

"Why the kid?"

"Rowan somehow knew we'd come for him."

"And you're going after the kid with a five-person army?"
Allyss shook her head. "You're going to need some help."

Dani and Miles discussed tactics with Allyss until fatigue
overtook them and they had to sleep. Dani gave Miles the only
cot inside the small shelter, and she slept on the ground next to
him.

The next morning, she was up early, crossed the camp, and
found Mary sitting next to Kelsey's cot. Cameron slept on the
ground a few feet away, and she didn't know where Alex was.
There was a scent inside the tent that Dani recognized as one of
death. It was the same smell from when she and Jace had found
the bodies of their father and Dani's mother after they were
slaughtered by the Wardens. The sickly odor of rotting flesh
turned her stomach.

Kelsey's face was gaunt and pale as he slept. He would have
passed for a corpse except he was still breathing. Mary stood
and stretched before stepping outside the tent with her.

"How is he?" Dani asked, though she already knew the
answer.

"Bad, but Cam knows his shit. He got the infection and
fever under control, but he needs to amputate Kelsey's arm.
The medic here didn't have enough experience to do it before
now without him bleeding out."

"Is he awake? Does he know you're here?"

Mary smiled. "Yeah."

"Good." Dani hugged her friend, then returned to the center of the camp where her gear waited. Her five-person army had just gone down to three. Cameron and Mary would stay with Kelsey. It made sense. Dani and Alex would have to take care of Miles while they looked for Oliver. Miles was asleep, and Dani changed out of her fatigues and into her layers of armor. She'd need Cameron to teach her and Alex how to work the MedPanel and instruct them on which meds to give Miles and when.

She adjusted her duty belt and slipped her pistol into the holster at her hip. Miles stirred, and Dani knelt next to him. She passed her fingers over his cheek. "How do you feel?"

"Like going to Boston. When do we leave?"

"As soon as you're ready, but don't rush."

Dani stood, and he kept her hand. She leaned down and kissed him before leaving the shelter with her pack in one hand and her jacket of exterior armor in the other. The camp began to wake as others moved about to cook food and prep gear. Dani and Allyss made a final review of the plans as they looked over the map.

Dani traced her finger over the map she'd marked with dots. "With the added explosives from our supplies, this is where your teams will move in and plant them. All along this perimeter and at Logan."

"Logan?"

"Uh, prewar name for the Boston airport. We attacked the airfield in Portland, so security in Boston will be tight as hell. Send only Brigands into that area. CNA sabs are too noisy and can't sneak around like we can. Alex, Miles, and I will set more devices as we move into the interior, and we'll control the detonations. Make sure your people are out of the city within forty-eight hours. I figure it will take us at least that long just to locate Oliver—if we're lucky. We'll have to sort out how to reach him inside, and these explosives will be our way to draw troops out. I don't want to set anything off with your people planting devices."

"I'll have them out. Sure you don't want any additional hands with you? I can go."

"No, but thanks for the offer."

Allyss nodded and left to organize her crews and distribute the explosives according to which teams would be in which areas of the city per Dani's plan. Dani took a deep breath and pulled her jacket on. Someone approached her from behind. She turned and spotted Mary in full gear with her rifle in hand.

"I don't understand," Dani said. "I assumed you'd be staying."

"You assumed wrong."

"But—"

"I talked to Kels. Cam is taking care of him and has the skill and the medicine to save him. There's no way in hell I'm letting you and Miles go into that city without me."

Dani smiled, thrilled to have her friend with her.

"Alex going too?" Mary asked.

"Yeah. Try not to kill her."

"No promises."

CHAPTER
34

The first night Oliver was in Boston, he woke inside a closet. He learned his captors' names by listening to the man and woman talking to a young boy and a gurgling baby. The woman's voice was tense the entire evening, and once the children were put to bed and the nanny was gone, the woman's voice turned into a shout.

"You bring that fucking *thing* into my home around my children. Are you insane?"

"I don't want him here either, but he's important to my investigation. Portland troops will come for him."

"So let the VR handle it. It's her job to blow the hell out of the CNA."

"I've told everyone he's my nephew."

Someone slammed something against something else. Oliver assumed it was Ana doing the slamming since her shriek followed. "*What?*"

"Keep your voice down before you wake the children. He has to stay here for now."

"No! Put it in a cell with the other captives. Get it away from me."

"I can't put a family member in a cell without people asking questions."

"*It* is *not* your family."

Footsteps stomped past the hall door, and Oliver shrank back. A pair of boots walked by seconds later.

"Ana, that's not what I meant. Just listen to me."

Their arguing continued in another room, but Oliver couldn't hear everything they said. He curled up into the back corner of the closet and tried to sleep. He wept instead.

The next day, the door opened only when the woman slid a small bowl of water on the floor through the opening before snapping the door closed again. Oliver wanted to gulp the water down, but he forced himself to sip it until it was gone.

Another argument between the man and woman erupted when the man returned in the middle of the day.

"You have to let him out to use the toilet, Ana."

"You let it out."

The closet door opened, and Rowan's frame loomed over Oliver as he sat huddled in the corner.

"Get up," Rowan said.

Oliver stood and exited the closet, blinking against the brighter light in the room. Rowan guided him down a hall to the toilet. Oliver relieved himself and stalled his imminent return to the closet. He could stand inside the closet but he couldn't do much more than turn in a circle. Stretching his legs felt nice. A sharp rap on the bathroom door startled him.

He washed his hands and opened the door. The man ushered him back toward the closet. Oliver spotted Gavin, and his brief moment of hope disappeared when Gavin looked at him, then turned away. Rowan sent Oliver back into the closet and closed the door behind him.

"Did you feed him?" Rowan asked.

"Feed it? Why?" Ana asked.

"I need him alive."

"It's a human, Rowan. We don't need any of them alive."

"Give him food and water. Take him outside once a day. If others are going to buy the nephew story, he needs to be seen with us."

Another argument ensued.

Once the man left, Oliver wasn't sure Ana would do anything Rowan had asked, but she did. Devon got yelled at each time he was caught near the closet door.

"What's behind the door, Mommy?"

"Nothing. Get away from there."

Oliver was let out every four hours to use the toilet and have a drink of water, but only when the children were out with the nanny or down for a nap. His stomach ached with hunger since Ana fed him very little. She didn't take him outside until the following day. She walked him to the stairs and up to a roof garden, and Oliver never spoke to her.

"We're up about ten stories," Ana said. "I'll happily throw you off the roof myself if you do anything I don't like."

He nodded and walked among the taller bushes. She kept her arms folded across her chest and glared at him the entire time. He stepped behind a tall shrub just to escape her hate-filled gaze. She rounded the opposite end to cut him off and ordered him back inside.

His routine remained unchanged, and he lost track of the days. On one evening, Rowan opened the door unexpectedly and Oliver tumbled out since he'd been leaning on the door. Rowan grabbed the back of his shirt and hauled him to his feet. He took him to his office in the home, and Oliver stood before Gavin and another man.

"*This* is your nephew?"

"No, Curtis. It's just the story to cover if anyone sees him when we let him out."

"Let him out? Where do you keep him?" Curtis asked.

"In the hall closet. You walked right by him when you came in earlier. I will say he's done a good job of staying quiet," Rowan said.

"You're sure Dani will come for him?"

Oliver gasped before he could contain his surprise.

"She'll come. Crow is certain she will and delivered him to me in person."

"You know Crow's identity then."

Rowan nodded.

"You created a side mission without telling me. That was a dangerous thing to do. I can't protect you if the VR or any chancellors find out."

"It'll be fine. You worry too much. Back to your hole, boy," Rowan said to Oliver.

Oliver left the office and returned to the closet. He didn't bother to look back to see if he was being watched; he knew he was. He pulled the door closed and sank to the floor. Dani *would* come for him and Rowan would be waiting for her. He needed a way to warn her.

The next day the routine changed a little. Devon, the nanny, and the infant were with him and Ana when she took him to the roof. Ana had given him strict instructions to not speak to or touch Devon. Oliver wandered away from the taller shrubs to a more open area. He enjoyed the sun on his face, and he looked out over the city. He peered down and saw there was another level to the roof below. He could climb down the rails then drop and run away. He didn't know where to go next, but he'd figure something out for how to get away from this place and the awful woman who hated the very sight of him.

He shuffled his feet closer to the edge. He couldn't escape.

He wasn't a Brigand like Dani. She could survive anything and take care of herself. Oliver knew how to draw pictures. Pencil sketches wouldn't help him here. If he ran away, he wouldn't know where to go. The best he could do was follow the coastline north to Portsmouth—another Warden-controlled city. He was screwed.

Devon's ball bounced across the grassy area and rolled to Oliver's feet. He picked up the ball and handed it to the boy. Ana spotted him and ordered Ella to take Katy and Devon inside. The boy waved at Oliver and smiled; Oliver waved back. As soon as they were gone. Ana's angry strides closed the distance to him. The first blow stunned him, and after the third, he put his hands up to protect himself. He tried to fight back and was hit again, much harder.

Ana pushed him against the railings and growled at him. "You filthy, fucking vermin. I feel like I need a shower after touching you. Never interact with my son again or you die."

Oliver's cheek throbbed as it swelled, and he nodded.

She dragged him back inside the home and threw him into the closet. He got no food or water for the rest of the day. The only reason he got to pee was that Rowan came home. Ana lashed out at Rowan again and told him what had happened on the roof.

"Goddammit, Ana, I'm using the story that he's our nephew. You can't beat him." Rowan pulled Oliver from the closet and took him to the bathroom. Oliver didn't want to pee in front of the man, but he might not get another chance to go until tomorrow. He emptied his bladder while Rowan removed various pieces of equipment from the drawers near the sink. Oliver washed his hands and wiped some water over his face.

"Stand here," Rowan said, pointing at the floor in front of him.

Oliver did, and Rowan used his equipment to heal the bruises on Oliver's face and arms.

"Thank you," Oliver whispered. He rocked back when Rowan's hand grabbed his throat.

"You do not speak. *Ever*," Rowan said into his ear.

Tears spilled from Oliver's eyes when he nodded.

He once again returned to his closet, sank to the floor, and wept.

CHAPTER

35

Dani and her team parted with Allyss's troops in Waltham, and they had spent the last two days moving ever closer to the center of Boston and avoiding Warden cameras. Their packs became lighter as they deployed their explosives on the way. They found the building Houston had told Dani was the high-ranking Warden living quarters. Rowan wasn't a vice regent or chancellor, so Dani split her team in half to try to figure out where the man lived so they could track him to where he kept Oliver. They'd spotted Rowan a few times, but never with the teen.

She and Mary lay among the debris near the top of what was left of Boston's prewar city hall. It had been partially demolished, but it overlooked the Warden headquarters. The VR and her associates lived in a fortified building next to HQ. Warden patrols moved around it constantly, with watchers on the roof. Houston had sent Gavin on an impossible mission. His team would have needed to drop a nuke on that building to assassinate the VR.

Dani wasn't concerned about the VR. She and Mary watched the arc-shaped building nearby on Cambridge Street where Rowan lived. The structure had once been a mix of office spaces and businesses with an underground parking area. Post-war it became Warden housing. Alex and Miles were watching the place where Rowan worked with his R&D teams in case Oliver was kept near Rowan's workplace. Each time Dani and Mary spotted Gavin walking with Rowan, Mary swiveled her rifle to put her crosshairs on Gavin's head, tracking him until he was out of sight. This morning was no different. Once they had gone into a building, Mary turned to Dani.

"I cannot describe to you how much I hate that asshole," Mary said.

"You don't have to; I can see it."

"What's the plan once we find Oliver's location? You've been tight-lipped the entire trip on this. You have a plan, right?"

"Yeah, but the plan won't matter much. We'll just end up winging it anyway when the shit starts."

Mary chuckled and returned to her scope to watch for Oliver. "We always do."

Dani scanned the structures around them. Much of the city had been leveled with the initial attack. The intact or rebuilt buildings were used by the Wardens on a daily basis.

"Roof. North side," Mary said.

Dani shifted her optics to focus on the roof. There was a garden on part of the roof with an area of high hedges. Oliver stood in a lower cut area of the roof and looked out at the city. Dani checked her watch and noted the time. Oliver strolled to the corner of the roof where there was a ten-foot drop to the next part of the roof. He looked down and shuffled closer.

"Stay where you are, kid," Dani said, wishing he could hear her. If he used his hands to first hang from the roof's edge, he could shorten the drop, but he wouldn't have anywhere else to go. If Oliver tried this, he'd land right in front of the four Wardens he couldn't see who were standing on the roof below him.

He brought his head up and passed his gaze over the area.

Dani knew he couldn't possibly see her, but as he turned his face in her direction, she gasped. His gaze moved on, and tears stung her eyes.

A green ball bounced out of the shrub area and rolled to his feet. Oliver bent and picked it up. He handed it to the boy who came to retrieve the ball. The little boy waved at Oliver, and he waved back. A woman holding an infant handed the child off to a younger woman who had appeared. The younger woman took the infant and led the boy away by the hand. Once the woman and Oliver were alone, she grabbed the front of Oliver's shirt and jerked him toward her. She hit him, and Oliver cowered under her blows. He tried to protect his head and face with his arms, but some of her strikes landed.

"Shoot her," Dani said.

"No."

"Fucking shoot her!"

When Mary's rifle didn't fire, Dani pulled her gaze from Oliver and grabbed Mary's shoulder. "Kill her."

Mary shoved Dani back. Dani moved to take Mary's rifle from her, and Mary slammed her elbow into Dani's jaw. She fell back from the blow, and Mary was on top of her with her tranq pistol pressed against the side of her neck.

"Goddammit, Dani, you know I'll knock your ass out. Breathe for a second. Think about this first. I kill her, and every Warden in the area knows exactly where to find us. We can't rescue Oliver if we're caught. As much as I want to snipe Gavin, I know I can't. Not *yet*."

"I want her dead."

"So do I. We'll get her, but not today. Not like this."

"I get to kill her."

"She's all yours when the time is right."

Dani nodded.

Mary released her and returned to her scope. Dani's jaw

ached, but she tried to ignore the pain. She found Oliver again with her optics. The woman had a grip on the back of his shirt and forced him toward the interior of the gardens, where Dani lost her view of him. She dropped her optics and buried her face in her hands. She took several deep breaths to try to regain control of herself, but the tears came anyway.

"This is my fault. Rowan wants me, not Oliver." She sniffled and wiped the tears from her face. She stood and started to leave.

"Don't even think of trading yourself for the kid."

Dani ignored her and kept walking. Something hissed and a bee stung the back of her leg. She turned and spotted the tranq dart sticking out of her lower leg. Dani glared at Mary.

Mary waggled her fingers at Dani and smiled. "Good night, darling."

Dani's initial step to charge Mary faltered; she was unconscious before she hit the floor.

When she woke to a throbbing headache, Dani groaned. She had been propped up in a corner of two pieces of concrete rubble. Mary lay prone in her place on the floor with her rifle ready. She glanced back at Dani, then returned to watching Rowan's building.

"Welcome back," Mary said.

Dani shifted to rub her face and realized her hands were bound with I-cuffs. "Wasn't enough to tranq me, but you had to restrain me too?"

"In case you woke while I slept. Are you done with your emotionally charged lunacy?"

"Yeah."

"Good. Sit there a bit longer while you regain the rest of your senses. Catherine's techies really ramped up the potency of the tranqs on Echoes. I heard it was good stuff, but damn, I never thought you'd be trashed for hours."

Dani writhed in her spot to get some feeling back into her legs and ass. "How long?"

Mary's eye left her scope to glance at her watch. "Twenty-six hours."

Dani sat up straighter. "Christ, Mary!"

"You were awake some in between to move. I helped you get up to pee a few times, but I doubt you'll remember any of that."

"No," Dani grumbled. She tried to rub her face to wake up a bit more and was irritated by the cuffs. "Take these fucking things off."

Mary left her rifle and stood. She stretched her back and shoulders, sighing when they cracked audibly. "You needed the sleep anyway." She dug through her pack and removed water and food.

"Not for an entire day!"

Mary took a drink of water and shoved a food wafer into her mouth.

"Stop ignoring me."

"Relax." Mary chewed as she removed a few more wafers and a second bottle from her pack. She squatted next to Dani and broke a wafer in half. "Open."

"I can feed myself if you take these off." Dani raised her bound hands.

"Open."

She sighed, then opened her mouth.

Mary placed the half wafer inside Dani's mouth and munched on the other half while she spoke. "When I radioed Miles to let him know we'd spotted Oliver, I told him you were taking a piss and unavailable. Since we have only seen Oliver in the garden—unless they're moving him underground—I don't think he's leaving that building."

"We only saw him the one time. That's not enough to establish a pattern."

"You saw him once. I saw him a second time two hours ago. Same time as yesterday. I think they've been bringing him out once a day, but he's been behind that hedge. We couldn't see him before. He's moving out into the open now where we can seem him."

"Was the woman there?"

"Yeah, but she didn't hit him. I think she's Rowan's wife or girlfriend. He was on the roof today too. They had quite the argument, but Oliver stayed well away from the fireworks."

"Did you tell Miles that Oliver was being abused?"

"And have him lose his fucking mind like you did? I had him and Alex change their location to focus on getting a low-angle view of the quarters. Maybe we can figure out which floor he's on." Mary adjusted the I-cuffs to release Dani's fingers but kept her wrists bound. She removed the lid to the bottle and placed the bottle in Dani's hands. Mary inserted another wafer into Dani's mouth and continued. "Alex thinks she can tap into the building's camera feeds, but I think that's too risky."

"Yeah. She needs to leave that shit alone unless she can do it remotely." Dani took a drink to wash down the food and froze.

"What?"

"Change of plans. How attached are you to that rifle?"

"Very. Why?"

"You're leaving it behind. Get these things off me. I have work to do."

Mary grinned and entered the code to deactivate the I-cuffs. "*This* is the Dani I need, not the freak from yesterday."

"You were right to tranq me."

"I don't have the patience to talk you out of doing something stupid like Miles does. Sedating you was easier. If you think I have a speck of guilt over doing that to you, you're wrong.

Dani nodded. "Fair."

"What's the plan?"

"Scavenging."

CHAPTER
36

attie leaned against the side of the building with her arms folded. She'd come to see Houston but stopped to observe the CNA in action. She grinned as she watched the flurry of activity on the base. It looked like chaos, but Hattie recognized the organization in the apparent mess. Teams of CNA troops prepped the transports. She couldn't see the airfield from where she stood, but she'd heard from others that the new planes were being moved out of the hangars during the day. The pilots had already put the birds in the air for flight trials, but that had been done only at night. Now everyone could see the new jets.

The details of what exactly they could do and what kind of weapons they carried remained classified, but that didn't stop the extravagant rumors. Houston had been careful to prevent leaks of information making their way to the Wardens. Although most of the rumors were far-fetched, the Wardens would take a beating from this new tech. Hattie left her place and headed for Houston's office.

She entered as four others exited. Six more CNA officers stood before Houston's desk receiving their orders, and Hattie waited.

"Take your troops south and secure this portion around Portsmouth," Houston said.

The colonel pointed at a map on the top of her desk. Hattie couldn't see exactly what Houston pointed at, but her interest was piqued. New Hampshire was never supposed to be a target.

"Leave today and sit on this spot until you hear from me," Houston said. "We'll have other troops joining you over the next few days. Dismissed."

Once the officers left, Hattie approached the colonel.

Houston glanced up at her while she dug through her desk. "What do you want?"

"Portsmouth? When the hell was that ever part of the plan?" Hattie asked.

"Now."

"Why?"

"Hattie, I appreciate everything you've had to offer the CNA on behalf of the Ancients, but I don't have to explain my actions to you."

"Oh, fuck you, Catherine. You have to explain everything. Troops are in motion to move out, and the last place they need to be is New Hampshire."

"Well, that *is* the state lying between us and Boston, is it not?"

"Fuck your mind games. What are you doing?"

Houston pulled a small bottle from her desk and opened it. She shook three pills into her palm and tossed them into her mouth. She swallowed as she replaced the cap and threw the bottle back into the drawer. "You don't give me enough credit for knowing Dani. Portsmouth is just a holding area for me to put troops and have them closer to Boston when it's time to strike."

"Good. Keep talking."

"Dani, Miles, and Mary were never going to stay here, but I

wanted to piss Dani off a little more. I gave her explicit orders to not leave the base and waited to see how far she was willing to go."

"You knew she would defy your orders to stay, so you manipulated her." Hattie's anger flared, and she stalked closer to Houston.

"I manipulate everyone, Hattie. Don't act surprised."

"If you were such an expert at reading people, you'd know I am not surprised. You fucked with her head and turned her loose, but it backfired. I heard about her visit to you the night she left."

"How? No one else was there."

Hattie shrugged. "I have more ears on this base than you'll ever know about. I wondered what you did to make her beat the shit out of you. Now I know. Well done, dearest Dani. Wish I could've seen it myself."

"Thankfully I had a med kit in my quarters to put my face back together before anyone saw what her fist did. I can't seem to fix the headache."

Hattie's cackling laugh filled the office. "Jace taught her how to fight, and Gavin honed her skills for years. Be sure to thank Gavin for the concussion she gave you the next time you see him. You *are* going to Boston, aren't you?"

"Yes."

"When?"

"As soon as I have a signal from Dani."

"A signal? Why would she signal you?" Hattie asked. She fell silent for a second and frowned. "You pushed Dani into action and let her go on ahead to stir the shit. You're using her as a decoy."

"I'm using her impulsiveness as an opportunity."

"You're a cold bitch."

Houston laughed. "Not the first time I've heard that. I didn't let her go alone or unequipped. I specifically ordered the security details to look the other way when Dani and her groupies started stealing everything. Once they were gone, I had the inventory reports sent to me so I'd know what she took. Dani has enough explosives to put a lot of holes in Boston. When she does whatever the hell it is she'll do to rescue Oliver, it'll be with a bang."

Hattie nodded. "Your signal to move in."

"Exactly. Dani met our contact near Boston and gave them comm gear, so we have communication with them again. I'm sending troops to them as we speak, but I can't move the bulk of our forces without the Wardens knowing. Portsmouth is a feint—sorta. We'll hit it, but it's only to try to draw Warden troops out of Boston."

"What if you piss off both sides and get your ass flanked north and south between the cities?"

"It's a risk, but the Wardens are so entrenched in Boston, I don't think they'll pour out of the city to destroy us. I have been building our reserves in western New Hampshire and Mass for weeks."

"How will you hit Boston and not kill Dani and the others?"

"I'm keeping tabs on them from here. I gave Cam a tracker. He stayed in Maynard to care for Kels and other wounded, so he moved the transmitter to Mary's gear."

"The Wardens can track that shit, Catherine."

"Not this model. One of your Ancients showed us how to bounce the signal so it's undetectable. The problem is they're so deep inside the city, the signal has been spotty, but we're trying to clean it up."

"You've taken too many risks at Dani's expense."

Houston shook her head. "Dani has a bigger problem."

"Bigger than waltzing into the middle of Warden HQ?"

"We ID'd the dead Warden Alex said she killed. Took a little time with his head gone and all. He was the bartender at your brothel the night Dani passed out."

"Kane? That asshole was never reliable. I didn't think much of it when he didn't show the next couple of nights. Kane was a Warden spy?" Hattie shook her head. "Fuck me. I'd gladly kill him myself if he wasn't already headless."

"Mary accused Alex of trying to drug Dani for sex."

"Yeah," Hattie said, and shrugged.

"I pulled Alex's CNA records, and nothing looked unusual. They show her being in Portland during the time she said she was, which coincides with the time Dani lived there. Everything was perfect. She had an exemplary CNA record."

Hattie's heart sank. "Shit."

"Yeah. What person on this planet hangs around Dani for any length of time and stays out of trouble? If they were in any semblance of a relationship, there is no way Alex could've kept a spotless record. When Miles was with Dani in Portland—I didn't know who he was seeing at the time—he went from a model MP to a shit show almost overnight. It all makes sense now. Alex wasn't after Dani for sex, or she was, but that wasn't the only thing she was after. Alex's record was faked."

"Oliver was a secondary target when drugging Dani failed. This was all Rowan."

"Yep."

"Who can you send in to warn her?" Hattie asked.

"No one. I didn't have comms with Maynard until after they'd left. I have no way to reach her."

"You said they took comm units with them. They have to be communicating with each other on the ground."

"I tried that. They're on a different frequency."

"Find the right fucking frequency! Get your guy who lives in the sim warehouse to find her."

"With the range we got from the Ancients, there are hundreds of frequencies. She could be on any one of them."

"Have your guy check every one. He can set up a scan to

run automatically and ping back when the frequency they use is active. It'll take him some time to set it up, but unless you're leaving for Boston in the next five minutes, he can at least get started."

Houston nodded and reached for her comm. "That might work."

"This should not have taken you so long to figure out and put into motion." Hattie stared at Houston for a moment. "Are you stalling on purpose?"

"You're seriously asking me that question?"

"You mean the one you're not answering? You've already admitted to using Dani and letting her leave with gear to start a fight you should have started weeks ago."

"I'm trying to win this goddamn war!"

"Are you? At what cost? If I find out you looked the other way while Oliver was taken so you could use his capture to better manipulate Dani, you'll pay."

"Threats now?"

"I'm telling you how it will be. Find her, Catherine. If she dies because of your bullshit tactics, I'll make you disappear, and it won't be painless."

Houston winced; Hattie wasn't bluffing.

CHAPTER 37

Over the next two days, Dani and Mary moved locations along with Alex and Miles to watch the different levels of the building where Oliver was held. They confirmed Mary's suspicion that Oliver was let outside only once a day, and they learned the woman's routine with ease. Rowan's routine was a bit more erratic, but he did have some consistent patterns. Dani and Mary waited in the lowest level of the building next to the biological waste reclamation center and food waste. They picked through the food, and Dani found a partially eaten, overripe pear. She wiped it off on her trousers before biting into it. She rolled the piece of fruit around in her mouth to taste it. There was no indication it had fermented, so she started chewing. She passed it to Mary, who took a bite.

With the pear in one hand and her pistol in the other, Mary had her weapon pointed at Alex's head as soon as the woman arrived.

Alex had her pistol drawn, but she raised her hands in a passive manner to Mary.

Miles arrived behind Alex, and Mary lowered her weapon.

Mary took another bite of the pear and passed it back to Dani.

"You're eating their garbage?" Alex asked.

"It's what Brigands do in a pinch," Dani said. Alex and Miles declined her offer of the pear, so she and Mary continued eating it. "This area is perfect for us—even the Wardens avoid it. Smells like the shit that's stored before processing, so there are no live camera feeds or patrols through this level."

Alex wrinkled her nose. "It's awful down here."

"You can leave," Mary said.

Dani half wondered if the tension between Mary and Alex would ever ease. She figured it wouldn't.

Miles stepped forward. "Alex thinks she spotted the floor they're holding Oliver on."

"I know I did," Alex said. "There are nine levels of living quarters. Ground level is the main entry and some shops for supplies and food. Second floor and up are residences until it turns into the roof and garden. I saw Oliver and the woman on the seventh floor, moving toward the center. I lost them after that."

"You're sure it was the seventh floor?" Dani asked.

"Absolutely," Alex said.

Dani discarded the rest of the pear and paced for a few minutes.

"Where's your rifle?" Miles asked Mary while Dani was lost in thought.

"Gone."

"How?"

Mary scowled. "I don't want to talk about it."

Dani was pulled from her thoughts when she spotted Alex kneeling near one of the walls and pulling wires out of a junction box by the floor. Dani rushed over. "Stop!"

"Let me tap into the camera feeds. We can find Oliver much quicker."

"Just leave it alone for now, Alex," Dani said. She pulled Miles aside and lowered her voice so only he could hear. "Does she know what she's doing? Do you think she can get into the cameras without setting off alarms?"

"I don't know," Miles said, shrugging. "You've done it before."

Dani shook her head. "I got into them and recorded data. That's it. I didn't go digging around looking for someone."

"You don't trust her."

"I haven't known her like I know you and Mary, and Mary fucking hates her. What do you think?"

"Dani, what are you really asking me?"

"We're inside the building where Oliver is. We're close, Miles. If we're to find Oliver, we need to split up. You've been working next to Alex for days now, so you've trusted her with your life. Do you trust her with Oliver's?"

He took a deep breath and considered his answer for a moment.

"You'd never take that long to answer if I asked you that same question about Mary."

Miles shook his head. "I'll stay with Alex as before. You and Mary will split up. We can at least cover the seventh floor in thirds."

"Okay."

"How are we doing this?"

"I'll review the higher-level stuff with the group and include Alex, but I've already told Mary the details. We need to draw the Wardens out of this building. Mary's rifle is positioned where we were on watch a few days ago. I rigged it so she can fire it remotely, and it's aimed at HQ. I'll blow the airport first. The Wardens will lock down this area, then Mary will fire shots into the glass at HQ where the VR will go once the shit starts."

"A rifle won't get through that glass, Dani."

"It doesn't need to. We only need it to impact the glass. Spook them. I figure they'll believe there is an exterior attack on the city and an interior assassination attempt. They'll secure the VR."

"Move their elite forces to the VR for her protection. Got it."

"When they determine our nonexistent sniper's location and go there, that building is rigged to come down. I'll blow other parts of the city to send them in different directions. This building should empty out. We can sneak our way up to the seventh floor, grab Oliver, and slip back out through here. It won't be easy, but they'll be looking for an army, not four people. Are you good with this?"

"Yeah."

Dani nodded and rejoined Alex and Mary.

"What's the plan?" Alex asked.

"Oliver will be taken outside for his walk in twenty minutes, so we're splitting up. Alex, you'll be with Miles, and Mary, you're with me as we work our way up the floors. Our best chance is to grab Oliver when he's coming back inside." Dani removed the panel from her pack, and the others gathered next to her while she pulled up a diagram of the building.

"The woman has been the only one taking him out lately. He'll be out for his walk, and I'll start setting off some of our explosives around the city five minutes into his walk. This will drive them back inside, and we'll be in position. Tranq the woman, grab Oliver, and we'll meet back at the septic reclaim tanks. Once we're together, we'll come here to the garbage and go out the rear of the building to the sewers. Good so far?"

Heads nodded, and Dani continued. "Mary, you'll cover this stairwell, and I'll be on this one. Alex and Miles, you'll cover these lifts here and here in case they come out there," she said, pointing at the places on the diagram.

"Miles and I can split up, cover more ground," Alex said.

"Nope. I want you to tap into the cameras to disable a few—not all of them, just the ones we need where we'll be stationed—and take out a few others so it looks like random outages. Understand?"

Alex nodded.

"Do *not* fuck around in their system any longer than necessary to disable the feeds. *Don't* look for Oliver. Get in. Get out."

"Yep," Alex said.

"Miles, you'll be her cover while her eyes are on her screen," Dani said. He nodded, and she hoped he understood her true meaning: to watch Alex to make sure she did her job and shoot her if she didn't. Dani wanted to trust Alex, but she couldn't— not with Miles reluctant to do so.

"Will do," he said.

"Use your tranqs on any Wardens you need to remove from your path. We're dressed like them, but if you have any problems, tranq 'em. We can't have a bloodbath or they'll know we're inside. The sedatives will put them down for hours. Stash the ones you take out. Stick them in a closet or office, or throw them down the garbage chute; I don't care. Just don't leave a blood trail."

Miles, Mary, and Alex nodded, and Dani continued as she passed two small devices to Miles and Alex.

"Mary pulled an access device off a Warden this morning, and I created three clones. It's a risk to use the same access off one Warden, but it was easier to hide one corpse than it would have been to hide four bodies. Questions?"

No one spoke.

"Alex, as soon as you have those wires back in the wall, we move out," Dani said. She checked her pistol and her pockets while Alex put the junction box back together. Dani mentally went through her list. She had the panel she needed to set off the explosives. Mary already knew she was the backup to detonate things if Dani was unable to. Once the first explosion went off, there was no retreat and no second chance.

Alex finished with the wires, and the group headed for the septic holding tanks. Dani stowed her pack in a utility closet, and Mary threw her gear in too. Alex and Miles tucked their gear behind one of the tanks. All eyes were on Dani once they were ready.

She checked her watch. "We have fifteen minutes to get in position on the seventh floor. Be careful and move quietly, but keep an eye on the time. Use the comm if you get delayed. We have a tight window. Let's go."

CHAPTER
38

"Alex is working on the cameras now," Miles said through the comm. "Dani and Mary, you're clear to enter your stairwells."

Dani's heart raced a bit more as she pushed the stairwell door open. She stopped and listened. The lifts were much faster, so she hoped the Wardens stayed off the stairs. She was tempted to race up to the seventh floor, but she forced herself to move upward quietly. The last thing she needed was to be caught loitering in the stairwell. If she met Wardens on her trip up, she would at least look like she was going somewhere instead of standing around and waiting.

She made it out of the four sublevels of the building to reach the ground floor. Dani continued upward and stopped for a moment to catch her breath on the third floor. She heard a door open above her, and the voices of a male and a female echoed as they started down the stairs. Dani skipped up a few steps to reach the next landing and left the stairs. She lingered near the door and listened. The two Wardens continued down past her level, and she allowed herself a moment to breathe before reentering the stairwell.

Dani altered her comm to link only with Mary.

"Mary, any problems?"

"No. You?"

"Just dodged a pair of Wardens. They never saw me."

"Rattled you, huh? I hear it in your voice."

"What level are you on?" Dani passed the door to the fourth level and continued up.

"Six. You?"

"Approaching five."

"Speed it up, slacker."

Dani smiled and some of her nervousness eased. As she moved past the door to the fifth level, it swung open unexpectedly. She leapt aside and dropped her hand to her pistol full of tranq rounds.

Rowan paced in his office. He had expected news of Dani's arrival before now, but the increased patrols hadn't turned up any Brigand or CNA captures in the area. He tossed his panel onto the desk, where it clattered across the top until it came to a stop. He sank into his chair and skimmed the R&D reports as a distraction. Curtis was a master at developing new tech, and Rowan's task was to sort which tech warranted more investigation. The VR often chided Rowan for the expenses his R&D team racked up, but once his crew demonstrated the new tech to Vice Regent Aubrey and the chancellors, the VR had no choice but to shut up.

Today Rowan couldn't focus on the reports. Gavin Marcus stood at his post just inside Rowan's office and never moved. Marcus was a model Warden, and Rowan wished he had fifty more of him. He'd lost his elite troops in Portland with his transfer to Boston, and Rowan desperately wanted them back. The chancellors continued to back him in his bid to attack Maine, but the VR was a problem. He leaned back in his chair and imagined the damage he could do to Maine's CNA with one well-planned strike across the state. His comm chirped with a call from his wife and brought him back to the present.

"Ana, how—"

"Rowan, I'm done with this human."

He sighed. "We've been through this."

"I can't tell you how badly I want to throw it off this roof. I'm done taking it for walks and feeding it. Get it out of my home."

"Not yet. Did you get him different clothes yet? He's been in the same clothing since the day he arrived. He's supposed to be my nephew, not a poor human Brigand."

"*It is a poor human Brigand!* You expect me to get it clothes? Fuck you! Get this thing out of my home or I'll leave you today and take the children with me."

He knew better than to tell her she was overreacting. The first and last time he'd made that mistake, she *had* left him.

"Ana—"

"Send your gorilla for it now. If it isn't gone within the hour, I throw it off the roof."

She ended the transmission, and Rowan sighed. Unless Dani showed up, the boy was more headache than he was worth.

"Marcus, go to my quarters and retrieve the boy. Bring him back here," Rowan said.

"Yes, sir." Marcus left, silent and deadly.

The female Warden who'd barged into Dani widened her eyes. "Oh, shit, sorry about that."

"Christ," Dani said.

"I didn't mean to almost hit you with the door."

Mary's voice sounded in Dani's ear. "If you have your hand on your weapon, remove it and act like this was just a simple mishap, which is exactly what it is. Do *not* try to lie your way out of this."

Dani shifted her hand from her pistol to the railing and dismissively waved with her other one. "Sorry. You startled me is all. I shouldn't have been walking so close to it."

"Next time I won't go barging through doors," the woman said before starting down the stairs. "Have a good one."

"Yeah, you too," Dani said.

"Nicely done," Mary said into her earpiece. "You do so much better when you just tell the truth."

Dani resisted the urge to respond. She continued upward and reopened her comm with the others. A door opened on a lower level, and Dani looked down, catching a glimpse of the female Warden leaving the stairs.

"Alex, do you have the cameras out in the stairs for the seventh floor yet? Mary and I are closing in."

"Yep. I have those out and a few others around the building," Alex said. "I set up a few to alternate going in and out so it all looks like a system glitch. Did we lose contact with you for a moment? I tried to reach you."

"Uh, yeah, brief loss of contact," Dani said. *Shit*. She knew better than to break comms with Alex and Miles to chitchat with Mary privately to calm her nerves. "What is it?"

"Oliver is out for his walk early with the woman," Miles said. "We caught a glimpse of him when Alex was taking the feeds down."

Mary hadn't mentioned seeing or hearing anyone in her stairwell, and Dani had encountered others only in the lower levels. *Unless they slipped in while I was hiding in the hall.* "Lift?"

"Yeah."

"Okay, we can do this," Dani said.

"The nanny or whatever is with them, as are the boy and infant," Miles said.

Dani growled. *Fuck!* "Uh, give me a minute."

Alex spoke up. "I can get roof access to see what's going on. Maybe we can take him up there."

"No!" Dani winced when her voice echoed in the stairwell. She lowered her voice. "I told you to stay out of their goddamn feeds. You are *only* disabling cameras."

"Understood," Alex said.

Dani noticed Alex's terse response. The woman was irritated with her, but Dani didn't care. This wasn't the first time she'd had to tell Alex to avoid digging around in the Wardens' security system. She buried her face in her hands and tried to think. She recalled the times she'd spotted Oliver on his daily walk, and lowered her hands.

"The woman always comes back in last. She follows Oliver when they return inside. This will be insanely close, but whichever one of us is there when they come back, the nanny should be carrying the infant and have the boy. Alert me as soon as you see them, and let them go by you. Oliver should be next with the woman escorting him. Tranq her, grab Oliver, and bolt. Don't do anything to the nanny and risk harming the boy or baby."

"The nanny will be able to alert the Wardens," Mary said.

"I'll blow the airport as soon we have eyes on Oliver. The Warden comm traffic should be jammed with reports of the attack, so if she alerts anyone of our presence, it should get lost among the rest of the reports for at least a little while."

"Shit, we're really rolling the dice on this," Mary said.

"This will work," Miles said.

Dani's shoulders relaxed. She needed Miles's approval of this new plan and was relieved when he agreed with her.

"Nothing else changes," Dani said. "Go to your spots on the seventh floor and wait for Oliver to show up."

She moved to the middle landing between the sixth and

seventh floors. Her idea was to be in motion going up to the seventh as soon as Oliver and the others neared it so she'd look like she was going somewhere. She could pause, pretending to be polite, and allow the younger woman to go through with the kids first. Then she could intercept Oliver and the woman escorting him. At least that was her perfect scenario. She tried not to think of how many times she'd seen her perfect plans go up in smoke—sometimes literally.

Dani took several deep breaths to calm her jittery insides and rapid heart rate. She pulled the palm-sized panel from her pocket and loaded the screen to detonate the airport and waited.

Her head snapped up when she heard a door on an upper floor open.

"Why do we have to leave early?" a young boy said.

Someone responded to him, but Dani couldn't hear what was said. Several sets of feet started down the stairs, creating a small thundering noise as they descended.

Dani needed to be sure who was coming down, so she inched toward the rail to look up. She didn't see the boy who had spoken, but she did see the woman who had beaten Oliver. Dani locked eyes with her for only a second before leaving the rail to duck back closer to the wall.

Rowan resumed pacing. He'd sent another batch of reports to the VR that morning on CNA and Brigand resources in the region, and again he'd gotten no response. Curtis entered his office.

"Should I come back, sir?" Curtis asked.

"No. I'm just frustrated. Ana is livid over the boy, so I sent Marcus to bring him here before she kills him. The VR is silent on my reports. I should be used to that by now, but that woman will be the reason Boston suffers casualties when the CNA attacks."

"You informed her of the odd CNA movements out of Portland and still nothing?"

Rowan shook his head.

Curtis grinned.

"What?" Rowan asked.

"I think it's time to move with the chancellors to unseat the VR."

"You mean this political game you've been playing will be over, and I will come into power?"

Curtis nodded.

"When?" Rowan asked. His comm alerted him to an incoming message from Ana. He was tempted to ignore it. "Ana, Marcus is already coming for the boy."

"I saw your Brigand woman in the stairwell," Ana said.

"I'm on my way," Rowan said. "Go to our quarters and stay there."

"Right after I kill her." She ended the link.

Ana was a skilled fighter as a former Warden soldier, but he didn't want her fighting the Brigand.

Dani took a breath to radio the others that she'd spotted the woman who had Oliver, but she stopped when the group halted and the door to the eighth floor opened. They weren't coming to the seventh floor, and Dani was out of position, as was everyone else.

"Eighth floor, not seventh. Move now!" Dani whispered into the comm as she drew her pistol.

She raced up the stairs as quietly as she could, but the door had closed behind the woman. Dani had missed her chance. She reached to pull it open and realized she had the panel in her hand and hadn't detonated the airport. She moved her thumb to blow it. The door flew open, catching Dani in the chest and face. She was thrown into the safety rail behind her, and both the pistol and the panel dropped from her hands.

She grunted with the impact of her back striking the rail and twisted to prevent flipping over it to a grisly fall to the lower levels. The door had caught her in the cheek, and she was wobbly from the impact. She clung to the rail to regain her balance as she turned to face her attacker. The woman charged toward her with something in her hand that Dani assumed was a pistol. Her vision was fuzzy as she tried to process what had happened.

"Ana, no!"

Oliver's voice snapped her mind into focus, and Dani straightened. He rammed his shoulder into the woman's back. She was knocked off balance enough that the pistol swung away from Dani.

"Was that Ollie?" Miles asked over the comm. "Dani, was that Ollie?"

She didn't have time to respond. Her friends should be able to hear everything, figure out she was eyeball-deep in shit, and find her. She just had to keep herself alive long enough for them to arrive.

Ana turned on Oliver. "Fucking human."

"Shit," Miles said.

Dani wanted to smile, laugh, be relieved, whatever, that Miles knew what was happening, but Ana was going after Oliver to kill him. Dani looped one arm around Ana's neck and reached for the pistol with her other hand. Ana's head snapped back and connected with Dani's cheekbone, but she refused to release the woman intent on killing both her and Oliver.

She didn't know if she'd successfully blown the airport or not before the door had struck her. The panel was somewhere in the stairwell, and Dani was too occupied to look for it. "Mary. Air—"

Ana's head collided with her cheek again. The woman then spun with Dani still attached, and both crashed into the wall next to the door. They bounced off and Ana spun again, this time deliberately tossing them both down the stairs to the middle landing.

"Dani, report," Miles said.

The armor mostly protected her during the fall, but when her wrist struck the edge of a step, she lost Ana's arm that had the pistol. They continued their tumble to the landing, stopping when they slammed into the wall. They separated, and Ana was on her feet first. She charged Dani and raised her leg, driving her knee toward Dani's head.

Miles, Mary, and Alex called to her over the comm, but she didn't respond.

Dani caught the woman's leg and shoved her aside. Ana brought her pistol down as she stumbled and clipped Dani's forehead with it. Dani was stunned, but remained conscious as warm blood flowed from her new cut.

Oliver tried to rush to Dani, and she held her hand up. "Stay back!"

Her distraction was enough for Ana to be on her again. The woman pinned Dani on her back and brought the pistol toward her face.

"Who stays back?" Alex asked.

"Dani, report," Miles said again.

She struggled to get her hands up and redirect Ana's weapon away from her head while keeping it from being pointed at Oliver. She wrapped a leg around Ana's legs and pushed off the wall with her other foot. The pair rolled. Dani was successful in getting the gun pointed in a safer direction, and she was briefly on top of Ana until they tumbled down the lower half of the steps to the seventh floor.

Dani scrambled away from the woman and winced with sudden pain in her ribs. "Airport. Mary, blow the airport."

Ana righted and Dani charged. She slammed the woman back into the stairs. Ana cried out in pain, and Dani liked the sound. She gripped the front of Ana's shirt to do it again, but the strength in her injured wrist failed. Ana brought her pistol up toward Dani's head again. She turned her head aside just before the pistol fired. The heat from the plasma pistol singed Dani's hair and blistered the side of her face.

Dani was more concerned about Oliver being hit by the wayward shot, but he remained on the middle landing, leaning against the wall, watching in horror as the women fought.

Where are they?

Dani's head snapped to the side when Ana's fist caught her jaw. She had had enough of this woman. She attacked Ana's hand with the pistol and grabbed her thumb. Dani suffered a few more punches, but she didn't stop. She twisted Ana's thumb until it snapped. Ana screamed, and the pistol fell from her hand to the floor.

Dani thought she'd gained an advantage, but Ana's burst of rage surprised her. The woman twisted to create space, then drove her elbow into Dani's chin. She was rocked by the blow, and Ana was on her again. They rolled on the floor and stopped against the rail. Ana drew her legs close to her core and used her feet to shove Dani through the space between the floor and lowest rail. Dani looped one arm around the rail to keep herself from falling. She reached through the rails and grabbed Ana's shirt, pulled hard, and smashed Ana's face into the rail. The woman's eyes flickered with the blow, so Dani did it again.

Ana sagged to the floor, and Dani pulled herself back through the rail to the safety of the floor and stood. She reached for Ana's pistol and missed it when Ana's kick caught her ankles and knocked her down. Ana picked up the pistol and stood. Dani rushed at her, but Ana spun and drove Dani's back to the wall. When the barrel of the pistol neared Dani's chin, she forced the woman back. They collided when Ana struck the rail.

The pistol discharged a plasma round, and Ana's head exploded.

Dani recoiled from the destruction and staggered back until she reached the wall.

Ana's body slumped to the floor, and a pool of blood formed and starting dripping down to the lower levels.

A spasm seized Dani's middle, and she leaned over to vomit.

When her stomach finished emptying, she leaned against the wall, trembling. "Fuck."

Oliver's small voice called to her. "Dani."

She looked up; he was curled into a ball, sitting in the corner on the midlevel landing. He stared at her with wide eyes, tears streaming down his face.

"Stay there, I'm coming." She took several deep breaths before leaving the wall holding her up. She picked up Ana's pistol with a shaking hand and started up the stairs to Oliver. "Miles, I have Oliver. We're in the east stairwell between seven and eight. Where the fuck are you?"

"Almost there," Miles said.

She set the pistol aside and pulled all upper layers of her armor off so she was left in her T-shirt. "Oliver," Dani said as she knelt next to him. "Put this on. No, don't look down there. Just put this on."

She helped him dress in the interior shirt of CNA armor, then put the exterior jacket of Warden armor on him. She fastened it closed, then pulled him to his feet to swallow him with her arms.

"I am so sorry you had to see that," she said. "It wasn't supposed to go that way."

He sniffled and nodded against her shoulder. "I was afraid you were going to die like Brody. He was hurt trying to help me.

I couldn't see what happened, but I heard him yelp when he was shot."

"We found him. He's going to be very happy to see you."

Oliver lifted his head. "He's alive?"

"Yeah," Dani said, smiling. "As soon as your dad is here, we're leaving. We aren't safe yet."

The stairwell doors on both the eighth and seventh floors opened. Dani moved Oliver behind her and brought her pistol up. Miles came through with Alex on the eighth floor, and Mary entered from below.

Miles rushed to his son, and Oliver dissolved into a sob in his father's arms.

"Jesus, Dani. You okay?" Alex asked.

Dani nodded, but she wasn't sure if that was the right answer or not. Her entire body ached. She didn't want to know what she looked like and figured she probably had bits of Ana on her too. She shuddered with the thought. A new wave of nausea hit, but she managed to avoid gagging or worse.

Mary moved past the corpse to join Dani. "So, considering the mess you made of Ana, the whole don't-leave-a-blood-trail plan is out, yes?"

"That wasn't supposed to happen," Dani said.

"You said you wanted to kill her."

"I didn't mean—" Dani shook her head and kept her gaze off the mostly headless body.

"Bitch needed to go." Mary calmly exchanged her pistol's tranq cartridges for live rounds. "C'mon," she said, and she began ushering everyone down the stairs.

Miles put his arm across his son's shoulders to guide him down. "Ollie, close your eyes and don't open them until we're off the stairs. I'll help you down and keep you from falling."

Oliver wiped at his tears. He drew in a shaky breath, closed his eyes, then nodded.

Dani was glad Mary had taken over for the moment. Her mind was too scattered after seeing Ana's head vanish in a horrific spray of organic material. She was glad she'd already emptied her stomach. While her feet moved down the stairs, her mind started to function again.

"You blew the airport, right?" Dani asked.

"You'd already detonated," Mary said. "Wardens started pouring out of their quarters when we were trying to reach you. That's why it took us so long."

"Dad," Oliver said.

"Keep your eyes closed," Miles said.

Dani said, "The rifle?"

"I took care of that and started the second wave of explosions across the city."

"Dad!"

Miles slowed his descent with Oliver. "Are you hurt?"

"No, but—"

"Then keep moving, and don't open your eyes."

Dani wished she could close her eyes. She tried to keep them off the blood dripping from Ana's body. Oliver didn't need to see this mess. She wished the fight with Ana had gone differently, but she couldn't change the outcome now.

Oliver stumbled when he reached the landing on the fifth floor. He opened his eyes, and Miles stood between Oliver and the view of blood dripping down the center of the stairwell.

"Dad, the woman, Ana—"

A door opened on a lower level, and someone entered the stairwell. Dani and the others abandoned the stairs to enter the hallway, and Dani eased the door closed with hopes no one would hear their movement or know what level they were on.

CHAPTER 39

"Curtis, alert the council that we have a breech in the—"
Rowan's words ended when a massive blast struck
across the harbor.

Combat alarms sounded in his department with alerts for
all senior staff to report to headquarters.

Curtis shouted over the alarms, "Sir, go to Ana and take our
weapon testers with you. They don't have recent tactical expertise as field soldiers, but they know the gear and how to use it.
I'll cover at HQ for you."

"Keep me updated. I want to know where that blast happened. I suspect it was the airfields. This is Houston's doing, and
there will be more targets."

Curtis nodded and left the office.

As Rowan followed, he activated his comm. Ana didn't
answer his hails, so he contacted Marcus instead. "Dani is inside
officers' quarters. Find her. I'm coming with backup."

"Yes, sir," Marcus said.

Rowan gathered his weapon techs. They geared up with
the newest armor, helmets, pistols, and rifles. After putting his
armor on, Rowan pulled his new helmet on, then picked up
the latest model of the plasma rifle. His team was slower than

elite Wardens, and the delay irritated him. He barked at them to move faster. They hadn't left the department yet when Marcus contacted him over the comm.

"Sir, your wife's body is in the east stairwell. Level seven," Marcus said.

"Stay with her until she regens," Rowan said. "I'll be there soon."

"Regen won't be possible, sir."

Rowan leaned against a table as he processed this information. Ana was gone. Forever. But he'd have to mourn for her later.

"My children?" Rowan asked.

"They're not with her."

"Any other dead present? The boy?"

"No, sir."

"Find the intruders. Capture Dani. I doubt she's alone, and I don't care if the others live or not."

"Understood, sir."

Rowan straightened and prepared to yell at his researchers again, but they were ready. "We have CNA intruders in the officers' quarters. Let's go."

His team might have been made up of techies, but they were eager, as Wardens should be, to hunt and exterminate humans. When they arrived at the ground level of the residence building, Rowan attempted contact with Marcus but got no reply.

He gestured to his team of ten techs. "Split into pairs. One pair for each lift; one goes up and one goes down. The remaining pairs cover north, south, and west stairwells. I'll take the east. Search every level and report your findings. Do *not* engage the enemy without contacting me first."

"Yes, sir," they said as a collective.

"Move out."

"Sir," Curtis said over the comm.

"Go ahead, Curtis."

"There was sniper fire directed at HQ in an apparent assassination attempt. No injuries since the rounds didn't pierce the glass. The VR ordered a search team to find the sniper, or snipers, in the adjacent building where the attack originated."

Rowan paused his trip to the stairs while he thought.

"Sir, do you copy?"

"Yes," Rowan said. "A sniper attack would be suicide. It's probably a decoy. Recall the search team."

"They have already left."

"Tell the chancellors who will listen that this is a trap and recall that team."

"Yes, sir."

Rowan's building trembled with a much closer blast.

"What the hell was that?" Rowan asked.

"Uh, the building the search team just entered has exploded."

"Goddammit! Shoot the fucking VR before she loses the city with her stupidity." Rowan terminated his connection with Curtis, knowing the man would never shoot Aubrey.

He jogged to his assigned stairwell and readied his rifle.

Rowan sprinted up from the ground level. He noticed spatters of blood dripping down from somewhere on a higher level and assumed it was his wife's. Rowan paused on the first floor and found no signs of blood or markings on walls or doors to indicate weapons fire. He could hear distant explosions outside and figured the CNA was acting as he'd predicted.

Curtis contacted him again. "Sir, more bombs have gone off around the city as you said. The Chancellors are aware that this information, including the warning that the sniper was a decoy, is coming from you. They're ready to follow your direction, not the VR's. Rowan, I need you at HQ as soon as you have Ana."

"Ana's dead, I've lost contact with Marcus, and I don't know where my children are."

Curtis paused before answering. "Yes, sir."

Rowan understood Curtis's implied condolences in his pause.

"Is the building contained yet?" Curtis asked.

"No."

"I'll send you a few more resources."

"Have them search the lower levels."

Rowan continued up the stairs. The amount of blood spatter increased as he neared the seventh floor. He knelt next to his wife's body. Three-quarters of her head was splattered against the opposite wall. He placed his hand on her shoulder and passed his fingers down her arm. He would have touched Ana's face one last time if she'd had one. He replaced the urge to mourn for her with rage.

"Dani will suffer for this, my love."

He stood and searched the areas of the stairs between the seventh and eighth floors. He spotted vomit on the landing floor and droplets of blood leading down the stairs. He abandoned the stairs to find his children.

CHAPTER
40

"Shit," Mary said. "They were supposed to *leave* the building, not enter it."

Dani touched Oliver's shoulder. "What about Ana?"

"She saw you in the stairs when we started coming down. She contacted Rowan before she attacked you. He knows you're here. This was all a trap. I couldn't warn you not to come."

Dani smiled. "It's not a trap when you know what you're walking into." Granted, none of them had really known what the fuck they were walking into, but she didn't need to tell Oliver that. "Alex, pull up a building schematic. We need a way out of here."

"Where's your exit?" Oliver asked.

"Basement, several levels underground," Miles said.

"The garbage depot?"

Miles nodded.

"We need to go to the other side of the building," Oliver said. "There's an access point where everyone chucks their garbage. I saw it when Ana took the trash out before taking me to the roof, and I know how to get there."

Mary said, "I put a tranqed Warden in a chute earlier so there wouldn't be a blood trail. I didn't know it was the garbage."

"Can we go down it without dying?" Miles asked, and Oliver shrugged.

"We'll figure it out when we get there," Dani said. "Mary, Alex, lead with Oliver behind you. Miles and I will follow."

Oliver told them which way to go and where the junctions were. They jogged down the hall, slowed at the turns for Mary and Alex to make sure the way was clear, then quickened their pace again. As they moved past the lifts, Dani wished they could use them, but lifts could stop on any floor to pick up Wardens. Without a way to override a lift to prevent unwanted passengers getting on, it was a death trap.

The group gathered at the final turn, and Mary checked the corridor before slipping out in front of them. They ran until Mary and Alex skidded to a stop at a junction with an adjoining hallway that Oliver hadn't mentioned, but it was too late.

Gavin slammed into the group, taking Mary and Alex with him. He smashed them into the opposite wall, then tossed Mary across the hallway so she struck the other wall. Both Mary and Alex slid down the walls to the floor. Oliver had been knocked aside, and he lay on the floor, clutching his shoulder.

Dani brought her pistol up, but Gavin disarmed her so quickly, the pistol skittered across the floor. He shoved her into Miles, and when Miles tried to catch her, Gavin attacked him. Dani fell as the men struggled to kill each other, but she was back on her feet in an instant. She pulled her knife and went after Gavin. He struck Miles in the face, and when Miles stumbled, Gavin attacked Dani.

She arced her blade and gave Gavin two nasty cuts across his forearms. Instead of him backing away, he came after her. He gripped her injured wrist and twisted. If it had been only bruised before, it was broken now. She screamed, and her knees buckled. He grabbed her arm and gripped a fistful of her Warden trousers. Gavin lifted her from the floor and threw her.

Dani skidded a few feet before she collided with Oliver. The teen had gained his feet at some point, and she took him back down. Gavin turned on Miles.

Dani coughed with the impact, and pain shot through her side. She didn't have time to assess her injuries; she held her throbbing wrist close to her body as she crawled to Mary and shook her shoulder. "Oliver, check on Alex. Mary, c'mon." Dani glanced back. Gavin was beating the shit out of Miles, but Miles was delivering his own blows. If she didn't do something to end the fight, Gavin would beat Miles to a very dead pulp.

Mary groaned, opened her eyes briefly, then closed them again.

"Alex isn't waking up," Oliver said.

"Stay with Mary."

Dani took Mary's pistol and fumbled with the weapon in her nondominant hand until she had a better grip on it. Shooting at Gavin like this was a terrible idea, but she was out of options.

"Whatever happens, don't come out around me," Dani said. "Try to wake Mary."

"Take the armor back," Oliver said.

"Keep it."

Dani stood and used the wall for extra balance. Miles had his pistol in his hand, and he and Gavin continued to trade blows, though Gavin had Miles's hand pinned against the wall. Dani aimed at Gavin, but the men fought so closely together; she feared she'd shoot Miles. If they separated even a little, she was prepared to fire on Gavin.

Miles slammed his forehead into Gavin's nose. Gavin's head snapped back, and he grinned despite streams of blood now coming from both nostrils. He drove his fist into Miles's side, and Dani knew exactly how that strike felt. Gavin had done the same to her many times when she trained with him. Miles took more blows, and his knees began to buckle.

She kept her aim on Gavin steady, slid her finger to the trigger, and applied pressure. She wished the men would separate for just *one* second.

Gavin held Miles's wrist. As Dani squeezed her trigger, Gavin pulled Miles's hand from the wall and slammed it back into it. Miles's weapon discharged, and Dani's shot missed Gavin when the plasma round from Miles's gun hit her in the gut. She stumbled, and the wall was the only thing keeping her up as she moved her hand to the new wound in her abdomen. Blood poured out of the hole, coating her hand.

The men stopped fighting for a moment, and Dani looked up. Miles stared in horror, and Gavin's scowl turned into a grin.

"You shot her again," Gavin said, and laughed.

"No. Christ, Dani, no," Miles said.

"You won't be alive to see it, but she'll be a Warden this time—no reconditioning needed. I'll raise her like a daughter," Gavin said.

"Asshole," Dani growled. "I'm not dead yet." She fired and struck Gavin in the shoulder.

Miles shoved the man back. Gavin drew his pistol and turned on her, lightning quick, his gun aimed before she could shoot again. But he paused. The flat emptiness in his eyes deepened to a look of longing.

Dani didn't move, wondering for a second if Gavin's reconditioning had ceased its hold on his mind. He removed his finger from the trigger.

Maybe he *could* beat the Wardens' lab experiment.

Gavin blinked and the Warden was back. He moved his finger to the trigger, and she fired several times. Most of her shots missed, but she got him in the arm, chest, and neck—the last one being a critical hit. He collapsed, and blood spilled from his wounds.

Dani slid to the floor and closed her eyes.

CHAPTER
41

Dani opened her eyes, but the mix of pain and growing weakness tempted her to close them again. Oliver and Mary arrived at her side, and Mary took the gun from her hand.

Miles knelt next to Dani, and his hand trembled when he touched her cheek. "I'm sorry. I'm so sorry."

Alex sat up, but she was unsteady.

Dani cried out when Mary's hands pressed into the wound on her side. Her friend was only trying to slow the bleeding, but the act made the pain much worse.

"I don't mean to hurt you," Mary said.

Dani nodded, but the pain was unbearable. Her breathing quickened, and she felt both cold and dizzy. She *really* wanted to sleep.

"We can't stay here, Miles. She's going into shock," Mary said.

"Dad, what do we do?"

Miles turned to his son. "Does this place have a med bay?"

"The only medical stuff I saw was a basic med kit in Rowan's bathroom," Oliver said.

Alex rubbed the side of her head when she spoke. "We have the gear we used on you in our packs."

"Packs are in the septic holding area," Mary said.

Dani turned her head when she noticed a blue light. Gavin.

Mary frowned and looked at Miles. "Finish that asshole."

Dani touched Miles's arm and nodded. "Kill him mid-regen." She took Oliver's hand. "Oliver, look at me. Only me."

He met her gaze and didn't turn around when his father moved to stand over Gavin. Dani kept her eyes on Oliver with Miles in her peripheral vision. He drove his knife into Gavin's chest. The regen glow stopped, and Gavin was gone forever.

Miles returned and scooped Dani into his arms. "Mary, take point. Ollie, help Alex. We're taking the lift."

Dani tried to control her breathing, but fear and growing weakness made concentrating difficult. She needed to tell him something about the lift but couldn't remember what it was. Miles held her close to him, but she was jarred when he ran. They entered the lift, and she remembered what she wanted to tell him. Dani threw her arm out to block Alex from programming it to the lowest floor.

"We can't go all the way down," Dani said. "Stop one or two levels below ground, then use the stairs. They know we're here, but we don't have to broadcast to them exactly what level we're on with a lift stopped in the bowels of the building where it shouldn't be."

Alex stared at Dani without moving, so Mary reached around her to program the lift as Dani instructed. The doors closed, as did Dani's eyes.

Miles shook her. "Hey!"

She opened her eyes a little. They opened more when Mary pressed her hand against Dani's wound again during the ride.

Dani groaned and spoke through a tightened jaw. "You're doing that on purpose."

"If it keeps you awake, yeah," Mary said.

The lift stopped, and Dani sighed when Mary released her

wound. Mary stepped out first and gestured for the others to follow. They headed for the stairs, with Mary in the lead. Oliver held the door open for Alex, and then Miles stepped through with Dani.

"Go," Miles said to his son. "Stay ahead of us."

Oliver headed down after Alex, and Miles tucked Dani tighter against him.

"This is gonna hurt like hell. Ready?" Miles asked her.

She nodded, but she could not have prepared for what came next. Each step sent bolts of pain through her. She buried her face in his chest armor to muffle her screams. She passed out before he reached the next floor.

Dani came to and turned her head when someone touched her face. There were voices around her.

"Is she dead?" Oliver asked.

"No," Miles said. His next words were whispered into her ear. "I need you to stay with us, Dani."

"Her blood pressure is low and her heart rate is too fast," Alex said.

"I don't need a MedPanel to tell me that," Mary said. "Put it down and help."

When Dani opened her eyes again, she was lying on the floor next to a septic holding tank. She yelped when her injured wrist was jarred.

Alex snapped vials into a patch on the back of one hand while Miles did the same to her other hand. Mary knelt at her side, her hands and forearms were smeared with blood. She worked furiously to stop the bleeding with different dressing types and a healing pen. The damage done by the plasma pistol was too much for the pen to fix. Oliver knelt by Dani's feet and watched her as his tears fell in silence.

Blood was everywhere—too much blood—and Dani knew she was dying. Her cycle of being killed by friendly fire and with a gun in her hand wasn't broken. Tears slid down the sides of her face while she stared upward. *I don't want to forget again. I want to remember.*

"Goddammit, I can't get the bleeding to stop," Mary said. She glanced up. "Alex, keep giving her the volume expanders."

"I'm out," Alex said.

"Miles, give her more," Mary said.

"I'm out too."

Mary shook her head. "No! There has to be more. Oliver?"

"I gave Alex and Dad everything I found that matched the medicine names you told me." He'd already emptied every pack. The contents were scattered across the floor around him. None of it was anything that could help Dani.

"Look again," Mary said.

Dani desperately wanted to close her eyes and rest a minute, but she forced her eyes to stay open. "Mary, stop."

"No," she said.

"I don't want to die. I don't want to forget. But every second you stay here working on me puts you and the others at risk. You can't save me." More tears spilled from her eyes.

Mary put her hand on Dani's shoulder. "I have to *try.*" She went back to work. "Alex, what else do you have in your stash?"

Alex shuffled through vials, calling out names of antibiotics and other things.

"Hit her with the steroid," Mary said. "It can't hurt at this point. Then look through what Miles has left."

Alex snapped the vial to the patch on Dani's hand before changing sides with Miles.

He leaned closer to Dani and kissed her. "I'm sorry I did this to you."

"It wasn't your fault or Oliver's. He needed the armor; I

didn't. I am sorry this is happening. I don't want to forget you."

Alex paused. "Forget? What does she mean?"

"Shut up and keep working," Mary said.

Dani wasn't afraid of dying; she just didn't want to forget him again. She'd regen and lose all her memories of Jace, Hattie, Mary, Oliver, and Miles. She'd even forget Brody. "I love you."

"I know. I love you too."

"There's nothing here but stuff if she arrests," Alex said after sorting through the remaining vials.

"We're not there yet, but keep them close," Mary said.

Dani was wondering if Alex had found something to give her when the pain lessened. Her vision blurred. She tried to fight the overwhelming fatigue taking over her mind, but she couldn't keep her eyes open any longer.

"No, no, no. Dani. Dani!" Miles said.

She tried to respond to him but couldn't.

"Her pressure is dropping," Alex said.

"Fuck. *Fuck!*" Mary said.

"We're dressed as Wardens. Is there a hospital on the base?" Oliver asked. "We can go in and tell them Dani was injured in one of the blasts. I can tell them I'm a regen to explain why I'm dressed like this and look young."

"Wardens just die and regen," Alex said. "They don't need a hospital."

"They have babies and children, right?" Oliver asked. "Don't those need some sort of care until they get older?"

"I don't know!" Alex said.

Dani wanted to respond. Oliver's idea was a good one, except he couldn't lie worth a damn. Neither could Miles. Plus, Oliver was wearing his school clothes from when he was kidnapped and now wearing a Warden chest piece over his top. It wouldn't work.

"Miles, put your hand here and hold pressure," Mary said. "There has to be something else in this kit."

The renewed pain helped pull Dani's mind from the darkness. She forced her eyes open finally, and Miles was with her.

"Stay with us," he said.

Dani forgot what she wanted to say—something about Oliver's clothes. She was dying; she remembered that part and figured her memories were already beginning their exit. Fresh tears filled her eyes at the sight of Miles and Mary trying so hard to save her. Miles attempted a smile at her, but she knew his heart was breaking again.

I don't want to forget.

I don't want to forget.

Her eyes closed. *I won't . . .*

Her head rolled to the side when unconsciousness took over.

CHAPTER
42

Rowan passed through his quarters, and they were empty. Items in the kitchen had been knocked over, but he noted that the missing ones were those needed to care for an infant. Ella must have left with his children, and that gave him hope despite the gnawing loss of Ana. He needed for Dani to be captured quickly so he could get to HQ and displace his ineffective VR. His long strides carried him out of his quarters and back to the stairs. He jogged down them to Ana's body and followed the trail of blood heading down the steps.

His Wardens provided updates over the comm for which levels they'd cleared, but Rowan didn't care. He only wanted to know when they found something. He wasn't paying attention to which level he was on when he followed the droplets of blood out of the stairwell.

The path he followed made no sense, but he continued on. He rounded a turn in a corridor and spotted Gavin Marcus. Blood was pooled all around the body. Plasma pistol shots to his body were partially healed but not the stab wound to his chest. He'd been murdered mid-regen. Rowan found another area of blood nearby. There were multiple smears on the wall and floor near another pool. In whatever fight had happened in this hallway, Marcus had lost, as had someone else. The blood that had been spilled was too great for a human or Echo to survive for long.

He had an easier time following the newest trail than he had had with the droplets. Rowan arrived at a lift where the blood ended.

"All teams converge on the lifts in the center of the building," he said, noting a marker on the wall. "I'm on level three. Cover all stairwells and floors, and work your way down. Do *not* recall the lifts. Contact me before engaging the intruders. They are armed."

Miles didn't want to believe that not only was Dani dying, but she was dying *again* at his hand. The horror of realizing he'd shot her had stunned him into complete disbelief, begging for it to not be real. He'd had the recurring nightmare in his sleep after shooting her the first time more than fifteen years ago. The dream always made his racing heart feel like it was going to come out of his chest, and he was soaked with sweat.

In her efforts to end his fight with Gavin, she'd put herself at risk, and it was going to kill her. Miles found it difficult to breathe, and he wished this nightmare to end, except with Dani alive and well. Mary barked orders at Alex as they continued to try to save Dani. Miles stayed out of their way the best he could without leaving her. He held her head with one hand and passed his fingertips over her face. She hadn't regained consciousness since the last time she passed out, and she needed a miracle.

"Ollie."

His son sprang up from his knees to go around Mary to join his father.

"Talk to her," Miles said.

Oliver shook his head and wiped at his tears. "I don't want to tell her goodbye."

"No, that's not what I mean."

"But she's dying."

"I know. I want you to talk to her for a minute while I talk to Mary. Let her know we're with her."

Oliver nodded and leaned down to speak to Dani.

Miles patted his son's shoulder and wished he could tell him everything would be fine.

"Mary, what else can we do for her?" Miles asked.

"I'm out of everything that might help. She needs a surgeon, and even that might not—" Mary shook her head.

"Will moving her do any additional harm?"

"No."

"We can't stay here. Rowan will eventually find us. I can carry her, but I think we need to find somewhere else to stay for a while."

Alex waved her hands at them. "Wait. What am I missing? We can leave now and let her regen on the way."

Miles frowned. "Dani will come back as a child younger than Ollie and won't remember anything, including us."

"What? Dani said she had memory gaps, but she never said she forgot *everything*. That's not normal. How is that possible?"

Mary turned on Alex. "How the fuck would we know anything about Echo biology?"

Miles passed his hand over his face. When he looked up, his eyes widened. Alex had turned away to draw her pistol so Mary wouldn't see the action. Alex's weapon came up, and Miles lunged across Dani's body to deflect the shot upward.

Mary rammed her shoulder into Alex's chest. The women tumbled to the floor, and Miles wrestled the pistol from Alex's hand.

"Fucking vermin." Alex drove her fist into Mary's jaw. "You don't deserve this planet. It's ours!" She struck Mary again.

Mary withstood the punches, flashed a vicious grin complete with blood-smeared teeth, and returned her own blow.

"Dad! She's not breathing."

Miles desperately wanted to go to Dani, but he couldn't abandon Mary until Alex was subdued. Alex and Mary exchanged strikes, with Mary delivering the more brutal attack. Alex's determination to kill Mary seemed to wane with the continued battering.

Miles pulled Mary off her and kept the pistol on Alex. "Mary, Dani needs us. Slap an I-cuff on Alex, and we'll deal with her later."

Mary nodded despite the rage in her eyes as she glared at Alex. Once the I-cuff was applied, Mary leaned close to Alex, now completely immobile.

Alex snarled at her. "I should have killed you when I had the chance."

"You won't have another chance. I knew you were full of lies. When I kill you, there will be no regen, Warden."

Miles couldn't feel a pulse in Dani's neck, and she no longer drew breath.

"Dad?" Oliver said with renewed tears.

Miles shook his head. He wanted to breathe for Dani, but it would do no good, she'd lost too much blood. Filling her full of stimulants for her heart wouldn't help with so much of her blood on the floor.

Mary left Alex and began pawing through the remaining vials of medication. "Here," she said, holding one out to Miles.

"No." Miles lifted Dani's upper body and held her close to him.

"We can save her," Mary said.

He shook his head.

Mary grabbed his sleeve. "Miles, please. We can't give up now."

"It's too late for the meds." He lowered his head to put his lips next to her ear. "Dani, listen to me. This body is gone. You're going to regen soon, but this time it will be different. You don't want to forget, so don't. Oliver, Mary, and I are here. We'll never leave you, so you can't leave us. Remember the people who love you. We need you."

The building shook when an explosion struck nearby.

"One of yours?" Miles asked Mary.

"Everything we set has been detonated already. CNA?" she asked.

Alex spat a mouthful of blood on the floor and laughed. "Houston knew we were coming for Dani and did nothing. She won't risk her toy soldiers for a rescue now."

"What do you mean Houston knew?" Mary asked.

"I almost had Dani that night. So close, but you fucked it up. It's your fault I had to take the damn kid instead. So when he's busy suffering from kidnapping trauma for the rest of his life, assuming he lives, he can thank you."

Miles tried to ignore what Alex said. He trusted Houston, or he thought he did. Alex was distracting them from their bigger problem with Dani.

"Dad," Oliver said, and he nodded at Dani's gunshot wound.

A blue glow began at the wound and grew brighter. Miles had never been this close when an Echo regenned. The glow traveled beneath her skin, and the wound started to heal and close. Miles resumed talking to Dani. He didn't know what else to do other than speak to her the way she'd spoken to him after the blast that had destroyed the planning room.

She writhed as she healed, and Miles held his breath, waiting for her to transform as she physically returned to a child. The bruises and cuts to her face faded and disappeared, but the blood remained. The bruised lump on her wrist shrank until it vanished as the bones repaired themselves. Her movement stopped when the glow faded, and her adult size remained unchanged.

Miles stared at her and removed the patches from the backs of her hands. She was healed and didn't need them anymore.

"She's supposed to regen to a kid," Oliver said. "This isn't the same as what Jace had in his journal. Keep talking to her, Dad."

"Dani, you're in control of this regen now. You won't return to that prewar child. The people with you now are the ones who will always be with you. Remember us."

Dani's eyes remained closed as she drew in her first ragged breath. Her breathing became easier as Miles continued to hold her.

The building trembled again as multiple blasts in the area shook the structure. A crack developed in a wall, and bits of debris fell from the ceiling.

Mary placed her hand on Dani's head. "Feel free to wake up any time now, darling."

Miles touched Dani's cheek, and her eyes fluttered open for a moment before she closed them again. She groaned.

"I thought she was supposed to be healed," Oliver said. "She looks like she's in pain."

"It'll pass," Miles said. He hoped it was true.

Dani took a deep breath and opened her eyes. When her gaze settled on Miles, she startled. He reflexively held her tighter, which only worsened her panic.

"Shit. Sorry." Miles relaxed his grip on her.

Dani thrashed in his arms until she broke free and scrambled away from him to sit huddled against the wall.

"You're safe, Dani," Oliver said.

She pressed against the wall. She lowered her head, buried her hands in her hair, and began to shiver.

Alex laughed. "The memory loss can't be the genetic

enhancement Rowan wanted from her. She forgot you despite your pathetic pleas."

"You're dead," Mary said as she rose to approach Alex.

"Christ, Mary, not in front of Ollie," Miles said.

Dani's head came up. "Christ, Mary. Christ, Mary?" She shook her head and frowned. "That's not right."

Oliver inched closer to Dani. "It is right. Mary is your friend." He removed his Warden jacket and eased nearer to her.

"It doesn't sound right," Dani said.

Miles had no idea what she meant.

The boy offered her the jacket. "Here. You're shivering."

CHAPTER
43

Dani was already pressed against the wall, so she couldn't back away from the boy and the jacket he held out to her.

"Keep it," she said, and wondered why the words sounded familiar.

The four people in the room watched her, but she didn't recognize any of them. Dani stared at her blood-covered, trembling hands. She picked at her bloodied shirt with a hole in the side. She slipped her hand under her shirt and felt the skin beneath it. There was no sign of a wound or scar. She looked up again. *Christ, Mary* repeated in her mind.

One woman was on the floor and bound. The other woman, the man, and the boy didn't move, and Dani noticed the man and woman were also bloodied. *My blood?* An image flashed in her mind.

"Uh, trees. Blood. A truck." She closed her eyes for a moment, trying to remember more. "'Christ, Mary, what's wrong?'" Dani said, and she nodded. "That's what I said before. That's the right one."

"What's she talking about?" the boy asked, and the man shushed him.

"Three trucks." Dani looked up and pointed at the woman. "And you."

"Yeah, I'm Mary. You and I were in one of three transport trucks when Wardens attacked. You saved my life that day."

As Mary approached, Dani pushed herself to her feet, taking a moment to steady herself. Her left side was sore.

Dani extended her bloody hands. "What happened?"

"You're an Echo, and you just regenned. I don't have the time to explain everything, but you can trust me. This is Ollie and his father, Miles. We're also your friends."

"You can't trust her, Dani. I'm Alex, and you belong with me. Mary is one of the humans who attacked our transport that day. That's why you remember her. She's dangerous."

Dani's gaze shifted to the woman on the ground.

Rowan's techs acknowledged their orders through the comm. He wanted to check every level down to where the lift was stopped on a sublevel. The Wardens radioed in various updates of cleared floors.

"Sir, we found a significant amount of blood on sublevel one. The lift is stopped here."

"Hold until I get there," Rowan said. He bolted down the stairs to rejoin his team.

When he arrived, he examined the blood on the floor. He hated not having his elite troops with him; they would not have stepped in and smeared the blood trail as the technicians had. It took him an extra minute to figure out which way the intruders had gone.

"With me," he said as he started for the far stairs.

His troops created a thunderous rumble within the stairwell as they marched down behind Rowan. He stopped and checked each sublevel for more blood in case his prey had doubled back instead of just going down into the bowels of the building. Once certain they hadn't left the stairs for that floor, Rowan led his team down to the next level.

"Sir, what is your location?" a woman said into his comm. "Curtis sent us to reinforce your numbers."

"Sublevel four," Rowan said.

"Copy. En route now."

"Negative. Hold on the ground level."

"Yes, sir."

Rowan split his techs. "I want you four to circle to the right. You four will go left. You two are with me, and we'll move through the center corridors. I suspect they're in the far edge of the building near the waste centers. They have at least one saboteur with them, so pay attention to where you are going and what you're stepping on."

"Yes, sir," the collective answered.

The Wardens began to split up, and Rowan started through the building. Dani and the others had nowhere else to go. The blood led to this level, and there was no way out.

"Sir, we found a blocked access point, and we'll have it cleared in a moment."

Rowan's feet slid to a stop. "Don't—"

A blast interrupted him. His comm filled with screams and panicked chatter as the other technicians rushed to help the injured.

"Stop where you are. Do not approach the blast site."

CHAPTER
44

"Shit," Mary said. "They found the entry I rigged with a few surprise charges." She moved toward the door and pulled a grenade from a pocket on her jacket. She armed it, yanked open the door, threw the grenade, slammed the door shut, and moved away from it.

The blast ripped through the corridor and shook the room.

"That won't buy us much time." Mary hauled Alex to a seated position. "Miles, put a gun on her."

He drew his pistol and aimed it at Alex. Mary deactivated the I-cuff and stepped back to draw her own gun.

"Remove your armor and toss it to Dani," Mary said.

"Dani, they're about to kill me," Alex said. "She just threw a grenade at *our* people. You and I are Echoes. They're humans, and they want us dead. They're not your friends."

Mary stalked closer to Alex with the gun. "Take the jacket off or I remove it after I relocate your head to the wall."

Dani frowned and shook her head. She wasn't sure of anything. She leaned forward to place her hands on her knees. She needed time to think, but her thoughts were unorganized, and the rising tension around her wasn't helping. She flinched when the heavy black jacket landed at her feet.

The boy picked it up for her. "You were injured before because you gave me your jacket to keep me safe."

His voice seemed familiar. "Ollie. Your name? No, that's not right either," Dani said.

"You call me Oliver. Or when you're irritated, it's Christ, Oliver."

"Street urchin."

Oliver smiled. "Yeah, you call me that too."

She straightened and took the jacket. "This is Warden armor." Dani remembered a war and terrifying people wearing the black gear.

Once Mary had Alex restrained again, she knelt and dug through a pack on the floor. The man Mary had called Miles approached Dani.

"We're not Wardens. We've taken their gear and are dressed like them to blend in. We live in Maine and came to Boston because that woman kidnapped my son, Oliver." Miles waved his pistol toward Alex. "There *are* Wardens in that corridor, and they're coming for us."

His voice sounded *very* familiar. *Maine. Boston. Kidnapped.* These words resonated in her mind as being true. *I'm a Brigand, not a Warden or Commonwealth soldier.* She knew the difference between the three entities and was somehow certain that she knew which one she belonged to. Dani pulled the jacket on and fastened it closed.

"Don't go with them," Alex said.

Mary grabbed the front of Alex's shirt. She drew her arm back as her hand formed a fist.

"Stop," Dani said.

Mary froze, her fist poised to strike. She lowered her hand and backed away when Dani approached Alex.

Dani knelt and touched Alex's face.

The woman smiled. "See? You know me."

Dani had recalled touching someone's face, but the face in her memory was blurred. *Faces.* The images in her mind cleared, and she saw both Miles and Mary, not Alex. "I don't," Dani said, removing her hand. "My mind is a fucked-up mess, but I do know you're lying." She turned to Mary. "Fully immobilize her. She's not to speak again." Dani stood and traded places with Mary.

"No! Wait!" Alex said.

Alex's struggle ended when Mary reprogrammed the I-cuff and Alex could only breathe and blink.

Dani wanted to know more about her ties to Mary and Miles, but she decided to hold her many questions.

"We need to leave now, yes?" Dani asked.

"Yep," Mary said as she pulled explosives from one pack, prepped them, then placed them in another. She then programmed a pair of detonators. Dani watched her as she worked and knew what Mary was doing, including configuring the devices properly. *Saboteurs. Mary and I are sabs.*

Mary left a charge next to Alex. "Miles, keep track of Oliver, and I'll make sure we don't lose Dani. Once we're out of this room, I'll set more charges during our exit to bring the place down or at least cripple the shit out of it." Mary tossed the extra pack to Dani.

"What about Alex?" Oliver asked.

"She's not going anywhere," Mary said.

"You're going to blow her up with the building?" Oliver asked.

"Alex attacked the base, injured and killed some of your friends at school, and kidnapped and dragged you to Boston so that bitch could beat you. Yeah, Oliver, Dani and I saw her hit you. Alex goes with the building. Miles, get him out of here through the garbage holding area to the back exit."

Miles didn't move and continued to stare at Mary.

"*Now!*"

Miles turned Oliver around by his shoulder. "Who hit you? When?"

"Ana. The lady Dani killed," Oliver said.

Miles put his arm around Oliver's shoulders and they left.

Dani was filled with a sudden horror, and her heart quickened. "Who did I kill, Mary?"

"Someone who deserved it."

"When?"

Mary didn't answer and placed Alex's pistol into the empty holster at Dani's hip. "You'll need that. Go." She ushered Dani out of the room.

Rowan's techs knew their gear, but they had spent too much time in the labs instead of in actual combat. They hadn't fallen for just one trap, but two.

He screamed orders into the comm, and finally his panicking techs began to listen. "Stay the fuck where you are. Do not move. I don't care who is down. *Don't fucking move!*"

Rowan led his group to the blast site and surveyed the damage and bodies. Curtis had just lost half of his R&D lab techs. The pair of explosions had ripped them apart, and a regen couldn't fix that kind of damage. A few others were badly wounded but alive.

He couldn't count on his squeamish techs to do what needed to be done, so Rowan pulled his knife. He knelt next to the closest wounded Warden.

"I can't wait around for you to bleed to death, then regen," Rowan said.

The man nodded.

Rowan called out, "I'll do this to each of you so you can regen now and get your asses back up and into the fight. We have humans to kill."

The man on the floor opened the center of his armored jacket, and the two other seriously injured Wardens began opening their jackets.

He rammed the blade into the man's chest. The man groaned for only a moment before he slumped to the side.

Rowan moved to the next injured Warden and the next. Once finished, he continued beyond the carnage to the garbage hold. He checked for traps, then eased the door open, spotting Alex lying on the floor and immobilized. Her eyes were wide, and an explosive charge lay on the floor next to her. Rowan ducked back into the corridor and closed the door.

"Are any of you equipped to disarm a bomb?" Rowan asked.

"Yes, sir," a female Warden said, stepping forward.

"Good. There is—"

The explosion threw him into the wall, and the door left its hinges and slammed into him. His helmet and armor protected him for the most part. He shoved the door off and stood. *These people will die so slowly once I have them.*

Dani walked ahead of Mary and spun when an explosion rocked the building.

Mary's stride never changed, and she tossed the detonator aside. "No more Alex."

"Couldn't you wait until we were farther away? Wait. Why isn't the building coming down on us?"

"That one was just for her. I'll nuke the building once we're out. If you can fish the rest of your memories out of that head of yours, darling, it sure would be helpful." Mary took the pack and urged Dani forward.

"Darling? Are you and I—"

"Nope, but you and Miles are."

"Miles? How—"

"Go, Dani."

After a few stumbling steps, she stopped resisting Mary's shoves to herd her forward. Mary stopped Dani periodically to remove an explosive from a pack and plant a charge. They made another stop in the garbage area for Mary to set her final device. Miles and Oliver came back to them.

"We can't leave that way," Miles said. "Wardens are all over this lowest level since someone announced our presence with a couple of blasts. We have to go up."

"The garbage chute." Dani wasn't sure how she knew that information.

Mary climbed up the side of a container and pulled open a hatch. She looked up into the chute, then peered down and grinned. "Found my tranqed Warden from earlier. He's in one piece, so I guess we can go up without getting ourselves mulched for compost."

Mary disappeared into the chute. Dani followed and helped pull Oliver into the tube.

"Oh, gross." Oliver gagged.

Dani didn't mind the smell; she'd been in worse situations. *Sewers.* She remembered being in those before and sometimes in them with Miles. *When?*

She helped Oliver climb up the tube a few yards by pushing her feet, back, and hands into the sides to scoot upward. Miles climbed in last, and when he pulled the latch closed, they were submerged in darkness. They continued their ascent until Mary stopped. She pulled her pistol from its holster and eased a hatch open.

Mary crawled out through the hatch and then popped her head back in. "Clear."

Dani moved up the chute and climbed out. She pulled Oliver through next and extended her hand to Miles to help him. Many of the glass windows on the ground level had been blown because of other explosions and a nearby building that had collapsed. Dust and smoke filtered around them, making it difficult to see and breathe, but the obscuring smoke would help them slip out undetected.

The quicker path out the front of the building was more dangerous, more exposed. "Go out the back and take the alley to the left of the courthouse," Dani said. "Make another left, then turn right on Beacon. Keep the park on your left until you get to Back Bay. We can disappear in there." Her brow creased. "Have I been here before?"

Mary took her arm. "More or less. C'mon."

Their boots crunched on shattered glass as they jogged to the rear of the building. Mary climbed up and over the frame first. Dani and Miles paused to help Oliver past the jagged shards and handed him off to Mary. A plane shrieked by overhead.

"Holy shit," Miles said. "The CNA is here. That's one of the new birds."

Rowan pulled a piece of shrapnel from his arm. The wound wasn't deep, but it made him furious. He needed a new plan for getting into the garbage hold.

"Spread out. They cannot leave this level. You've seen what they can do. They will kill us without a second thought. I want them captured so they can pay for the murder of your friends and colleagues."

"Yes, sir."

He enjoyed his techs' interest in revenge on a personal level. *Revenge. Great motivator.* Ana deserved to have waves upon waves of human blood shed for how she'd died, but by the end of their search of the sublevel, he had no prisoners. "*Fuck!*" Rowan took a deep breath to calm his anger. He needed to remain in control.

"Intruders spotted on ground floor," the female Warden from Curtis reported into his comm.

How the hell did they get past us? "Pin them down if you can." Rowan gestured for his remaining techs to come with him as he started back toward the stairs.

He raced up and emerged on the ground level with his Wardens behind him.

The whine of a quake rifle caught Dani's attention. She glanced back and spotted multiple Wardens in full tactical gear, armed and approaching. She tackled Miles, taking him out through the window with her before the shot struck the side of the frame. It blasted the metal and concrete around the window frame. It shuddered and began to crumble. They were pelted by debris, but nothing large enough to crush them—yet.

Rowan rounded a corner in time to see Dani dive out a broken window.

"Circle around," he said, and he gestured to his team to split them again. He addressed the Warden wielding the quake rifle. "Put another shot on that frame to drop debris on them."

Rowan strode forward. He slipped his plasma rifle strap over his shoulder and pulled his knife. When he attacked Dani, he would make it personal.

The quake rifle's whine began again, and they had nowhere to go. If they stood to run, they'd be shot. If they stayed where they were, the Wardens could just keep shooting parts of the building to drop on them. Dani and Miles pulled Mary and Oliver closer to them, and they huddled together outside the building next to the wall beneath the half-destroyed window frame.

The plane released a rocket that obliterated several buildings southeast of their location. The impact tore through the lower levels of the officers' quarters, with smoke and dust billowing out of the broken windows and shattering the rest.

When debris blasted through the ground floor. Rowan was caught in the destruction and tossed. His spine was broken, and part of his chest was crushed with the impact. He was dead before his corpse finished sliding across the floor.

CHAPTER
45

Dani coughed and was disoriented for a moment. She couldn't see much, but figured the Wardens standing in that lower level had to be dead—for now. She took a deep breath before climbing over the window frame to reenter the building.

Her boot snagged on the frame, and she pitched forward. Her less-than-graceful entry landed her on a Warden body. Her hand squished into something soft, wet, and gross. She yelped, losing part of the breath she was holding, and scrambled away from the corpse. She was hastily dragging her hand across her armored jacket to wipe away the mess when the burning in her chest reminded her why she'd reentered the building.

She crawled back toward the body, and her eyes burned and teared from the smoke and dust. The Warden lay facedown, turned away from her, and she couldn't see his face through the faceplate. She was glad. Dani slipped her hands under the seam between the Warden's helmet and jacket and removed it. The inside of the helmet was mercifully free of gore, and she slipped it over her head.

The mechanisms inside the helmet adjusted to her head, and internal filters removed the smoke. She drew in a small breath, grateful to find it free of dust and smoke, then took a deeper one. Her visibility improved without the smoke burning her eyes. The optical mechanisms in the helmet enhanced her vision in the smoke-obscured conditions. She saw the Warden's body clearly now. He was so twisted at the waist that no spine could remain intact with that kind of trauma. There was a tear in his side that left a loop of intestine exposed. That's what she'd put her hand in when she fell, and she almost gagged.

She needed helmets for the others, so she moved away from the body. The helmet-to-helmet vision made her able to see through the faceplates of other helmets, but somehow she'd already known they worked like that. She bypassed two bodies where blood had spattered the insides of the faceplates. Another corpse's head and helmet had been flattened by falling concrete, so she didn't bother to go near that corpse except to grab the higher-tech rifle lying next to its former owner. She continued her scramble among the bodies until she had three rifles and three helmets taken from Wardens not crushed by building debris.

She spotted a fancier rifle and approached it. Her insides knotted with nausea when she found the broken body of one Warden missing a head. The nausea worsened when another image of a mostly headless woman filled her mind. For fear of puking inside her helmet, Dani had to leave. She exchanged one weapon for the fancy one, slipped the rifle straps over her shoulder, and carried the helmets in her arms.

She returned to the blown-out window and turned to sit in a mostly glassless base of the frame. The armored trousers protected her from any cuts as she shifted to swing one leg over the frame and out.

Arms appeared and wrapped around her torso. She was yanked through the window and slammed to the ground on her back. She lost the helmets in the fall and held her hands up when the end of a plasma pistol was rammed under her helmet and pressed against her neck. "Don't shoot!" she said.

"Jesus, Dani." Mary withdrew the pistol and coughed against the dust.

Miles helped her back up with an apologetic smile. "Sorry."

Oliver picked up one of the helmets and put it on.

"You weren't answering on the comm," Miles said. "Why the hell did you go back in there?"

"This is much better," Oliver said. "Dad, put one on. Way easier to breathe with it on."

"What he said," Dani said with a wave of her hand toward Oliver. She removed her helmet as Mary and Miles put their helmets on. The comm had become dislodged at some point, so she tucked it back into her ear canal. "This thing working now?"

Miles nodded. "Yeah."

Dani put her stolen helmet back on, slipped the rifles from her shoulder, and passed a standard plasma rifle to Miles and kept the other one. She handed the advanced-looking rifle with more gadgets and mounted optics to Mary. "Thought you would like this one."

Mary took the weapon and looked it over. "Yes, indeed."

"What is it?" Oliver asked.

"Not a damn clue, but it's fancy as hell and I already like it," Mary said. "I'll figure out how it works."

Dani waved toward the building. "Lots of dead Wardens in there, but some may have survived. I don't think we should stick around to finish dispatching the dead. They'll start to regen any minute now."

"Agreed," Mary said. "I can blow the rest of my charges once we're clear. Ideally that will drop the building on them and permanently end several of the bastards at once."

"Let's go," Miles said. He moved to the front, and Oliver

followed. Mary and Dani jogged behind them, keeping Oliver between them and his father.

Rowan tried to roll to his side, but soreness in his back made him stop. The dust and smoke were suffocating, so he had no choice but to move. His helmet was gone, as were his knife and rifle. The blast had almost torn him in half. He coughed and successfully rolled over on his second attempt. He stood and staggered to the window where the smoke filtered out. He climbed over the frame and sank to his knees.

Breathing was a bit easier, but he wasn't sure what had happened. Regens used up a lot of energy, especially when they required multiple repairs to a damaged body. Rest was the best way to recover, but Rowan had humans in his city who required killing. A few other Wardens tumbled out of the building through the shattered windows. He grabbed the shoulder of one wearing a helmet.

"Get your ass back in there and gather weapons from any of our people who won't be coming back."

"Yes, sir." The woman climbed back through the window.

"Curtis. Status."

"Sir, most of the attacks are on the city's perimeter. Coastal, primarily, with some inland assaults."

"Is there a main force?"

"No, sir. They're scattered around. There are numerous detonations all over the place, so we can't pinpoint where the attacks originate."

"It's all distraction bullshit, Curtis. This is classic Houston tactics, and Aubrey falls for it every fucking time. Stop focusing on the smaller blasts. Houston will be sending in a larger assault. Prep for that, not this small shit."

"Yes, sir. I'll advise the VR."

I recommend shooting her instead. "She won't listen. Persuade the chancellors to override her."

"I will. Sir, I saw the feed of Ana. I am sorry, sir."

"I don't want your condolences. Give me Houston's head while I take Dani's."

"Yes, sir."

Rowan took the rifle offered by the returning Warden. She distributed a few more weapons to others who had lost theirs, then went back inside the building. He gestured for his current troops to regroup and head out. Rowan led them and scanned the ground for blood. He was again thrown when multiple blasts tore through the sublevels of the building.

This time he wasn't killed, but his collision with the concrete when he crashed into the ground left him battered and scraped. He cursed as he returned to his feet. Flames fanned out from the ground floor and leapt up the sides of the building. Any Warden inside the structure during the blast couldn't self-heal if they were ash.

Rowan trembled with rage and spat blood. It didn't matter that he'd provoked the Maine forces into action by abducting the boy. The death of his wife and the destruction of the city was not his fault. If the vice regent had just let him destroy the CNA in Maine, everything would be different.

Two Wardens in the rear of the group were dead, again. He didn't have time to wait for them to regen, so he moved on with the ones he had left.

Dani tried to sort through a mix of memories in her mind. "You and I are sabs, and Miles is an MP. Well, I think he's an MP. Do I have that right?"

"Yeah," Mary said.

"You had a special rifle before, yes?"

"Not as fancy as this one, but yes. I double as a sniper when needed." Mary nodded toward her new rifle. "I can't wait to try this thing out; Wardens always have the best tech. You're remembering more. This is good."

"Is it? A headless woman. Who was that?"

"The person who beat Oliver and tried to kill you. The only times you've ever killed up close have been in self-defense."

Dani's pace slowed, and she grimaced. "I've done this before?"

"Once before to another person trying to kill you and Oliver. You need to remember how much you love that kid first. Then you'll understand why those two people don't matter."

"But—"

A louder rumble made her glance back again. The top corner of the building buckled, then crumbled toward the ground. Additional pieces of the structure did the same. Dani stopped moving and turned to stare when half of the building collapsed. Her mouth went dry as her heartbeat thundered inside her chest and ears. She'd seen this happen before, somewhere, and it had terrified her then as much as it did now. She wanted to run away, hide in a hole, and never come out again—but she remained frozen.

Her next breath came in a gasp, and a violent shiver gripped her.

Mary touched her arm. "We don't have time for sightseeing."

Dani eyes remained fixed on the building.

"Shit. Miles, she's losing it!"

Dani's knees weakened, and she dropped to the ground. She closed her eyes against the dizziness and felt like she was falling. When she opened her eyes, she was on her knees, and Oliver stood between her and the destroyed building. Her visor was open, as was Oliver's, and he had his palms on the sides of her helmet.

"Look at me," he said.

Dani trembled. "It's the hospital, the one for the children."

"It's not. You saw the hospital destroyed the day the war started, but that was a long time ago."

"Jace is with me."

"Jace was your brother."

"Was?"

Oliver winced before answering. "He died last year."

"Do I have other family members?"

"Yeah."

"Where?"

"We're here with you now." Oliver leaned closer to her face, and whispered. "You're my best friend."

Dani stared at him. "We like to skip rocks across the river," she said.

He smiled and nodded.

Dani mirrored his smile. "Oliver." She remembered several instances with the boy, and most of her fear faded. "Brody chases the rocks."

"Yeah."

"I remember you."

"That's good," Oliver said. "We should go instead of staying here in the middle of the street." He closed her visor before closing his own. "C'mon." He took her hand.

Dani nodded, and shifted to stand.

CHAPTER

46

Rowan tried to ignore the pain as he increased his pace to a jog, moving with his team around the buildings in the area.

"Sir?" Curtis asked in his comm.

"Go ahead."

"The chancellors are requesting your immediate presence. They're ready to vote no confidence in Aubrey, but they won't make that move on the VR without you here."

"I'm busy trying to save this city."

"They're aware you're tracking the CNA spies, but they want you to hand it off to another Warden to come here. Sir, VR Aubrey has given orders for you to return."

"I don't care. I'm not done yet."

"The VR is citing treason if you don't."

Rowan laughed—a genuine laugh—in the midst of the chaos and destruction. His wife had been murdered, and countless Wardens had been slaughtered, blown up, crushed, burned, and suffered all manner of torment in death—sometimes permanent death—and Aubrey was threatening charges of treason against *him*.

"Rowan, please," Curtis said.

Rowan had capable people on his team now—not the technicians, but the reinforcements Curtis had sent him. He slowed and glanced at his team to see who would be the best at leading, but he wasn't ready to give up. As they rounded the corner of a building, Rowan stopped. Dani knelt in the street with the boy standing in front of her.

"Sir?" Curtis asked.

Rowan slipped the plasma rifle from his shoulder. "Tell Aubrey to fuck off. Rowan out." He brought the weapon up and looked through the sights. He couldn't stop a grin as he watched his targets. Their helmets hid their faces, but he knew them by their size and shape.

Captain Jackman stood to one side of Dani and the human Brigand called Mary Smith stood on the other side. *They're like bookends.*

He lined the crosshairs up on Jackman's head, then Smith's. Rowan shifted the rifle slightly, but Dani's head was blocked by the teen's body.

One shot, and they would panic and scatter. He wanted to try to capture them alive. They had a lot of suffering to do before he killed them. He wanted to incapacitate Dani first, but the boy never moved. He could easily shoot Jackman or Smith in the helmet and put them down. The helmets could withstand an energy weapon shot, but the wearer would be unconscious before they hit the ground.

Rowan trained the rifle on Jackman and slid his finger to the trigger. Dani was reportedly attached to this man, and Rowan could use him against her. He shifted his sights back to Smith. He remembered her face from the photos Alex had sent him. He imagined humans found Smith attractive, but to him she was detestable. He'd love to put a plasma shot through her face, but her stolen helmet was in the way.

Dani had risked everything to reach Oliver. *He* was the best way to torture her. Rowan moved the sights to the back of the teen's helmet. It was a little too big for his head, and there was a small seam at the base of his neck between the armor and helmet. Dani shifted her position slightly, and Rowan saw that her visor wasn't activated.

The way she knelt meant that if Rowan took the boy's head off, he'd likely take Dani's off with it. He couldn't risk the shot.

Rowan shifted the sights downward a little to the center of Oliver's back and squeezed the trigger.

CHAPTER
47

O liver cried out when the impact from a plasma rifle struck his back and slammed him into Dani. She dropped her rifle and threw her arms around him. A different kind of terror filled her when he slumped against her.

The barrage of shots that followed caught Dani by surprise, and she didn't know what to do. Miles circled around her to put himself between the incoming attack and Dani and Oliver. She lifted Oliver as she stood, and Miles took him from her.

"Leave it," Miles said when she reached for her rifle. "Go!"

Dani drew her pistol and added her return fire to Mary's.

"Holy shit," Mary said. She fired several more shots. "This rifle is amazing. You do *not* want to take a hit from this thing. Goes right through the armor."

Dani tugged on Mary's arm with her free hand. "Can you shoot and retreat at the same time, please."

Mary adjusted a setting on the weapon before firing again. "These optics are fantastic. I can't permanently kill a Warden with a round, but I can put them down for a while before the next regen." Mary fired two more times and laughed. "Fuck me, this thing is deadly! I think I'm in love."

"Move, Mary!" Miles said.

She grumbled as she shifted her position. Dani tried to continue covering their retreat since her pistol could fire faster than the rifles. She just wished she knew who or what she was hitting. The attacking Wardens scattered, giving Dani and the others time to vacate the street. A shot struck Mary in the shoulder, and she fell. Dani fired her weapon as fast as her finger could move, not aiming at any Warden in particular. Her barrage caused the Wardens to thin a little more.

Mary groaned when she tried to stand.

Dani helped her up, and they rejoined Miles. Oliver whimpered in his father's arms, and Dani's relief to know the boy was alive almost made her weep.

They gathered behind a mound of rubble near a scorched crater in the ground. Miles tore at Oliver's jacket to get it open and inspected his son's back. Oliver stirred and yelped when his father's fingers touched the blackened area on the inner layer of armor.

"How bad is it?" Dani asked.

Miles glanced up at her and smiled. "The inner armor you gave him saved his life. Plasma shot went through the jacket. Their energy weapons are better than our outdated armor."

Dani helped Mary sit and began checking her friend's shoulder.

Mary batted Dani's hands aside. "I'm fine. Just pissed off."

Dani glanced at the crater. She assumed the charred, almost lifeless area of ground was a result of the war, but for a reason she couldn't explain, she remembered this area as a park. *Boston Common.*

Oliver groaned.

"It's just a nasty bruise, son. You'll be fine," Miles said.

Dani remembered being shot in the back of her armor before and being unable to move for a moment. A Warden had pressed a pistol to the side of her head while she lay sprawled on the floor. Other memories that followed that event filled her mind, and she blinked several times. She remembered a Warden's face and part of a name. *Rowe? Roman? No. Rowan. That's it.*

Rowan had had Oliver kidnapped to draw her to him, and Dani had accidentally killed a woman while trying to get Oliver back. Ana, Rowan's wife, was the mostly headless woman with her brain splattered on the wall in a stairwell of the building that had just semi-collapsed.

"Fuck," Dani muttered. More memories returned from the battle in Portland, Rowan's attempt to recondition her, and several other events leading up to now. Her hand with the pistol shook, as did the rest of her. The Wardens would regroup and come after them in force. Mary, Miles, and Oliver would be slaughtered and Dani captured for reconditioning if they didn't escape.

Mary touched Dani's hand. "Hey. Did you hear me? Are you injured?"

"Uh, no. No, I'm fine."

"You're shaking."

"Yeah, I do that sometimes." Dani took a deep breath to refocus her thoughts. "Oliver, can you run?"

He nodded, but grimaced when he tried to stand.

"Miles, carry him and take the lead. Mary and I will cover our retreat to Back Bay." Dani peeked around the rubble and saw what she had feared. The Wardens were reorganizing. One man among them wore no helmet and stood among them giving orders. *Rowan.* Two small groups broke off from the larger one. If Dani and the others waited any longer, they'd be flanked in minutes.

Miles knelt, and Oliver crawled onto his father's back. He hooked his legs around Miles's waist and looped his arms around his neck. Miles stood with his rifle, and Mary was ready with hers. Dani was the last one to her feet, and they left. A few shots were fired their way, but Miles led them to an area with more cover. The additional navigation around debris slowed their progress, but they didn't have a constant barrage of shots fired at them during their retreat.

They stayed close to what was left of Boston Common, taking the more direct route toward Back Bay. Dani's idea was to disappear into the many remaining structures, hide, and hope the Wardens decided to deal with the larger attack on the city instead of three adults and a teenager. Correction. Rowan wouldn't stop hunting *her*; he was a fucking madman.

"Miles, up ahead there will be rows of multilevel buildings—what's left of them," Dani said through the comm.

"Yep. I know what you're thinking," he said.

"Oh." Dani was about to ask how he knew, but an unfamiliar woman's voice broke through the comm.

"Dani! Took you goddamn long enough, Anton. Dani, report."

"Uh," Dani said.

"Dani, you copy?"

She wasn't sure who this new person in her ear was or how she knew her. "Yeah? Who is this?"

"*What?*"

Dani winced with the woman's shriek inside her ear, and Mary snorted a laugh.

"Colonel Houston," Miles said between labored breaths as he continued to jog with his son on his back. "We ran into a complication."

"Oh, shit. Please don't tell me she died and her mind reset to ground zero," Houston said.

"Sort of," Mary said. "It's in the process of rebooting."

"Speed it up, goddammit! Captain Jackman, report. Is Alex with you?"

Dani didn't know if Captain Jackman was another title for Mary or Miles.

"Negative," Miles said. "We learned she was a Warden; she's dead."

Oh. At least she had that question answered.

"We've been trying to reach you with that warning, but couldn't find the right frequency until now. Do you have your son?"

While Miles updated the woman called Colonel Houston, Dani wondered how she had managed to piss off someone she didn't know. "Why is she so angry?" Dani asked Mary.

"She's always like that. Don't worry about it."

"That's right. I am. Mary, you and Miles will catch hell for letting Dani die," Houston said before returning to her discussion with Miles.

"They didn't let me die," Dani said, glancing at Mary. "It wasn't anyone's fault." She recalled more details of the incident; Miles had accidentally shot her. Again. Dani stumbled with the distraction and rush of more memories.

Mary slowed to stay with her, and Dani waved her forward. "I'm good." She returned her attention to the other conversation happening over the comm.

Houston continued. "Negative. Ground support is too far out to assist. We're monitoring a tracker on Mary's boot so we know your general location, but the signal distorts once she's inside buildings."

Mary slowed to search for the offending device on her boot. "She's been tracking me? What the *fuck*?"

Dani shoved her forward. "Doesn't matter now. Go."

"We saw one of the jets," Miles said. "Can you get a helo in to pick us up?"

"Not in Back Bay," Houston said. "You need to find a more open area for extraction."

"Pick us up from a roof," Dani said.

After a brief pause, Houston spoke again. "I'm not hearing

shrieks of protest from Miles or Mary, so make it happen. Radio when you're almost in position and ready for pickup. Houston out."

They neared rows of tightly packed buildings southwest of the overgrown Boston Public Garden. Dani glanced back and spotted three Wardens pausing their pursuit to take aim.

"Take cover to your left!" she barked, and Miles veered left.

A rifle shot passed just above and to the right of Mary's head. She cursed and started to turn to shoot back, but Dani grabbed her friend's jacket and yanked hard to keep her moving. Mary passed in front of her to join Miles behind part of a crumbled building. Dani shifted to follow, but a sharp pain bit into the side of her hip when a plasma rifle shot struck. She twisted with the impact, and her tumble continued when she hit the ground.

"Dani!" Mary started to leave the protective cover.

"Stay there." Dani scrambled to her friends. She winced and held her palm against the now very tender spot on her right hip beneath the charred armor. "The armor absorbed the hit." It wasn't a complete lie. She didn't have a hole torn through her leg, but she'd now have a significant limp. "We need to get off these streets."

Miles had lowered Oliver to the ground, and the teen was able to stand on his own while Miles gasped to catch his breath.

"You and Miles get Oliver to a roof," Mary said. "I can slow these assholes down."

Dani shook her head. "You're out of your goddamn mind if you think that's our new plan. We'll cut a path through here to go three blocks in, find a way into one of the buildings with stairs to roof access, and go from there. If we can't get in, we'll go up using a fire escape." She had some recollection of being on a fire escape before and it not going well, but she couldn't remember the details. "Oliver, you have to run instead of ride. Can you do that?"

"Yeah," he said.

"Dani, you know this area better than any of us," Miles said. "Lead us where you want, Oliver stays behind you, and Mary and I will protect our flanks and rear." He fired several shots at the Wardens while the others left their cover. He followed as Dani led the group on a convoluted route through Back Bay.

They lost the trailing Wardens—for now—but Dani couldn't get into any of the buildings through a door. The proximity tags in the armor wouldn't deactivate the locking mechanisms. A broken window would leave glass that the Wardens might spot. She paused at the base of a building and looked up. Every fire escape was rusted, but the one she stood beneath was at least attached to the structure all the way up.

Dani holstered her pistol and leapt for the lowest part of the fire escape. Mary placed her hand under Dani's boot and pushed to assist. Dani pulled herself up to the base of the fire escape, and when the whole thing didn't detach and fall on them, she reached down. Miles lifted Oliver, and she pulled the boy up to the landing with her.

"Start climbing," she said.

Oliver did as he was told, and Mary was next.

"Mary, can you get high and snipe them as they come down the street?" Dani asked.

"On it."

"Catch up to Oliver and move ahead of him. Shoot when you can, but we must keep moving. We're too exposed on this thing and need our asses on that roof."

Mary gave a sharp nod and started up the stairs.

After Dani helped Miles onto the fire escape, the structure shuddered under their weight and the movement of Mary and

Oliver. A few memories from the last time she was on a fire escape surfaced. Miles had been with her, and she recalled a lot of glass and a damaged ankle.

She touched Miles's arm. "Is this a good idea?"

"Guess we'll find out. C'mon."

Shit.

CHAPTER
48

Rowan roared at this team. "Where the hell did you learn to shoot? We have them outnumbered and outgunned, yet not one of you can manage to put a hole through them?"

His Wardens were at least smart enough to remain silent.

Rowan strode up to one of the remaining techs and snatched the high-end rifle from his hands. "This is the best rifle we have, and it's wasted in your hands." He thrust his plasma rifle at the technician, who took it and stepped back in submission. "You're fucking useless. Who has a quake rifle?"

He was answered with silence until one Warden finally spoke up. "They were all lost in the building with the blasts, sir."

Rowan moved around one of the longer buildings in Back Bay and spotted Dani as she and the others moved upward on a fire escape attached to a seven-story building.

"Perfect!" He gestured to a portion of his troops. "I want you to get inside and use the interior stairs to find roof access. The rest of you are with me. We're going up behind them. I want them captured."

They reached the base of the building, and Rowan gazed up the length of the fire escape. He climbed on, and the structure shook with his added weight. He started up the stairs, but stopped when his comm activated.

"Sir, our access isn't letting us in," one of his Wardens on the ground said.

"Curtis, this is Rowan."

"Yes, sir. Go ahead," Curtis said.

"I'm in Back Bay. Override any building locks for sector two-three-six. We have the intruders located and almost pinned."

"Yes, sir. One second."

More seconds ticked by than Rowan wanted. He started up the fire escape so the rest of his team could begin the climb too.

"Curtis!" Rowan said.

"Working on it," Curtis said. When he spoke again, his voice was lower. "Vice Regent Aubrey is furious. She's monitoring everything I'm doing for you."

Rowan wished he were there with Curtis to put an armor-piercing round through Aubrey's head. It wouldn't completely blow her head off, so she would regen and he'd get to shoot her again. This thought tempted him for the briefest of seconds to abandon his chase of Dani. *No.* He'd capture Dani first, return to HQ, *then* shoot Aubrey. That was the better plan.

"Remind her that we have spies on the ground who I'm actively trying to apprehend, which is a lot more than what she is doing in her Ops chair."

"Sir," Curtis pleaded.

"I understand you're in a horrible position, Curtis. I will be there as soon as I am able. Can you at least get the override?"

"Yes, sir. It's done."

"Start lining up air support for this sector."

Curtis groaned before he responded. "I'll do my best, sir."

"Rowan out."

He really did owe Curtis for every trick he had turned to help Rowan pursue Dani. His soldiers at the building entrance entered, and Rowan returned his attention to Dani. He resumed his ascent. The lowest portion of the fire escape rattled and broke off, taking one of his Wardens with it.

He glanced down at his dead Warden and growled; he would need time to regen. The only way to go was up.

Rowan couldn't hide his annoyance and frustration. Hunting one Brigand Echo had cost him more Wardens than he wished to admit. "Curtis!"

"Sir?"

"Bring in that air support. Intruders are heading up to roof level in Back Bay. Send me more troops too."

"I—"

"Why are you hesitating?"

"Sir, I'm receiving new orders. The CNA jets are too close to taking Ops out entirely. We're moving to our secondary operations center. I need you to meet me there."

"I will as soon as I have our enemies here secured."

"I can send a couple of helos to support you at Back Bay, but the extra soldiers will take some time."

"Send what you can as long as they aren't R&D techs. They can't shoot worth shit."

"Yes, sir. Curtis out."

Rowan halted his ascent so he could stop and aim more accurately. Dani had moved higher up the fire escape and was obscured by the ironwork. He continued after her for another flight, gaining on her position before he paused. She was limping, and he didn't have a clear shot at her. He could put a round through her leg and stop her in her tracks. Rowan shifted his position and found the angle he needed.

He rested the rifle barrel on part of the fire escape for stability, but the foot traffic up the steps caused too much movement. He pressed the stock firmly into his shoulder and watched her through the scope. One of his Wardens stopped next to him, which caused the fire escape to shudder and alter his view through the scope. He'd just missed his window at a clear shot. He ground his teeth, angered with another lost opportunity.

"Don't fucking move!" Rowan said to the Warden next to him.

The man froze and signaled *halt* to the others behind him.

Rowan at least had another viable target going up the stairs after Dani.

"Captain Jackman," Rowan said with a small laugh. He aimed his rifle at the small opening between the rails and steps, put his finger on the trigger, and waited for Jackman to enter his crosshairs.

CHAPTER

49

Dani mentally begged Mary to move faster. Oliver had stayed with her, but Mary had stopped a few times on her ascent to shoot at the Wardens. This just pissed off the Wardens more. Windows shattered around the stairs as they climbed, and their boots crunched over glass. Dani's cheek bled where shards had nicked her face. She and Miles didn't want to risk moving faster and shaking the entire fire escape loose, but they would eventually get shot if they stayed on it any longer.

Mary leaned over a rail and shouted down to Dani. "They're entering the building from the ground."

Dani and Miles picked up their pace, and the fire escape continued shuddering. The entire structure trembled with the Wardens climbing the fire escape.

"You've got company," Mary said.

Dani rolled her eyes. *Company* was the last word she'd use to describe genocidal Wardens, but whatever.

Bolts continued to loosen, and part of the level Dani was on began to pull away from the building. She glanced up and spotted Mary helping Oliver on his final part of the climb. "They're on the roof," she said, and she recklessly scampered upward as fast as her limp allowed, Miles right behind her. He cried out, and Dani's heart sank as she turned.

Mary called to her over the comm, but Dani was focused only on Miles. He crumpled as his knees folded, and his upper body pitched toward the rail. He was going to fall to his death.

She leapt off the step she was on, and her boots struck the landing hard. That portion of the fire escape pulled away from the building, causing her to almost lose her grip on his arm. They swayed toward the rail until Dani put her arms around him. If he fell, he was taking her with him. Her sore hip slammed into the rail, and she grunted with the mix of pain and stress of holding Miles up. His rifle fell from his hand and clattered down a few steps until it made a final bounce before flipping into the air and off the fire escape.

Blood spilled from both openings of a golf-ball-sized hole extending from his lower back through to his abdomen. *Fuck!* Dani holstered her pistol and adjusted her position to try to hold some form of pressure on at least one of the wounds. "Move your feet and get your ass up those last few stairs. Mary, call the helo. Miles is hit."

"On it."

Miles took his first step, groaned, and began to sink to his knees as his head lolled forward. Dani jabbed her fingers into his wound, and he cried out again.

His head came up, and he glared at her. "Christ, do you *want* me to pass out?"

"Move!"

Their progress was too slow. Dani knew she shouldn't do it, but she glanced down anyway. She counted at least six Wardens on the fire escape coming for them. The one in the lead was Rowan. He held the rifle with the fancy gadgets and special rounds like the one Mary had. He had been the one who had shot Miles with a round that his armor couldn't stop. Dani fired her plasma pistol at him until it didn't work. Her pistol was depleted of either rounds or energy. She tossed it aside and pulled Miles's pistol from the holster at his hip.

She looked down again and spotted Rowan half seated and half slumped against a portion of the stairs, grimacing. His head remained intact, but she'd hit him in his armor with enough rounds to slow him down and cause pain. "Ha! Fucker," she said before returning her full attention to Miles.

Mary started to climb back onto the fire escape.

"Stay up there," Dani said. "This thing can't take much more weight. Just grab him when we're close."

Mary nodded and shifted to lie prone on the roof. She extended her hands and pulled on Miles's jacket as soon as he was within reach.

"Where's Ollie?" Miles asked.

"He's waiting a few paces away from the edge to stay clear of the ground fire," Mary said.

Miles nodded. "Good."

Dani hated the weak sound of his voice. He'd bleed out soon and die. She and Mary wrestled him to the roof, and Dani climbed up behind him. They didn't bother trying to get him on his feet again and instead dragged him away from the roof's edge. Oliver rushed to them and trotted beside his father. They had no cover on the roof. It was a great place for a pickup but terrible for hiding and waiting. Before she could ask about the helo, she heard them approaching. *Them?* "Did that colonel person send more than one?"

"Just one with a jet as cover," Mary said.

"Ours either has some extra sounds or we're about to be blown to bits. The fire escape is crawling with Wardens."

"Got it," Mary said. "Houston, tell your jet to come around our position and do a strafing run to take out the Wardens on the fire escape. Miles needs immediate evac."

"Copy that," Houston said.

The jet's weapons could decimate the Warden ground troops in one pass, but Dani and the others didn't have much time left. Wardens began emerging from a roof access point.

"Shit." Mary released Miles and slipped her rifle strap from her shoulder while Dani fired at the ones coming onto the roof from the fire escape.

The pair of helos that arrived belonged to the Wardens. Mary started firing at them, and Dani frantically alternated targets between the two batches of Wardens coming toward them. The Wardens were clearly under orders to capture their prey since they could have shredded Mary and Dani with the amount of firepower they possessed. Instead they fired shots to drive them toward the center of the roof.

The CNA jet swooped around from one of the taller buildings. It arced up and sprayed the side of the building and the fire escape with hundreds of rounds in an instant.

One Warden helo fired a pair of missiles at the jet. The jet counterattacked with its own missiles. The battle above the roof sent Mary and Dani scrambling to cover Miles and Oliver.

Scorching hot air washed over them, and Dani was glad they had their helmets on.

Another helo arrived, and a British voice filled Dani's comm.

"We're landing on the eastern corner of the roof. Can you make it to us?"

"Cam!" Mary said. "Took you long enough. Miles is down and unable to move on his own."

"We'll land and send someone to help you," the Brit said.

Dani and Mary hoisted Miles to his feet. Oliver's face was almost as pale as his father's.

"As soon as you see our people, run to them," Dani said to Oliver. "We'll be right behind you." She hoped he knew the Cam person; she certainly didn't.

The jet providing cover and shooting at the Warden helos created a deafening mix of noise that lessened a little when the Warden helos turned to leave. They were no match for the CNA jet. Instead of pursuing, the jet remained to protect the CNA helo as it landed on the roof.

Oliver sprinted forward, and Dani almost shouted at him to stop until she spotted the two men approaching with rifles and a third person on the deck-mounted gun inside the helo. Miles couldn't stand, so Dani and Mary dragged him across the roof. Her eyes widened when she spotted more Warden helos coming their way.

The roof and surrounding buildings suffered from the onslaught of weapons fire as they tried to destroy the jet.

Blanketed by swirling smoke, Dani lost sight of their helo, but she continued in the direction where she had last seen it. Rather, she *thought* she was going in the right direction. She couldn't see shit.

Men appeared in front of them through the smoke, and Dani yelped, startled by their arrival until she realized they were in CNA uniforms.

Miles collapsed when they reached the helo, and Dani did a quick head count. Oliver was inside the helo and moving closer to the door when a man pulled on Miles to get him inside.

"Stay back," Mary said to Oliver. Then she looked at Dani. "You got him?"

"Yeah." Dani holstered her pistol and looped her left arm around Miles's waist. She used her right hand to grab a fistful of his armored trousers to try to push him up while Mary jumped into the helo to help the man pull Miles in the rest of the way. The door gunner fired several shots at silhouettes approaching through the smoke. Shots were fired back at him, and he was hit.

Dani released Miles and was going for the other man

covering their retreat when he went down. He was able to stand with her help.

"Thanks, Dani. I can always count on you."

"Uh huh," she said to the stranger with a name patch identifying him as Dresden.

Something near them exploded, and the blast sent a tremor through her. She and Dresden were bathed by a wave of hot air. Whatever it was that blew was too close for her to want to stick around another second. Thick, roiling smoke billowed around them, making it difficult to see anything.

"Get us out of here!" the man with the British accent said to the pilot as he pulled the injured Dresden into the helo.

Dani guessed the Brit was Cam since his uniform ID'd him as Cameron. She had her boot on the skid and reached for Mary's outstretched hand. Someone slipped an arm across her throat, and she reached for her pistol only to find the holster empty. Rowan's head appeared next to hers as he brought her pistol up. Mary pivoted with her rifle to shoot him, but Rowan fired first.

The shot struck Mary's faceplate, shattering the visor and causing her head to rock back with the impact. Mary collapsed, and as the helicopter lifted unsteadily from the roof, Mary spilled out, crashing into both Dani and Rowan.

Dani was desperate to know if Mary was alive, but she had to deal with Rowan first. Mary fell to the roof while Dani struggled with the arm around her neck. Another explosion smothered them with smoke that was violently whipped around them by the helo blades.

Dani heard Miles's voice through the comm. "We lost Dani and Mary."

"Where? What happened?" Cam asked.

Dani couldn't reply as Rowan dragged her away. She twisted until she got one foot under her. She rammed her shoulder into

Rowan's side. He didn't release her, but she had enough space to move a little more. She brought her hands up and gripped his wrist. She pried his arm away from her throat and almost had him in an elbow lock. He fired the plasma pistol directly into her chest armor. She was thrown back with the blast, and pain filled her chest. Instead of striking the roof's surface, she continued past the roof's edge. Her next impact would be with the street below.

CHAPTER
50

Air rushed from Dani's lungs when her back slammed into the roof of the adjacent building. Her helmet struck the roof and mostly protected her head. Minus oxygen, the discomfort in her chest plus the new pain in her back and head threatened to make her lose consciousness. She managed a small grunt mixed with a cough as she rolled to her side and tried to take enough tiny breaths to refill her lungs while the rest of her body continued to complain. She wasn't a splattered mess on the street below, so she was glad—despite how she felt—that she'd only fallen to the roof of the next building. Still, it was a far-enough drop to make moving difficult.

She had a bigger problem.

Where's the asshole with my gun?

Dani forced herself to roll over the rest of the way. Her chest ached from the shot she'd taken in the armor. *Fuck, that hurts.* She grunted and pushed herself to her hands and knees while taking a few bigger breaths.

"Dani, Mary, respond!" Cam said through the comm. "Swing us back around … I don't care. Take us back. You can take the wounded out after you bring me close enough to the roof to jump out."

"Stay with Miles. I'll go," another voice said. Dani assumed it was the person on the deck-mounted gun in the helo and the only person she hadn't heard speak before now.

Mary wasn't answering either, and that terrified Dani. She tried to reply, but the only thing that came out was a strangled cough.

"Dani. It's Oliver. I have Dad's comm. He's bad, and I need you. The pilot is making us leave. Please tell us where you are."

Dani's face was protected from the smoke by her helmet, but the boy's voice in her ear made tears form in her eyes. "I'm—" Her voice was too weak. She straightened her upper body while she continued to kneel and took an almost normal breath. "Oliv— Shit." The form that emerged from the smoke charged toward her.

Dani was almost to her feet when Rowan grabbed her by the shoulders to ram his knee into her middle. She snatched his pistol from his holster as she twisted to avoid the full blow, but she lost her balance.

The side of her helmet struck the roof. Rowan approached, and Dani rolled to her belly. She used one hand and her feet to push-pull away from him, keeping the hand with the pistol tucked beneath her. Cameron and others continued to call for her over the comm, but she didn't respond. Her heart leapt when she heard Mary's voice.

"Where are you? Answer me!"

She wanted to call to her friend in the worst way, but she needed to focus her attention on Rowan.

He stalked her while she continued her slow crawl. "I want you dead for so many reasons, but I will keep you alive. I'll recondition you after I torture and kill your friends in front of you." He grabbed the collar on the back of her jacket. "That is what your future looks like."

He rolled her over, and Dani brought the pistol up. He

wasn't wearing a helmet, and his eyes widened. Rowan reached for his pistol to find it not there.

"Is it?" she asked.

Her finger remained on the trigger as she stood when he backed away. She wanted him dead, but she couldn't bring herself to depress the trigger the rest of the way. Firing recklessly at Wardens shooting at her was one thing. Holding an unarmed Warden at gunpoint was another—at least for her.

"Dani, I can hear you," Mary said. "Where are you? Who are you talking to?"

"Rowan," Dani said. "I have him."

"Do *not* engage. Run!"

"I *have* him."

Rowan sneered. "Just the two of us facing off again in the middle of this goddamn war. This is the fourth time. What are the odds?"

Dani tried to ignore him. *Four times?* Aside from today, she remembered only one. *What happened the other two times? When did the other two times happen?*

Mary was in her ear again. "If you have a gun on him, kill him now. Permanently."

"No!" Houston barked into the comm. "We need him for intel."

"Don't fuck around with this guy, Dani. Kill him," Mary said.

"Dani, I'm giving you a direct order," Houston said. "Spare him for capture. Do you copy?"

Rowan's sneer faded. "Why did you murder my wife and the mother of my young son and infant daughter?"

Dani wasn't sure how to answer him. She only partially remembered the woman. "I—"

The jet shrieked by overhead, and the smoke billowed in waves around her. She lost Rowan for only a second, but it was enough time for him to disappear.

"Goddammit," Dani said.

"What happened?" Mary asked.

"The fucking jet stirred up the smoke. Rowan's gone." Dani spun while holding the gun out. He'd vanished, and she didn't know from which direction he'd attack again.

"Where are you?"

Dani needed a new plan. "Houston, send a helo to pick up Mary, then come for me. I'll move to the other end, away from the smoke. I'm on the roof next to and below the one we were on. Mary, Rowan didn't run off. He'll be back, and I can't deal with him while you're in my ear."

"Don't you dare take the comm out."

"I'll call in when I'm clear. Pick me up from the far side of the roof."

Mary's string of curses filled her ear as a response. Dani continued her turns, watching for Rowan as she touched the side of her helmet with her free hand to slide the visor up. She pulled the comm from her ear and slipped it into her pocket. Smoke filtered into her face in those few seconds before she got the visor closed again. Her eyes watered and burned. She blinked to clear her vision while the helmet removed the smoke.

Dani had turned so many times, she'd lost track of which way she needed to go to reach the other end. The jet screamed by overhead, and she resisted the urge to look up. She knew Rowan was stalking her.

The smoke seemed to thin until more explosions erupted. The jet continued to fire at the remaining Warden helos as they tried to retreat. The noise was too much. A helicopter slammed into part of the roof near her, taking a massive chunk out of it with its spinning blades as it skidded across to the other side to fall off and drop to the street below. Dani was shaken to her knees with the impact.

Something crashed into her side. Rowan grabbed her wrist

and smashed her hand against the roof. She held the pistol until he slammed her hand down again. The pistol skittered a few yards across the surface until it disappeared into the hole torn into the building by the crashing helicopter.

Rowan gripped the front of her armor and pulled her up. She drove her knee into his groin. The armor protected him, but only to an extent. He growled when he shoved her away, then leaned forward. Dani didn't run from him. She rushed Rowan and rammed the faceplate of her helmet into his face. The impact dizzied her a little and created a crack across her visor, but he suffered worse.

He stumbled a few steps, and blood began pouring from the bridge of his nose; it now had a bend that it hadn't had before.

Dani pulled her knife from the inside of her belt. Someone had told her to always keep a third knife on her, but she couldn't remember who that was.

"You won't kill me with that again," Rowan said.

Again?

He stalked toward her, undaunted by the weapon in her hand. He was taller and stronger than her, and he had a longer reach. To use the knife, she'd have to be close to him.

"Dani!"

Mary's shout filled Dani with fear for her friend's life. Rowan would follow through on his threat to murder her friends in front of her; his sudden grin confirmed it. He shifted to go toward Mary's voice, and Dani charged. Rowan's grin widened, and Dani realized that he'd tricked her into a desperate move.

He caught Dani's wrist and gave it a violent twist. She yelped as her fingers opened and the knife flew out of them. He grabbed her side with his other hand and stepped in close. He twisted his upper body and flipped her over his hip. As soon as her back hit the roof, she rolled to avoid him pinning her down.

Dani contorted to pull one leg close to her center to clear his body. She threw her leg out and hooked it around his neck.

She sat up and rolled back toward him, peeling him off her by his neck while he grappled to remove her leg. Dani's left fist connected with his face while he was trapped beneath her. She cried out when he stabbed a knife between her armored jacket and trousers. Her grip on him weakened, but she turned her focus to the blade.

They fought for control, and Dani withstood his strikes while she wrenched the knife from him. The knife bounced out of his hand and down into the hole in the roof. She didn't know when or how they'd gotten so close to it.

Another explosion rocked the area, and Dani's head came up. She saw Mary and the silhouette of someone else before smoke smothered them. Rowan's fist struck the laceration on her side, and she released him. She rolled away to a crouch despite the pain in her side the position created. She despised Rowan's confident grin as he rose to his feet.

"That trick of hiding a small blade, I stole from you," he said.

"And I'm stealing this one from your wife." Dani charged, threw her arms around him, and took him with her into the maw of the hole in the roof.

CHAPTER
51

D ani caught glimpses of the interior of the building as they fell. Her boot clipped something on one of the upper floors, sending her into a flip. She and Rowan separated as a result. She curled into a ball before hitting a piece of a wall left somewhat standing after the helo had torn through the building. She bounced off and continued her fall to the next level. She closed her eyes, not wanting to see what object in someone's former home would impale her. Dani's upper body collided with something hard. Her scream was shortened when her head hit another object.

Pain everywhere brought her mind back to the present. The side of her face was wet, and even the smallest of breaths caused her chest to protest, sending bolts of lightning through her right side. The taste of blood filled her mouth where she'd bitten the inside of her left cheek. She was in a seated position and hung her head. Blood dripped from her lips. She had no memory of sitting up. Dani shifted and grunted when the motion caused more discomfort.

"Wake up," a voice said.

Her eyelids were impossibly heavy. Fingers gripped her hair, using it for leverage, and the person rapped the back of her head against something hard. "Wake up!"

The insult to her already aching head made her wince, but she opened her eyes when the worst of the headache eased a little. She recognized the man before her, and her shoulders slumped a little more. "Fuck."

Rowan released her hair and grinned.

His previously broken nose was in perfect alignment now. He was covered in smears of blood, but he was uninjured. He'd gone through another regen, recovered, and was now crouched in front of Dani, who felt like she'd been hit by a train or two. He'd removed her helmet at some point and left it on the floor next to her leg. The visor was covered in a spiderweb of cracks. Her fall hadn't killed her—somehow—but it had battered the hell out of her. She'd been out long enough for Rowan to regen, find her, and prop her up against a cabinet in what looked like the remnants of a kitchen.

The helo had wrecked this level of the building. Part of the floor was missing behind where Rowan crouched in front of her, and Dani wasn't up for making another blind leap into a hole.

"I have had to *really* restrain myself from killing you, Dani."

She didn't respond.

"I expected a bit more gratitude for sparing you."

"Fuck off."

His strike to her cheek sent her sprawling to her side. Her vision went dark for a few seconds, but Rowan jerked her back upright again. Her ribs and the knife wound to her side gave her stark reminders of their presence. Dani groaned and rested her hand against the stab wound. Fresh, warm blood coated her fingers. Rowan's blade had caused more damage than she'd realized.

"I want to show you something," he said.

He picked up the helmet and used the sleeve of his jacket to wipe the bloody smears off it, revealing the name of its prior owner: Rowan.

"I got caught in the mess when that building went down near the officers' quarters. Killed. But you already know that part, because someone stole my helmet off my body." He placed the helmet back on the floor next to her. "Was it you who took the helmets off me and my other Wardens to put on your people?"

Because of her headache, she resisted the urge to nod. No point in lying. "Yeah."

"Goddamn, you've got some balls. I died again when you took us into this hole," he said, nodding toward the destroyed building behind him. "Twice in one day. The last time I managed that was during the hottest fighting with Earth's military forces. That was before we kicked their asses and they regrouped to form their useless Commonwealths." Rowan paused. "What is it, Curtis?" he asked. He didn't speak for a moment. "Stall them. I don't care how, just do it. I have her and will come to you shortly from Back Bay. Send me a team to escort her back."

Shit. He was calling for backup. *Shit.Shit.Shit.* Once more Wardens arrived, she was fucked. "I'm sorry," Dani said.

"What?" Rowan scowled and shook his head. "No, not you. I'm talking to her. Hang on."

"I'm sorry." She tried to sit up straighter and placed her palm on the helmet to push against it.

Rowan's brow creased. "For what? Never mind. Shut up for two seconds." He diverted his attention back to his comm. "Goddammit, Curtis. Fine. Stall the chancellors and the damn vote. I'm on my way. Rowan out." He glared at Dani. "What the hell are you talking about?"

She slid her hand to the base of the helmet. "I didn't mean to kill your wife."

Rowan grabbed her upper arm and hauled her to her feet.

"I'm also sorry I took your helmet. You can have it back." Dani slammed the helmet into the side of Rowan's head. He rocked, but not enough. She swung again. His head snapped back, and he staggered into the hole in the floor. She dropped the helmet and groaned. Dani leaned forward to see where he'd fallen. He lay two floors down—twisted at a horrible angle with a ragged piece of metal sticking out of his abdomen that had pierced him through the back. A pool of blood formed beneath him.

"Asshole."

She wanted to rest but forced herself to move away from the hole and lean against the counter. Sweat burned the cuts to her head and face while she took a moment to breathe. Dani pulled the comm from her pocket and stuck it into her ear.

Comm traffic was a mix of Mary and someone she called Elmore talking to each other as they searched for Dani with periodic input from Houston. Dani wanted to hear Miles's voice and know he was okay, but neither he nor Oliver spoke over the frequency.

"Mary," Dani said. She coughed, said her friend's name a second time, and her voice was stronger.

"Fucking hell, Dani, where are you?"

"Uh, you know the roof where the falling helo made a crater in the building?"

"Elmore and I are on that building now. I don't see you."

"I'm in the crater."

"Of course you are."

Dani laughed and immediately regretted it. "Rowan's dead for now but will regen soon. I can't be here when he does."

"You injured?"

"Somewhat."

"That bad, huh? We're coming to you. Elmore, contact the

helo, see if they have gear to lower down for an extraction using the gap in the roof."

"How is Miles?" Dani asked.

"On his way to the field hospital with Oliver. Cam is taking care of him."

Dani looked around the apartment. She didn't want to get too close to the hole for fear of it crumbling and her ending up like Rowan. Her best exit was just outside the window. "I'm coming up the fire escape. Meet me there."

"Copy that."

Dani limped to the window and climbed out to the fire escape landing. She sucked in a breath when the entire structure groaned. She started up and winced each time bolts shook a bit more brick and dust from their anchor points.

"Hey!"

Dani looked up and smiled to see her friend. Mary's helmet was gone, and the side of her face bore smears of blood and swelling under one eye.

"Wow, you look like shit," Mary said.

"So do you."

"I'm coming down."

Dani shook her head and winced. "Stay there. This thing is rickety as hell. I can make it to you."

"Hurry. The jet took out the enemy helos and the Wardens on the roof. Elmore tossed them off, but we'll have to deal with them again once they regen and come back."

Dani focused on her friend's voice as a way to help ignore her injuries for a little longer. Each step got harder as her strength faded. She didn't know how much blood she'd already lost, and she tried not to think of her internal injuries.

"Faster, Dani."

Moving faster wasn't an option. She paused on the next-to-last landing before reaching Mary. Dani leaned her hand against the rail and pressed her hand to the knife wound to slow the bleeding. She glimpsed movement behind the window where she'd stopped.

Rowan burst through glass and rammed into her.

Curtis passed his hand over his face and sighed. Rowan had asked the impossible. He couldn't delay the chancellors any longer. Rowan said he was on his way, but Curtis didn't believe him. He had overheard only a few pieces of Rowan's conversation with Dani. His commanding officer was beyond obsessed with her, and Curtis now doubted Rowan's ability to effectively lead the Wardens. His duty should have been to the Wardens and the VR no matter how much he hated Vice Regent Aubrey. But no, Rowan was fucking around with the Brigand. Curtis hoped that Rowan's capture of her was final and would be the end of this madness of hunting her.

"They're leaving. We must go now," one of Curtis's aides whispered to him.

Curtis nodded and gathered among the others to leave the primary Ops center. The CNA jets had already taken down almost every building in the square, and the glass windows overlooking the city were cracked in many places. The building could withstand more abuse, but there wasn't a need to risk exposing the city's leadership to another CNA surprise. The new CNA jets were a big enough one. Their stealth, mobility, and firepower had easily knocked Warden jets out of the sky. The helos never stood a chance against them, but Curtis had ordered their pilots and crews to their death to follow Rowan's orders.

As they moved through the building toward the secondary Ops, Curtis pulled up the archived camera feeds from the officers' quarters. When he found the video of Ana and Dani in the stairwell, his steps slowed. He hated seeing Ana's death, but he backed up the feed and played it again.

Dani recoiled from Ana when the pistol discharged, taking Ana's head with the blast. Dani stumbled back until she reached the wall, horror-stricken. She even vomited after the event. Ana's death had been an accident, but it didn't matter. Curtis wanted Dani dead. He knew his rage was only a fraction of the pain and anger that Rowan felt. And Dani was the direct cause. She needed to be caught and executed. Fuck reconditioning. She wasn't worth adding to the Warden ranks.

Curtis worked on the clip from the camera feed while they walked. He rendered the clip and froze it the moment the plasma pistol discharged. Dani's face was distorted because of the exertion of her battle with Ana, but Curtis planned to use her expression to convince the chancellors that Ana's murder was done with hate. He removed the part of their struggle showing how the pair fought, tumbled down stairs, and struggled for control of the pistol. He only needed to show them the few seconds containing Ana's brutal death at the hands of a Brigand that Rowan had identified to the VR as a hostile threat months ago.

The aides and other Wardens began powering up the gear in the new Ops center as soon as they arrived. The chancellors and VR were already reviewing the latest reports on their individual panels.

Vice Regent Aubrey looked up from her panel and scanned the room. "As soon as Rowan arrives, I want him arrested for dereliction of duty."

Curtis's temper flared, and he stepped forward as he moved his hand over his panel.

"Chancellors, I urge you to review the files I sent to your devices," Curtis said. "Please note the date stamps. Multiple times Rowan sent such files to Vice Regent Aubrey regarding CNA and Brigand activities in Maine and their likely presence in and around Boston. Please note the individually flagged files and note the photograph of the Bangor Brigand called Dani."

"Goddammit, Curtis, not this again," Aubrey said.

Curtis sent another file to the leaders in the room.

"Please open this next file. This is a clip from earlier today. The Brigand you just saw is the same one who murdered Rowan's wife while she defended the lives of her children." Curtis tapped his screen and the video played. Several of the leaders gasped when Ana's head exploded. He froze the image at that point, which perfectly showed Ana's fatal destruction and the expression on Dani's face.

"You're looking at pure hatred, ladies and gentlemen. Rowan warned everyone that this was coming, and he was ignored and shunned. The primary Brigand he hunted is the same one who took his wife's life. The attack was personal and deliberate. Ana was targeted because of Rowan's efforts, and now the VR wants to arrest him for hunting the people who invaded our city and started this attack."

The scowls on the leaders' faces while they stared at the image on their panels made him smile inwardly.

Curtis wasn't finished. "I propose a no-confidence vote of Vice Regent Aubrey, who is directly responsible for denying Rowan's plans of action against the CNA and Brigands."

Heads nodded and the chancellors began to speak. Several hurled angry words at the VR, who responded with defensive rage. Curtis waited until the shouting escalated to a roar. Aubrey had no choice but to back down.

"There's only one person guilty of dereliction of duty in this room," one of the chancellors said.

Another chancellor, Saket, agreed. He ordered Aubrey's arrest and removal from Ops.

Curtis nodded to his aide, who drew his weapon and escorted Aubrey away.

"Chancellor Saket, I urge you to elect Rowan to the role of vice regent," Curtis said. "No one knows Colonel Houston's tactics better than him. He's the one who can save Boston."

"Save Boston?" Saket asked. "You're implying that we're losing the city."

"I'm saying we wouldn't be victims of this attack if Aubrey had listened to Rowan months ago."

"The other chancellors and I have been listening to *you*, Curtis, not Rowan."

That caused Curtis to pause before answering. "I'm not sure what you mean, sir."

Saket turned to the other chancellors. "Curtis has been in our ears since the day he and Rowan arrived with the others from Portland. We've been advised by Curtis all this time, not Rowan. I propose we elect Curtis as the new vice regent."

Curtis's mouth dropped open before he could hide his surprise. This wasn't how it was supposed to happen. He wasn't supposed to be the next VR.

He managed to snap his mouth shut, but swallowing was almost impossible. He activated his comm and lowered his voice while the chancellors spoke with each other. "Rowan, come in. Please, for fuck's sake, Rowan, *respond*."

He was answered by silence.

"Rowan, respond, please."

Saket's voice rose again. "Do we need to have any other discussion on this? I don't think we do."

The other chancellors were agreeing before Curtis had a chance to speak. Saket called for a formal vote, and Curtis was unanimously elected vice regent.

Saket turned to the new VR. "Congratulations, Vice Regent Curtis."

Curtis was stunned into silence.

CHAPTER

52

Had Rowan not been trying to kill her, Dani would have been impressed with his tenacity. Instead she was just pissed off. As soon as she'd seen him through the glass, she'd started bending her knees. This prevented him from taking her off the fire escape entirely when they collided, but they rolled down the stairs. When they stopped, he struck her several times in her stab wound.

She was weakened by the attack and repeated waves of pain. Dani couldn't fight back enough to get him off her. The fire escape trembled. Mary was coming down to join her, and Rowan couldn't see her. Dani swung her leg out and clipped Rowan's knee. His leg buckled, but he was enraged and focused only on beating her to death. She needed to keep him busy until Mary could get a clear shot at him.

"How did you like your wife's new look after I was done with her?" Dani asked. She couldn't believe the words coming out of her mouth, but she needed Rowan's attention on her. "That was nice work on my part, right?" She questioned the brightness of this plan when he smashed her ribs with his fist.

"Best Wardens are the headless ones," she said.

His fist caught her cheek, and Dani's head hit the step

beneath it. She retained enough consciousness to see a hole tear through the left side of his chest. He sank to the landing and rolled to his side. His eyes stared into nothingness as blood poured from the wound where his heart used to be. He could regen from that wound.

Mary helped her up, and Dani paused. She leaned against the rail and closed her eyes for a moment. The dizziness was almost too much. It began to pass, and she opened her eyes again.

"The rounds in your rifle, you said they won't take a head off like a plasma shot, right?" Dani asked.

"No, unfortunately. They do a lot of damage but go right through. He can regen."

Dani placed her boot against Rowan's corpse to shove him off the fire escape.

"Wait," Mary said. "Let him start to regen. I'll pop him with another round while he's glowing, and that'll end him for good."

Bolts pulled free from the concrete, and the fire escape shook. Dani and Mary shared a quick glance before they both put a boot to Rowan and pushed him off. He flipped in the air until he smashed into the street below.

Dani gripped the rail and closed her eyes, trying to stay upright and conscious. "Any chance he landed on his head to make it explode so he can't come back?" She opened her eyes a little.

Mary leaned out over the rail and gazed down. She frowned and shifted to slip her arm around Dani's waist. "No such luck, my dear."

Mary helped Dani up the fire escape, and each step sent renewed waves of pain through her. Dani's vision oscillated between blurred and doubled, and she feared she'd collapse soon. She tried to distract herself from the overwhelming sensation of feeling like shit. "The one you're calling Cam, his uniform says Cameron."

"Yeah. Same guy. He said Kels is recovering in Bangor and doing well."

"Kels?"

Mary shook her head and sighed. "This is going to be a long process, isn't it?"

"I'm sorry."

"It's a good thing I love you."

Dani looked at her.

Mary glanced at Dani. "Figure of speech, darling. You love Miles. Keep your feet moving. We're almost there."

"I think I'm going to pass out."

"We don't have time for that. One foot in front of the other. Elmore is waiting for us."

"Elmore?"

"Jesus. Really?"

Later, Dani didn't remember much of the events that followed. Elmore and Mary helped her into the helicopter waiting for them, and Dani closed her eyes once Mary had her strapped in. Elmore asked her a few medical questions that Dani tried to answer with nods and shakes of her head. Someone stuck something to the back of her hand, and she opened her eyes. Elmore snapped a vial into the patch on her hand, and her head lolled forward with unconsciousness a few seconds later.

"Sir?" Saket asked.

Curtis recovered. "I am just surprised and honored by the trust you are placing in me." He wasn't sure how he even managed to speak, much less express his gratitude.

"What are your orders?"

He needed Rowan's tactical mind more than anything else, but Curtis had to hide his reliance on Rowan or he'd be out of his new position in an instant.

"Send a platoon of elite Wardens to Back Bay to assist Rowan and his retrieval of the intruders," Curtis said. "I want every aircraft we have in the air now to take out the CNA jets. Get me the latest reports of all blasts across the city since this shit started. Color-code them according to time of detonation. Put analysts on the data. There will be a pattern to the assault. Once we find it, we'll know where the real attack is coming from."

Everyone went into action, and Curtis began poring over the reports coming into the feed on his panel. The Wardens had been able to retake a few areas of the city from the CNA, but the bitter fighting had left his forces thinned. A commotion at the entry to the Ops center brought his head up. Curtis immediately left the station to go to Rowan since the guards refused his entry to Ops. The man was covered in a mix of blood, dirt, soot, and other debris stuck to his armor.

Curtis waved the guards off. "Release him. We need his expertise here."

"Yes, sir, Vice Regent Curtis," the guards said, and stepped aside.

Rowan jerked his arms from the guards' hands and approached Curtis. "Did they just call you Vice Regent?"

"Yes, s—" Curtis checked himself. He was the ranking officer in Boston and no longer answered to Rowan—at least not in an official capacity. He lowered his voice. "Rowan, I tried to contact you, but they voted in a rushed manner. We can work this to your advantage, but not right this second."

"How?"

"The city is falling. Use your tactical genius, save the city, I'll pass the title to you, and no one will question it. If we can't save the city, I'll take the blame, step down, and put you in my place."

Rowan frowned. "Vice Regent Curtis."

"Please continue to trust me as you always have, Rowan. You're the right man to be the VR of Boston."

"Not if we don't have Boston. Goddamn Aubrey. Oh, she's dead. I blew her useless head off when I came in."

Curtis rubbed the bridge of his nose. Rowan's impulsive murder of the former VR wouldn't help efforts to get Rowan into the vice regent role. Curtis would have to figure out something later to get around that. He lowered his hand. "Let me bring you up to date on the reports we have thus far."

"It's alive!"

Dani startled awake and stared at an older woman grinning at her from the foot of her bed. She glanced around and realized she was in an infirmary. *How? When?*

"Get your ass up, honey," the woman said, and she tossed a knapsack on the bed. "Get dressed. We have shit to do."

Dani continued to stare. *Jace. No, Jace is my brother. This woman is connected to Jace. Her name is … no clue.*

"Nothing? Really? Mary said your memories were a mess. She wasn't kidding. I'm Hattie. I married your brother, Jace. Remember him?"

"Name, yes. Face, not so much. Hattie. Aunt Hattie?"

"Yep. Let's go. You've had enough time to lie around and sleep."

She rolled out of bed and took a moment to work out some of the soreness. Her boots were on the floor next to the chair by the bed. She pulled the small pack closer and removed the clothes from it.

"Do you know Miles and Oliver?" Dani asked.

"Of course."

"Where are they?"

"I'll take you to see them if you can manage to move a little faster."

Dani pulled off her hospital-issued shirt and touched a blinking healing patch stuck to her left side where Rowan had stabbed her. She had another patch over her right ribs. She probed her cheek with her tongue, and the ragged cut where she'd bitten it before was now only a thin, raised line. Dani touched her head and passed her fingers over another patch extending from the left side of her forehead, behind her ear, to the base of her skull.

"You concussed the hell out of your brain, but you're healing well. The patches will come off tomorrow," Hattie said.

Dani felt around the patch, and her fingertips brushed scars that used to be gaping lacerations. Her fingers traveled to an area on her neck, where she expected to find another scar, but her skin was smooth. The regen had made it disappear, and for some reason she couldn't yet explain, she didn't want that scar gone.

"Are you done making sure you're in one piece? Or you just want to stand there half naked the rest of the day?"

"I—" Dani recalled that arguing with Hattie was often a wasted effort. She clamped her mouth shut and slipped her new shirt on. "Where's Mary?"

"Busy."

"Doing what?"

"A favor."

Dani huffed at Hattie's evasiveness. She finished dressing, then sat in the chair. Hattie helped her put her socks and boots on. "Miles hates wet socks," Dani said.

Hattie's brow creased. "Oh, good, you're remembering the useless crap now."

"Sorry. Sometimes these little things come back to me at random times." Another memory surfaced. "Oh shit."

"What?"

"Oh, uh. You're not—" She whispered the next word. "Human."

"Do you remember the other stuff about me?"

Dani nodded.

"Good. Take it to your grave."

"I will."

"Ready?"

"Yep."

"In a minute. Sit tight," Hattie said.

Dani remained seated, and the older woman pulled another chair over.

Hattie leaned in close and lowered her voice. "You can't trust Catherine."

"Catherine?"

"Jesus, you're a disaster. Colonel Houston."

"Oh. Yeah. I know who you mean. Sort of."

"She used you, Dani. She knew an assault of some sort was likely coming, and her response to the Warden attack was delayed on purpose once she knew Oliver was missing. She let you and Miles go after the boy because she knew you'd be a perfect distraction for the Wardens while she moved in for the primary assault."

Dani let the information sit in her mind for a few minutes. Just as she somehow knew when Alex was lying to her, she knew what Hattie had said was the truth.

"What's the status on Boston?" Dani asked.

"The Wardens started their evac an hour ago. The city will be ours by morning."

"How did that happen so quickly?"

Hattie chuckled. "Honey, we pulled you out of the city three days ago. Fighting has been horrible. Loads of dead and wounded on both sides."

"Three days?"

"Whatever Elmore gave you on that helo put you on your ass. Once the initial waves of wounded came pouring in and were stabilized—including you and Miles—you were shipped up to Portland to make room for the other wounded coming into the field hospital. You don't remember any of that?"

Dani shook her head.

"You are the cheapest damn date I've ever seen."

"So, Houston's plan worked."

"It did, but you're missing the bigger point."

"No, I'm not, Hattie. I understand what you're telling me."

"If you're smart, you can get what you want out of this."

Dani paused. "Oh, you lost me there."

"You'll figure it out." Hattie stood and took Dani's arm.

"I will? Are you sure? I haven't a fucking clue what you're talking about now."

"I know," Hattie said, and she laughed.

Oliver and Brody bolted from the oversized chair they shared when Dani neared Miles's healing pod. She hugged the boy and freed one hand to greet the dog as he bounced around her. Her last memory of the dog was of him bloodied and wounded, but he was fine now. Miles opened his eyes, and a slow smile spread across his face.

"Are you better?" Oliver asked Dani when he released her.

"Yeah."

Hattie interrupted them. "Hey, kid, let's go find some food to smuggle back in."

Oliver went to his father's side. "Can I?"

Miles nodded. "Sure, but don't let Aunt Hattie get you arrested."

"I make no promises," Hattie said, which made Oliver grin.

When Hattie and Oliver left with Brody trotting beside the teen, Dani realized Hattie had planned to get her here only to leave her alone with Miles.

She approached the pod and noticed the swath of blinking lights beneath Miles's shirt. "You've been in one of these before, right? Recently, I think."

"Yeah." He reached for her hand, and she slipped hers inside his. "Thank you."

"For?"

"I would've died had you not gotten me on that helo. I'm sorry I wasn't able to help you when you needed it."

His hand moved over hers until he interlaced fingers with her.

"You helped me plenty." She watched his fingers, and a mix of memories flooded her mind. She blinked several times and gripped the side of the pod with her other hand for extra balance as more memories returned.

"Dani?"

She pulled her hand from his and placed her palms on the sides of his face. "It was your voice I heard when I was dying. You told me to remember everything. I didn't, but I remember enough now." Dani leaned down and pressed her lips against his.

He smiled and pulled her into his arms. He ran his hand through her hair and held her close. His scent triggered more images of when they had lived in Portland during her prior life—now two lives prior. She recalled an intimate memory when he'd had his hands in her hair and his mouth on hers while he was inside her. She shuddered to remember how it felt to be with him. When he released her, she opened her mouth and kissed him again.

The pod began to alarm, and Dani released him. "Sorry." She took a step back and stared at the pod. It stopped beeping, and Miles grinned. His eyelids were heavy as fatigue, meds, or both took over. "Maybe you should rest."

"I don't want to."

"I'll be here when you wake up."

Miles nodded and closed his eyes. She kept her hand on his, and his breathing changed to longer, deeper breaths as he fell asleep.

An older man approached, and although Dani thought he looked somewhat familiar, no name came to mind.

"Figured I'd find you here," he said.

"You are?"

"The rumors are true? You forgot everything when you died?"

"Not everything," Dani said.

"Uh huh. I'm Javi. Colonel Houston wants to see you. She's on a video comm from Boston. I'll take you to her office here so you can speak with her."

"No."

Javi's eyebrows went up. "This isn't a request."

She shrugged. "I don't care."

"This isn't the time for your bullshit."

Dani released Miles's hand, approached the man calling himself Javi, and stood in front of him. "You *will* keep your voice down. I'm not leaving."

"Houston has ordered—"

"I'm. Not. Leaving."

Javi's face reddened, but he turned and left.

Dani settled into the chair Oliver had occupied and recognized the boots—one upright and one lying on its side—beneath Miles's pod. She caught the attention of a tech as she passed by and asked for a couple of items. When the tech returned, Dani thanked her and took the tin and cloth. She retrieved the boots and polished them while Miles slept. The action felt familiar, so she assumed she'd done this for him before.

CHAPTER
53

Dani stood at the counter in the kitchen, lost in thought, while her piece of toast remained uneaten on the counter before her.

"Hey."

Dani looked up and gave Mary a partial smile. "Morning."

"Morning?" Mary shook her head. "How long have you been standing in here?"

"Uh." Dani looked out the window. "Not long." The length of the shadows told a different story.

"Horrible liar. You gonna eat that?"

Dani shook her head and passed the bread to her friend.

Mary took a bite and leaned one elbow on the counter. "This is stale as shit," she said while she chewed.

"Where's Hattie?"

"She was in Boston already scoping out a place for her new brothel and pub. She got back a couple hours ago but has been in meetings with her food and ale suppliers. How is Miles?"

"Good, I guess. He was discharged from the infirmary last night."

"And you haven't gone to see him today? What's wrong?"

Dani shifted to lean against the counter and folded her

arms. She frowned as she tried to figure out how to relay her thoughts to Mary.

"Just spit it out."

"I've been able to remember more, and I've come so close to losing you, Miles, and Oliver to this war. I already lost Jace. I had a scar on my neck from the day he saved my life and lost his." Dani passed her fingers over the smooth skin on her neck before dropping her hand. "That reminder of him is gone now too. Mary, I don't want to fight anymore."

Mary shrugged and set the bread aside. "We're vols. We can quit when we want. If you bail, I bail too."

"What about Miles? He's CNA. He can't just walk away."

"Why don't you talk to him first?"

"Oliver once told me that he didn't mind when Miles and I both were gone on trips related to recon or whatever. He said he knew we'd take care of each other to get us both home again. I can't leave the war and help Miles at the same time."

"Talk to Miles. *Now*." Mary took Dani's arm and guided her toward the back door.

Dani walked through the door when Mary opened it. When she turned back, Mary waved her hand to shoo her away, then closed the door.

"What the hell just happened?" Dani muttered. Mary was acting weird, and Dani didn't know what else to do but start walking toward the CNA base. A few people greeted her on the way. She gave them a nod but didn't know who any of them were. Her mind was like a book with missing pages—*lots* of missing pages—yet she remembered how to get to Miles's home.

Before she could signal her arrival at his door, Brody yipped from the other side. Oliver opened the door and smiled.

"Hi, Dani," Oliver said.

"Hey," she said, smiling. She knelt to greet the wiggling dog. He licked her face, then buried his head under her hands while she scratched his head and ears. "Am I losing my mind, or was he injured recently?"

"He lost his right front leg, but the vet grew him another one. He just has a tiny scar here." Oliver traced his finger over Brody's shoulder.

Dani couldn't see anything more than a hint of a line in the dog's fur.

"You're staying for dinner, right?" Oliver asked.

"Uh ..."

"Dad, Dani's staying for dinner," Oliver said, grinning.

"Can you let her inside instead of standing there at the door?" Miles asked from somewhere.

Dani entered, and Oliver closed the door behind her. She stopped and stared at the totes spread around Miles in the kitchen. His feet were bare, and he wore jeans and a faded gray tee. *Holy shit, that's sexy.* Dani recalled that she always liked it best when he wasn't in uniform. Something about the CNA uniform irritated her, but she hadn't resurrected that memory yet.

Dani waved her hand at the totes. "What's this?"

"More packing." Miles said. "You're already finished?"

Her brow formed a deep crease.

"Oh." Miles stopped sorting through items on the counter. "General Ramos hasn't talked to you yet?"

"Who?"

Miles guided Dani to a chair at the table. He sat next to her and took her hand. "You met the general once before. He was present when a lot of other people came to hear you speak about Portland."

She shrugged.

"Okay, he was there whether you remember any of that or not. He's ordered me to join him on a diplomatic mission of sorts. Major Cameron—Cam—remember him? The Brit."

"He was part of the roof rescue."

Miles nodded. "He and General Ramos have already started setting up our itinerary."

"You're *leaving*?"

"*We're* leaving."

Dani yanked her hand away and stood, tears burning her eyes. She couldn't lose Miles *and* Oliver. "No!"

Oliver was at her side, and he touched her arm. "You're misunderstanding Dad. We're all going."

"What?"

"You, me, Dad, Brody, and Mary, if she wants."

Dani shook her head and looked at Miles. "I came here to tell you I don't want to fight anymore. There's so much death everywhere, and I killed a woman I didn't mean to kill. I'm terrified of the memories I don't have back yet. What if they reveal that I'm a terrible person? I don't know who I am, because I can't remember everything." She didn't bother trying to keep the tears from spilling down her cheeks.

Miles pulled her close. "You're not a terrible person. We'll help you fill in the gaps."

She nodded but kept her head against his shoulder. His touch, *this* she remembered. "What is this mission?"

"It's diplomatic. I can't say we'll never be shot at again, but we won't be in the thick of the fighting like before."

Dani shifted to step back and look at him. "What are we supposed to do?"

"You'll be the face of Brigand unification."

"Huh?"

Miles smiled and led her back to her chair.

Oliver hopped into the chair next to her and grinned. "You're gonna love this."

Dani wasn't so sure about that.

"Our job is to represent Brigands," Miles said. "Not the CNA or other commonwealths. You created the Brigand-CNA partnership, which is the only reason why we were able to retake Maine from the Wardens and reclaim Boston. You are a person Brigands will listen to when they don't listen to others. You're being elevated for your charisma."

"What?!" Dani laughed at the absurdity of the idea. "Charisma? You've lost your mind worse than me."

Miles continued. "General Ramos wants the partnership momentum to continue, and he wants you to be involved in the talks to bring in more Brigands to join forces with commonwealths across the globe."

"The *globe*? Are you serious?"

Miles nodded. "Think of it, Dani. A civilian military that is worldwide. It'll be incredible."

She couldn't believe she was actually having this conversation.

"First stop is Manchester," Miles said.

"Okay. Fine. Start small with New England, right?"

"Manchester, England," Oliver said. "With Ambassador Ireland!"

Dani frowned. "Who is that?"

"Uh, Ollie, we'll work on that part later."

She didn't know what Miles meant, but apparently Oliver did, because he changed topics.

"We get to go on a British ship to England," he said.

Dani remained silent while this information sank in. A vague memory of Hattie saying something about Maine and the rest of the world surfaced, but she didn't have enough recollection of the event to sort it out. She'd have to ask Hattie about it later.

"What did Catherine say?" Dani asked.

"Oh, she's livid," Miles said, chuckling. "She had her role in the original partnership, so she's pissed that she's been passed over. But there's nothing she can do to stop him from taking me."

Dani's brow creased into deep lines, and she tilted her head as she looked at him.

"What's wrong? You have a really strange look on your face," Miles said.

"Well, I have been stressed all day with thoughts of quitting the war, but I was worried about you and what that would mean. I didn't know what to do, then Mary told me to come see you, but—shit." Dani shook her head and rolled her eyes. "She already knew about this diplomatic crap, didn't she?"

Miles nodded and smiled. "I saw her earlier today."

"Christ. Why couldn't she just tell me that instead of messing with my head?"

"She really enjoys screwing with you," Oliver said.

"She *is* a friend, right?"

Oliver laughed and nodded. "Want to help me pack?"

"Sure," Dani said, and she followed him to his room.

The single tote in the room was already full of the clothes he was taking with him. He didn't need her help. Oliver sat on the floor, and Brody sat on his right side. Oliver patted the floor to his left, and Dani settled in next to him. He pulled a book from a drawer beneath the stand next to his bed and handed it to her.

The battered book looked familiar as she turned it in her hands.

"This is Jace's journal that he kept when he cared for you during your prior Echoes," Oliver said. "It might help fill in some gaps. You even wrote yourself a note that's in here too."

Dani opened the book and flipped through some of the first pages. Oliver turned pages for her to the back of the book. Dani's eyes widened upon seeing detailed drawings of faces.

"Since your memories kinda short-circuited when you died, I started drawing faces once we got home to help you recognize people in case you died again. Well, I mean, I don't want you to die again, but just in case, you know?"

She nodded and marveled at the portraits. Hattie, Mary, Miles, and Jace were all there.

"Jace," she said. "I had no memory of his face until now." Tears burned her eyes. "Thank you, Oliver. These are great. You perfectly captured that smirk Hattie always has."

Miles leaned against the doorway. "Turns out the little turd has been hiding his artistic talent from everyone, including me."

She flipped through more pages and pointed to one. "This guy, Anton. He spends too much time with electronics."

Oliver nodded. "I told him you had some memory problems, and he thinks your brain is just taking time rendering everything back into the right sequence."

"Rendering?" Dani asked.

"When Anton makes an update to a sim program, it takes time for the data to render, or compile. The buildings and landscapes you see in the sim are sharp, realistic images. When he first makes a change and applies it to the program, the images start out blocky and crude, but as the details render, a block starts to look smoother and cleaner until it eventually turns into a field covered with wildflowers and lots of detail. Your memories were so fragmented, you didn't remember us at first, but now you're picking up more and more details."

"Okay. I get it. I think," Dani said.

She flipped through more pages and stopped on one. "Rowan. Why did you draw him?"

"You need to remember him too. He wants you deader than dead."

Dani nodded and Oliver continued. "Each entry in there where Jace wrote about you dying, you regenned as a child around ten years old. You remained an adult this time, although you never had before. Do you know what changed to cause that?"

"I'm not sure, but I suspect it had something to do with your father talking me out of it." Dani glanced at Miles and smiled before she turned her gaze back to the teen. "I remember being more afraid of forgetting my friends than of the death itself. I didn't *want* to forget, Oliver, and I think that was a factor too."

"If you die again, will you return to the age you are now?"

"I don't know."

Oliver's eyes widened. "I mean, I don't want you to die just so we can find out, but—"

Dani chuckled and squeezed his shoulder. "Relax, street urchin. I know what you meant." She passed the journal back to him. "There is a huge problem with this book."

"What? What's wrong?"

"There isn't a picture of you. If this is to help me remember everyone just in case my memories crap out on me again, you must be in it too. Can you do a self-portrait?"

"Yeah."

She enjoyed her time with them, and Oliver and Brody went to bed shortly after dinner. Dani helped Miles clear the table and clean the dishes. She placed the last plate in the cabinet and felt Miles's hand at her lower back. He slipped it around to her side, and she turned to face him.

"I'm glad you're here," he said.

"Me too." She took his hand and walked with him to his bedroom. He closed the door, and she helped him remove his shirt. He had a lot of scars on his body. More than two decades in the CNA had not been kind to him. She passed her fingers over the healing patch extending from his abdomen to his back. "Does this hurt?"

He touched her shoulders, then slid his hands down her upper arms. "It's just a little sore." Miles moved his hands to her waist and slipped his fingers beneath the edge of her shirt.

She recalled the feel of his fingertips on her skin from before and closed her eyes for a moment.

"Are you okay?"

"I'm rendering." She grinned with her eyes closed.

Miles laughed, then kissed her.

Dani opened her eyes and smiled. She removed her tee and then her tank, and he pulled her close. He placed his lips and tongue on her shoulder and moved them along her skin toward her neck. Dani felt herself unraveling with his touch. More memories of being with him surfaced in a rush, creating a wave of dizziness that she concealed by clinging to him until it passed. She forgot all about the war while he finished undressing her on the way to his bed.

CHAPTER 54

Dani lay partially across Miles's body with her cheek against his chest. One of her hands lay between the back of his neck and his pillow. Her arm was a little contorted, but she loved the feel of his hair against her palm. Her other arm was draped across his abdomen. His chin rested on her head, and she enjoyed the sound of his breathing while watching his chest rise and fall as he slept. He had an arm around her back, and his hand rested in the curve between her waist and hip. She closed her eyes, lulled into a peaceful doze by his rhythmic breathing.

A comm chirped, and Dani ignored it. The chirping continued, and she groaned when Miles shifted to slide out from under her.

"Leave it," she said.

He kissed her forehead and got up. She settled into the warm spot he left on the sheets and stole his pillow. He pawed through clothes on the floor until he found his jeans and the offending comm in a pocket.

"Oh, shit. Dani," he said, returning to the side of the bed.

She kept her eyes closed and mumbled into the pillow. "What?"

"We have to go. Now."

She grumbled an incomprehensible refusal.

He shook her shoulder until she opened her eyes to glare at him.

"Houston needs you," he said.

"I'm done with her." She attempted to roll away from him, but he stopped her.

"She's in Boston with a bomb strapped to her chair. She's sitting on a dead man's switch, and no one knows how to disarm the device."

Dani sat up. "You're serious?"

Miles nodded. "Javi has a helo waiting for us, and Aunt Hattie is on her way to stay with Oliver."

She frowned but slid out of bed to retrieve her clothes. "Why me?"

"In the training sims, you were the only sab to beat every disarming scenario Javi threw at you." He pulled his jeans on, then sat to put his socks on.

Dani dressed in silence for a moment. "Sims. The warehouse with lots of sensors, blinking things, suits with more sensors, and fancy helmets?"

"Yeah."

"I remember getting covered in paint when a training bomb went off."

"You'd already disarmed it, but when you dropped your helmet on the thing, the paint cartridge went off."

"Oh."

Miles paused, holding one of his boots. "Did you polish these for me the other day?"

She turned in a circle looking for her other sock. "Uh. Yeah. Ah!" Dani found her missing sock and retrieved it from the corner of a table. Her face felt a little warm, and she smiled, remembering how it felt when he—

"Ready?" Miles asked.

She pulled her thoughts back to the present, put her sock on, then yanked her boots on. "Yep."

Dani followed him out of the room and to the front door. He opened it, and Hattie was waiting.

"Good to see you here, finally," she said to Dani. "It's about fucking time you two bedded each other. I'll look after the kid and mutt till you get back."

Dani started to speak, but Hattie spoke first. "Have fun with the bombs." Hattie pushed past them to enter Miles's quarters.

"Thank you," Miles said, and herded Dani out.

Dani's mind was preoccupied. *Wait. Bombs?*

The jog to the airfield helped wake her up a bit more, and the helicopter was already running by the time they arrived. Javi stood next to it, shielding his face from the wind the blades created.

"Took you long enough," Javi said. "Get in."

Mary was already strapped in, and Dani smiled to see her friend. The older man climbed in, and once Dani and Miles were inside, he slid the door shut.

The blades increased in speed, and Mary leaned close to Dani's ear.

"It's 0300 and you show up with Miles. Please tell me you finally slept with him."

A smile spread across Dani's face as her answer.

"Finally!" Mary said. "He had to be better than Gavin, right?"

"Who is that?"

Mary's head rocked back as she laughed. "Perfect! That is *so* perfect."

Dani didn't know what she meant, but Mary seemed thrilled.

"What's that about?" Miles asked Dani, and he nodded toward Mary.

"Inside joke maybe? One I can't remember, I guess." Dani shrugged. "I don't know."

They put on helmets with built-in comms so they could speak more easily during the ride. Javi passed Dani a panel. She looked at the image on it while Mary and Miles leaned in for a closer look.

"This device is unlike anything we've ever seen before," Javi said. "The complexity is off the charts."

Dani moved through the images of an I-shaped explosive with a wiring configuration that looked more like a knotted mess. She examined another image taken from a different angle. The wiring wasn't a mess at all; there was a pattern to it.

"Can you disarm it?" Javi asked.

"There are two ways to answer that question, depending on if I come out in one piece or a million," Dani said without taking her eyes from the screen.

"That's not funny," Mary said.

Dani glanced at her friend before returning to the panel. "I'm not joking." She wasn't sure if she could disarm the device.

The remainder of the trip to Boston was quiet. Mary took the panel from Dani when she leaned her head back and closed her eyes. Her evening with Miles had been amazing, but she was paying for the sleep deprivation now. The helo touched down before she was able to doze.

Javi rushed them from the field to a truck waiting to take them somewhere. She wondered why they hadn't landed at Logan, then remembered she'd been the one to blow the airport up—and it wasn't called Logan anymore. She didn't bother trying to sort out which life she'd lived when she knew areas of Boston by different names.

Dani followed the others to a tent full of equipment and

weapons. She and Mary put on protective gear, then gathered the tools they wanted for the bomb into a pair of packs. Javi and Miles escorted them to a perimeter set up around the field tent that served as Houston's office.

Miles kissed Dani before she passed beyond the perimeter. "Be careful."

"I'll relay info back to you once we have a closer look," Dani said, pointing to the comm in her ear. "Javi, remove it. I don't want you screaming in my ear."

He scowled as he pulled his comm out.

Dani turned to hide her surprise that he had complied so easily. Apparently, she was in charge now, and that caused a nervous flutter in her gut. She just hoped she didn't get herself and Mary killed. Dani entered the tent, followed by Mary.

She recognized Houston from Oliver's drawing. *I love that kid.*

Houston was pale with dark circles under her eyes while she sat unmoving in her chair behind a desk. Her jaw worked like she wanted to speak but was unsure what to say. Dani recognized the expressions on the woman's face as a mix of anger and relief.

"Do you have a comm on you?" Dani asked.

"Yes," Houston said.

Dani turned to Mary. "Toss it," she said while she moved to the other side of Houston's chair.

Mary approached the colonel, pulled the comm from the woman's ear, then walked back to the tent entrance to throw it out. She then rejoined Dani. They placed their packs on the floor, knelt, and peered under Houston's chair. The bomb looked even worse in person than it had on the panel, and Dani's mouth dropped open.

Mary turned to Dani with widened eyes. "Ho-ly fuck."

Dani nodded.

"What do we do?" Mary asked.

"Uh, give me a minute."

"My confidence in your ability is steadily dropping," Houston said.

"Catherine, shut the fuck up while I think!" Dani wasn't sure where her sudden burst of anger came from—perhaps lack of sleep, perhaps something deeper. The colonel fell silent, which was exactly what Dani wanted.

CHAPTER
55

Rowan hated the never-ending vibration that rumbled through the ship's hull. He, along with the rest of the remaining senior staff in Boston, had been evacuated to ships in the harbor. Three carriers had been sunk by the CNA's new jets, but the Wardens had managed to take one down. The Wardens were too busy escaping Boston as the Commonwealth reduced vast swaths of the city to rubble to bother with trying to retrieve the downed bird. Rowan was desperate to know what was in the new jets that made them invisible to all Warden scans until it was far too late to respond. It had been easier to track the jets using their destructive paths as vectors than trying to locate them before they unloaded their missiles and bombs.

His children and the nanny were also on the ship, but Rowan hadn't gone to them yet. They had left the city a few days earlier, and he already regretted leaving. If he'd stayed, he could have continued fighting. Boston was lost, but those who remained gave their lives so others could escape. Rowan wanted to die with them instead of being on this ship headed to wherever the hell it was going.

Rowan had used Curtis's new title to issue orders in an attempt to regain portions of Boston lost to the CNA, but those efforts had failed. Aubrey's ignorance had allowed the CNA forces to get too deep into the city for Rowan to turn things around.

Rowan's officers' quarters in Boston were now reduced to rows of bunks with other Wardens on the ship. He sat in the galley late that night while only those on night duty remained awake. Curtis brought him a mug of coffee and sat across from him.

"Vice Regent," Rowan said without looking up from the reports on his panel.

Curtis sighed and wrapped his hands around his own mug. "Stop calling me that. The title vanished with the loss of the city. I begged you to return to Ops for the vote. *Begged* you. At least this goes against my record, not yours."

"Doesn't it? Like you, I am assigned to sleep in rows and rows of bunks with foot soldiers, most of them reconditioned Echoes you and I created." Rowan sighed and downed half of his coffee in a few gulps. "Do we know where this ship is headed?"

"I haven't been able to get that information yet. The ships are being divided. Some will head north to Canada, others south to Virginia, and the rest are going to England."

"Let England deal with England. North America is our territory. Our ships should stay here."

Curtis shifted in his chair.

"What?" Rowan asked.

"Battles have broken out all across the US. Houston coordinated with the CNA across the country to begin simultaneous attacks." Curtis held up his hand before Rowan could ask his next question. "No, we never intercepted that kind of intel, which means their tech now exceeds ours. No one knows how she did it, but Houston fucked us good."

"We need to pull everything we have on comm equipment, ours and theirs. R&D can—"

"Rowan, there is no R&D anymore. We're on this ship and under orders to go wherever they take us."

Rowan slammed his fist on the table. "We can do more than just ride this fucking boat!"

"We can't, actually."

"We can make a massive strike just like we did against the humans when we started this war."

Curtis shook his head. "The regent will never allow that. We can't deplete our resources like that again. The Commonwealth has proved they're no longer in a prolonged defensive mode. Their aggression is working in their favor now."

"It's fear that controls the regent and vice regents now. *Fear*," Rowan said. He had no tolerance for cowardice. To back down to the Commonwealth was an act of treason against Ekkoh. He finished his coffee and leaned back in his chair. Minutes ticked by.

"I know what is going through your head, Rowan. We have our new orders, and we must follow them."

"I would swim back to Boston this instant to continue fighting."

"I know you would. Your children are on this ship, and you haven't gone to them yet. Devon is asking for you. He's asking about Ana, and I don't feel I'm the one to tell him she's gone."

Rowan stood and slipped his panel into his pocket. "Tell them whatever you want. I have work to do."

"Rowan, there is the matter of Aubrey."

Rowan listened.

"You should have allowed the VRs to bring her to trial and convict her of dereliction of duty. We had more than enough evidence to prove it, but you blew her head off while she was unarmed and under guard. Now you will have a trial."

"Spin the story as you always do, Curtis. Aubrey was incompetent, we were under attack, and my wife had been slaughtered as a result. I was overcome with grief or whatever you want to call it."

"No, sir. I can't spin this one. I'm forbidden from representing you on this case."

Rowan faced his former friend. "So, the betrayal comes full circle. You stole the VR title and now leave me to defend myself at trial. Well done, Curtis. I played right into your plans."

"Sir, that was *never* my intent, and you know it."

Rowan left the galley. He didn't care how the trial went or what Curtis said. He needed to go wherever the Warden leaders were sending him and figure out how to return to New England later.

CHAPTER
56

D ani took a deep breath and released it slowly. She took a moment to figure out her plan, then stood.

"Miles, double the distance of the perimeter," Dani said.

"Shit. It's that bad?" he asked.

"Just a precaution."

"Liar. You don't have to do this."

Dani dragged her hand through her hair. "Mary, grab your gear."

Mary stood and frowned. "We're leaving?"

"You are."

"Fuck you." Mary resumed her position on the floor next to Houston's chair.

Dani rolled her eyes, and Houston snorted.

"Sucks when you think you're the boss, only to find out you're not," Houston said.

"You really think this is the time to play the bitch card?" Dani asked.

Houston grinned.

Dani remembered what Hattie had said about getting what she wanted if she was smart. She picked up the panel sitting closest to Houston on the desk.

"What are you doing? Put that down. Deal with this bomb."

"Careful in that chair, Catherine. Move too much and we all have a quick end," Dani said before turning her attention to Mary. "General Ramos is commandeering Miles for his diplomatic whatever, which includes me. You in?"

"You're going?" Mary asked.

"Yes."

"Fuck yeah, I'm in."

Dani passed the panel to Houston. "Send a note to the general that Kelsey will accompany us as a medical liaison. Also let Ramos know that you recommend Miles for a promotion. 'Major Jackman' sounds nice."

"Christ, Dani what are you doing?" Miles asked.

She ignored him.

"No," Houston said.

"Enjoy your bomb." Dani retrieved her pack from the floor.

Mary stared up at her, and when Dani bent to grab her pack, she flashed her friend a quick smile. Mary picked up her pack and stood.

"Wait!" Houston said. "This is extortion."

"You would know."

Houston growled, and tapped on the panel. Once finished she turned the panel toward Dani. "There. Kelsey has my blessing to go and Miles has his promotion submitted."

"Good. Forward that to the rest of the brass above you."

"There's no need. I've signed it."

"Except you sometimes fail to submit *all* your paperwork. You document only the parts you want. My memories are fragmented, but you've been guilty of falsifying documents before, yes? Send it to the brass. Now."

"Dani, what are you doing?" Miles asked. "Don't push her like this. She's a good leader."

"I disagree, Miles." Dani returned her attention to Houston.

When the colonel gave the panel back to Dani, she confirmed that Miles's files had been updated and transmitted to Commonwealth brass. She smiled. "See? It wasn't that hard. Mary, ready to tackle this thing?"

Mary nodded and resumed pulling her tools from her pack to organize them on the floor. Dani pulled her helmet off and rolled to her back. She looked up at the I-shaped explosive and sighed. Mary passed her a light, then lay next to her. They examined the mechanisms for several minutes in silence while Dani used her finger to gently move wires to see what they were up against. She lowered her arm and stared at the packs of explosives attached to the myriad of wiring and blinking chips.

"What are you thinking?" Mary asked.

"Nothing good. Miles, you have everyone moved?"

"Yes. We're clear. You and Mary, please be careful. I love you."

Her face flushed hot, and she smiled.

Mary nudged her shoulder. "Say it. You know it's true," she mouthed.

Dani nodded and said, "I love you, too." Her smile faded when Houston spoke.

"Just shoot me now."

"That can be arranged," Dani said, and Mary laughed.

Twenty minutes had passed by the time Dani got the first layer of the casing around the wires off. Mary had taken her helmet off halfway in. The helmets wouldn't protect them, being so close to a device that could blow a respectable crater in the ground. They weren't playing with paint cartridges this time, and the stress of possibly dying at any second while wearing suffocating armor had them both sweating.

Dani turned the casing in her hand and sat up. She snipped three wires and placed it inside her bag.

"Done?" Houston asked.

"No." Dani pulled her armored jacket off, and Mary did the same before they resumed lying on the floor under Houston's chair.

"The wiring pattern and chips make no sense," Mary said as she pointed to the device.

Dani nodded. "This schema is like fucking hieroglyphics."

"It's layered."

"Yeah." *Hieroglyphics. The comm units were Ekkohrian. No, they were Ancient Ekkohrian tech, and I am dealing with more than one bomb.* Dani tilted her head, and the I-shaped explosive device became an H-shaped one. *Hattie. Fuck.*

Houston had never been in any real danger. The bomb had all the right parts, including the ones to obliterate human and Echo lives, but the mechanisms weren't hooked up in a way to make the thing detonate. It was built to confound the disarmer, and Hattie had succeeded.

Dani pointed to the device. "Put two clips on this wire and loop them to the one directly opposite."

Mary stared at her for a second. Then she placed the clips where Dani wanted them.

Dani resumed working once Mary's hands were clear.

"More clips here and here," Dani said. The clips were useless, and Mary had caught on. Dani was just using the periodic instructions as filler for Houston.

She removed the next layer of the harmless device and added it to her bag. Hattie's bomb—*bombs*—had been beautifully constructed. If Hattie had wanted Houston dead, she could have done it hours earlier with the push of one button from a detonator. Instead, she'd rigged the device to activate when Houston plopped her ass in her chair, and let Dani have a moment of leverage against the colonel. She wanted to both hug and strangle Hattie.

After removing the final layer, she signaled to Mary to

remain quiet. Dani rewired the last piece to be an actual, working bomb, and Mary's eyes widened.

"Miles, bring up a containment rig for controlled detonation," Dani said. "Leave it near the tent entrance and let me know when you're clear." She needed to continue the ruse a little longer. If anyone got their hands on the device and figured out its Ancient origins, Houston would execute Hattie.

"On it," he said.

"You're done?" Houston asked, unable to keep the excitement from her voice.

"Not yet. Don't move," Dani said.

Mary grinned at her, and Dani smiled. Tormenting Houston for a change was fun.

"What does it look like?" Houston asked.

Dani remembered—though she didn't know how or why she retained this information—that lying to the colonel was futile. The woman could smell a lie a mile away, so Dani went with the truth. "It's far more advanced than anything we've ever used in the sims or otherwise."

"Fucking Wardens," Houston said.

Dani let Houston go with her assumption. In an official capacity, the colonel had orchestrated a significant Warden defeat and captured a major city for the Commonwealth. The idea that the Wardens would try to assassinate her was a valid one. Hattie was safe with Houston blaming the Wardens.

"Dani, you're clear for controlled det," Miles said.

"Understood." Dani slid out partially from beneath Houston's chair. "Mary, we'll gear up again once I'm ready to finish disconnecting this thing from the chair."

"Okay," Mary said.

"Catherine, you've been sitting for a while now. Use the desk for support and rise slowly. Don't try to walk until you're certain you can. I don't want you falling on us while Mary and I finish. Got it?"

Houston scooted to the edge of the chair. She used the desk to leverage herself up. Dani snipped another—but pointless— wire to the switch in the seat. The colonel took a few tentative steps.

"Leave when you're ready," Dani said. "We'll meet you beyond the perimeter."

Houston nodded and left. Dani sat up and pulled her armored jacket back on. While Mary did the same, Dani finished disconnecting the device from Houston's chair, then tinkered with a detonator for another few minutes. She stood and picked up the panel she'd had Houston use earlier. Dani saw responses from CNA generals approving Miles's promotion given his recent service and role in victories in both Portland and Boston. General Ramos had responded with a personal message to Houston agreeing with her recommendation to include Kelsey on their team. Pleased, she placed the panel back on the desk with her bomb on top of it.

"Almost done, Miles," Dani said. "You have Catherine?"

"She's here," he said.

"Stand by."

"Copy that."

Mary nudged her arm and shrugged. Dani pulled the comm from her ear and waited until Mary had hers out.

"I'm setting this thing off and taking Houston's shit with it. I don't want her to have the chance to try to undo or retract documents. Miles has his promotion, and Kels is coming with us."

"Sometimes you scare me."

"Shit, Mary, sometimes I scare myself."

"I like it. So, we pretend we're taking it to controlled det but instead frantically run out and you blow the thing, yeah?"

"Yeah. I have it on a timer so we really do need to bolt out of here." Dani put the comm back in her ear. "Miles, this thing is unstable. Confirm the area is clear."

"It's clear. No one is inside the perimeter."

"Completely clear? I don't even want a dog or bird near us."

"You're clear. Javi has people outside the perimeter monitoring. There's nothing near you."

They put their helmets back on, gathered their packs, and walked toward the tent's exit. Dani had the remote in her hand and looked at her friend. Mary nodded. Dani pressed the button, then tossed the detonator under Houston's desk. The lights on the bomb started flickering, and they sprinted from the tent with shouts for others to take cover. They'd almost reached the barriers creating the perimeter when Houston's tent was engulfed by a thunderous explosion and ball of flame.

Dani didn't need to fabricate her look of surprise with the blast. Maybe she should have set the timer for a little longer.

Miles helped her and Mary up. "You okay?" he asked. "You're both okay?"

They nodded, and removed their helmets.

"What happened?" Houston asked.

Dani again went with the truth. "I pissed it off. The lights on it started blinking faster, and we got the hell out."

Houston grumbled in response.

"She just saved your life, and you can't even thank her?" Mary asked.

"No." Houston growled when she glared at Dani. "I hate you."

"I know, Catherine. I send all your pretty plans right into the shitter, yet you get all the commendations off the success of others. You will fight your future battles without me."

Houston ground her teeth. "You're the perfect weapon against the Wardens. Do you realize that? You're like a fucking hurricane. Unpredictable and destructive as hell. You wreck everything you touch."

"Yeah, that's probably true."

"I *hate* you, Dani Ireland."

Dani's eyebrows went up as she turned to Mary and Miles. "I have a last name?"

Houston lunged at her, and Javi stepped in. "Stand down, Colonel."

"Step aside!"

Javi shook his head. "Our Commonwealth doesn't attack civilians." He turned to Miles. "The helo will take you back to Portland."

The colonel kept her glare on Dani. "You can't leave this war."

Dani turned her back to Houston and left with her friends. Her steps slowed when she recalled her earlier conversation with Miles and Oliver.

"Ireland." Dani frowned. "Miles, was Oliver talking about me when he said Ambassador Ireland?"

He glanced at her. "Uh …"

She touched his arm. "No. Miles, *no!*"

"Oh, yes." Mary grinned and kept Dani moving forward.

CHAPTER
57

The sun was up when they landed in Portland. Mary and Miles had slept on the trip back, but Dani couldn't. Miles had contacted Hattie with his comm, so they went to Hattie's brothel instead of back to Miles's quarters. They met Oliver, Brody, and Hattie in the kitchen where the older woman had prepared breakfast. Instead of bounding toward them when they arrived, Brody stayed near Oliver at the table, waiting for dropped food.

Hattie flashed Dani a fiendish grin. "Well, look who's in one piece."

Dani wasn't amused, and approached the woman. "Have you lost your goddamn mind?"

"Oh, far from it, honey." Hattie sipped her coffee. "Want some?"

"No!"

Hattie shrugged, apparently unaffected by Dani's outburst. "You sure? You're kinda cranky."

Mary was already helping herself to eggs, toast, and fruit while Miles poured three mugs of coffee.

"What's wrong?" Oliver asked Dani.

Mary placed her plate back on the counter before turning to Dani. "Holy shit. You think *she* did it?"

"I know she did," Dani said.

"The bomb?" Miles asked. "We're talking about the bomb, right?"

"Yes," Dani said, glancing at him before returning her glare to Hattie.

The older woman smiled, took her cup to the table, and sat next to Oliver.

"Do I need to leave?" Oliver asked.

"Not at all," Hattie said. "Finish your breakfast."

Dani approached the table and removed a piece of the explosive device from her pack. Hattie glanced at it and smiled before taking another sip of coffee.

Mary gasped. "Oh my God. I know that smile." She sank into a chair at the table and stared at Hattie. "You planted the bomb."

"I did far more than that, honey," Hattie said.

"She *made* it." Dani paced near the table, refusing to sit, while Miles dropped into a chair next to Oliver. Miles looked like if he didn't sit, he'd fall.

Hattie nodded. "Fine piece of work too. My finest, I'd say. What gave me away?"

"Oh, God," Miles groaned.

"You practically signed the damn thing," Dani said. At the questioning looks from the others at the table, Dani held the device upright. "Every image we had of it made it look like an I." She turned it ninety degrees.

"It's an H," Oliver said. "How is tha— Oh."

Mary laughed, and Miles turned an interesting shade of green.

Dani slipped the device back into her pack and finally sat.

"The only good thing is it was never rigged to blow. Houston was never in danger."

"But it *did* blow," Miles said.

"That part was me. I destroyed Houston's little field office so she couldn't recant her approval on your promotion or Kels going with us on the general's field trip." Dani rested her elbows on the table and dropped her face into her hands. She desperately needed sleep.

"And destroyed the deadly part of the bomb so no one could ID where it came from," Mary said. "Jesus, Dani, you're smarter than you look. I am so impressed." Mary slapped her on the back.

"Don't be," Dani said, and she lowered her hands. "Hattie, what errands did you have Mary doing the other day when I was in the infirmary?"

Hattie flashed another grin. "She was an unknowing accomplice at the time. I had her digging in the cellar to bring up totes so I could make Catherine's present."

"You didn't go to Boston for business expansion," Dani said.

"Oh, I absolutely went there for that. Found a great spot. It's nothing but rubble right now, but it's perfect. Great view of the harbor. Of course, customers won't be doing much sightseeing while they're being entertained. But I made time to stop by Catherine's tent while she was out."

Mary shook her head. "But you were back here for hours, long before the bomb was discovered."

Hattie chuckled and nodded.

"How did you do it?" Mary leaned forward, eager for the answer.

"I can't tell all my secrets, honey. You know that."

Mary nodded, got up, and retrieved her food from the counter. Her appetite was back, and she started eating as soon as she was seated.

Hattie left the table and fixed two plates of food. She placed one in front of Miles and one in front of Dani. "Eat, then get some sleep. You four are heading to Bangor in a few hours. Ramos is meeting you there."

"I'm not done packing," Miles said.

"I sent some people over to finish up while you were gone," Hattie said. "Mary, Dani, your things are packed too. The transport truck is already loaded. Kels will meet you there, Mary. He's fully recovered with his new arm and was transferred out of Catherine's recon division to the Bangor barracks as part of their med staff. But it sounds like he's going overseas with you now." Hattie left.

Dani's middle rumbled with hunger, so she picked up her fork and started eating because she didn't know what else to do. Miles also began eating while Mary and Oliver chatted about their return to Bangor. Oliver ate, then took Brody out for a walk. Dani and Miles finished eating while Mary cleaned the kitchen.

Mary waved Dani away when she tried to help. "Get out of here. Go to bed."

Dani didn't argue, and left with Miles for her room. Her books and a few other things were gone, but the furniture and everything else remained.

The table in the corner held two basins of water with cloths, towels, and changes of clothes next to them. Hattie had planned everything down to the last detail. Houston had said Dani was the perfect weapon, but Dani believed she was wrong. Hattie was a mastermind.

She dipped her hand into the basin; the water was still warm. She assumed Hattie had filled it once she'd left the kitchen. Dani stripped and washed while Miles did the same. Standing naked next to him didn't last long before they tumbled into the bed together.

Hours later, a knock on the door woke them.

"Aunt Hattie says we're leaving soon," Oliver said from the other side of the door.

"Okay," Dani grumbled.

When Miles and Dani arrived at the transport truck, Dresden waved at them from the gun mounted on the roof while Mary sat behind the steering wheel. Dani froze for a moment. *Why does this look familiar?* She approached the front passenger door, and Oliver and Brody were in the seat. Oliver had rigged the seat belt across him and the dog.

"You're in the back with Dad," Oliver said, smiling. "Mary wanted me up here with her."

"Figured it would be fine," Mary said. "Dres insisted on staying up top. He swears it won't be like the last time we made a transport run."

Dani recalled only a portion of what Mary referred to but decided not to ask any questions.

"Fine with me," Miles said.

Dani opened the rear door and climbed in, followed by Miles. He closed the door, and Mary started the engine. The sound brought back memories that filled the rest of the gaps of the day Mary and Dani had been part of a three-truck transport that was attacked.

Miles said, "You good?"

"Huh?" Dani blinked and realized that he held her hand. "Yeah. I'm good."

Her thoughts wandered, and an hour into the trip, her eyelids became heavy. Dresden never left his post on the roof, and Mary chatted back and forth with Oliver while they kept their eyes on the road and surroundings. Miles put his arm around her shoulders, and Dani settled against him.

He passed his hand through her hair and lowered his head to put his lips next to her ear.

"I love you," he said softly so only she could hear.

She smiled and turned in the seat. He adjusted his position so she could lean back against his chest. He wrapped his arms around her, and she rested her head against the inside of his upper arm. Dani closed her eyes and was asleep in seconds.

ACKNOWLEDGMENTS

These writing adventures would not be possible without the support from my friends and family.

Special thanks to my friend and adviser on military tactics, Major Mike Henderson, USMC, retired. I buy the pints, and he supplies the stories while I furiously take notes. He is also a wonderful human to be around even when I'm not planning fictional invasions. If there are any tactical errors in the story, they are mine.

I'm also thankful for the patience and feedback of my test readers: Jennifer Elmore, Rebecca Hardman, and Mike Henderson. They had the task of wading through the first draft to sniff out any early story problems. The time they spent reading and then dealing with me and my questions is proof they are magnificently patient people.

I am grateful for the editing magic of Ray Rhamey and his help on this project. His attention to detail is truly spectacular.

Anytime I get lost in the fog of writing, editing, publishing, and other work around the release of *Echoes* into the wild, Sarah Miniaci is my lighthouse.

Heaps of thanks to my Massachusetts family: Chris, Allison, and Helen Clements. They provided a crash pad for me in their home that allowed me to more easily access and complete my research in Boston for this novel. Only in Maynard. Wink.

Thank *you*, reader, for your time and for taking this adventure with me!

ABOUT THE AUTHOR

Irvin Serrano of Irvin Serrano Commercial Photography

Cheryl Campbell was born in Louisiana and lived there and in Mississippi before moving to Maine. Her varied background includes art, herpetology, emergency department and critical care nursing, and computer systems. When not traveling as a nomadic wanderer, she lives in Maine—the state she calls home.

To follow her blog, visit cherylscreativesoup.com or facebook.com/cherylscreativesoup. She is also on Instagram @cherylscreativesoup.